Caffeine N

A C
WITNESS

The second novel in the
Michael Strange series

Spencer Coleman

Fiction aimed at the heart
and the head...

Published by Caffeine Nights Publishing 2014

Published in Great Britain by Caffeine Nights Publishing

www.caffeine-nights.com

British Library Cataloguing in Publication Data.

A CIP catalogue record for this book is available from the British Library

ISBN: 978-1-907565-82-3

Cover design by

Mark (Wills) Williams

Everything else by

Default, Luck and Accident

Spencer Coleman

Martin Spencer Coleman was born in 1952, Leicester, England. He has been a professional artist and gallerist for over thirty years handling the work of artists from all around the world. A keen sportsman he is an avid follower of Portsmouth football club. Over the years, he has written several magazine articles and been regularly interviewed on BBC radio in connection to his artistic endeavours. His paintings are collected worldwide and one of his fine art prints "Bottoms Up" was an international best seller. He currently lives in Lincolnshire and has one son, Jordan. This is his second novel.

www.spencercolemanfineart.com

Email: martinspencercoleman@gmail.com

To both my parents, who taught me to always face adversity head on

Acknowledgements:

Eternal gratitude to Darren Laws from Caffeine Nights for helping to bring this book to publication. This process is always a long road to undertake. I would also like to thank my family for their support and belief and to those who offered unflagging encouragement over the years. You know who you are. I'll need you all again in the future, I'm sure!

The Poisoned Carnival

There is more to light in the morning
When demons have been playing at night
In that cage of broken doubts
And death comes but at a price

Too late for a call to witness
Where uncertainly is the winner
Where dark lies, crawl and bell
As red tears drop and crush under foot

Revenge is sweet but twice bitter
When your life is on the line
You do not betray your shadows
Echoing Hell and past devotions

When others collected vengeance
Even flames were far too dark
Whatever the dreamer said
It's too soon to drop our mask

Jorge Aguilar-Agon, B.Agr., AEA, AAPB, FRSA.

PROLOGUE

A million deadly shards of glass lay sprinkled like jewelled confetti outside the vandalised grand façade of the gallery. A fine drizzle fell from the midnight sky. From afar, the distant rumblings indicated an approaching storm.

The glazier trod carefully, crunching glass under foot, as he expertly removed the last of the razor-sharp fragments lodged precariously in the window frame. It was hazardous and noisy work, hampered by the slippery pavement as the rain intensified, the droplets illuminated by the artificial light from the row of elegant Georgian street lamps. With the remainder of the splinters cleared away, the man and his colleague worked methodically on the boarding-up process. It was a laborious task, one they had undertaken perhaps a thousand times before. Between them, they heaved several enormous sheets of heavy MDF into position, covering up the gaping hole which had, hours before, been part of the most impressive shop-front on the street. It was now a repaired wreck, a sorrowful sight set among some of London's finest shops.

The loud retort of the nail gun fractured the air, repeatedly. Those who lived in the apartments opposite peeped through curtains to express their displeasure at the continued disturbance to their sleep. One or two late night revellers gathered on the pavement, watching the activity as the alarm continued to shrill. The flickering strobe lighting danced off the walls of the wet buildings.

Within the gallery (made up of four interconnecting high-ceilinged rooms), a man, standing forlorn, looked on at the surrounding chaos, his eyes as dark as the night that engulfed him. For a fleeting moment, he was content to remain anonymous in the unlit gloom, alone with his puzzled thoughts. In the choking dust and debris, he saw a parallel scene of his own making: a fading picture of ruin.

He managed to clear his head of such a mundane judgment and dragged his weary limbs to the pavement, a mobile stuck to his ear as he tried to contact his absent colleagues.

The workmen, meanwhile, had momentarily downed tools and one of them busied himself with documentation. The other lit a cigarette, his beer belly protruding flabbily over his trouser belt. Thankfully for all concerned, the alarm automatically ceased, and in the relative calm, the man with the phone took the opportunity to punch in fresh numbers on his keypad. He waited, agitated. He buttoned his jacket against the invasive cold as the wind swirled in from the west. The first clap of thunder reached them high above.

'It's Michael. I'm here now,' he explained. On the surface he remained unruffled but his voice wavered and betrayed his thin pretence of control. 'No, no. The paintings are fine. No damage, but it's a miracle, I can tell you.' He waited, listening to the response; then added, 'I need you to come in early in the morning to help with the cleaning-up operation.' Pacing back and forth, he listened again, then said, 'Thanks.'

With that, he clicked off, pondering the next move. Under the lamp light, his silver hair glistened. Rain settled on his jacketed shoulders. Punching the keypad once more, he spoke quickly. 'Toby, it's me. I hope you get this message. Just an update from our earlier conversation… everything is under control. I've just spoken to Ronald. He's coming in early tomorrow to help. The alarm company is on the way now. I'll stay until the premises are secure and the police have done their report. No need for you to come out. Luckily, there is no damage to the artwork. It appears that someone threw a brick at the window, probably some drunken yob ejected from the nightclub down the road. It's happened before.' He yawned, aware that a police car was parking up opposite, and continued: 'The glaziers are here, and should be finished shortly. I'll speak to the insurers first thing tomorrow.' He fell silent again, checked his watch and then said, 'Should be wrapped up within the hour. Hope the concert was good. Perhaps I'll grab a cup of tea but, in the circumstances, a double whisky would be preferable. Anyway, get here when you can in the morning. I'll open as normal. OK. Bye for now.'

Michael clicked off and suddenly felt the unseasonal chill of the August night clatter his bones. A flash of lightning illuminated the sky. Retreating once more into the gallery, he offered tea to the workers and moved to the kitchen, switching on the interior lights as he went. This incident with the broken window spooked him more than previous occasions, however seldom they occurred. The shock never diminished. You just have to deal with it, he reminded himself. Usually, it was an empty beer bottle that did the damage, never a brick as the glazier suspected. This was a deliberate act of destruction, he sensed, not just an impulsive booze-induced prank. He recalled that many years ago someone even pissed through the letterbox on New Year's Eve. This was more sinister, however. It implied a personal statement of attack. *You don't just find a brick lying in the road.*

In his increased anxiety, Michael dropped a mug of tea onto the floor, smashing it. Scalding water splashed his trousers, instantly saturating his legs. He cursed as his skin reacted to the burning. *Fuck.* He towelled down as best he could and tried again, refilling another cup with trembling hands. *For Christ's sake, get a proper grip this time.*

Out on the street, he encountered the workmen and offered the hot beverage. One of them (the one with the gut), handed him a piece of blackened rock.

'That's what did the damage, Boss. Found it at the back of the window.'

Michael took the offending missile, turning it in his hand. 'What is it?'

A policeman approached, nodded to them all and reached out and inspected the evidence.

'Flint,' he muttered, then pondered: 'Unusual... especially in this neighbourhood. This is the kind of thing more suited to a country barn, hardly a Mayfair mansion.'

Michael's heart pounded, his mind racing. *What did he just say?*

The officer, peering at a notepad, said matter-of-factly: 'Our station had a call-out from Red Care. I'm looking for a Michael Strange, the principal key holder...is that you sir?'

Ashen-faced, Michael stared at him, preoccupied suddenly by a ghost from the past. He nodded his reply but it wasn't picked up. He felt the jagged edges of the piece of flint as he took hold of it again. His world almost somersaulted in that second. *Christ: a barn.* That's what the officer implied. His brain shifted gear, shuddering at the memory – and acrid smell – of flames and burning flesh from the inferno at the barn over a year ago. Terrible images flashed before him: He was still haunted by his lucky escape from the fire at Laburnum Farm. This incident brought it back so vividly, with the reference to the chunk of flint. Was there a connection between the two incidents? Surely, surely not...he closed his eyes for a moment and thought first of Lauren O'Neill, and then Maggie Conlon: the two psychotic sisters who, not so long ago, had almost destroyed him and those he was closest to, Kara and Marcus.

Lauren was dead, killed by a falling roof beam. Was this the work of her mad sister hell-bent on revenge? It didn't bear thinking about, but the possibility was strong: compelling, in fact. He opened his eyes, felt dizzy and in the same instant nervously scanned the road in either direction. Maggie was a very dangerous fugitive with murder in her heart. She had tried to kill him once before. She would try again, given the opportunity. All she needed was proximity and chance.

'Sir..?' the policeman repeated. 'Are you the key holder?'

Michael caught his breath and thought of the double whisky again. No amount of firewater would calm his unease on this night. He nodded his reply again and stood aside as the policeman inspected the damage to the property and made notes as he went. Michael was more concerned by the whereabouts of the perpetrator to this criminal act.

It had to be *her,* her with the poisonous eyes of the devil. He scanned the street once more, nervous of any simple movement that would spook him still further. A light faded from the window opposite, the curtains yanking tight. He twitched. A taxi pulled into the street further down, forcing him to take a step back. Maggie had that affect on him. Two lovers alighted and disappeared into a building, a frenzy of sexually-charged laughter following their unsteady footsteps.

Relief washed over him. Then the street was deserted once more, but still he wanted to be sure...of what? He stared intently, startled by another thunder roar and a fork of lighting too close for comfort. He stood his ground though, determined to show his mettle. She was out there somewhere, watching his every move from the shadows. *He was sure of it.*

CHAPTER ONE

Michael Strange caught the central line train to Piccadilly, and then hurriedly walked the short distance to the Churchill Fine Art gallery on Cork Street, his business address for the past twenty odd years. It was a sticky morning, the storm failing to shift the humidity of the past few days. The first of the falling reddish leaves dotted the wet pavements around Berkeley Square. Michael wore his customary cream raincoat, unbuttoned, the waist belt dangling in his wake. Although his stride was purposeful, he was mindful of the slippery surface underfoot. However, he knew the sorry image of the smashed window would shortly take the spring from his step, bringing an air of despondency crashing down around him. Something had to spoil his misguided optimism on this morning: Another day, another problem. And the thought of Maggie, which had disturbed his shallow dreams during a fitful night, was definitely a big problem. However, once he got to the premises he knew it would be a case of heads down and "work as usual". There wouldn't be time to wallow in self-pity. Hopefully, Ronald would have arrived early, as he had promised when they spoke on the mobile the night before. Ronald was dependable. Michael missed having Kara around though, his old sidekick. She was always a rock in a crisis. That she hastily left the gallery in difficult circumstances, pushed out by his then estranged wife during his recovery in hospital from the injuries he sustained in the fire, was a big regret to him. Adele, his ex-wife. The very name turned his stomach: Now the ex-business partner too. That had a good ring to it. Many long months had now passed since Kara had departed. Christmas had come and gone and big changes had occurred: He underwent two more operations, the divorce settlement all but wiped him out, Toby, his son, saved the business with renewed investment and Kara, well, she was heavily pregnant and no doubt preoccupied by all things maternal. He felt like old news and debated the obvious question: Would she ever return to work? He hoped so, but here was the rub. Although Adele was gone, he and Kara had drifted apart. They hadn't spoken in nearly nine months, since she announced her good news. This saddened him, but he knew he had to let go. Marcus had made this point forcibly. They were now the team. He was excluded. He shrugged. All things were possible though. *Life staggers on*, he muttered solemnly under his breath.

As he'd predicted, he was suddenly stopped in his tracks. The boarded-up façade of the gallery was indeed a dreadful sight, more of a shock now in broad daylight. The new replacement window hadn't arrived, and a few tiny shards of glass remained scattered in the gutter, a sharp reminder of the carnage from last night. The entrance door was ajar, and the overhead spotlights ablaze. As he entered, Ronald spotted him approaching with a frown and, eyes averted, scurried around with bin liner and broom, oblivious to the dust that still seeped into the display area where he had just cleaned diligently. Michael shook off his raincoat and closed the door behind him. Catching sight of the fragment of flint, discarded upon a desk, he once again felt threatened by this brutish act. What he didn't want to do was force his paranoia onto the shoulders of others…notably his trusted colleague. The less he knew about the sisters of doom, the better.

The implication that Maggie had thrown the missile was, at this stage, unfounded, and possibly far-fetched. It gave him the creeps though. The last thing Michael needed was unnecessary hysteria from the staff. For the time being, he would keep counsel…and wait. Anything else just fuelled gossip, and he had enough of that to last a lifetime. He just knew though that he, Kara and Marcus would spent the rest of their lives haunted by their past deeds.

He exchanged pleasantries with Ronald as if every woe that befell them could be taken in their stride. Ronald, though, was having none of it on this morning, mumbling aloud as to who he thought was responsible for the vandalism. He suggested a late night boozer. Michael just nodded at the conjecture, keeping everything as low-key as possible. Ronald then swore aloud, venting his frustration as a splinter of glass lodged in his finger. It was going to be one of those days.

Michael made coffee, switched up the air conditioning and largely confined himself to the job in hand: It was important to get the gallery presentable to the public as soon as possible. He retreated to his office and spoke with the insurance company to submit a claim for damage to the shop front. The conversation proved predictably dull and time-consuming. He then phoned the police to check the film footage from the CCTV camera in the street, only to discover that it was out of order. More expletives followed.

The new office girl arrived at midday, excused the morning off to attend a dental appointment for a nagging toothache. She appeared dazed at first, but Michael had difficulty working out if this was a reaction to the mess in the gallery or from the injection into her gums, and no doubt the overzealous drill that followed. If the truth be known, Michael also found it difficult forging a close friendship with Gemma after so many years working alongside Kara. It was an odd situation, but one he had to get used to. He missed Kara desperately, and wished for her to breeze into the gallery just like the good old days. She would have taken everything in her stride. *Just like the old days.*

Nostalgia was a fine thing, he reflected, but the past was the past. It was a new regime now, with Toby taking the reins which, in turn, allowed Michael to find his feet again after many weeks in hospital, slowly recovering from the burns and smoke inhalation that so nearly killed him. Of course, the new girl knew nothing of how this enforced change had altered lives so drastically and affected the status quo. How could she know? She was the outsider, taken on by Adele after she unceremoniously dumped Kara. He sighed. People come and go. No one was indispensable... but he hated the change. He missed Kara. Get on with it, his ex-wife Adele would have said bitingly. He certainly didn't miss *her*.

On reflection, Toby was just what the gallery needed after the financial hardship of the past couple of years, which nearly brought closure to the premises after over two decades of sustained success. This was the real damage that divorce brought to the table, Michael reflected ruefully. Well, that and the demands of the taxman and a certain Lauren O'Neill, his former lover. Christ, she was now an afterthought but the truth of the matter – his downfall – lay in the catastrophic liaison between them. It nearly caused the death of everyone he held dear. What was he thinking at the time? Was he so far from reality that his pursuit of lust and greed overwhelmed, even buried, his sense of common morality? Was she *that* intoxicating..?

The straight answer was yes. It was a shattering time, one in which he so nearly lost his life too. Lauren sadly did, and he felt utterly responsible for this terrible loss, even though she was perhaps the architect of her own demise. A blackness descended over him. It took several minutes of intense argument with himself before he gained a welcome release from the vice-like grip of depression which often imprisoned him. He felt sickened by such morbid recollections. He breathed in deeply and counted down, trying to relieve his sense of panic. Now, thankfully, he was free again...the demons pushed away temporarily. But for how long?

He thought of Toby once more. His youthful enthusiasm in the business was a breath of fresh air. He hit the ground running, leaving behind the financial stock market of New York and encompassing the world of art with a vigour that reminded Michael of his own zest for life three decades hence. If the truth be told, it was the very best thing when his son joined the business and brought in much-needed investment. Without it, the gallery would have folded. Michael's world would have folded too. Instead, he rediscovered his son into the bargain and, in spite of his own obvious and old-fashioned way in doing things which was bound to rattle Toby's cage, he had great admiration for how the new broom swept in and guided Churchill Fine Art back to rude fiscal health. Once again, they were at the forefront of leading London galleries, marketing and selling prestigious international fine art to the rest of the world. It felt good, even if there was a big "but" in the equation...Toby was the future. It was the gradual endgame for Michael, and perhaps not a bad thing, given the way in which he had cheated death. His presumption of natural health would definitely never be the same again, but working a couple of days a week allowed him a certain dignity, and the chance for him to bow out gracefully over a period of time. He felt like a liability, especially to his son, but Toby, he knew, recognised the limitations and sidestepped them, allowing his father to make a decent contribution before declining ill-health and enforced retirement became a certainty. He wasn't old, for heaven's sake, but he felt ancient. The mind was willing, but the broken body screamed for help. The healing from the wounds was terribly slow and unforgiving, particularly the painful skin grafts to protect his flesh. *Christ, the ravages of the fire...*

Even now, many months later, Michael detested the smell of smoke, even a single whiff of a lighted cigarette from a passer-by in the street made him feel nauseous. Such a simple intrusion caused misery, and sent him back into the rolling fireball of hell, where the heat scorched his eyes and the flames melted his skin. He was sickened whenever a news bulletin on the TV featured a building ablaze... he imagined people being trapped inside as white-hot debris engulfed them. He had been in that god-damn hellhole, and survived. *Got the T-shirt*. Sometimes, at his lowest point, he wished he hadn't escaped from the burning barn. Sometimes, he cursed the name of Marcus for saving him. It was a living nightmare, this burden of life, but he didn't dare share these darkest thoughts with anyone. Time was not a healer. Time just prolonged the agony. He kept quiet about it though.

Gemma's voice cut in: 'Mr Strange, telephone in reception for you.'

Michael looked up from his desk and knew his mind had wandered. He caught sight of Gemma, who was staring at him strangely. He guessed she was balancing on an edge somewhere between leaving him to his bizarre parallel world or disturbing him once again with the same message, hoping that it would eventually get through to his brain. He imagined he looked oddly vacant to her. Utterly lost. Sadly, he was.

She decided to repeat her words.

He knew that he had let the subconscious wasteland in his tortured head overtake the more pressing matters of the day. For a split-second, he thought Gemma held pity in her eyes and he realised that he had not been aware that she was standing there; such was the intensity of his...what was it?...

propensity to dwell in the shadows of his gloomy past.

'Mr Strange…?'

Michael stood and followed her from the room. He took the phone and surveyed his surroundings, checking up on Ronald. The gallery looked half-decent, given the difficult circumstances his colleague worked under. Good on him, Michael thought. He then caught Gemma's attention once more and mouthed the word 'tea' to her, raising an invisible cup to his lips. Watching her turn smartly in the direction of the kitchen, his mind focused on the call. The usual patter kicked in on autopilot:

'Michael Strange, the Churchill gallery. How may I help you?'

'Christ, good to hear that you're back at the helm.'

'Terry, is that you?' Michael's face lit up in an instant. He thrilled at the sound of his old drinking pal's voice. It had been several months since they had last spoken, and then at a time of great tension and sorrow as Terry, a journalist, helped him come to terms with the destruction in his life and the aftermath of Lauren's shocking death. Suddenly though, Michael's fleeting elation at hearing his friend's voice turned sullen. His eyes narrowed. Was this phone call a return to the dark days? He recalled a conversation they had several months ago, when Terry brought the terrifying news that Maggie was back on the scene and on the prowl again, intent on revenge for her sister's death.

Michael spoke guardedly, not wanting to disturb the hornet's nest. 'Where are you, Terry? What have you been up to?'

'I'm about to run a story on Northern Rock. My investigation has revealed a cash shortfall in the bank. I'm predicting a loss of confidence in the financial markets. Ever heard of the term sub-prime?'

'No…'

'Well, you soon will. Read it: The shit's about to hit the fan. I have a lead story out tomorrow. Should be fun. My editor is nervous. When I did a similar exposé last month comparing the US banking situation with our credit woes, he suddenly had both the financial regulators and the government on his case. I was accused of scaremongering.

But this is going to be big. Bloody fucking big.'

'Have you phoned just to tell me that?' Michael knew the answer already. The history between the two of them didn't usually involve monetary tips and banking regulatory gossip. He caught his breath.

'No.'

'Thought not.'

There was a silence, before Terry said: 'We need to talk.'

Michael took up the reins: 'About global fiscal policy?'

'Not exactly…'

Michael was tired and impatient. *Spit it out, man!*

'How about a pint?' Terry asked.

'When?'

Another silence as Gemma placed a cup of tea beside him.

'Michael,' Terry urged, 'I think we should get together pretty sharpish.' His tone was flat. 'How about tonight? Drinks on me.'

'That important, eh? Do you want to tell me what this is about or is it just an excuse to drown ourselves into a drunken stupor?'

'Ah, those were the days! Rather more serious than that, I'm afraid. Meet me at the Wessex at seven. They do a two-for-one bar meal and a bottle of house plonk for a tenner. As I said: my treat.'

'The last of the big spenders.'

'After my newspaper article, there'll be no more big spenders. You'll be grateful for my generous offer. Beyond that, it will be worldwide melt-down for everyone. See you later. Oh, and if you have shares in the Rock, sell now.'

Before Michael had time to reply, the line went dead. And so did his sinking heart. The proposed meeting would have nothing to do with international banking, nor global Armageddon, of that he was sure. No, Terry had other business too sensitive to discuss over the phone. Michael knew the subject of their forthcoming conversation. He just knew. Then he searched his memory: He did have shares in the Rock!

They were as safe as houses, surely…

He let the tea go cold.

***

The rest of the day ran relatively smoothly, despite Michael's foreboding after Terry's call. Toby arrived at just after twelve. and the glaziers followed at two. The activity of the workmen made business impossible and Toby decided to close the gallery to the public, until the dust and noise had abated. After his earlier efforts, Ronald was going spare, much to Michael's amusement. Gemma, bless her, made copious amounts of tea and coffee for everyone. At four, Michael got the alarm company to reinstall the security as the glass was cleaned down after the workmen had finished. It had been a horrible day, both frustrating and dirty. Eventually, Michael finished at just after five, took the tube, bought a copy of the *London Evening News* and got back to his apartment in Chelsea, where he showered quickly and then changed into a long sleeve polo shirt, jeans and chinos. He had a sneaky gin and tonic and scanned the paper for city gossip, picking up on the problems at Northern Rock. Terry was on the button again: A real pro. Then the worst kind of headline hit him between the eyes on page three:

TOP ART DEALER TO BE QUESTIONED AGAIN

Michael's insides somersaulted. Sweat formed on his brow. This fucking story would never go away. He read on:

The eminent art dealer Michael Strange of Churchill Fine Art in Mayfair is to be questioned again by police about the death of Lauren O'Neill, a client of his, also, allegedly, his lover, who was the victim of a devastating fire at her home in Surrey last year.

What really happened at Laburnum Farm on that fateful day remains a mystery, and Strange is expected to help with ongoing enquiries. The 43-year old woman died, trapped in the burning barn with her sister, Maggie, who miraculously survived alongside Michael Strange and his assistant Kara Scott and her boyfriend, Marcus Heath. At the time, it was suggested that they had gathered at the farm to discuss the sale of valuable paintings. However,

24

**the events leading up to the tragic incident have never
been fully explained , due to a court order protecting the
true identity of Ms O'Neill –As a minor she was convicted
of a murder and served her custodial sentence in a
psychiatric ward in Dublin before being released in the
1980s. Until the recovery of her body, Lauren's
whereabouts had remained unknown. The inquest, held
behind closed doors, recorded a verdict of death by
misadventure.**

Dizziness overcame him. He took a gulp of his drink and
slumped in an armchair overlooking the Thames far below,
which churned its silver coil into the distance …much the
same way as his gut churned, in turmoil. He tried to avert his
eyes from the text but something compelled him to prolong
the agony:

**Since the day of the fire, questions have been raised
about the relationship between Mr Strange and Lauren
O'Neill, how the fire started and why the five people were
at the farm that fateful day. It has been suggested that an
argument ensued over the ownership of the paintings by
the deceased artist, Patrick Porter.**

**Our enquiries have been hampered by the court order
protecting the identity of the victim, although we are now
in possession of her real name. The police have refused to
be drawn on why further investigation is necessary, but
we understand it concentrates on the fraudulent nature of
how the paintings were to be sold secretly on the black
market. Michael Strange has always denied this
allegation.**

**We understand the police wish to interview all those
present on the day to re-establish the motives of each and
dismiss the persistent rumours that Ms O'Neill (who was
separated from her husband) was killed in a
confrontation over the art collection. Were there other
mitigating circumstances held back from us? Some
newspapers have suggested that Laburnum Farm is now
a murder scene. Lauren's older sister, Maggie Conlon, is
wanted urgently for questioning. Clearly implicated in**

this mystery, she is believed to be still on the run. A police spokesman has warned she is a danger to the public and should not be approached. Both sisters had a history of violence..

Michael Strange has always maintained his innocence in relation to Lauren's death and emphasised that his role, as that of his colleague Kara and her boyfriend, was purely professional in all dealings with the deceased. He was badly burned in the inferno and has only recently returned to work.

A spokesman for the police stressed that Mr Strange has fully cooperated with the investigation and his eyewitness testimony will help shed further light on the case. Lauren O'Neill is survived by her estranged husband, Julius Gray, who lives in Venice with his long term Italian girlfriend and their daughter. He too is expected to be interviewed.

Michael discarded the newspaper and searched the mail and found what he was looking for: A formal letter from the police instructing him to arrange an appointment for the interview at the earliest convenience. They weren't wasting time.

The phone rang, and instinctively Michael knew who it was. He listened with all the enthusiasm of a blind man trying to cross the road.

'It's Toby. I've just read the *London Evening News…*'

Michael sucked his breath in. 'I'm so…'

'This will kill us, Dad…when will it end?'

'I didn't expect this, Toby.'

'Well, we got it that's for sure. All barrels blazing.'

Michael refrained from responding.

'We need to talk in the morning,' Toby said, and then disconnected the line.

Michael felt horrible; there was a feeling like a bottomless pit in his stomach. Somehow the meeting with Terry now filled him with renewed horror: more grief on the horizon. He downed a second gin and tonic and slowly headed off to the Wessex on the King's Road.

The bar was surprisingly noisy, with many late night shoppers taking advantage of the bargain half-price meal for two. If Terry's earlier pronouncement of universal doom and gloom was true, then Michael surmised that this was to be the Last Supper. To die, die full.

He searched around and found Terry, who had grabbed a table at the rear of the building, in a darkened corner. This instantly worried him.

'I've ordered,' he said matter-of-factly as Michael approached timidly. 'You're late, and I wasn't going to lose the deal.'

Michael sat down. 'Great to see you too…'

Terry ignored him, and replied, 'Red chicken curry and a bottle of Tiger beer. Can't beat it. You get a choice of wine or beer.' Then he stared back, examining his visitor's face. 'You look like shit.'

'And you haven't changed. Still the same rude fucker with the ugly manners of a farm pig ready for slaughter.'

'Maybe, but I'm also the best journalist in London with a nose for a cracking story…which reminds me.'

Michael dived in: 'A hack, working on the cheap end tabloids. And don't mention the bloody news story on you-know-who. I've already had an earful from my son.'

'It's unavoidable. These things never go away,' Terry countered, 'it's how you deal with it that matters. When are you going to speak to the police?'

Michael frowned. 'They can wait…'

As if by magic, the food and drinks arrived, courtesy of a cherub-faced young girl who looked like the singer, Sarah Brightman.

'Thanks, Luv,' Terry said, as she placed the plates and cutlery on the table. He tossed some coins on her tray. 'Give my regards to Sir Andrew.'

She stood back, studied him in bewilderment, and murmured, 'Watcha say?'

Michael rescued her. 'Forgive my friend.'

'Whatever…' The girl said and disappeared into the crowd.

The two men clinked bottles, grinned and downed the beer.

'Great to see you,' Michael said, swigging greedily and tucking into the piping hot curry. It wasn't bad either. Good pub grub.

'Chelsea are still crap,' Terry responded. 'Wait till the Gooners thrash you at the Emirates next month. I have tickets... fancy the humiliation?

'Are you treating me?'

'Winner pays. Game on?'

Michael sensed his moment to strike. 'How much do I owe you then?'

'Smart-ass.'

The table became littered with beer bottles. Eventually, Michael checked his watch and ordered coffee. His patience was wearing thin: When was Terry going to raise *the* subject, the one that was too sensitive to discuss on the phone? They had covered most banal subjects and the conversation was becoming exhausted. Michael picked up that Terry was becoming somewhat agitated.

'Well?' Michael asked during a prolonged silence. 'What's so damn awkward that you avoid the very topic that brought us here in the first place. We're suitably pissed not to feel aggrieved or embarrassed by what needs to be said. Spit it out. What's the problem, Terry?'

Terry fidgeted on his seat, and said: 'Two things, actually. One *is* a bit embarrassing, and ultimately damaging to your reputation and could...'

Michael laughed and jumped in: 'Embarrassing? That's a word I seldom associate with you!'

Terry lowered his eyes and folded his arms. '...And could threaten our friendship. The other issue, personal to me, has certainly got me fucking angry to the point of despair.'

'Christ, Terry. You'd better talk.'

The two old friends stared at each other. They both had a haunted look. The intervening years hadn't been kind. Terry's eyes suddenly became moist and his mouth tightened. Michael detected fear in the air.

'We have a problem,' Terry said, lowering his gaze once more. 'I've been commissioned to write a lead story for a weekend glossy magazine. Piece of bollocks, normally. Good money for me and high profile readership material that will add weight to my CV. A no-brainer. However, it's a controversial piece, and highly damaging to the reputation of the main protagonist who the editor wants me to take issue with. I've been told to dig up all the dirt. It's called character assassination in the trade. You know the type of thing: Lurid headlines.' He waited, frowned, then said, 'It concerns an infamous London art dealer.'

'Fuck,' Michael said. He hadn't seen this coming.

Terry swallowed hard from one of the unfinished bottles. 'Michael, it's an investigative story. No stone unturned. Heavy hitting, do you understand what I'm saying?'

Michaels's face turned ashen. 'I can see it now: "Inferno at farm!"'

He shook his head slowly, then continued: 'Rich Mayfair art dealer caught in web of deceit, trying to offload paintings for a shed full of cash. Woman found dead in suspicious circumstances. How did she die? Was she silenced? Who killed her? Is that the kind of thing, Terry? It would leave my professional standing in tatters: utterly destroyed. It would bring my ex-wife Adele out of the woodwork as well, and she would revel in it and then blame me for failing to protect family privacy, blah, blah, blah. Her vendetta against me would not be a pretty sight in the newspapers. Not to mention what a story like that would do to Kara and Marcus.' He shook his head violently. 'Jesus fucking Christ, Terry, this is becoming a witch-hunt!'

Terry leaned forward and grabbed Michael's arm. 'This story is big because the public have a thirst for it. It's going to be written, Michael, and whether you like it or not, published and syndicated right around the world. It has all the ingredients of high drama and intrigue and, dare I say it, enough sex to entice the movie men as well. Listen to me. Let me do the story, this way I keep control. I can protect you. If it goes out to commission you'll get hammered by a third-rate journalist who will portray a juicy tale of lust, betrayal and grandiose greed. I can at least bring a degree of dignity to the proceedings. You're going to have to trust me on this, OK?'

'Can we stop it?'

'No.'

'Can we delay it?'

'No, not if you want me on board.'

'I can sue the bastards, take out an injunction.'

'Not a chance. The story is already in the public domain.'

Michael gripped Terry's hand and squeezed. 'Keep me informed of every development…and I mean everything. I need to speak to people. Find me time, OK?'

'We can do better than that. We'll work together on the project. This way I can emphasise your support for the truth and bring credibility to your character and the reason for your actions. I'll keep Kara in the margins. I can also gain sympathy from the reader, especially in regard to your injuries but – and I must stress this point – I cannot hide from the facts, Michael. A woman was killed, and a damned glamorous one at that, even if she was a mental case. Work with me and you will survive the sneers and pointed fingers that will inevitably come your way. It won't be pretty, the tabloids will hunt you down like a pack of wolves. Don't hide, show your face. Damage limitation is the name of the game.'

Michael slumped in his chair, overcome by a mist of uncertainty and absolute terror. The devil had returned to the table. Terry was right, they had to collaborate on this one. He felt light-headed and sick. The coffee had gone cold, as had the conversation. Michael was in meltdown.

They sat in silence, two worlds apart, unable to speak. The bar was virtually empty, save for the angelic Sarah B. clearing the tables of dirty glasses. One day soon she could be reading his bloody life story in the papers, Michael pondered with a shudder. He thought, hoped, that everything had calmed down. Yesterday's news. Not a chance. There was always someone wanting to rake up the past. Then he turned to confront his pal, a thousand thoughts whirling around his head.

'You said there was two issues to discuss. If my sordid life history is the so-called embarrassment, then what could possibly make you any more angrier than me at this point in time?'

Terry pursed his lips and exhaled breath. Then he lit a cigarette and didn't care that he was killing himself. He blew a spiral of smoke into the stale air and locked into Michael's gaze.

'I've got prostate cancer,' he announced.

***

The following day, Michael awoke slowly and painfully, acutely aware that a pneumatic drill hammered away at his skull. He tried to recall the number of beers he had consumed in the pub, but the count wasn't necessary... the inner thudding of his head told him everything. The last time he felt this bad was...with Terry. *Christ.* Would he ever learn? He soaked himself under a blissfully hot shower, towelled down and dressed casually in red cashmere crewneck and corduroy slacks. He made his way into the kitchen and drank copious amounts of steaming black coffee. Pulling back the window blind, he peered down to street level and saw workmen digging up the road. He felt marginally better in the knowledge that the pneumatic drill was not imaginary, nor confined to his head.

Terry. Dear God! His thoughts returned to their conversation last night, cut short by his friend's sudden admission of prostate cancer. Michael felt a natural obligation to jump in and offer both moral and financial help. Yet at the moment of support it was typical that, like most men, the severity of the situation was suddenly diminished by a series of jokes. Basically, they elected to sweep it conveniently under the carpet and have another beer. He recalled one awkward moment, punctuated by a Terry sideswipe that the side-effects of surgery was incontinence and loss of an erection. What was the problem then? He had joked. Michael reluctantly shared the humour but felt unease at not being able to talk seriously through the diagnosis, as a woman would do in the same circumstances. In a man's world, illness and especially a terminal sentence was to be avoided at all costs because...well, it might just go away in their fantasy world, and besides it was uncomfortable for men to dwell on such mundane matters as life and death. Football was more important than life and death, as the great Bill Shankly had once remarked.

It baffled him that Terry had been more concerned with Michael's welfare than his own private issues. Typical of the man, Michael thought of his friend: dismissive of his own serious health problem, which he had referred almost bizarrely as just an afterthought to the evening. Shit. In reality, his friend was desperately crying out for help but was too afraid to ask for it.

Michael dialled the extension number at News International in Wapping and got straight through to Terry.

'I can help,' Michael said. 'I know a top physician who has helped pioneer laser treatment for prostate sufferers. It's less invasive than surgery, and apparently you get to keep your hard-on.'

Terry laughed and said, 'Thanks for that. This call was on audio and so you've just informed fifty other people in the office, including my secretary who is just twenty-two, that not only am I dying of cancer but I can die with an erection if I so fancy it.'

'Jesus, Terry. Switch to private. This is serious.'

'I have, and thanks.'

'What is the prognosis?'

'…With the cancer or my dick?'

'Cut the jokes, Terry. How far has the cancer spread?'

'I'm due for a MRI scan which will tell me. So far the biopsy result has revealed a localised central cancer, moderately aggressive. My Gleason reading was 3:3 which indicates early malignant growth, a type which can be managed successfully with the right treatment but the specialist is uncertain at this stage. Basically, I'm fucked. Left alone, it will kill me eventually, like the fags. But I like a hard-on as much as the fags. Life goes on, eh?'

'Listen, Terry, cut the fags and booze. As from now you need to eat healthily and drink pure pomegranate juice…'

'You sound like my mother.'

Michael ignored him. 'I'll organise an appointment with this consultant at Chelmsford. I've been doing some research and he is the top guy.'

'I can't afford him, Michael.'

'I can. I won't take no for an answer. Will you see him?'

'Call it a loan and you're on.'

'No. I want to help…'

'Is this a bribe, so that I'll go easy on you in the news story?'

'Fuck that, Terry. No bribe. We go back way too far. Money is irrelevant in the circumstances.'

'I thought you were wiped out from the divorce?'

'I was, but let's just say I can get my hands on the amount that is required. I'm not destitute. I can always sell my shares in Northern Rock, what do you think?'

'A wise move, but do it quickly. The financial markets are getting very twitchy.'

'Then that settles it.'

Terry went quiet, then said surprisingly, 'I'm meeting my editor in an hour to outline my take on the events that led up to Lauren's death at the farm. I intend to tell her that I have approached you and you are fully compliant with my line of enquiry. So much so that you are willing to cooperate in all aspects of how you all came to be engulfed in a fire which ultimately killed someone. I need to convince her that you wish to support the storyline and not jeopardise it. This way I can tone down the context, make it less sensational, but she will insist that my approach is hard-hitting. It is fair to point out that things will get a little uncomfortable, but I have to ask the right questions or she'll see straight through me. I mention this because I can easily be replaced if I sway from the original idea for the piece. Are you on board with this?'

Michael pondered. 'Will the police be brought into the equation?'

'Undoubtedly.'

'Will I be quoted in your piece?'

'Naturally.'

'Kara too?'

'As I said last night, I'll keep her on the margins but she will need to be informed of what I'm doing. Will you do this?'

'Yes, with reluctance.'

'Remember, trust me on this. We can wash our dirty linen in public but in this case I can make sure that the public ultimately see only the whites blowing squeaky clean on the line. Within a fortnight everything will be forgotten. Fish and chip paper. Then the story can be buried.'

'Deal. Now let's get this medical treatment sorted and quickly, so that the story is not the only thing we are burying.'

Terry laughed again. Only this time his loudness was subdued, rather like the gravity in Michael's pointed tone.

Both knew he wasn't joking this time.

'Piece of advice,' Terry said. 'Sell your shares first thing tomorrow. Take whatever price is being offered. There'll be no recovery.'

There wasn't a trace of amusement in his voice either.

CHAPTER TWO

Gripping the metal railings, her balled hands turned knuckle white with fear. She peered tentatively into the dark waters of the lagoon below and caught sight of her reflection, which sent an icy shiver rattling through her spine. It was as if the ghosts of her past stared back and haunted her, bringing first terror and then tears to her eyes.

Was this a movie? Was this a dream? Unnervingly, whichever way she viewed it, the logic in her brain told her that this was for real. But how could it be so? She was on the footbridge, but now, in a second instance, she also stood observing this odd situation a few paces away: in a parallel world, unable to make contact, as if separated by...what exactly? It was like a weird out-of-body-experience, the sort of thing people try to explain, but fail. This young woman, wrapped in a red woollen overcoat, hesitated on the precipice of the subconscious world and thought of...well, murder; and then the consequences of her own demise. It scared her witless. And she wanted to scream, but no sound would come.

Although feeling nauseous and ill-at-ease with her predicament, the young woman somehow regained her composure, and in spite of everything, remained surprisingly firm and defiant in the face of adversity. Killing, after all, was the reason why she was here in Venice. This was ordinarily a place for lovers to meet, certainly, and sworn enemies too, it now seemed.

Love and loathing, separated only by the whisper of betrayal and broken promises.

My name is Kara Scott, she lamented so quietly, fearful of revealing her identity to the unseen eyes of the forgotten. They were out there, somewhere, for sure. You'd better believe it, she reminded herself forcefully, shouting the words aloud this time: My name is Kara Scott! She was determined not to hide away, stepping meekly into this world of the unforgiving. Her booming voice unsettled a flock of seagulls and they erupted into the sky, leaving behind a widening arc of glistening foam on the surface of the black water. A line of canal boats, held together tightly by rope, creaked and moaned, their polished timber hulls rhythmically colliding as the ripples unsettled the moorings.

This city: a place of poetry, for sure; never of death. From somewhere above her, a window shutter clattered open, revealing a bare-chested man on a balcony. The dazzling light caught his rough, unshaven face. Beguilingly, he then played a violin recital to sweeten the ears of those blessed to be so close. Such magical repose...just then, this same sunlight sliced through the shadows and illuminated the decayed houses, signalling church bells and people gradually awakening to their daily chores and early morning Mass.

Kara marvelled, and then came back to earth, reminding herself of why she was here...An eye for an eye. She walked a solitary path, leaving music and dreams to others. Slowly, the streets came alive. Behind closed doors, idle chatter began to emerge and daily life infiltrated the deserted alleyways once more. She was no longer alone. Yet in her mind, she was alone for eternity.

Meandering across a pretty, cobbled square, Kara cherished the first of the sun as it caressed her pale skin. The aroma of bitter ground coffee and fresh oven-baked bread invaded her nostrils. Before, when death had not become her constant companion, she would happily embrace the sights and smells of the world, rather like a child would her first rag doll. But now though, it was almost impossible. For Kara Scott, the bloody violence of her history was a burden too great to carry.

This was the reason for being here, in this bejewelled city: to confront her demons, and force a path to a new beginning. A renewal of her faith; was how she best summed it up. One problem plagued her, though. Was she capable of a cold blooded killing, when it really came down to it? Her own life was on the line. She had to be prepared to forsake it in order to rid the world of the evil that forever followed her.

In her tortured mind, betrayal and trust was a two-headed monster, with far-reaching tentacles that lured her to a place too dark to speak of. Marcus, dear, dear Marcus spoke of it as a form of depression, something that she should merely 'get over'. Not so. Revenge was silent like the assassin, ready to explode with deadly intent. If asked, she would tell it like it was...

Why were these images so vivid...so haunting?

She hated herself for thinking such shocking thoughts...the very notion of retribution made her feel violently sick. But it came nonetheless, and now she had to deal with it. A tooth for a tooth...

If need be, she was prepared to die here on these ancient streets. The prospect was both chilling and repellent, and very, very dominant in her head. The enemy was close, after all.

As quickly as she contemplated this, she instinctively turned to look over her shoulder. In the darkness of an archway, a slight movement in the shadows made her jump. It was nothing of course, just the scratching of a water rat. But her fear could go beyond the aroma of coffee and bread, and her acute sense of smell picked up danger in the air. She knew she was being stalked. In fact, she had been aware of it for some time, ever since her echoing footsteps carried her off the main promenade and into the unknown streets. This meandering path took her over the Accademia bridge and into the narrow Dorsoduro district.

It was at this point that Kara halted, took stock, and entered impulsively into the Academy of Arts, knowing that hidden eyes were mapping her unplanned course. This stain from her past almost touched her now, she could even detect the stench from the breath of the beast itself, not far behind her.

Every now and again, Kara deflected her gaze from the gigantic ornate biblical Titians that adorned the walls and paused, listening acutely...Ah, there it was again, that whisper on the wind, a footstep too far, a sigh beneath the quickening heartbeat. So very close...

It was maddening to be the quarry, but the rules of engagement would be set by Kara when she was good and ready. For now, she would play the game and portray herself as the willing victim, drawing her foe into the lair of her making. It was a necessary diversion. Kara wanted the upper hand at the precise moment of combat.

Out into daylight once more, Kara felt the first drops of rain hit the pavement. The early sun had by now vanished behind restless dark clouds, leaving a solemn cast over the faded ochre-coloured houses. Such beauty so saddened.

It did not matter. Beyond the downpour, a rainbow emerged, as yet undiscovered. That was the way with nature. It held surprises, some of which were spectacularly beautiful, some of which were savage. This day, this hour, and the days to follow...well, Kara was sure of one thing. A mighty storm was gathering on the horizon, known to her, undetected by all others. This knowledge kept her ahead of the game.

Or so she thought. A lengthening shadow suddenly reached her from behind, touching her toes, and extending beyond. It made her stiffen. In the square, nobody paid any attention to this, except for a scabby dog that stopped, stared, tilted his head and then looked beyond her. Do dogs see ghosts? This one saw something that it didn't take too kindly to. It yelped and scampered off with indecent haste, disappearing down a blind alleyway.

Just then, a man, familiar to her, came out from the same spot and glanced in her direction. A shaft of bright light obscured his identity, but it made her heart race. Then he vanished. Michael, is that...could that possibly be you?

Kara opened her mouth to scream his name, but held counsel, dismissing such notion. It was improbable of course, although she always held a belief in the truth of angels on this earth.

Turning carefully, the shadow still remained defiantly under her feet. What surprised her was the sudden nerveless energy she felt. It empowered her, knowing that Michael was also close by: her protector.

Such false hope: In an instant, the strength of her resolve evaporated. Her eyes met those of another, and the blood in her veins turned to ice. Sheer terror crept up and rendered her defenceless. She felt totally disengaged from reality, gripped by paralysis.

It wasn't meant to be like this. It wasn't how she imagined it. Confronting the future was as cruel as facing the past. No *angel here, for sure. The glinting blade came down upon her throat with lightning speed. This vision was death itself, and crushed everything she held dear to her heart. Kara wobbled, and felt her legs buckle as her life slowly ebbed away...*

She gasped. Everything happened so fast. It was her call to witness, dashing all hope of recovery.

Kara Scott awoke with an almighty jolt, compounded by a headache from hell that seemed destined to tear her head from her shoulders. *Christ.* The shock of the dream made her feel nauseous and dizzy with fright. This was the third successive night that the nightmare had returned to haunt her. Three fucking nights... she was exhausted by the awful repetition of it all. And to make matters worse her sudden awakening coincided always at the pivotal sequence, that dreadful moment when her life was abruptly terminated, when her very existence ended, in such savage fashion, by the downward thrust of the knife puncturing her throat. Not once, but again and again the blade fell, until consciousness failed her, and blood misted over her eyes. Then there was nothing; just a silent compressed void, like being trapped in a coffin. Like death itself.

From somewhere though, a rasping sound somehow penetrated the stifling air and Kara knew it was her own voice – her own scream – that saved her in the dream. On each occasion, she had sat bolt upright in bed and clawed at the darkness of the room with her outstretched hands, her breath caught dry, trying desperately to fend off her unworldly assailant. Bad things always came in the dead of the night. Now, in the hour before dawn, she was safe once more from the wilful invaders of her mind. Damn, how she wished for an escape from such torment. Shaking her head, she imagined being alone with her irrational fears, but then her thoughts turned to untroubled Marcus...who slept serenely beside her. Dear Marcus. Then she cursed silently, knowing he was somewhere else, at peace with the world. How she envied his ability to switch off from all that was rotten at the edge of reason: for her reasoning, at least. All that remained for her was the clammy, weird feeling of her enormously stretched skin, which was a stark reminder of her maternal responsibilities. *Oh, Christ.* In the darkened room her hand rested upon a protruding belly which, surprisingly enough, she discovered was her own. She simply couldn't get used to being pregnant. Impending motherhood: not so much a surprise, more a realisation of utter shock. And like the bump she touched, the shock never diminished. It just grew and grew.

The bedroom was stiflingly hot, like the Sahara desert scorched by the midday sun. The air had been sucked from the room. Reaching out in the dark, Kara knocked over the bedside glass of water with her fumbling hand. Shit! The sound of the glass thumping the wooden floor forced Marcus to swear under his breath and turn over, away from her. Kara remained motionless, overcome by the heat. Perspiration trickled down her neck. The recurring nightmare terrified her, but she needed to keep quiet about it in the knowledge that Marcus was near breaking point with her constant worrying about what it all meant. It was eroding their close emotional bond, and lurking in the back of her brain was the nagging suspicion that her attacker was out there and ready to do harm. And this attacker was very real. It all centred on the absurd sisters of doom (as Michael, her former boss, always referred to them), and the terrible destruction they had caused…and Maggie was still hovering somewhere. This dream was a foretaste of what was to come, she was convinced of it.

Slowly, Kara lifted herself from the sodden bed and shuffled to the bathroom, had a pee and gulped water from the sink tap. The headache still raged. This dream was strange to the point of surreal. Kara reluctantly re-enacted in her mind what happened. The attacker who confronted her with the sharpened blade was framed by a rainbow, their face hidden behind a Venetian mask, a grotesque shiny white mask with ruby encrusted decoration and slit-eyed perforations to see through. The wearer of the mask was unknown to Kara, which further intimidated her and caused confusion and panic. Was it Maggie? Then there was the downward thrust of the dagger, blood profusion, the last gasp of breath. What person, or demon, wanted to harm her? Was it..? Who possessed such a sheer evil intent to destroy life?

She knew of course, but it was as difficult to say the name as imagine the face behind the mask.

It was all too much. With the bathroom spinning insanely, Kara threw up.

***

The dawn light crept through the window slats, bathing her face in a soft glow. Kara awoke slowly, finding herself propped against the side of the roll-top Victorian bath. Her spine ached, and cramp besieged her left leg which was twisted awkwardly beneath her right. She yelled out, stretching her limbs and massaging furiously with her hands until the pain subsided. She managed to stand and wobble to the sink, splashing cold water onto her face. Searching her reflection in the mirror, Kara winced at the ghastly image that stared back. She hardly recognised herself. Beneath her, on the floor, a sticky mess squashed under her foot. God, how did it come to this? The smell of sick turned her stomach. Grabbing a tissue, she wiped between her toes, tossed a towel over the offending mess, and retreated from the bathroom.

Whatever was happening to her life – right now – Kara resolved to get help before the remnants of her sanity was overwhelmed by these terrifying demons that infiltrated her subconscious world. Marcus, dear Marcus, knew of her fears, but he was so strong and able to compartmentalise his own horrors, if they existed at all. She was envious of his calmness. Damn him, the conceit of his confidence. But then she regretted her verdict and realised that this morbid outlook on all things that threatened their happiness was really wrapped up in the child she was carrying. This precious baby, this beating heart…if Kara couldn't handle the reality of the past, and the bloody consequence of how she survived that past, then how the hell was she going to face the future and all the uncertainty that it entailed? She had to get a grip on reality, and fast. This should be a great time, she reminded herself, to no avail.

Motherhood freaked her out, if the truth was told. She just wasn't ready for it, physically or spiritually. Christ, she could hardly clean her teeth in the morning, such was her feeble resolve. Before the fire at the barn, Kara had the strength of a lioness and the capability to tackle whatever life threw in her direction. But now...*Now?* Even the tiniest problems in her life became insurmountable. For example, just yesterday she despaired at the difficulty of unscrewing the lid from a jar of pickle, which refused to budge. What happened? She saw fit to throw the offending item into the sink, smashing it, rather than do the simple thing and ask Marcus to open it. Although he laughed at the incident, she knew she was out of control. Everything was an issue, a big deal; one that her brain could not fathom out. Kara was aware that Marcus was beside himself with worry, but he always had the capacity to hide his anger and frustration at her bizarre behaviour. This infuriated her. Deep down, she asked herself a thousand times how he managed to cope with her tantrums. But still she challenged him, pushing him constantly to the limits of his endurance. It was as if she wanted to break him...punish him for infecting her with this embryonic seed of life. This was *his* child. She was not ready, not prepared, her mind and body recoiling from the rejoicing of new birth, a blessed cycle of nature that for her was a form of cancer. The latter thought slammed home. How could she think such a thing? Was she going mad?

For the second time, Kara imagined her responsibility to motherhood, and in that same moment, she saw that she did not possess the inner strength to see it through. This intrusion...it invaded her body and threatened what was truly important in her life right now. The brittle truth dawned: how was she able to protect her child when she was not able to protect herself? What kind of mother would that make her?

Staring at the sleeping figure of Marcus, half-submerged beneath the sheets, Kara somehow managed to draw strength from envisaging him being an angel of light: someone who held pure love for them – mother and baby – to lean upon. And this child she carried would prevail, and help uplift her beyond negativity and finally banish this nastiness to another dimension: one that could not harm them.

God, she had to believe this. In order to survive, as any mother would testify.

***

Earlier, Marcus Heath had stirred, turned over and reached out for Kara, only to discover that he was alone in bed...again. He cleared his head, and knew precisely where he would find her. He stepped onto the wooden floor, trod a strange dampness and retrieved an empty glass from underfoot. In the darkness, with the curtains drawn, the only light came as a thin blade from under the bathroom door. He sighed, knowing that this is where he would find her, huddled on the floor, her back propped against the bath, her eyes red raw. He felt inadequate, powerless to break into her hidden world of imaginary demons. However much he tried to sympathise, he felt he was a spectator, unable to reach out and truly help. Here was the rub. As long as Kara continued to keep him at arm's length he felt defenceless to protect her from harm's way. And there was a monster out there, a very real monster. Inside, Marcus was as scared as his girlfriend of the power and destruction that Maggie – he could hardly breathe when her name was mentioned – possessed.

Marcus padded into the kitchen and made tea, scalding his fingers on the boiling kettle as he tried to handle things as calmly as possible. It was going to be a long day. Silently, he entered the bathroom again and nestled beside her. She smiled thinly and sipped from the welcome cup that he handed to her. Through the slats of the window blind, the majestic outline of Tower Bridge stood silhouetted against the crimson sky. A new day beckoned. He felt useless in the circumstances of her suffering, but she hugged him anyway, and he in turn was silently grateful, the hug bringing comfort to them both. In this strange vacuum, Marcus reflected on their lives and knew he had a more practical sense of what was happening. He offered words, he offered explanation, but she was not ready for this. Kara needed nursing, it was that simple. She was in denial, and the impending birth of their baby was simply too soon. They had been thrust together just months earlier, in adversity and unexpected intensity, finding a path of sorts to real love, and as a consequence of this collision they had no fortitude, no grasp, of how they were going to bring this little bundle into the world and care for it.

They had no reserves of energy. Trauma was debilitating, and neither of them had the capability to restore their dormant batteries.

Parenthood was terrifying. Slowly, he ran this over in his head once more. Then he cast the thought from his brain, changed the subject (for the hundredth time), and offered other words, kinder words as far from the truth as he dared, to a lost soul. He knew that practicality, from a man's point of view, would not do the trick. Eventually, he went back to bed, insisting she join him. She nodded, but stayed alone for a while longer, gathering her thoughts for the day ahead and what it might bring.

***

It was a Sunday. Marcus made a late breakfast, knowing he didn't need to open the gallery until 11.30 am. Owning his own proper gallery still bewildered him, and brought a rare smile to his face. He was a grown-up now, an entrepreneur...no longer the pompous artist. Who would have believed it? He was a player of sorts, mixing with the adults in the real world! Like a bad actor though, he had his insecurities and feared being found out: that he couldn't actually hack it. And then what? There was no going back. He liked the new-found status of pretending to be a businessman...and, in spite of his shortcomings and inexperience, he was making a decent fist of it. The label of businessman fitted, much to his astonishment. So much had happened since the fire at Laburnum Farm. He took a moment to reflect on what a weird transformation had taken place. For him, defying death prompted a new direction in his professional life. He'd quickly taken stock of the situation and, to his utter astonishment, abandoned art – in the sense of making a precarious living from actually painting pictures. His heart went out of it. The light switched off. He preferred instead to open a sculpture and glass gallery with his girlfriend on Butler's Wharf in the east end of London, just a few minutes' walk from where they now lived. It was a real turn-up for the books which surprised family and friends.

He vowed to no longer starve for a living, preferring a

steady 9 to 5 job to bring in a respectable income. Fed up with being the eternal struggler with little or no cash, he conformed, begrudgingly, to a different work ethic and planned to make his fortune this way instead. This abrupt change of direction was somewhat forced upon him by two unpalatable truths. Firstly, his pissed-off acceptance that his own work was not of the standard required to make the necessary inroads on the glittering path to stardom and, secondly, his desire to guide Kara back to a normality of existence once again. She had nearly lost her life in the fire. She had lost her job at the gallery, and the status it brought. She had lost her income. She had lost her close friendship with her boss, Michael Strange. He felt he owed her, and a commitment to work was a good starting point.

Kara needed closure. Marcus knew this and in his heart he felt the unspoken trust had eroded between them. Both survived the inferno: but at what cost to their sanity? So he fumbled on, in the background, just being there, showing that he cared. This was all that mattered. Marcus reckoned that she despised herself for being so helpless and devoid of emotional longing. Before the fire, she was feisty. But now? She was a broken woman. He had a word for it: It was called inadequacy.

***

Staring at him over breakfast, Kara read his thoughts and wanted to weep. She longed to get back on track in her relationship with not just Marcus but everyone else: Michael, especially. It was hugely unfair on all of them, but she felt incapable to contribute toward, well, social interaction: a basic need to communicate. She was devoid of intimacy and emotion, on any level.

Maggie, this dangerous fugitive, consumed her every thought. While she was still free, this woman stood between her happiness with Marcus and also diminished her lust for life. Day and night, Maggie loomed over them like a spectre, hiding in the shadows, ready to re-enter their lives.

There was another cause of tension too; an unspeakable shocking pact made between her and Marcus, never to be broken for fear of recrimination. It was this: Marcus had started the fire that killed Lauren O'Neill. This horrendous fact gnawed away at them every waking hour. No one had to die that fateful day. Both she and Marcus were complicit in withholding this information from the police, and as a result they were now bound to secrecy forever. The thread of their relationship was stretched to the limit and Maggie would play on this weakness and seek revenge for the death of her sister. Kara was sure of that.

Kara reflected on the long, difficult months after the funeral of Lauren O'Neill, when police suspicions were at their most intense. Rumours persisted as to which sister actually died that day. Who could be sure that it was Lauren who perished, the body in the barn having been burnt to a cinder? As far as Kara understood it, DNA from the corpse (taken from the hip bone, which was all that remained) was not conclusive until a comparison could be made with a family connection: hence the need to find the errant sister. The police only had Michael's eyewitness report that he saw Lauren fall, but he, according to the pathologist, was undoubtedly confused at the time, near to death himself. Nothing would be resolved until Maggie (whom they all assumed was the one to escape) was apprehended. Then the doubts could be put to bed. Until then, however far-fetched it seemed, Kara had to ask the question: Suppose it was Lauren who escaped and was on the run?

In the meantime, the three survivors tried desperately to live with the guilt of what happened at the farm, and how each of them conspired to hide the cause of the fire from the police. This was the fucking problem. They were struggling to keep the secret. The burden was becoming too great.

Yes, Marcus took steps to protect Kara from this dreadful scenario as best he knew how. They grieved for what might have been: a safe and loving world in which to live. This was Michael's promise, snatched away in a heartbeat. Her pregnancy then came unexpectedly, but it was a joy to behold in the beginning. A blessing. Their lives turned topsy-turvy and they initially basked in the wonder of it all. However, looking back, they were too young to cope with the impending responsibility of parenthood.

Kara was too young to cope with most things, if the truth be known. To escape the press attention, the police investigation, to recover from her wounds, she first sold her flat in central London and moved, with Marcus, to the east end at Tower Hamlets, north of the Thames. Home was now an old warehouse conversion, with extra light and space in which to stretch and breathe and ultimately for the both of them to recover in, physically and spiritually. Additional funds from the move to a cheaper area in the city gave them choices as well. The gallery idea was a joint decision, allowing them both to find structure and focus and a steady income, especially as she wasn't working. The months of recuperation meant she had to rest during the pregnancy, doctor's orders. This period of time brightened their lives: For a while, at least.

Then the fear crept in. Kara would go about her daily business and nod complacently to those friends who smiled back, and preferred to listen to the wise words of Marcus instead. She was too exhausted to argue, and a gentle nod here and there saved so much explaining, so much bother. Who was listening anyway?

Inwardly, the utter heartbreak that she endured, and endured alone, in spite of Marcus being the rock on which she stood, was known to her by another name. Her suffering was abiding grief and it pained her that he could not enter into this world that she inhabited. This grief, the loss of innocence, was embedded within her very soul, to the exclusion of all others. Sometimes it took her to the edge of madness.

But gradually, over the ensuing months, something had changed. From the womb of grief came a tidal wave of anger. It consumed her brain with terrifying intensity and would not abate. She was becoming angry with everyone.

***

Marcus was exhausted by Kara's submergence into despair and depression. He felt wholly pathetic in dealing with her continued vulnerability, but he always reminded himself that he had made her a promise: a solemn promise to keep her safe, and provide a home and stability for the family. In his own dark moments, he reinforced this pledge to help her overcome the remorse she so painfully experienced. He tried to share everything with her but he could never quite reach beyond his own limited capabilities, given their grim history. And this was the difficulty.

There could never be a normal existence while the secret remained buried and unspoken to others, for them to carry to eternity. Perhaps even worse, they always needed to look over their shoulders, for fear of Maggie creeping up on them. In his head, it was *never* Lauren creeping up on them.

When Maggie escaped the inferno, evil escaped that day too.

Eventually, Marcus looked up from washing the pots in the sink and asked, 'Do you want to talk about it?'

'I'm too exhausted…actually, too scared,' Kara said.

So they avoided the topic, again. He hugged her, and then put his jacket on. This signalled the start of the day for him. Finally, he was off to work, burdened by the price they had to pay for the sins of others.

***

Marcus hoped for a busy day at the gallery. The rent was due on the premises and money was needed urgently through the till. It had been a difficult time recently, with the credit crunch taking hold. The City was particularly affected, and widespread redundancies were predicted within the banking corporations. These were his customers, so things were looking bleak.

London had that effect, always on the edge, forever teetering between boom and bust. As the world's leading financial centre, this was where mega fortunes and unwarranted reputations could be made. Or lost.

On this day, Marcus was caught somewhere in the middle of such vanity. As a budding businessman, he lacked the necessary experience and guile to weather the slowdown in trade, preferring to bury his head beneath the parapet, for fear of getting shot at. On top of the impending rent demand, business rates for the month were also due, plus the quarterly electricity bill. This was no fun, he acknowledged privately to himself. Making money was bloody hard. Still, he had to look on the brighter side, the bankers were still pulling in the bonuses, in spite of continued failure. This screwed with his brain: How could they sleep at night?

Then he remembered: they didn't sleep. They partied the nights away on Champagne and cocaine. Screw the world was their motto. On the one hand Marcus envied their mantra of work hard, live hard. But he wanted above all else to sleep at peace with himself. And Kara swore he slept for England. He did, actually, despite his worries. But here was the thing. On reflection, above all else, he wanted money in the bank, that degree of financial clout which meant he was not answerable to anyone who came knocking on his door. In other words: he sought financial freedom by any means. Marcus decided there and then he would fight dirty to get it. He had a plan...and pondered on the killer deal he secretly had lined up.

Marcus opened up at 11.30 am, after a short stroll along the boardwalk of St. Katharine Docks. It was a fresh morning, the still waters reflecting the gleaming hulls of the yachts tied to their moorings. A swan glided effortlessly in the blinding sun. Passing the array of shops, Marcus grabbed a salt beef sandwich, a latte to go and the *Daily Mirror* and settled in behind the desk, ready to charm the ladies who shop. He switched on the lights and desktop Apple, placed the A-boards outside and waited for the rush. It never came.

***

Kara cleaned up the apartment from the night before, filled the washing machine, and wrote a scribbled list to herself itemising the week's food requirements. The trip to the supermarket and back would take her to lunchtime, and in the afternoon she normally joined Marcus in the gallery. This morning Kara changed her schedule.

***

It took nearly two hours before the first customer of the day purchased a hand-painted glass vase. Marcus was pleased, as the piece sold for £150. Perhaps things were looking up. Twenty minutes later, he was on a roll, selling a bronze ballerina and a ceramic dish for a combined £650. Marcus punched the air. Kara would be delighted. He checked his watch, knowing she usually came over by two. Plenty of time for a hat trick of sales...trade remained unpredictable but at least he was selling at last.

By 2.30 there was still no sign of Kara. He tried phoning the apartment, then her mobile. No response. He pushed through another sale, his mind momentarily taken away from his concern for her. He kept himself busy, redressing the main window, making coffee and phoning again: still no answer. This was odd. Usually reliable, he figured that other things had got in the way of her routine. He shrugged. No big deal. But still, something was eating away at him: Should he be worried?

* * *

Kara was shocked that she made the call. What possessed her, for fuck's sake? Maybe it was an overwhelming need for plain comfort and reassurance from an old acquaintance at work. Surely Ronald, dependable Ronald, would be approachable, wouldn't he? Or perhaps her need to meet up again was a pathetic desire to meddle in the affairs of others...Michael, Toby and Adele. She missed the gallery so much. No matter what her motive was, Kara just needed to know...well, anything.

Marcus would be worried by her absence, but she avoided phoning in, choosing to turn her mobile off. Sitting in a café, her hands trembled as she brought a coffee cup to her lips. Christ, how bizarre was this, a secret meeting between former colleagues, one which she elected to hide from Marcus. Why the need for secrecy? It was only Ronald, for God's sake. He wasn't going to bite her. He was an old softie, a relic from the past. A dinosaur still roaming, as she'd once ungallantly described him.

Then she saw him, and nearly dropped her cup. Why was

she so nervous? Her eyes were riveted to the street as he crossed the road with a swagger. Her initial response was to notice how much older he looked, thinner too. His complexion and receding hair matched his pinstripe grey suit, which hung loosely on him. Oh dear, she thought, even just a few months had not been kind to him. Perhaps he would think the same of her. Suddenly, Kara felt uncomfortable as well as apprehensive.

***

Ronald entered the café and spotted Kara at the table by the window.

Even from a distance, she looked ghastly. He was momentarily shocked but tried to hide it. In his memories of her, Kara was always radiant, with jewel-like eyes and a welcoming happy smile for everyone who crossed her path. This picture was different. After all, he had to acknowledge that she had come close to death and now looked like she carried the ills of the world on her shoulders. In the circumstances, who was he to pass judgment? They had all been through the mill.

Ronald was surprised to get her call. He hadn't heard from Kara since she left the gallery on Cork Street. He hated to admit it, but they had gone their separate ways. Perhaps the past had embarrassed them or they had become plain obstinate in avoiding each other: they had unresolved issues, that was for sure. The trust had gone.

They had worked together at Churchill Fine Art for over four years, and for the most part they were fantastic colleagues. It was only at the end –*bloody hell* – when things went horribly wrong. This left a nasty taste in the mouth. After the incident at the barn, Kara quickly resigned from the gallery for health reasons as he recalled. That was the official line. Off the record, he knew that Kara and Adele were at loggerheads, and for some reason (he didn't know why) the working relationship between them broke down. Something had to give, and Adele wasn't known for backing down. Kara was out. He, fortunately, didn't have a problem with Adele (Hey, he knew how to sit on the fence!) and was kept in his job by Michael's son, Toby, who joined the gallery immediately when his father's fight for life became apparent. It was a case of all hands to the deck after the 'terrible thing' at the barn and Michael's subsequent lengthy stay in the hospital. Toby was vital to the cause and he needed strong support while he got his feet under the table. Ronald was happy to oblige, and admittedly he needed the financial support himself, so remaining at the gallery was just as vital to him.

At his advanced age, this enabled him to keep a steady income and hold onto the self-esteem of still being useful to someone, anyone, in fact! Who else in the city would employ an ancient, gay and burnt-out salesman, well past his sell-by date. This was his last chance, and he wasn't going to let it pass him by. The young guns on the block would eventually line up to replace him…but not yet, if he had anything to do with it.

Perhaps that's why Kara distanced herself from him, in the knowledge that he somehow kept his allegiance to Adele, Kara's sworn enemy. Why they became enemies he again did not truly know…there was so many secrets, so much aggravation in those last days. It was like a battlefield. He was mystified as to what really happened, finding out most of the juice from local gossip and the newspaper coverage. And just occasionally, the odd stilted conversation with Michael who was reluctant to really talk about it. But Kara was entitled, perhaps, to know the bitter truth of the matter as to where he stood amid the debris. Hence this meeting, he surmised. He didn't want to hurt her, or show mistrust, it was simply a matter of…well, absolute survival in a brutal world. Dog eat dog. He wanted to keep his job, first and foremost, and she made him nervous.

His maxim in life was simple: "Keep your bloody head down and get on with it, without fuss". Surely Kara, of all people, would see that in reality he was never truly comfortable with the scenario at the gallery? This was largely forced on them all by horrendous circumstances that no one could have predicted or fathomed. He was still unsure of the true facts, or how intelligent people could so easily cock-up their lives. Ultimately, it was a power game between Adele and Michael. He, as an employee, was just a puppet, a sideshow. However, at the end of the day, he went with what was on offer: Needs must.

Just like now. Kara had called, and he responded. But he was uncomfortable all the same. Ronald was perplexed, a little angry, first with himself and now Kara for requesting this impromptu get together. Why couldn't she let it go?

The call came out of the blue: would he meet her for lunch, today, at Carlo's on Duke Street? That quick...Why the urgency? He could hardly say no, although his stomach churned at the prospect. What the hell could he say to help her now? He approached with trepidation.

'Hello, Kara.'

She stood nervously and they hugged.

'Coffee?' she asked, catching the eye of a passing waiter.

Roland ordered a double espresso and then sat down, his hands fidgeting out of sight. A pretty red-checked gingham tablecloth spread between them, giving enough space for both of them to breathe in and out and take stock of each other: there were boundaries to cross, after all. Atop the table, a little glass vase holding an array of yellow pansies took centre stage, surrounded by silver salt and pepper shakers and a sugar bowl.

'I'm thrilled with the news of your baby,' Ronald said, trying to break the ice. 'You look great,' he lied.

'Hardly.' She patted her bump. 'It's a struggle, this motherhood lark, perhaps I'm just not cut out for it.'

'Nonsense. You'll be a great mum, and Marcus, is he well?'

'Excited by the arrival...'

'When is the baby due?'

Kara used her fingers to count on. 'Six days overdue.'

The coffee arrived and Ronald downed it in one gulp. A silence dropped between them.

'Another,' Ronald said to the passing waiter.

'And for you, madam?'

'I'm fine, thank you.'

The waiter scuttled off. Alone again, they grinned and sat awkwardly.

'So. How is the job going?' Kara asked.

'Fine,' he shrugged. He declined to mention the broken window which happened just a few days before. Something spooked him about the incident but he couldn't put a finger on it. Michael seemed to be on guard, apprehensive, hiding something. He decided to keep conversation with Kara on an even keel. 'Not the same as before, of course.'

Kara jumped in too quickly. 'I miss the old days and I miss working with…'

'Michael.'

'Everything was spoiled.' Her shoulders dropped. 'Why was everything so fucked in the end?'

'*Everything* was spoiled,' he echoed, lowering his gaze.

His refill arrived and they remained stiff with each other, drinking quietly.

'And Toby, is he finding his feet?' Kara asked.

Ronald smiled thinly. 'Let's say he has his own methods…'

'…A clash of personalities?' she suggested.

'Something like that, but he is good and gets the job done efficiently, if a little less flamboyantly than his father.'

'And Michael, how is Michael?'

Ronald popped a sugar cube into his mouth and loosened his tie. Clearing his throat, he said, 'Michael's absolutely fine, if a little traumatised by his slow recovery and, dare I say it, costly divorce. I'm not sure which is the most painful – the skin grafts or Adele's financial demands.'

Neither of them saw fit to smile this time. Kara said, 'I haven't seen him since I told him I was pregnant. So much has happened in the meantime, and so fast…it's been difficult to keep in touch.'

'You mean Marcus has kept you both apart.'

'Something like that.'

'Is this the reason for our little meeting?'

Kara bit her lip. 'I feel out of the loop, somehow.'

'Better that way, my dear.'

'Is it?'

'From how I see it, your health is the only issue to worry about.' Ronald shuffled on his seat. 'And, I'm sorry to say, you don't appear to be doing a very good job of it…usually someone in your position positively blooms. What's the matter, Kara?'

'Everything, and nothing. Are you happy, Ronald?'

He laughed for the first time. 'We certainly didn't come here to find out if I was a happy bunny, now did we? I see anguish on your face and bones sticking out from your body, in spite of your bump. Frankly, you look terrible. Marcus must be beside himself with worry, at a time when you should both be rejoicing.'

Tears welled in her eyes. 'We are rejoicing, and I was so happy when I first realised I was pregnant. It was the best thing that could possibly have happened. But the police haven't been successful in apprehending Maggie, and the fact that she overshadows all our lives is having a damaging effect on my health...and attitude. If I'm brutally honest, I want her caught and arrested or...found dead. It's that blunt. Until then, she haunts us to the point of hysteria.'

'Strong words...does Marcus share that view?'

Kara slumped in her chair. 'Not exactly, no. He sees the danger, but refuses to bow to it.'

Ronald checked his watch. 'Can I bow to an alcoholic drink?'

Kara grinned. 'A coke and lime for me, but you kill whatever it is you need to kill.'

He summoned the waiter again, who cleared the table as Ronald repeated her request and added: 'A large gin and tonic with lime, plenty of ice, thank you.'

'Hmm, how I would have loved to join you.' Kara said, patting her stomach. 'Give me a few months...'

'And you'd finish the bottle, no doubt,' Ronald interrupted. 'You could always drink any of us under the table.' Laughter at last rebounded between them.

'The good old days,' she said wistfully.

Relaxed, Ronald continued: 'Call Michael, it's so easy to lose touch. He's not the rock we all think he is, though. He's back on his feet and, thankfully, regaining his old swagger. But things are still tough. Toby has his own ideas at the gallery and is trying to impose his way of doing things and, naturally, treading on toes in the process...'

Kara frowned, and proclaimed: 'Namely on your toes and those of his father.' Then she insisted, 'the Boss.'

'Partner, actually.'

'Ouch. I'd heard a rumour. Does that sit well with Michael?'

'He had little choice in the matter,' Ronald said. 'Toby invested heavily to save the gallery from going under. Therefore, it stands to reason that he wanted to protect his capital investment by taking control of the day-to-day running of the business. He works most days. I do three mornings. Michael comes in two days a week, between hospital visits and physiotherapy sessions. It works well, until tensions rise and egos clash. Then I keep a low profile.'

'Is Adele involved?'

'The She-Devil? No. As part of the deal, Toby asked her to leave and retire gracefully, which she did with great reluctance. Of course, the money he offered as a sweetener would have been most persuasive in her reaching the correct decision. This enabled Toby and Michael to clear the tax debt and form a partnership without interference. They're winning through, gradually. When Michael is fully recovered, both physically and mentally, they will make a formidable team...'

'Is there a question mark there?' she asked.

Roland dropped the conversation as the drinks were served.

'Toby could decide to go it alone,' he then said. 'Michael sometimes struggles with his fitness. If that happens, I'll retire gracefully too. I only want to work with Michael. I won't get the cash incentive that Adele got, of course. I'll go quietly. Life's unfair, don't you think?'

'Totally.'

'You miss him, don't you?'

'Absolutely.'

'Why have you lost touch then?'

Kara hesitated, fiddling with her necklace. 'It's just that...I don't know. Marcus is trying desperately to carve out a new life for us, a new beginning, and for him that excludes the past and everyone connected with it. He sees Michael as a past relic.'

'And who can blame him?'

'I know, I know. I think Marcus is a little jealous of Michael as well. But I miss working with Michael. The past was my anchor. We haven't lost touch, it's simply that our paths no longer cross. I suppose the events leading up to the fire, and his crazy obsession with Lauren has somehow driven a wedge between us...as if we are too embarrassed to talk about it. Therefore, we avoid each other. That's my theory, anyway.'

Ronald emptied his glass with a satisfied gulp. 'He needs you, Kara. Don't turn your back on him. He is trying to confront his own demons, as you are too. But the news of your pregnancy gave him a tremendous lift, believe me. He sees this as the only good thing to come out of the whole damn tragedy. For that reason alone, don't become strangers. Marcus will understand the situation, your needs, I'm sure. Would you like me to arrange a meeting? Is that what this rendezvous is all about?'

Kara was silent for a few seconds. 'I suppose it would be good...but I'm frightened that the pain of the past will be dragged up again.'

'My dear, look at me.' Their eyes locked. 'The pain has never gone away, for any of you. It's time to talk, cry, shout, whatever – because the way I see things, well, unless you all find peace of mind then you're screwed for life. I admit I was apprehensive about seeing you, but I'm so pleased I did: Time to bury the ghosts of the past, yes?'

Kara recalled her recurring dream, and nodded apprehensively.

Ronald stood, buttoned his jacket and smiled. Then he wiped his puffed, ruddy face with a handkerchief. 'Leave it to me.' He prodded his chest. 'You can rely on this silly old sod to arrange something, especially for you. I'm just a fool with a tear in his eye.'

'Sentimental to the last,' Kara said, squeezing his hand for reassurance. He returned the gesture, and smiled knowingly.

Then he was gone. She sat for a while, staring into space, feeling calm and reassured. Ronald was a dear. He would fix it. Eventually she paid up, crossed the road, and headed toward home, thinking of Marcus. She was carrying a baby, their precious baby and it began to feel good. From afar, unbeknown to her, someone else crossed the road and, gathering speed, followed a few paces behind, monitoring her every movement with poisonous eyes.

Kara was unaware of this person's identity, just the proximity. It wasn't enough to make her turn, so she was unaware of their hidden agenda as well. If she did, she would know that they had a cold conviction to fix it too.

CHAPTER THREE

One week later

Preoccupied by all things which complicated her life, Kara missed a message on her mobile. Her heart jumped as she finally read it. It was from Michael, suggesting that they got together for coffee, sooner rather than later. She was perplexed: surely Ronald hadn't broached the subject with him so quickly? She wanted to answer Michael immediately, but decided to wait and gather her muddled thoughts.

Marcus was proving awkward again, not talking freely to her after she had explained (rather sheepishly) that she had met Ronald at a café, behind his back. Bingo! They had argued again. What a surprise. Now they had endured days of awkward silence. Raking up old issues was how he saw things. "We need to move on," was his stock response, as always. He had a point, of course. Kara acknowledged that her health was important with the birth of their first child so close, and according to the good book of Marcus, anxiety was not conducive to a healthy mind and body. Her spirits were low again, she had to admit. She needed Marcus desperately, but each time she tried to claw her way back in, he in turn moved away from her emotionally, creating a void in their relationship. What he failed to grasp was her basic need to find the very answers that would then help to transform the irrational fears she felt for their future as a family.

The fucking dreams didn't help either. For her, the future was planted in the past, these very roots on which she could grow and nurture the child she carried. Marcus, of course, saw danger in doing this, seeing the past as a kind of foreboding snake pit from which he had once climbed out. He had no intention of falling back in accidentally or intentionally, and in the process losing everything dear to him. She saw danger in *not* doing it. In her mind, happiness could be destroyed in the blink of an eye. For this reason alone, Kara could not, would not, embrace his viewpoint. Even though she was acutely aware of what it was doing to her sanity, and their fragile connection. Ronald had put things into perspective. Why couldn't Marcus at least just recognise this?

Her decision was made. Marcus *had* to understand the perception of her whole fear. If he doubted this...this... obsession, then she would take control of her own destiny and unearth those buried building blocks so necessary to aid recovery. She would do it on her own, if need be: with a little help from Michael perhaps. Her stubbornness knew no bounds. Then, in the fullness of time, she was sure Marcus would accept the situation, and they could at last slowly gather in their precious (but fractured) dependence on one another once more. Kara craved for this kind of normality, bringing stability back into their lives. Above all, she would seek protection for herself and Marcus at any cost.

It was this desire to dedicate her life to him and their imminent family which drove her forward, perversely, from the remnants of their shared, yet troubled, history: a bloody history. And that was the rub of course: to find this stability meant entering the snake pit once again...and face the viper and its deadly venom.

Kara steeled herself and phoned Michael, her throat as dry as parchment. She hated this deception, keeping secrets from Marcus. But, damn it, he was equally obstinate and cocooned in his own little world. For the moment, until she decided to come clean, he would have to remain in this suspended state of childlike self-denial.

Michael's reassuring voice came through on the third ring. She hesitated, her pulse quickening.

'It's me,' she announced meekly in reply.

'Hi,' Michael said. 'Great to hear from you. I hope my text didn't startle you, a blast from the...'

She picked up the cautiousness in his voice, as if the common ground they once shared so perfectly had shifted.

'Not at all,' she cut in nervously. *Why was she such a bloody contradiction?* Kara composed herself nonetheless.

'It's been such a long time and we need to catch up: old

time's sake and all that. I was thrilled to hear from you, actually.'

'When's the baby due?'

'Don't ask! I'm like a capsized hippo most of the time.'

'Christ, where have the months gone to?'

'Believe me, I've lived every long one of them.'

'Nervous of the big day?'

'Terrified!'

'Let me buy you lunch...How about tomorrow at one?'

'Where?'

'Zizzi's on the dock. Is Marcus around to join us?'

Kara bit her lip. 'No.'

'Everything OK between you?'

'This would be too soon for him, Michael. Better we just meet up on our own. Is that what you had in mind?'

'Exactly...'

'Then one o'clock it is. You'll still need to book a table for three. Two chairs for me, I'm afraid. I've got an arse as wide as a baboon's.'

Michael laughed.

'You'd better believe it,' Kara said, smiling inwardly at the thought of renewing her friendship with her old boss. It was just what she needed.

When she switched off her mobile, the first rays of sunlight crept out from behind the leaden clouds. Perhaps things were looking up, at last.

***

Michael planned his strategy, knowing that Kara was vulnerable and not ready for a sudden shock to her system: He couldn't just throw the name Maggie into the conversation. Ronald had warned him of her poor disposition. Childbirth was about to unleash itself upon her body...could she cope both physically and emotionally with everything that was going on? On top of that, he detected a strain in her relationship with Marcus. He had to tread carefully. Strangely, even before Ronald had taken him aside and suggested that Kara had wanted to meet him, he was thinking the same thing. Coincidence? Michael shrugged it off, not buying into a possible conspiracy by a member of staff to get her back working with him again.

He had Gemma, full stop. Then the new girl knocked over a painting and damaged a frame, and in the chaos, he so wished for the impossible to happen. The old yearnings came flooding back.

That night, he relaxed for the first time in weeks, happy that he was at last weaned off painkillers permanently. His damaged body still ached and stiffened though, constantly reminding him to remember the drill the surgeon recommended: a daily routine to moisturise his new skin grafts which concealed the hideous injuries from the fire. Naked, he tried to apply the cream without catching sight of his disfigurement in the bathroom mirror. The surgeon had performed miracles, but the burns had left their mark. If he was brutally honest, he was lucky to be alive. He finished the daily routine, shrugged on a white towelling robe, poured himself a Hine brandy and sat in the spacious lounge, overlooking Chelsea harbour. Through the window, he watched as the slate grey river below snaked lazily into the distance before being swallowed up by the towering metallic and glass metropolis which never dulled his sense of wonder: This was his town. He watched, awe-struck, as this hypnotic vast monster majestically spread upwards and outwards to the blue horizon and then slowly, as if by magic, disappeared into dusk's last orange flame. It was a truly spectacular landscape, as the lights of the city then suddenly and systematically flickered on in their millions, like a stellar sunburst as nightfall descended. Tomorrow, the promise of a new day would bring him and Kara together again.

Normally, he would embrace such a reunion but somehow his heart grew heavy. He loved Kara like a daughter. Over the past year and a bit he had perhaps distanced himself from her deliberately, knowing that she now had Marcus. Their life together was a cherished thing, and he wasn't going to crowd it. Now, after what Terry had told him about the forthcoming tabloid story, this was exactly what he was going to do.

What happened at Laburnum Farm would haunt them all forever. What happened between him and Lauren would trouble him forever: The intensity of their lust for each other

62

was overwhelming. There was no escape from this, except in sleep and drunken stupor. He took another brandy, and kept pouring. It seemed a good option. Who was there to stop him? In the gloom, Michael saw the spectre of loneliness on the darkened horizon, a forbidding solitary prison for those without connection. He drank greedily. The future appeared to be remorselessly mapped out, and he was alone to face it.

***

The following morning, Kara awoke refreshed and felt seemingly more in charge of events. She had a sparkle in her eyes. Marcus noticed it too, and after breakfast he kissed and cuddled her before leaving to open the gallery. The absence of the cursed dream meant she had slept undisturbed, a rare luxury these days. The baby kicked more frequently. She took a long soak in the bath and stroked her protruding belly, marvelling at nature's wondrous gift of life.

In spite of her ill-founded dread of motherhood and inadequacy, she still felt deeply privileged to have nurtured this child in her womb. God, it made her weep with unbridled happiness. *Her first baby. Her first baby!* She repeated the words over and over in her mind.

The phone rang. Kara ignored it and eventually climbed from the bath and towelled herself down. She was excited and a little apprehensive at the thought of meeting Michael for lunch. She checked the time and dressed in a cream smock over black tights. For the first time in ages she took extra care of her make-up and hair. Silly cow, get real she said under her breath. Next: nails, shoes, beret, coat. There, the perfect look for a has-been city slicker, out to pasture and redundant for the first time in her life. She had heard of Gemma on the gossip grapevine, no doubt a younger, sleeker, thinner model...Kara laughed. She hated her already. She checked herself once more in the bedroom mirror and vowed to give Michael hell for not replacing her with a five-foot dwarf with ginger hair. Then she thought about it. It was just not his style. He always liked to be surrounded by glamorous types.

Gathering her handbag, she made for the door. The phone

rang for the second time. She lifted the handset and made the usual greeting. There was silence: a strange metallic silence that suggested to her that someone was listening; without wishing to talk to her.

Kara persisted. 'Hello? Is someone there?'

The line went dead.

Kara dialled 1471, and heard the recorded voice announce flatly that the caller had withheld their number.

She closed the door behind her, took the lift and hailed a cab for the short journey to the docks. Somehow, and without warning, her new found confidence had evaporated in an instant and her legs turned to jelly. The phone call had spooked her. She tried to dismiss it but something nagged at the back of her mind.

***

Michael felt like shit. He had fallen asleep in the chair and remained in the same position all night. His neck creaked as he lifted himself to go to the bathroom. On his return, he noticed the upturned empty bottle of brandy on the floor and a small stain on the carpet. Then, in a panic, he checked the time. *Christ.* Ten-forty five! He showered, shaved and dressed in record time, drinking black coffee as he went and swallowing aspirin as if they were Smarties. This drinking would have to stop. It was the second hangover from hell in one week. His body simply couldn't cope any more. Get real, his brain demanded. He had made this same futile promise a hundred times before. He looked in the mirror and saw a man he barely recognised: flabby jowls, red sunken eyes and skin the texture of a moonscape. He was a wreck. He splashed cold water on his face to tighten his skin. Even his tousled hair was speckled with grey, and he saw the first visible signs of thinning at the scalp-line. Fuck. He frantically searched for a positive sign in all the misery. Maybe he could convince himself that the craggy, vacant style was in: the Serge Gainsbourg look was still hip, surely?

Reality struck home. He had to admit defeat...he wasn't remotely hip. The good news in all this? Kara would endeavour to soothe his faltering ego, and allow him to think that he somehow defiantly retained his debonair good looks. That was the plan anyway. *Dream on.*

After dressing in black denims, open necked cotton shirt and plain brown woollen jacket, he reluctantly phoned the police station to arrange the interview they had requested. Then he took the elevator down to reception. The Concierge checked his mailbox and handed him an array of envelopes. He skipped through them and elected to collect the batch on his return. One caught his eye though.

'Nick, this letter isn't mine: It says Ms Byrne. I don't recognise the name. Is she a new tenant? '

The young man behind the desk raised his eyebrows and took the letter back, placing it in the mailbox marked with her nameplate.

'Just moved in, about a week ago,' Nick replied, stifling a yawn.

'Is she young and gorgeous?' Michael asked optimistically.

He had known Nick for a couple of years now. They had good banter usually, but Michael could tell it had been a long shift behind the desk by the reluctance in the conversation.

'Hardly your type, Michael,' he said. 'She can barely muster a "hello"or "goodbye" whenever she passes my desk. Always dressed in dark clothes. Covers her head in a silk scarf and wears sunglasses.'

Michael smirked. 'Garbo…esque?'

Nick grimaced. 'Looks a mean one to me: Eyes averted and acts as cold as ice. Luckily, it's a short-term let.'

Michael turned the smirk into a smile and buttoned his jacket, ready for the chill as he reached the revolving door. 'I assume you're not relying on a Christmas bonus from her then?'

'Nope, but I don't recall getting one from you either last year…'

'Ooops.' With that, Michael made his timely escape and headed for the docks.

***

Typical Kara. Her first words to him on entering the restaurant were unflattering, and made him recoil at her

65

bluntness. He had already been kept waiting for over fifteen minutes, so this really took the biscuit.

'Michael, you look ghastly. You've either been to an all-night rave, or recently joined a boxing class and lost your first ten bouts…'

'You look fabulous too,' he replied, standing up from the table and hugging her as best he could, avoiding the huge bump that separated them.

'Liar,' she remarked.

Neither of then heard the subtle camera click from the far side of the restaurant.

The waiter took her coat and Michael helped her into the chair opposite to his. She was right, one chair was barely adequate, and it made him laugh. It was a shock to see her like this: oversized and a bit like a beached whale. But he refrained from saying it aloud.

'I ordered mineral water for you,' he said, refilling his glass from a bottle of fine Argentine Malbec.

'Good idea, and thanks.' She cast a disapproving glare in his direction. 'Do you intend to finish the entire bottle? Am I that scary? I'll hazard a guess that you're boozing too much…I'm not joking Michael.'

'Christ, you sound like my ex-wife.'

'Someone has to say it. I can see it in your face. Is Gemma –or whatever her name is – *that* useless that you have turned to drink?'

'Under 60 seconds.'

'What..?'

'I had a bet with Ronald that you would mention her name in under five minutes. He was rather more kind to you, he reckoned within half an hour, tops. Gemma, by the way, is delightful.' He grimaced, waiting for the inevitable low shots coming his way.

'Delightful?' Kara shrieked. 'Is that in reference to her pert bottom? Which, incidentally, I no longer have owing to my enforced weight gain… or is she delightful to work with because she is less demanding than me?' She narrowed her eyes. 'Bearing in mind you had the best secretary in the world working for you just a few months ago – and my arse wasn't bad either – reply with caution. One of the side effects of pregnancy is a short temper and a pathetic tendency to wail uncontrollably at the slightest provocation. Don't push your luck with a clever response.'

'You were – are, as always – irreplaceable.'

'Correct answer. I'm starving.'

Michael beckoned the waiter. They ordered a shared plate of antipasta, followed by seafood Linguini for two. They ate in comfortable silence, as old friends do. Pipe and slippers: a perfect match. Anything else didn't really matter to them. They sat at a window overlooking the array of gin palaces that bobbed gently in their moorings. The reflection of the water in the dock dazzled from the sunshine. It made them feel special.

Michael finished his food and stared at Kara. In spite of what he had heard, she looked pretty good if a little tired. Her tongue was still waspish though when something had to be said. They talked endlessly now, with much laughter, which seemed to lift their spirits beyond what each of them had expected after their time apart. Good food, good company. Like old times. Eventually, they fell into a secure calm once more, where words were not always necessary.

Michael ordered coffee, Kara choosing Earl Grey tea to finish.

'Can we do this again?' Kara asked.

'You bet.' He smiled and took her hand. 'Kara, do you want to talk about the…past. Or is it too painful?'

'I thought you would never ask…'

Then in a rush, she poured her heart out.

***

Arm in arm, they sauntered across Tower Bridge and caught sight of the angled sunlight bouncing off the towering office columns of Canary Wharf in the distance. Oddly, the tall buildings resembled a line of silver bullets protruding from the white and emerald green sheen of the Thames. A sudden breeze whipped up and cooled their faces. Beyond the Victorian iron bridge, they descended the stone steps on the south embankment which led to the narrow passageways that made up Butler's Wharf, a labyrinth of warehouses now converted into chic apartments. They idled through the row of coffee houses, estate agents and numerous posh restaurants. They kept their distance from Marcus's gallery. *Click.* Kara turned, staring at the passers-by. Then walked on. Within the narrows, the sun did not penetrate here. Instead, Kara shivered and was thankful to Michael, who removed his jacket and draped it over her shoulders. *Click.*

Eventually, they stepped onto the wide promenade beside the river, busy with tourists and businessmen, and felt the cold of the shadows give way to the warmth of the sun once more. The high tide was hectic too with pleasure boats and industrial barges jostling for space on the foaming waters. Michael marvelled at it all. He never tired of *his* London. A metropolis of forsaken dreams and killer ambitions of those who lived here: Hard cases, rich entrepreneurs, poor folk, the forgotten. No one wore their heart on their sleeve for fear of looking weak. In his opinion, you had to dig deep beyond the brittle façade of human behaviour to find this beating heart, a heart of a nation, but it was there hidden away.

As far as he was concerned, you could take any city, any city on the planet, and anyone who lived this daily existence always wore a coat of armour, a steely mask of independence. *Keep away, I am invincible, each would say.* It was mainly just for show, this mask, as a deflection against expressing emotion or vulnerability in a hardened environment…and the evidence of this stood beside him. Michael stared at Kara, and wanted to remove her mask. She had been to hell and back, and was still in denial.

'I'm sorry that this has been so difficult for you,' he said. 'I offer no defence on my part. I have overlooked the suffering of others, and you in particular. I've selfishly concentrated on my own frailties, which to be frank have been too numerous to look beyond. What you have just told me in the restaurant brings everything into sharp focus.'

He touched her cheek. *Click.*

'I hate the fact that I've kept my distance, Kara. I should have been there for you…and Marcus.'

'And we should have been there for you too.' Kara took his hand in hers and squeezed. *Click.* 'From now on, we do just that. Agreed?'

'Agreed.'

They crossed the narrow bridge at St Saviour, and walked along Bermondsey Wall West before finally turning back on themselves, once again retracing their footprints over Tower Bridge. Beyond, the Tower of London loomed into view in the gathering mist. The ravens circled.

'Do you believe in ghosts?' Kara asked.

'Not really...'

'I keep getting weird phone calls. They scare me. Do you believe in bad dreams coming true?'

'I hope not. I have enough of them.'

They laughed awkwardly and took the steps down onto the promenade.

'I have a recurring dream,' Kara continued. 'I'm being pursued by a woman in a Venetian mask, her identity concealed from me. She has a knife, and in this dream this woman attacks me, slashing at my throat with the blade. I sense that I know her, and, as I claw at her mask, I awake with a scream...never knowing her identity. I have a premonition, Michael, that this woman really exists and that our paths are destined to cross – just as the dream foretells.'

Michael could see that she was shaking, her skin sweating. Finally, he dared to say *the* name.

'Is it...Maggie in the dream? He asked.

Her eyes closed and then she took a deep breath. 'It has to be, I suppose.'

'I'll try to do everything I can to protect you.'

Their eyes met and locked. Just then, Kara became distracted and pointed at the crowd standing on the bridge high above them 'Who's that woman taking our picture?'

Michael turned and looked upward, squinting in the light.

'Where...?'

'There...on the left. She's moving away! Can't you see her, Michael?'

He tried to follow the direction of her moving finger. He was losing patience quickly. 'There are hundreds of people up there, Kara. Loads of them are taking photos.'

'No! She was focusing on us, I'm sure. She disappeared when I started pointing at her...'

'It's just a tourist.'

'No. I'm sure it was…her. Christ, Michael! I'm sure it was…'

He took her arm. 'Let's not get paranoid.'

'Easy for you to say.'

'Forget it, Kara. It's just your imagination playing tricks, that's all.'

The mood changed as heavy clouds moved in.

'Oh, fuck you, Michael.' She pulled away in disgust and then faced him again in an instant, anger in her eyes. 'Don't bullshit me. It's Maggie. That was her on the bridge.'

Michael didn't doubt her for one minute. He tried to defuse the tension and hurriedly changed the subject. 'Does Marcus know about the dream?'

'What..?' she hated his clever tactics. 'Yes, of course he bloody knows.'

Michael held her arm and marched her away. Of course Maggie was out there. He could feel the imprint of her prying eyes on the back of his head. It was red-hot. She was getting brazen in her approach.

Out of sight, Michael got to the point. 'Bad news: You're right about Maggie. Marcus needs to know. We'd better call an emergency meeting between the three of us, and plan for eventual warfare. I reckon that she is here in London and right under our noses. She's baiting us.'

'What does she want?'

'Revenge. She blames us for Lauren's death. She wants our blood. An eye for an eye. I have the evidence to back up my theory.'

'What evidence?'

'The smashed window, for starters,' he murmured.

'What smashed window?'

'The gallery was vandalised. It's no coincidence that the attacker only picked out our premises on the entire street. It was a wilful act, her first warning shot. The flint was a sign too.'

'Flint…?'

'The missile.'

'Jesus.' Kara laughed nervously. 'This is getting too close to home.'

Michael wasn't finished. 'The second indication is the

numerous phone calls you mentioned.'

'I'm not dreaming them up.'

'I know. The list is getting longer...now we have the happy snapper on our trail.'

Kara swayed against him and momentarily caught her breath. 'I thought for one moment you weren't taking any of this seriously.'

Michael refrained at this stage from telling her about the dud calls he was getting too. Enough for one day, he reckoned. 'I'm just trying to keep everyone calm, until we can be absolutely sure that she's back on the scene. Then I can deal with the situation. Marcus would think I'm stirring things up.'

'Tell me about it! He thinks I'm off my rocker...'

'There's another thing, too,' Michael said. 'I've spoken with Terry Miles, remember him? He's a journalist. The tabloids are writing a feature on me, an investigative story uncovering the events of Laburnum Farm. Apparently I'm going to be seriously big news soon...Again! Terry, by the way, is the commissioned writer.'

'I thought all of this had died down?'

'No such luck. The police want to interview me again. Did you not see the write-up in the paper?''

'I try to avoid such crap. Why do the police want to talk to you again?'

'Because of the suspicious nature of Lauren's death: They don't think it was accidental, as they first believed. And in view of the continued press coverage highlighting the case and Lauren's protected status under the laws of the land they are beginning to smell a rat. No smoke without fire, if you forgive the pun. And why wouldn't they be suspicious? According to our testimonies, there was no crime committed, and yet the circumstances of why we were all there that day, under the same roof so to speak, doesn't add up to many people. And remember Lauren and I were ill-fated lovers...the public crave for that kind of story. None of us can truthfully explain our actions that day without giving away the game...and our guilt.'

'And what game is that?'

'Get real, Kara. Fraud, for starters.'

'How the hell did you get us into this mess in the first place?'

'You know only too well,' Michael snapped. 'I was at a very low point...I needed money fast, Adele was about to skin me alive in the divorce courts and I saw a way out...I was greedy and foolhardy and fell in with Lauren's crazy plan to make a fast buck...or a million quid to be exact.'

'You were bonkers, more like...'

Michael's voice softened. 'I should never have involved you. I pushed you into cooperating in the secret disposal of paintings by Patrick Porter, and it was foolhardy to the extreme. But I was desperate and I reckoned on dealing mostly in cash, thus avoiding tax and VAT payments. I thought I could get away with it and keep the money out of the clutches of my wife.'

'I can't say I blame you on that score, the scheming bitch.'

'It got more complicated, as you know. On top of that little scam we were also associating with a woman who I later discovered was a former convicted criminal...banged up for murdering her father. She had history. If I had known that I would never have got involved. I was out of my depth but in too far...it was a kind of madness.'

'I was frightened, Michael, but I got caught up into it as well...so don't blame yourself entirely. Who were we to know that Lauren was also, over many years, painting on the sly under the assumed name of her dead brother, Patrick? But that's in the past. Outside of the three of us, no one is any of the wiser, including the cops. Most of the incriminating evidence which would have exposed her lie and your scam was destroyed conveniently in the fire at the barn, namely in the destruction of her studio and what was contained in it. So we got away with it.'

Michael raised his eyebrows. 'Shall I go on? All is not forgotten. We also have the slight problem of a dead woman who cannot be officially identified as Lauren O'Neill at this stage, even by using DNA methods because the police need to match these findings with that of her sister to prove conclusively who the real victim is.'

Kara said in bewilderment: 'But you were adamant it was Lauren...'

'At the time, yes.'

'Have you changed your mind?'

'No! But there has to be an element of doubt until the proof is conclusive, and that means apprehending the wayward sister. *She,* as you well know, is on the run and therefore cannot be identified either. The police need to find her, bearing in mind that the body in the barn was burnt beyond recognition, so visual identification is impossible from their findings. What a fucking mess. So whoever is on the run needs to be caught, and bloody quickly. Then we'll know who really died in the fire.' He took breath. 'The police believe the remains are those of Lauren. The coroner too. I testified to this fact. However, I repeat: until we have absolute proof then it is all conjecture. But I remain convinced it is Maggie stalking us and in that case who knows what will come out of her vile mouth?'

Kara was aghast. 'She can implicate us again, is that what you are saying?'

'Yes.'

'You swore an oath that it was Lauren who died. Why are you suddenly doubting yourself?'

'It was impossible to be absolutely sure. I could just make her out in the dense smoke and flames, fighting with her sister. It was hell in there and I was confused and fading fast…my memory plays tricks on me, even to this day. I try to remember things and then everything goes blank.'

'We were all victims that day, not just you.'

'I know, I know…'

'But Marcus saved you.'

Michael dropped his shoulders and sighed, his vacant eyes betraying his inner struggle with everyday survival. 'Did he?' he muttered in feeble resignation.

'He endangered his own life to do so.' Kara saw the defeat etched on his face, felt compassion and then suddenly lost it. 'Don't be so fucking ungrateful. He could have died trying to save your skin. How dare you –'

Michael grabbed her fist as she threw it in the direction of his chest in sheer frustration and anger. Her eyes blazed.

He had to cool it, and quickly. 'I'm sorry, Kara. I'm not thinking straight…'

She unclenched her hand and pulled away, folding her arms instead. An awkward silence fell between them as they circled each other like two wounded animals, neither giving ground.

'Marcus saved me, I know,' Michael said quietly, trying to mend the sudden distance between them. 'Maggie escaped...*someone* escaped... now we live with the terrible consequences. That was what I was trying to explain...'

'She was a coward. She ran...'

'She ran for sure. She was only interested in saving herself. Now she has to be caught. Or silenced.'

'Jesus.'

'Until then, none of us can resume our lives for fear of reprisals. And not just us either. There is Julius and Antonia to think of as well.'

'Christ, Michael, you can't be responsible for everyone! There was no love lost between Julius and Lauren, his crackpot wife...'

'Remember, he is a party to this deception. He knew the real identity of Patrick Porter. He knew Lauren was attempting to swindle him by selling the paintings through me, without informing him. Well, lucky in love or not, he'll eventually inherit the farm and the remaining paintings and be set up for life. The estate is worth a fortune. It's in his interests that Maggie is found and then he can prove the demise of his wife. Until then...he is in limbo, so how do you think he copes in all this? He can't even lay claim to what's rightfully his. Either his estranged wife is laid to rest...or seven years needs to elapse before the estate is lawfully transferred over.' He caught his breath again with a sharp intake, his brain spinning with all the confusion. 'Is that enough of this so-called game for you to be getting on with?'

Kara took the point. She turned and reached for his hand. 'What do we do?' she pleaded meekly.

'Clawing at each others' throats is akin to playing right into Maggie's hands. We need to be strong. Keep our heads down, our mouths shut and our eyes open. At the moment we are in the clear, until the story breaks or the police uncover the truth. Lauren died by misadventure, in the words of the coroner, and that suits us just fine. But this will start to get messy from now on. No stone unturned etc. You and Marcus need to leave London for a few weeks while I get Terry to bury a few ghosts, if that's possible.'

'Will we be questioned by the police again?'

'Unavoidable, I'm afraid.'

'We won't run, Michael.'

'I didn't suggest that option. Just keep a low profile. That will leave the heat firmly on me. I have broad shoulders.'

'I don't like it. First Maggie, then this garbage…'

They walked slowly toward The Minories just off Tower Hill. Then Michael faced her again with more harsh words. 'Hard unpalatable facts: The police want to open the files again, and the press are sniffing around for more lurid details. Both are like a dog with a bone. This story was inevitable and someone wants to bury me once and for all,' Michael said. 'I have enemies in high places. I'm just surprised it's taken them so long to start digging the grave.' He tried to lighten the mood. 'If they do the movie, I rather think Daniel Craig would do me proud.'

His mocking tone worked. They were back from the brink of killing each other.

She dug him in the ribs. 'Such an ego!'

He was indignant. 'Who would you choose to portray me?'

Kara walked on ahead of him. 'Dale Winton,' she muttered.

At the junction with the Royal Mint, Michael hailed a cab. 'Speak with Marcus. Explain to him my concerns. We can meet up if he so wishes. We need a plan of action. Are you OK with this, Kara?'

'Yes, providing he will listen to reason.'

'He has to. You need to convince him that none of us are safe. I'm seriously thinking of hiring a private detective to help uncover the whereabouts of Maggie. If she's in London, we need to find her and fast. I don't have the resources but I know a man who does. We also need round-the-clock protection. The police can't provide that.'

'Seems extreme, Michael, but I like the idea.'

They kissed and hugged. *Click.*

'You all right to get home alone?' he asked.

'No problem, a five minute walk. Speak to me soon.'

'I'll catch up with you tomorrow.'

Michael took one last look at the sea of faces surrounding them, searching for *her* in the crowd. Warily, he closed the cab door behind him and settled into his seat. Within seconds, he disappeared into the heavy traffic heading down the embankment towards Westminster. Tiredness overtook him.

His mobile rang. When he answered, the line went dead. He checked missed calls and noted the caller withheld their number. He shrugged, then felt uneasy. This was the third such call in the past 24 hours.

***

Kara watched the cab vanish and then crossed the road toward The Highway, the road which separated Tower Hamlets from Wapping. She entered Leman Street, bought milk from a corner shop and made her way home. The baby kicked. At the first junction, she waited at the crossing lights as the flow of cars intensified. Her phone went. She fumbled into her handbag, caught the signal and shouted above the din as the lorries passed by.

'Hello?'

Silence.

'I can't hear you…'

Someone was listening. Kara was seriously pissed off as the bastard clicked off. This was becoming a regular occurrence. Then the lights changed, allowing her to cross the road. On the far side, she mingled with the late afternoon crowds.

Behind her, just twenty metres away, a figure in a dark-hooded raincoat had moments earlier followed her path undetected. Under the railway arches on Dock Street the figure stopped; withdrew a phone and dialled a number. Hidden by the shadows, the observer scanned the crowd on the pavement ahead and watched as a young, pregnant woman seemed to halt, listen, shake her mobile and curse aloud. People stared and dispersed around her, startled by the inappropriate language from an expectant mother.

The mysterious figure reappeared and mingled

anonymously with the onlookers, before vanishing quietly into the impending darkness of night: Like a phantom. As if never existing in the first place.

Unaware of this, Kara hurried home. She was acutely embarrassed by her pathetic outburst in public. It was a further sign of her distress. *This* and the mysterious photographer magnified the nervousness she felt from even the slightest intrusion into her life. The rant was so undignified, she had to admit. It made her cringe. She unlocked the main door to her apartment block, turned, and surveyed the street. *For what?* She was terrified of ghosts. They were everywhere in her mind.

Inside, she took the lift and managed to calm down at last. Had time to catch her breath. *Grow up, for chrissakes!* She screamed inwardly, admonishing herself like a child. Her brain raced. Only one thing for it at a time of crisis: Have a mug of tea and a muffin.

She stood by the window, munching. *Click.*

Then the phone rang.

This time she was ready. She took the call.

'Fuck off, whoever you are!' she shouted. 'If you've got something to fucking say, then say it to my face, you fucking piece of shit, you cowardly cunt, you pathetic loser, what kind of asshole hides behind a withheld number, eh? Speak god damn it...say it now, fuck face, or never bother me again!'

Silence.

'Well, dickhead?'

Faint breathing.

'I can't hear you, wanker. Well...?'

A familiar voice cut in. 'It's just your mother, dear. Just checking to make sure you are OK. I can always ring back if it's a bad time to call...

Kara recoiled in horror. That really did it. She was in serious need of therapy.

CHAPTER FOUR

'You said what?'

Kara was mortified. 'I know, I know.'

Michael suppressed a giggle on the phone as Kara relayed the story of the abusive rant at her mother. He could barely contain his devilment as he imagined the crazy scenario that took place between the two of them. Bloody hell, what a comedy duo they made. He had to ask rather mischievously: 'Are you two still talking?'

'Haha!' Then she realised that they hadn't indeed spoken for a few hours, but she was in no mood for his mickey-taking 'There is a serious side to this, funny man.'

Michael hesitated, and then remarked: 'And what would that be? Marcus will be delighted that he doesn't have to tolerate a visit from your mother quite so often...'

'Jesus, Michael. Do you have to be so facetious? Get focused. I'll ask again: Have you had a similar experience to me?'

'What, swearing insanely at my mother? Or your mother to be exact? Not recently, no.'

'That's it, smart ass. I thought I could depend on you for a shoulder to cry on. Marcus too thought it was hilarious. Why are men so childish?'

Michael smiled to himself. 'Perhaps you should question your own bizarre actions before throwing accusations in our direction. After all...'

'All right! Point taken. I was the fucking idiot, the fool who flipped. Now talk to me seriously for once. You've had your fun at my expense. Have you had the same type of calls?'

Michael hesitated, and got focused. He owed her that. 'Yes.'

'How many?'

'Six, seven...maybe ten.'

'This is scary.'

'We shouldn't read too much into them. I quite like a bit of heavy breathing...'

Kara drew breath. 'What did you just say?'

'Okay, we should take them seriously. I was just trying to calm the situation down as I explained yesterday. Yes, it appears that you and I are being targeted.'

'Stalked by a weirdo more like.'

Again, he hesitated. 'It looks that way. Either that or your mother is a secret psychopathic mass murderer and she's been finally caught out...'

'My God, Michael. Listen to yourself. Piss off.'

Then she slammed the phone down on him. Christ, when it rained it poured. He was trying to lighten the mood. Now they were at war again.

***

Michael bitterly regretted his crass comments. He phoned back to no avail. She obviously had the hump with him. He would try later when she had a chance to calm down. He was acutely aware that the anonymous calls to the both of them did appear sinister, he now knew to his cost. She was so bloody hypo though. He took stock. The jokes had to be put aside. He had clearly offended her. Everyone was so touchy...Toby, Ronald, Kara, Marcus...which wasn't surprising taking into account what they had been through over the past months. On top of that, he had to contend with the impending soap story and Terry's despicable illness...well, bad things were piling up like a gathering storm. The best course of action he decided, from past experience, was usually to sit it out, ignore the crap or steel himself for the onslaught. In this case, he was beginning to fear the worst. They *were* being watched. He could sense the smell of fear in the air. Kara, in her heightened emotional state, was handling things poorly, he concluded. Marcus needed to know the true picture, especially as the baby's birth was getting very close. She was on a knife-edge and had to be protected at all costs.

From his office drawer, he extracted his address book and flipped through the pages. He found the name he was looking for: Martin Penny, private detective. *Penny for your thoughts* was how he advertised himself. This always struck a chord with Michael. He had used him a couple of years ago during a time of several unaccountable thefts from the gallery. Mr Penny 'joined' the staff and soon apprehended the culprit: a part-time cleaner on nightshift. She stole small, less valuable works from the overstocked storeroom, not so easily detected as missing due to lazy accounting on their part. It was a case of being out of sight, out of mind. Eventually, Michael recovered some items on eBay. The woman was dismissed, but never charged. Since then, the stockroom was under constant camera surveillance. The database of listings was regularly updated too, so that it would never happen again. Martin had done his job well.

Michael thought long and hard and tried to weigh up the necessity of bringing an expert on board once again. He thought of Kara... and the frightening scenario of trying to protect her newborn from harm's way. He jotted down Martin's number and vowed to take action.

Slowly, he sifted through the mail: Usual bills and circulars. Only one caught his attention. An invitation to the Annual International Art Gala, held this year on *Star Cruiser,* a new floating five-storey restaurant/hotel ship moored at Excel, the exhibition site based near City airport.

Michael always attended and took the staff for an evening jolly as reward for their efforts in the gallery. It was usually a glittering affair, held at a different venue each year, with much merriment and a chance to gain national recognition in the industry by way of the award ceremony. In the past twenty years Churchill Fine Art had only ever won one award, for Best Exhibition in 1999. He always lived in hope of a further prize but he wasn't holding his breath. Each year he would always take a special guest too. He vowed to take Kara and Marcus as part of the gang on this occasion. Why not invite Julius and Antonia too? *The Night of the Survivors.* He chuckled. Then he raised his eyebrows as he noticed the theme of the Ball: A Venetian Extravaganza.

Inexplicably, he felt a little uneasy and remembered Kara and her recurring dream. What had she said to him? Was his mind playing tricks? Did she imply that someone in her dream was attacking her, their identity hidden behind a Venetian mask? He wanted to dismiss such a fanciful notion as silly paranoia on her behalf, a state of play which only she took seriously. It had no bearing on the realities of life. Then he studied the invitation again. It was full fancy dress, in festival attire to mark the special night: Masks and all. The smile was wiped from his face. *He hated masks.*

***

Terry Miles had a plan. For it to work properly, he would turn detective: fancying himself as some kind of Columbo, his favourite gumshoe. Looking back to the start of his career, investigative work was the reason for being attracted to journalism in the first place. He had an eye for skulduggery as a means of extracting the truth, and *his* story (any story) had to be authentic. Integrity was the keyword for him. Many in his profession would not agree with this statement, but it was how he tried to operate. And turning detective was part of the process. His late beloved wife had instilled this need for integrity in him after they first hooked up. He couldn't let her down. She was always looking over his shoulder from above, protecting him. It gave him comfort in a hard, brutal world of cynicism and now illness. And he wanted to join her, and wished for God's consent when the time came. In the meantime, he bent the rules of his profession just enough so that He didn't notice. Integrity was one thing, discovering the truth by other means was also permitted... if the bigger injustice was uncovered for the good of all. This was called *Terry's World.*

His primary task, therefore, was to stake out the territory that he was going to write about, and in this instance the one which had been under surveillance by the police (and insurance companies) for several months, and discover the brutal reality of what happened there: And this location was the farm. He wanted to keep this visit a secret initially, even from his editor-in-chief...who would be looking to sensationalise the story with as many dark deeds as possible. And, Terry had to admit, there were plenty of those on offer. He was caught between the devil and the deep blue sea, but he would be damned if he would bow to pressure from above until he had got a grip on what really happened that fateful day and in the days leading up to it. He was the observer. Later, he would be the judge. The central players were a bunch of liars and thieves. And Michael was supposed to be a friend. God would love this one, for what it was worth.

At this juncture, some things were best kept quiet and at arm's length until he had formed his own opinion of people and events. Liars and thieves was just the gossip on the grapevine. No one had been arrested. Not yet. First, he had to see first-hand the stage on which they played. Besides, he didn't know how he would react to the infamous farm or what he anticipated on his arrival. It was that kind of road trip: maybe even leading to a dead end.

He drove out of central London in silence, hitting the A3 without the customary snarl up at Roehampton. Forty odd miles later he found the village of Old Hampton, due south of Guildford. Although it first struck him as a sleepy hamlet, he knew only too well that the close-knit inhabitants had tried to hide their shame from the national press when it put the spotlight firmly on them. They retreated behind closed doors: quickly closing ranks to discourage the public from visiting and gawping at the calamity that had befallen the village just months before, when its previously uneventful history was altered forever in just one gory day of carnage. Now it was a place of notoriety. He sensed that no one here would want to speak of it voluntarily.

Just beyond the pretty village of affluent clapboard houses, set amid rolling hills, lay the ruins of Laburnum Farm, formerly the home of Lauren O'Neill and her estranged husband, the artist Julius Gray. As Terry approached the long gravelled drive, he noticed the KEEP OUT sign attached limply to the five bar gate, which hung precariously upon its hinges. According to the local estate agents that he had spoken with, there was no one enquiring to buy the property. He wasn't remotely surprised. The smell of death still lingered in the air.

Parking his Rav4 on the verge, he grabbed his camera and ambled toward the forsaken house, partially obscured by dense, overgrown shrubbery and tall, spidery black trees, almost turned to charcoal from the intensity of the fire. The gardens were unkempt, the half-timbered house silent, dark and sickly: The house of ghosts. There was no love here. The decorative bay trees, now brown and brittle from lack of water, stood pathetically to attention in matching terracotta urns either side of the main door. It was a sad reminder of former glories. Terry stood transfixed by the prevailing sense of evil and, turning slowly, surveyed the wreckage. Beyond, his eyes spotted the great tithe barn. Or, to be accurate, what was left of it after the ravages of the inferno. On first impression, he likened it to a mammoth whale, now stricken and skeletal, seemingly beached and slowly rotting in the sunlight. Great blackened beams protruded from the ground like an exposed ribcage thrusting skyward. The stench of burnt wood still reached deep into his nostrils. He hardly dared to look inside the remains. It was a tomb.

This was where Lauren perished. This was at the point where they all had so nearly died. He approached cautiously. Across the now defunct entrance, where huge oak doors once hung proudly, police tape flapped in the breeze. A placard stated boldly:

POLICE. CONDEMNED. NO ADMITTANCE.

Terry took stock and felt a chill run through his bones. Christ, he could only imagine such an inferno from Hell. This had once been a vast building, now reduced to rubble and sacrifice. In one corner, close to where he stood, he could make out the carcass of a burnt-out car. Beyond, a scorched gable wall remained upright and defiant, propped up by a mass of tangled heavy roof beams which had piled up and fused together from the explosion and subsequent intense heat. He looked around and saw only sadness and neglect. Would anyone dare to buy this property now? The entire estate carried the weight of despair upon its broad fallen shoulders. The soul of this house, he reasoned, died when the first sparks ignited. It was a horrible place, a bad place...lonely and beyond spiritual repair. On the undamaged roofline of the main house, ugly black crows perched and fidgeted and stared down on him, as if he was an unwanted intruder. Which he was, of course. From the undergrowth, a hare bolted across his path, disappearing fast into the cover of the thicket. A shaft of sunlight broke the heavy cloud, causing him to squint unexpectedly. For a split second, Terry was sure he detected a faint shadow move across an upstairs window at the front of the house. He looked again, deciding it was a simple trick of the light. Just then a crow swooped and stood close, his talons scratching at the scorched earth. Its beady eyes gawped at him with relish.

Bollocks to this, Terry decided. He removed the lens cap from the camera. Get the job done. Get the fuck out. *Doom House* was now his private codename for Laburnum Farm. It was apt.

Hurriedly, he took a series of photos with an unsteady hand, and ventured gingerly into what remained of the barn, treading carefully wherever he could get a firm footing. He didn't get far. In the ruins, he somehow envisaged the utter chaos and imagined he heard the screams of a woman dying at this infernal spot. It turned his stomach. This was Lauren's resting place. Her graveyard. Apparently, she was burnt to cinders, emulsified. There was no hope here either. Let the departed rest in peace, he concluded. He retreated as fast as he could, with the bitter taste of soot lingering on his tongue. He didn't take a last look.

Glad to get away, he drove speedily to the village pub. It was called The Royal Oak. Michael had mentioned it. Above the entrance, a banner swung in the breeze. It read: *UNDER NEW MANAGEMENT.* He entered, washed his hands and face in the Men's Room, and settled at the bar for a very welcome beer. His lips were parched. Looking around, he was the only customer. A young punkish girl, dressed all in black with a tattoo on her neck, slowly approached from behind the bar and took his order. She possessed all the enthusiasm of someone who had better things to do with their life. Terry knew how she felt. He didn't want to be here either. She returned to her stool at the far end of the bar. He searched around tentatively: the place was unkempt and devoid of atmosphere. He wasn't surprised. Perhaps the villagers had abandoned their local too, fed up with being the victims of answering so many intrusive questions from the media. He drank greedily.

'How much do I owe you?' he asked.

'Two-sixty,' the girl replied, without looking up.

Terry dropped three quid on the bar. She made no effort to move , preoccupied instead with a magazine resting on her lap and a mobile in her hand, which she was texting manically on.

He tried communication. It usually worked. 'What happened to the previous tenants?'

'Dunno.'

A good start. 'Have you just taken over?'

'Do I look like a landlord?'

Terry noticed that she had the same beady eyes as the crow that stared him down at the farm. *This really was horrorville.*

She surprised him by making conversation. 'Not sure when the changeover will happen...I'm just keeping things ticking over. The new owners arrive next week I think.'

'Do you live in the village?'

She looked up again, distracted from her mobile. She viewed him with the same disdain as someone would view shit on their shoes. He clearly wasn't making a good impression on her. He tried again.

'Perhaps you knew the woman who tragically died in the fire, up at the farm?'

'What fire would that be? I've been away at Uni.'

Terry cut his losses. 'I'll be on my way,' he said. He went to his car, disillusioned (using that time-honoured cliché) at what had got into the youth of today. He suddenly felt old and culturally detached. He then had an urge to look over his shoulder. She had followed him.

'You forgot your change.'

'Keep it.' He couldn't help himself, adding mischievously: 'And thanks for the conversation. It was riveting.'

She came closer, revealing a silver nose piercing. 'I have a degree in sociology and economic history if you must know.'

'I don't remember asking. But I'm pleased for you, really.'

'I'm just holding the fort. Then I'm off to Belgium, where I start my new job at the EU headquarters in Brussels.'

'Congratulations.'

'I was thinking about what you said earlier. I do recall

something about a fire in the village. The tenant's name was Dougie. Anyhow, he showed me the ropes, so to speak, but there's not much to do here…it's a bit of a dead hole these days. He was a nice man, but a bit twisted I'd say.'

'And why was that?'

'The rumour was his wife, who ran the bar, left him and never returned. Her name was Sheila, I think. She'd run away before, so it was nothing unusual. But this time she disappeared for good. He was devastated apparently. Never said a word to me directly, just gossip I picked up. After a while, he too upped and left. Now it's just me. I live about twelve miles away, in that direction.' She pointed.

'Who pays your wages?' Terry asked.

'The brewery.'

'Not as much as you'll get in Brussels, I bet.'

'My first salaried job… and I get to travel first class on Eurostar,' she added in triumph.

Terry smiled. He liked her impish grin. 'You'll go far, young lady.'

'Cheers.'

He was warming to her. 'Be careful in Brussels: It's a strange place. Just being there afflicts everyone…especially those who work in central office, believing that money really does grow on trees. You'll see when you get there. What's your name, by the way?'

'Lilly.'

'Well. Good luck, Lilly.'

Then he drove off, back to London: never wishing to return. At the back of his mind, though, he had a nagging feeling his wish would fall on deaf ears. Lilly would never return though, that he could confidently predict. Just as he could confidently predict that both the current world fiscal collapse and the ever-insatiable demand for an unrealistic increased EU budget from Brussels Headquarters went hand in hand.

Some things would never change.

***

Michael sold his shares in Northern Rock, against the advice of his broker. The grand total came to just short of twelve thousand pounds. Enough, he reckoned, for the laser surgery which he had promised Terry. He felt good. While on a high, he phoned Kara. No answer. He decided against leaving a message. At work, the hours passed slowly. Business was non- existent in the city. Everything was too quiet for his liking. The *Financial Times* spoke of rumblings in the US stock markets. For the first time, he read about sub-prime. He searched his memory. Hadn't Terry vaguely mentioned this term on the phone? It meant nothing to him, of course. What was happening over the pond could, quite frankly, stay that side of the pond. He searched for news on Northern Rock. Sure enough, a piece on the front cover of the *Financial Times* warned of a run on deposits as confidence evaporated between the major high street banks on matters of internal lending policy. Basically, as he saw it, the Rock was being squeezed of cash flow. Just like Churchill Fine Art. If the punters dried up, so did the ability to trade. Liquidity then disappeared. Bills couldn't be met. You were basically fucked. He read a disturbing report that the Bank of England was issuing a statement that a period of reflection was needed, in order for the volatile markets to settle down. Michael scanned the pages again, then switched on the portable TV in his office. He caught the tail end of *Sky News*. The commentator spoke of thousands of ordinary people, simple account holders, queuing outside their local bank branch seeking assurances that their deposits were safe. Christ. When did that last happen in Britain? No one was looking for a period of reflection: They wanted decisive action now. The Chancellor looked like a rabbit caught in the headlamps. Michael urgently rang Toby, who was out on the road seeking new artists for the gallery.

He got him on the second ring.

'Have you heard the news?' Michael asked.

'As much as you, I guess,' Toby replied.

'Are you driving?'

'Yes.'

'Switch on the radio.'

'Is there a problem?'

'Maybe I'm being alarmist, but there is unrest in the city. A friend of mine warned me of a global meltdown. I'm sure he is misinformed, but perhaps we should curtail our spending and watch and wait until the economic upheaval settles down. We might need to increase the overdraft facility to tide us over.'

'Makes sense. Let's meet shortly and draw up a contingency plan in case the shit hits the fan. I've spoken to former colleagues in New York and I'm picking up on their nervousness. No one is saying anything to the contrary, but I can tell when a market collapse is imminent. The US dollar is in freefall. Our Government is dithering. Sometimes, silence is deafening.'

Michael had one instruction: 'Stop spending.'

He clicked off, and returned to the extended news. The Prime Minister was uttering assurances (with a thin smile) to the nation outside Downing Street. He looked shell-shocked and weary, Michael observed. That spelt trouble.

***

Terry got back to International House in Wapping at three o'clock. The news floor was chaotic with fellow reporters screaming into their phones, seeking updated information on the looming financial crisis. Terry's hard-hitting front liner on the evening editions would bring the city to a standstill. He was certainly not going to be flavour of the month, with a story of impending doom and gloom but he had to tell it as it was. His editor would be delighted: sales of the newspaper would go through the roof. In the good ol' USA, he somehow imagined the reverse: no one would have a roof to speak of.

Amid the clatter, Terry got his head down at his desk and started on the follow up piece, headlined succinctly: 'World in Freefall'. He thought of his cancer and the comparison to world disorder: The enemy within. The hidden disease. Nothing was as it seemed on the surface, whichever way he looked at it. Everything and everyone was in freefall. Then he started to write his story, fast. Accordingly, his great journalistic page grabber spoke of the disease in terms of unprecedented banking greed and risk-taking on a scale never been seen before, fuelled by wide- boys chasing their inflated bonuses, knowing that the rewards of their endeavour was wholly out of context with the false dream they promised: unimaginable profits. There was a fundamental problem here though. The profits were unsustainable and where there was a profit, there was always a loss to someone else. It was a trade-off. Someone would get hurt. In this case, the sucker was the public: in other words the tax-payer. Eventually, he stopped writing on his computer. The screen was filled with emotive language, and damning statistics. It was a hard and brutal condemnation of all that was decaying in western commercial civilisation. *Someone would get their fingers burned. Eventually, someone would go under…but who?*

The words stuck in his throat. It then dawned on him that everything he expressed in his pent-up anger was actually mirroring the state of his crumbling body: the disease had taken hold, at first hidden, now exposed by the biopsy. Just like the nation's woes had been highlighted by the government. But it was too late to offer words of comfort, either to him or to the country's population. The bottom line was that everyone would have to pay. Everyone carried the bloody tumour. For some poor souls, they just weren't aware of it yet. The cancer was the big society, out of control; manifesting itself and growing inwardly and outwardly until it consumed everything in its path. It was bloated beyond repair. There was no stopping it on its path to self-destruction. Terry could not remember the last time he cried. It just wasn't something he did. But as he resumed his typing, he felt a tear falling on his cheek. And he realised just how upset he had become since the doctor sat him down and explained how this unwanted malignant tumour would impart on his life. He finished the story and sat back in his chair. The official line at the end of his report contained words of optimism to the reader. His own line was this: Do not believe the politicians, and certainly not the bankers. Think of the deepening crisis as a piece of fruit. The core of the apple is rotten. They will try to convince you otherwise.

On the outside, the skin appears to be ripe and golden. It is an illusion. There is no ripe juicy apple because within days, it will have shrivelled and turned to pulp. So will your savings, dear reader, if you do not take an early bite while the fruit is still edible. In other words, grab your money.

He too felt just like the bad apple: Rotting inside.

***

At just before five, with Gemma and Ronald now departed, Michael closed the gallery. He had switched off the lights, except for the one illuminating the reception desk, normally occupied by his secretary. He took a final call.

'Churchill Fine Art,' he said wearily.

'Could I speak to Michael Strange, please?'

'That would be me.'

'Allow me to introduce myself. My name is Theo Britton, spelt B-R-I-T-T-O-N and I represent a company called Britton on the Map.' He hesitated, adding, 'I hope you like the play on words.'

Michael was too tired for this, but humoured him anyway by means of a small snigger.

The man continued. 'Some time ago, my father died and as an only child, I inherited his entire estate. My mother had passed away many years before. The point is, he had three homes and it is only recently that I had the opportunity to examine the last house, and the contents held within. The house, or piazza, is in Venice. My father was a secretive man. I didn't even know that he owned a property abroad. On my visit, I discovered a rather good collection of decent fine vintage wine, Chinese porcelain and antique paintings which, in the latter case, I am not sure of their value or desirability. I collect clocks and vintage wrist watches, Mr Strange. Those are my passion. And so I am at a loss as to what to do with all this additional clutter in my life.'

'You could drink the wine,' Michael suggested.

'That I will happily do… However, I need your help with the artwork. I want to liquidate the entire collection.'

'Have we met before? Did I have dealings with your father? I wonder because usually there is a connection between client and gallery. Why did you choose us?'

'We certainly haven't met, but here is the intriguing thing, and the reason why I chose to ring you. On the back of one of the paintings is a label marked Churchill's Fine Art, dated 1986 - so it was purchased just over twenty years ago. I did a little research on the internet and discovered your father established the business before you so I presume the painting was bought from him, perhaps?'

'Certainly, that fits.'

'Basically, I need the various works valued and then put into auction. You will, of course, be amply rewarded for your endeavours. I need someone I can trust. You come highly recommended.'

'By whom?'

'I visited a gallery while in Venice, run by a woman called Agnes, who mentioned your name. I have her business card somewhere…'

'Agnes Olivetti.'

'The very same.'

'We go back a long way. We worked together in London, before she returned to Italy.' Michael's faltering voice conveyed his tiredness. 'As she is in the vicinity of your newly acquired home, and comes equally highly recommended by me, I suggest you use her instead. Her local contacts will be better acquainted with the paintings, and it will be cheaper for you as well.'

There was a long pause. Michael began to lose interest and tidied the papers on the desk.

The man cleared his throat and spoke. 'Mr Strange, most of the work is by English artists, mainly by minor masters, I think. Forgive my ignorance in these matters. There are, of course, one or two Italian scenes, which might not be your cup of tea. But there is a rather special one which warrants expert attention. That is where you come in. Take a look and tell me if it is authentic. My father collected good art, but I was surprised that, in this case, he acquired great art.' He fell silent once again, then added, 'I am not averse for the two of you to work together. Name your price, Mr Strange. I require you to travel to Venice, do the inventory, organise the sale and authenticate the masterpiece in question. I am a wealthy man, and will pay handsomely for your services. If you do your job properly, I will be a seriously rich man and you will benefit greatly as well. Shall we say ten per cent of the sale price?'

Michael was becoming slightly irritated by the over-confidence in the man, but was reminded of the fiscal meltdown on his doorstep and pressed ahead. He liked the sound of the commission.

'Can you reveal the name of the artist that merits such special attention?'

'Not on the phone, no. I need you to travel over soon. Within the next, say, seven days. Then you can feast your eyes on the work and report back to me, ensuring the utmost confidentiality of course. Do we have a deal?'

'In theory, yes. I'll draw up a contract of service, including expenses for you to consider...'

'Already agreed, your expenses will be met. Paperwork is not necessary. But I like your efficiency. It is late. In the morning, my secretary will phone you with all the details of the entire transaction, and what I want you to do in the case of the supposed masterpiece, if that is what it turns out to be. One last thing: I will pay you in cash, in advance, no questions asked. I will arrange for someone to drop in the key and address details, that sort of thing.'

'Just email me the details. I'll pick up on it.'

'Too many prying eyes, Mr Strange. This is a private commission, do you understand? I am happy for a partner to be involved with the general auction, but not with the main event. I've heard you can do this?'

Heard? Was this a trick or did the stranger know things that he shouldn't? He had to be careful with this guy. The last private cash transaction he got involved in was the ill-fated sale of the twelve Patrick Porters: and look what happened there. It nearly killed him. It resulted in the death of Lauren O' Neill. His mind began to focus on these matters. The voice on the phone cut through his meanderings. '...Therefore, I have hidden it from view in the house. You will find it, eventually if you search the property thoroughly... I am looking forward to your reaction. If you can place a private sale – discreetly, of course – then I am happy for you to receive a bonus...shall we say a fifteen per cent cut on this one?'

Michael's brain came back sharply into the present. The figures were getting better.

The man continued: 'That, I can assure you, will be

considerable money.'

It was Michael's turn for reflection. It took him three seconds. He was in. Then he said, 'I look forward to meeting with you, Mr Britton.'

'And I look forward to doing business with you, Mr Strange.'

'Michael.'

'Very well, Michael it is. I am Theo. Once you confirm the date of travel, I will forward the cash to your door. Clean and simple. Of course, as I have already stressed, I will expect total confidentiality in this little matter…'

'Of course.'

'Then good night.' The line went dead.

Michael immediately switched on the desktop computer and typed in a search request on Britton on the Map. He waited in anticipation. He checked Google and was rattled to discover that no such company existed. He wasn't going to sleep well tonight.

CHAPTER FIVE

He was right on that score. He slept dreadfully, tossing and turning all night. And the next night. By the third night, the bizarre phone call had become as troublesome as a toothache. It kept nagging at him. In the intervening days, he tried to put it out of his mind. No chance. His first thought awakening on this morning was to decline the job. Then curiosity kicked in. What mysterious painting did Theo Britton have in his possession? So prized he had taken the trouble to hide it. Why not put it in a bank vault? A hideous thought crossed his mind: Was it a stolen work of art? Oh, Christ…He had to put that notion right out of his mind. Looking back, he'd had enough drama in recent times to last him two lifetimes. But there was the money to consider and business was business. He wasn't going to let a competitor steal it from him. When the going gets tough…

***

Kara showered and felt the baby kick. Harder this time and more frequent. She allowed the hot water to soothe her aching body, aware that her stress levels would register an almighty 9.5 on the Richter scale, if one in fact existed for people being measured for the equivalent of a human earthquake. Feeling the kick again, she was clearly ready to explode in more ways than one. Last night, she had tried to talk to Marcus and at first they had reached an amicable truce. It went swimmingly until she mentioned her recent lunch date with Michael. Then he really let rip, accusing her of having secret trysts behind his back. First Ronald, now her former boss. His parting shot on storming out was something on the line of 'fuck you' and he hadn't been seen since. He'd probably slept in the gallery, she guessed. With an IQ of 126 she knew that their little conversation hadn't gone well, to put it mildly.

She decided to let him stew. He could be so juvenile sometimes. So competitive, believing that he and he alone could protect her and that the likes of Michael was intrusive and melodramatic to the point of always, in his words, making mountains out of a molehills. He could talk!

That's how he saw it in magical *Marcus World,* according to her. She was equally incensed and repeated the same words – fuck you – under her breath.

She dressed, made coffee, and pottered around the apartment. There were things to do, but her mind would not focus properly. Certain issues did her head in. Firstly, she needed to see her mother and grovel big time for her outburst on the phone. Then there was the forthcoming magazine story that Michael told her about, which now threatened to lift the lid on all their lives. Exposure and ridicule would follow. Jesus, she hadn't even got to that part before Marcus threw a fit. She would leave that tasty morsel for when he had calmed down. Never a dull moment, she had to concede.

She emptied the washing machine and chucked the wet clothes into the dryer, switched it to fast spin and pretended that it was her boyfriend who was gyrating inside, with her holding the control button. The world was screwed. She checked the time: 10am. If Marcus was at the gallery, he would need a fresh shirt at the very least. She collected one from the wardrobe, grabbed his deodorant and planned to make her way over shortly, and in the process make-up big time with him. She thought too of her rash behaviour in slamming down the phone on Michael. She would have to grovel to him too. *Men*

Attempting to lift a basket of wet sheets, her back went into spasm, forcing her to cry out in discomfort. She dropped the heavy load and reached out for support, grabbing the bedroom door handle. She felt nauseous, and her head began to whirl insanely. An excruciating pain, like a dagger ripping at her womb, shot through her protruding belly. She gulped for air, and in an instant felt a warm sensation overcome her. Looking down, she saw a strange puddle gathering at her feet. Normally, she would freak out at seeing this. So she freaked out.

Marcus got the call at the gallery at just after ten. He felt like shit, having drunk a bottle of cheap red plonk from the local supermarket the night before. Kara's hysterical rant took maybe two seconds to register before it dawned on him what she was babbling on about. He did the arithmetic: nearly three weeks late! He locked the gallery and raced home like a madman, knowing the birth of his child was about to happen right in the bloody apartment if he didn't get her to hospital, and fast. He found Kara slumped against the stairs, breathing erratically and sweating profusely.

Her clothes were soaking wet. He knew her waters had broken. Although they had rehearsed this moment, right now he went into panic mode, then regained his composure. He snatched an overnight bag, lots of towels, grabbed Kara and, in what seemed like a blink of an eye, drove like a wild man toward the hospital at Whitechapel, barely half a mile away. In his confusion, he must have done something right, miraculously remembering to call in and tell them to expect their imminent arrival. It was utter relief to see the wheelchair and two attendants waiting on the pavement. After that, everything was a blur. Two hours later…fuck, just two hours later… Marcus Heath, artist extraordinaire, budding entrepreneur, and all round good guy was a proud first-time father to a newborn son. He was a Daddy to a son he had already secretly named as Harvey. It just seemed to fit perfectly. Harvey Heath! Kara would just have to get used to it because he wasn't going to change his mind. He was going to have to marry her now. He was actually thankful that he had a baby boy. Firstly, because his name would be preserved for the next generation…but more to the point the girl's intended name was going to be Heavenly.

That would have taken some convincing.

***

Michael got the news from Marcus at one o'clock and rushed over to join him at the maternity ward. The baby was in an incubator as a precaution. In the corridor, they hugged and, for the time being at least, put their differences behind them. Michael saw the utter exhaustion and pride on Marcus's beaming face. In a moment of supreme exhilaration, the new Dad burst out shouting with unrepentant joy the simple news that mother and child were in perfect health. Then he wept for England.

Michael stayed for several hours, waiting for a fleeting moment to see Kara and catch a glimpse of, dare he say it…Harvey. Both were asleep when his chance came. Both looked utterly beautiful, the newborn wrapped in his mother's embrace after her son was removed from the incubator. Michael too had a tear in his eye. Then he went home, a very happy man.

That night, unlike the previous night, he slept beautifully too.

***

Kara could now believe in miracles and the strength of angels. God, how they helped her push the little blighter out! He was several weeks overdue and finally came out into the world in a rush. Never had she experienced such a contrast between agony and ecstasy, and for something so tiny, precious and…adorable. She sat up in bed, cradling her son, watched over by her adoring Mum and Marcus. Gorgeous, gorgeous Marcus. What a hero he had been. Through the window, she could see early morning shafts of light cascading down on the buildings opposite. A ray of light! A new day, a new beginning. Although she was shot through, she felt a surge of strength that simply overwhelmed her. She, Kara Scott: a Mother! Get that!

She took Marcus's hand and looked him straight in the eye. 'I love the name, Marcus: H-A-R-V-E-Y. It's perfect. Like father, like son.' Then she closed her eyes and slept deeply.

Marcus gathered his newborn baby to his chest, kissed his forehead, and asked Kara's mum what she thought of their son's name.

She looked at him witheringly, and said, 'I'd hoped for something more dignified. Wilfred would have been lovely, named after Kara's granddad, but I suppose we have to move with the times. As long as you two are happy, then the decision is made. Don't concern yourselves with my feelings.'

Ouch. Marcus kept his cool. Nothing could faze him at this moment.

'If we have another baby, even if it's a girl, I promise we will call it Wilfred. Then everyone will be happy.'

For the first time in her life, he guessed, the woman was speechless.

***

Michael got to work early, refreshed and energised. He phoned Marcus to check on Kara's progress, ordered flowers for her bedside and bought premium bonds worth £500 for little Harvey. It was a start. He met Toby to discuss their master plan for survival in the event of a serious economic downturn, which was now widely predicted in all the newspapers. Michael read Terry's analysis and was thankful that he had sold his shares in the Rock. His story was a great journalistic triumph, full of damning rhetoric. The words were punched home by a true wordsmith.

The meeting with his son took three hours. At lunch, they grabbed a ham sandwich and, over a pot of Earl Grey, drew up a tight budget which would see them weather the storm over the next twelve months. If a tsunami was on the horizon, then nothing would save them. They gambled on a hurricane instead. Battening down the hatches usually did the trick. They had seen this sort of thing before, over the previous generations, and Churchill Fine Art still stood firm on its foundations, if a little wobbly at times. Like now.

In the afternoon, business was surprisingly good, with three sales. Michael's spirits lifted: First the news on Kara, now a good day on the shop floor. Gemma came to him and handed over a sealed parchment envelope, handwritten in ink and addressed as follows:

The attention of Michael Strange/ Confidential.

Gemma raised her eyebrows. 'You know all the right

people in high places,' she remarked, sounding more and more like Kara.

He smiled thinly. 'Gemma, find out all you can about a firm called Britton on the Map, will you? I tried Google and found nothing. See what you can dig up.'

She nodded.

Michael then retreated into his office. He removed the contents from the envelope. The note was short and to the point. Most annoyingly, there was no address at the top. It was handwritten and signed simply 'Theo'. It contained an address in Venice and box number for a key to the property. There was also a PS, which read, *I will arrange delivery of your down payment by courier at five this evening.* That was it. No phone number. No email address. He regretted that he had not dialled 1471 when he last spoke to Theo, although probably the number would have been withheld anyway. He took stock of the situation. He was beginning to smell a rat. He reconsidered the proposition, decided against it and would now maintain a policy of doing nothing, as he was unable to contact Theo directly with his sudden change of heart. Let the courier go back with the cash. He was sure that Theo would then call again. Then he could get the measure of the man.

The courier arrived at five. He was sent packing at one minute past. Michael decided to stay the extra hour, just in case. The phone remained silent. He eventually went home, via the hospital, and stayed with Kara for half an hour. She was radiant. Marcus shared a coffee and a natter with him at the cafeteria and then he got home at eight. He was knackered. He kicked off his shoes, stuck a curry dish in the microwave and opened a bottle of chilled wine. The phone rang.

'Michael Stra...'

'It's Theo Britton, do we have a problem?'

Michael was aghast. 'How did you get my home number?'

'There are ways.'

'Do you always get your own way, Theo?'

'Generally speaking. I can be very persuasive.'

'In this instance, I think not.'

'We had an agreement.'

'I've broken it.'

'I thought my terms were more than generous.'

'They are, but I like an open line of communication to those I work with. We need to meet, to discuss matters. I want to know something about you. At the moment, you seem to know a great deal more about me. I have questions I need answers to.'

'Go to your window, Michael. In the car park below you will see a black Mercedes saloon. I will be waiting for you, if you care to join me.'

Michael checked. He shuddered at the thought that this man even knew where he lived. He snatched his jacket and made for the elevator. Outside, it was cold. Michael approached cautiously. Within a few feet of the car, the rear door swung open. A portly, silver-haired man got out, smoking an Havana cigar. He was perhaps in his early sixties, groomed impeccably, his shoes polished to perfection. His cashmere topcoat looked like it cost a few thousand. Even in the gloom of the car park, his eyes shone with rapier intent. When he spoke, Michael detected a decorative and highly polished diamond lodged in one of his front teeth.

'Good evening, Michael, so happy to make your acquaintance,' the man said. He didn't offer a handshake. The uniformed chauffeur then got out and hovered like a jittery protector, eyes peeled, hand in pocket.

Michael searched around. He didn't like this one bit. 'Theo,' he said sharply. He buttoned up his jacket and shivered.

Theo gestured with his hand. 'Would you care to step inside where it is warmer?'

'I'm fine just as I am, thank you.'

'Shall we walk then?'

'Just the two of us?'

'Vladimir can keep his distance, if that's OK?'

Just what he needed: fucking Russian mafia. Michael nodded valiantly. In truth, he was as nervous as a cat on a hot tin roof.

They strolled into the adjacent avenue, with Mr Heavy hovering fifty paces behind. It was a typical tree-lined road like many others in the neighbourhood, made up of handsome and expensive three-storey houses painted in Chelsea pastel shades. Sleek cars parked nose to tail. The street lamps made eerie pools of light on the pavement which they had to pass through on their journey to nowhere. In one of these illuminations, Michael spotted a long jagged scar down Theo's neck. *Who was this man?* A man of means, apparently: but with no registered company to speak of. *Don't go there.*

'Who are you, Theo? I can't work for someone who hides all traces of their identity from me. I have no means of contacting you.'

'I'm here now.'

'That's not the same thing.'

'I wish for my identity to remain unknown, for security reasons. Vladimir will be our go-between. I am not a British citizen, although I do conduct business here throughout the year and have a home in London. I am based in Monte Carlo. I am known as a Shifter, I shift things: People, cargo, weapons, governments.'

'Governments..?'

'I am well connected. For instance, look ahead. Do you see those two men standing by that Range Rover? They work for me. If you glance to your right and look above, you will see someone on a flat roof. See him?'

Michael blinked and stared.

'I own him too.'

'Own him?'

'A figure of speech.'

'Do you intend to own me as well?'

'I've done my research, Michael. You are clearly your own man. That's why I chose you.'

'This painting in Venice, is it stolen?'

'You be the judge of that. I value your opinion. It could be many things to many people. Depends on your prospective and your need for the money.' He halted and shivered. 'Shall we go back?'

'Tell me: Is the story of your father's death true?'

'Yes. He had three homes, although I only knew of one, as I had previously explained on the phone. I now have six to contend with. A burden of sorts. The expenses of maintaining them are enormous.'

Michael didn't answer or offer sympathy or weep for the man. They turned. Vladimir held his ground as they passed. He looked Michael straight in the face. Eyes like ice.

As they reached the Mercedes, Theo smiled generously for the first time.

'Michael, let us be clear on this. You do not need to know who I am, just whether I can deliver what I promise. I always deliver. The point is, can you do the same? I ask very little of you, in return for a great deal of money. I am paying for your expertise. It is in your interests to know as little as possible about me. Do a job. Get rich. Forget about it.'

'You said you were a Shifter. If you can dislodge a government, then surely you can dispose of a simple painting if you see fit?'

The driver rejoined them and unlocked the car. He waited.

Theo settled into the rear and looked up at Michael. He flashed his diamond smile. 'Not this one. I need a real shifter in this case. You'll have your money in advance, tomorrow. I don't need a contract, nor an inventory of your expenses. Spend whatever is necessary. Enjoy your trip to Venice. Authenticate the painting. If it is genuine, we talk again. If it is a fake, throw it in the bin. You still get paid. Don't look for me, Michael. I cannot be found. But I will be watching you. As you know, I have eyes everywhere. My colleague will be in touch. Goodbye.'

Michael watched as the door closed and the Mercedes glided out of the car park and disappeared like a stealth bomber, swallowed up by the night. He felt shaken and a little stirred. He needed a stiff brandy. Several, in fact. He then remembered the curry in the microwave. It would be frazzled by now. *Just like him.* He'd have to settle for beans on toast. In truth, his appetite was gone.

He shivered. What in God's name was all that about? Who was this Theo Britton, a man with a diamond in his teeth? A man who could shift things...Whoever heard of anyone who could do that? It was the stuff of fiction, dreamt up by the like of Ian Fleming. He'd read about this sort of thing in novels, but never in real life. Lauren O'Neill was a pussycat compared to Theo, he was sure. He wasn't even being given a chance to cut and run. The job was now expected of him, full stop. He breathed in the cold air and steadied himself. It would be a barmy ride, if it wasn't so scary.

Back in his apartment, Michael locked his door and checked the nearby rooftops from his window. There was no one to be seen. There was a certain perverse humour to all this, though.

Theo, the Shifter. As he had earlier predicted with misplaced confidence, he had got the measure of the man. *As if.* He wanted to laugh. Instead, his gut twisted.

***

The following afternoon, Harvey Michael Wilfred came home to a house overflowing with flowers and balloons and banners proclaiming his arrival into this world. Marcus had done all the fancy decoration, and Kara cried with delight. They were now a family. While she and baby rested, he cooked lasagne and drank several bottled beers in celebration. From the kitchen, he couldn't resist a peek into the lounge to catch sight of them, both fast asleep, his dozing son contentedly spread-eagled across her chest.

He popped Champagne and was so relieved that they were at home: just the three of them. Yes, Kara's mother was great, Michael was great, the hospital staff absolutely brilliant but...this was blissful. After Kara had woken up, they shared dinner and then gawped at Harvey and realised what a little marvel he was: All 7lb 2oz of him. The two of them drank a celebratory toast.

Marcus kissed Kara, and said, 'Any idea what we do now?'

Kara smiled, and took his hand. 'Haven't got a clue,' she answered.

***

Ronald raised an eyebrow and said, 'You have a visitor.'

Michael could tell by his expression that his colleague was troubled. Looking beyond him he saw Mr Heavy waiting in the gallery. He was carrying a package, and a vacant expression. Menacing, all the same. He stood over six feet six

103

tall.

'It's OK Ronald, I know him.'

'*Really?*'

'Really. Don't be alarmed. He can kill both of us with expert ease, but only one at a time. I'll distract him, you make a run for it. He's big but he's slow.'

'Very funny...'

Michael walked into the gallery.

'Hello, Vladimir.'

Ice eyes returned his gaze. 'I have a package for you. Can we go somewhere private?'

'Here's just fine.'

'My Boss sends his regards. I believe you will find this will take care of your needs. For now, at least.' He handed over the brown paper parcel. Michael took it, without blinking. Outwardly, he was cool personified. Inside, he was a bag of nerves.

'You can contact me on the cell phone which is contained in the envelope. I do not expect to hear from you, except in an emergency.' He turned and departed, his long black leather coat making a swishing noise as he went, like Darth Vader.

From a safe distance, Ronald said, 'Is he your new best friend?'

'Better to be a friend than an enemy,' Michael replied.

He returned to his office and shut the door. Atop his desk, he unwrapped the parcel and extracted a wad of cash. He counted £10,000. That, he knew, was for the trip to Venice. He now had the address, the whereabouts of a house key, a phone and the money to travel. He sighed heavily. Then he thought of Agnes. It would be great to see her again.

For old time's sake. As students in London, they had a thing going on but that was a very long time ago. He reckoned he could go to Italy and undertake the task in three days and have a little fun...a piece of cake. What could possibly go wrong?

CHAPTER SIX

'Do you still see Adele?'

Michael was somewhat taken aback by Kara's comment. This was the very last question he would expect to be asked. They strolled in the park near Limehouse basin, which overlooked the Thames, Kara pushing the newly acquired pram along the wharf, with Harvey wrapped up inside. He was now eight days old.

Michael looked at her and shook his head. 'Why do you ask?'

'Because you were married for many years, and I assume that for a long time you were happy with each other.'

'Yes, we were.'

'Why would it go wrong, if you love each other?'

'Heavy stuff,' he replied.

'Will you keep in touch? After all, you built something special with the gallery, the magazine, and you have a fine son between you...'

They stopped. He was uneasy with her inquisition. He took a bar of chocolate from his pocket and shared it with her and tried to answer truthfully.

'We have no reason to see each other,' he said. 'The divorce went through, I'm broke and she lives in isolated splendour on an estate in Herefordshire, with you-know-who. Thankfully, Toby bought into the business, cleared the debts and asked his mother to resign from the company. She kicked and screamed but saw the light. She now has no part in my life. Sad, but true. We move on, but secretly I hope their house burns down.'

'Careful what you wish for. Not bitter then?'

'Not at all, just when I breathe.'

'And Lauren, do you still think about her?'

'Christ, Kara, what's this all about?'

They continued their journey, Harvey oblivious to the complexities of human strife heading his way.

'I don't think any of us have given you enough credit for flipping your life around,' Kara said. 'We are all so busy wrapped up in our own little worlds that we sometimes forget to ask how other people are feeling about things. Now I'm asking.'

'I miss her because of the mind-blowing sex.'

'Too much detail.' She punched him playfully on the arm.

'Ouch!'

'Baby.'

He thought about it. It was hard being reminded of such pain. He cleared his throat. 'Lauren was a minefield of contradictions, a woman with an unquenchable thirst for thrills and drama, who sought vengeance on those that she felt betrayed her. She gave everything and expected everything in return. She lived on a knife-edge. Remember, the abuse she suffered at the hands of her father throughout her childhood marked her for life. Her illness was destructive, her troubled personality split by trauma. She was wrongfully accused of manslaughter. She took the rap for the crimes of her sister. No wonder she was off her head. Her passion was all-consuming, but flawed. She couldn't tolerate the weakness in others. Had she lived, she would have killed the both of us eventually.' He buttoned his coat tight around his neck, the cold biting into his skin. 'I too am flawed. I was letting this destruction happen because I was greedy. We were on a fast downward curve, being sucked into oblivion from our obsession for each other. Perhaps I loved her too much, but she was a curse.'

'I like the bit about passion being all-consuming. You had that with two unique women. Some people never experience that feeling in their whole lifetime. Personally, I thought that both Adele and Lauren were off their fucking heads.'

He grimaced. 'What does that say about me?'

'Exactly.'

'Thanks.'

Then she smiled. 'But I love you, sometimes.'

They linked arms as they walked. It felt supremely good to him.

'How about you and Marcus?' he asked.

Kara remained quiet for a few steps. 'I too want that aching passion. I gave you a hard time because I want answers. I want *real* love. I don't want to make a mistake with my life, I want to make the right decision.'

'And what decision is that?'

She smiled radiantly, her eyes ablaze. Then she surprised him. 'Marcus has asked me to marry him!'

He was taken aback. 'What was your answer?'

'I'll go with the barmy-army chorus line, of which you are a fully signed-up member of. I said yes of course!' Then she added with a smile, 'I'm stupid, I know. I need my head testing.'

'Off your fucking rocker!' Michael said laughing, and took over pushing the pram, leaving her standing there, perplexed. He turned and faced her.

'Best decision of your life,' he said.

***

Later, over supper at their apartment, Michael confronted Kara and Marcus with some unsettling news: 'I'm going to Venice for a few days.'

From past experience, they all knew this meant trouble.

They sat in the cluttered lounge, surrounded by baby clothes and toys, gifts from family and friends. Michael overdid it with a giant panda and a Chelsea football kit (for future use). You had to get them young, he surmised. They ate cross-legged on the floor, tucking into pizza and salad and chips. Harvey lay between his Dad's open legs, alert to the mysterious big balloons that dangled from the ceiling above his head. His eyes twinkled in wonder.

'Venice?' Kara echoed. The atmosphere suddenly became brittle.

'A business proposition. Couple of days holiday break as well…'

'Will you see Julius and Antonia?'

Michael hesitated. 'Depends. I don't want to open up old wounds, but I'll let them know I'm about.'

'I think they would love to see you,' Kara said.

Marcus pulled funny faces at Harvey. He was keeping out of it.

Kara made coffee in the kitchen. Michael took the chance to speak candidly and turned to Marcus.

'We need to talk, privately, Marcus. Can I ring you at the gallery tomorrow? There are things you need to know, especially as I am going away.'

'Sure.' Marcus eyed him suspiciously. They still hadn't become entirely comfortable with each other. 'Why can't you say those things in front of Kara?'

'Because she is a young mum, and very fragile at the moment. You are stronger, and can evaluate the situation better.'

'And what situation is that?'

'Someone from the past...'

'Ah, the past. It never seems to leave us alone, does it?'

Michael picked up the scorn in his voice, and dropped the subject as Kara re-entered the room and placed their drinks down on the table.

'Having fun, guys?' she asked.

'Solving the problems of the world,' Marcus said, turning his attention his son, who screamed as loud as a baby can.

'Time for a nappy change,' Kara announced. She picked her son up. Then she looked at Michael. 'Do you want to do it?'

'Time for me to go,' Michael said quickly, raising his hands in protest. Those days were over. He gulped the remains of his coffee, kissed Kara good night and walked to the door with Marcus. There was a awkwardness between them.

'I'm not trying to cause problems, Marcus.'

Marcus fidgeted. 'Sure.'

'Hear me out, and then you can decide if I'm overreacting.'

'Is this a rumour based on fact or fantasy?'

'A bit of both. But you need to know what's been happening.'

'You know where to find me. If this is all bullshit, I'll put an end to this friendship once and for all. I've had enough, OK?'

They stared each other down.

'I'll ring you tomorrow,' Michael said.

***

The next day, Michael reflected on the situation with Marcus. He knew he was treading on thin ice with all this conjecture about the return of Maggie. The very mention of her name would threaten the balance of their delicate three-way relationship, which was strained at the best of times. *A poor relationship,* he corrected himself. On the one hand, he understood this young man's concern for privacy and stability, especially when he considered what they had all gone through over the past year. Equally, Michael had to make him understand the severity of the situation if they chose to ignore the potential harm that Maggie could inflict on them. To turn a blind eye was, in Michael's opinion, perilous in the extreme. If his constant warnings meant friction between them, then so be it. This was a real danger. After surviving the fire, it was a case of regrouping and seeking closure. They each did that on their own terms. For Marcus, this meant stubborn denial. For Michael, it meant awareness. Kara just saw fear on the horizon. They all dealt with it in a fractured and unhealthy manner. It ate at them. Marcus had to be made aware of his responsibilities to Kara and his newborn son. Naivety was a wrong turn in Michael's book. He too had responsibilities. He was older and wiser and overly protective because of the fatherly role that he adopted.

In the past, he had been foolish in love and very nearly paid with his life. Lauren was gone, and Kara's earlier probing in the park once again brought the immense hurt of the past to the surface. Perhaps he had loved Lauren...but what was love? Was it just lust? She was always there in the background though, consuming his muddled thoughts. Over the past months, he had managed to subconsciously bury his feelings (he lied to himself), and had felt numb with the lack of emotion he felt (he was in denial). He recognised this was shock. Both his body and mind were in total shutdown. Kara made him reawaken his desire for physical need and comfort. Sometimes, he had to admit that he desperately missed Lauren.

Yes, she was cursed, but in the short time that they got

together, the extreme passion they shared was overwhelming. Their lovemaking was intense and almost brutal. Although she almost took him down into Hell, he acknowledged that she had also lifted him to a height of ecstasy he'd never experienced before. Oh, how he missed it...She was an intensely exotic creature, a one-off creation. And a great artist too...truly great. She never got the credit she deserved, hiding her immense talent behind an assumed name in order to keep the memory of her dead brother alive. Perverse, yes, but she was mentally disturbed by the trauma of her upbringing. If only he had known earlier...

Sometimes, it saddened him that he would probably never fulfill this spiritual and sexual dimension again with another human being. She was off this planet. Although this was an almost crazy view of their headstrong obsession (that seemed to hold them like glue) toward each other, it was true for him. He ached for her. She really did exist in his life, and for a short time he found what he was looking for: sheer yearning and the abandonment of commitment. No ties. Just sex. Looking back, he and Lauren used each other. It suited them. They took everything from each other, but rarely gave anything back. Yes, it was a relationship based on carnal gratification, selfishness and voracity, but in conjunction with that, they lived on the bittersweet razor blade edge between intense love and loathing.

Call it what you like, everyone would have an opinion – but for Michael, as of this moment, he missed her dearly. He craved her. He would have died with her. So nearly did. It was Marcus who changed his destiny. Sometimes, he hated him for it. It was the first time in ages that he had confronted this anger within. This rage. It still existed, and he guessed that it existed in Marcus as well.

They had something so common – so raw – that, whether they liked it or not, it held them together in spite of themselves. It was like an invisible rope which structured their destinies. They could push and pull on each other but, in the end, their fate was entwined. It bound them. Michael understood; he doubted that Marcus would see the same picture. They were of a different generation.

He phoned Marcus at his gallery, expecting an ear bashing.

The response took him by surprise, pushing him off guard.

'You'd better come over,' Marcus said. 'We've had a window broken, so I'm a bit preoccupied with clearing up at the moment.'

Michael's heart sank.

***

He got to the premises within the hour. The main window was shattered, although it remained partially intact, with great splinter lines drawn deep into the glass which still hung precariously within the frame. It was a dangerous situation, especially to those walking by. Michael could see the impact hole. He entered and found Marcus clearing away the window display in readiness for the glaziers to arrive. He looked flustered, so Michael nodded silently and kept his distance, trying to make himself useful. Immediately, he repositioned two chairs from the gallery in front of the window on the boardwalk to protect passers-by from possible injury, then re-entered the premises and scanned the wooden floor. He knew instinctively what he was searching for. To the rear of the building, he approached a multi-tiered free-standing glass cabinet and got down on his hands and knees. He felt underneath and grasped the hard-edged object.

Marcus looked over. 'What are you searching for?'

'This.' Michael stood. He opened his hand.

'A stone,' Marcus observed. Then he looked at the window. 'Was that the missile?'

'Not stone,' Michael said. 'It is a piece of flint, exactly the same type which was used to break our gallery window recently. This is not a coincidence, Marcus. Like me, you have been targeted.'

'Targeted? It was probably one of the homeless passing by, high on meths. They live in a hostel just around the corner from here. It happened last month to the coffee shop next door.'

'No, Marcus. This just reinforces my view that my suspicions are well-founded.' He took breath and steadied himself. 'Maggie is back, make no mistake. We need to talk seriously, Marcus. And you need to listen to me, very

111

carefully.'

Marcus sighed, 'Another of your conspiracy theories, huh?'

Michael placed the flint on the desk.

'Don't mock me, Marcus. You've seen the damage she can inflict first hand, and she is capable of more than just smashing windows. This is just her way of cranking up the pressure on us: First me, now you. The flint is from the barn, it is her calling card. I'm convinced that she is on a mission of revenge. She blames us for Lauren's death. Maggie has the money she took from the farm, which gives her the power to move around anonymously. Possibly, she has changed her appearance, gained a false passport. You won't like this Marcus, but both Kara and I have received numerous phone calls by an unidentifiable source. It's her…be sure of it.'

Marcus gave him a withering look but calmed sufficiently to put the kettle on.

'Suppose it isn't,' he said. 'Suppose it's just your warped sense of latching onto the past for whatever reason suits you. You don't have the evidence to support your theory, Michael. The flint doesn't signify anything. In the meantime, you put the shit up Kara and me, just when our lives are looking up. Kara has time for all this mad stuff, but I don't.'

'She sees the danger, Marcus.'

'She sees whatever you want her to see,' Marcus snapped back.

Marcus poured coffee and pushed a mug in Michael's direction. He in turn took the drink and moved away, giving them space. He ambled around the gallery and examined the glass sculptures that adorned the wall shelves and those that sat atop the Perspex plinths. It was an impressive stock, he acknowledged. Marcus had the talent for display. One piece of bronze captivated him, a beautiful elongated figurine of a female nude, with arced back and a mass of cascading hair. It stood over twenty inches high on a polished marble base. Momentarily distracted from their conversation, Michael vowed to buy it. He finished his coffee and checked the price of the limited edition piece: £3000.

'What do you propose we do?' Marcus asked finally.

Michael was taken aback by his conciliatory manner. The

aggression had gone from his voice. 'We watch our backs, for a start,' Michael began, returning to the small kitchen at the rear. He suddenly noticed something – a canvas, maybe? – wrapped tightly in a grey blanket. This struck him as odd, as everything else propped against the wall was protected by bubble wrap. His mind moved on. 'I'm going to Venice, as you know. I intend to speak with Julius, to see if he too has experienced any problems. I suggest that you keep an eye on Kara. Bring her into the gallery, with Harvey. Don't allow for them to be left alone. Maybe her mother can stay over? I know a private detective. Seems a bit extreme, but I'm willing to pay him to dig around and also watch over you all. When I get back, we can sit down and plan a course of action. Do you remember Terry Miles? He is a journalist friend of mine. I'll get him on board too.'

'What about the police?'

'They will only act upon hard evidence, not our paranoia as you put it. Besides, after dropping the case against us in regard to Lauren's death, the last thing we want is to have them fishing into the case again. I propose we get them involved when we have a fix on Maggie.' He elected at this stage to refrain from telling him about his forthcoming interview with the police, in order to quell any further panic.

'Agreed. Who is this detective?'

'His name is Martin Penny, ex-army. Served in Bosnia. I've used him before. With your permission I'll pass on your address details to him. He will then contact you direct. Best Kara is not aware of this, although I had mentioned the idea to her. What do you think?'

'Yeah, keep it quiet. Kara doesn't need the hassle of a minder on her shoulder. It'll spook her.'

'Be aware, Marcus. This is for real. If you become suspicious of anything, then be assured that you need to be suspicious, OK?

'OK.'

Michael moved to the door. 'Have you called the glaziers?'

'Yeah.'

'I like this bronze,' he said. 'How much to me?'

'Three thousand pounds'

'Best price for the trade?'

'Three thousand.'

Michael laughed at the arrogance, raising an eyebrow. 'You make a crap businessman. We need to look after each other...'

'I just won't be taken advantage of.' Then Marcus offered for the first time a broad grin, adding: 'I know you want to protect us. Thanks, Michael.'

As he walked along the boardwalk beside the dock, Michael felt a begrudging degree of solidarity at last, although it was a flimsy stand-off. But he would take it. He would negotiate the price of the bronze at a later date. His stride quickened.

***

Back at his apartment, Michael poured himself a glass of Chilean Merlot, adjusted the lighting to a more ambient mood and turned on a CD of Mozart's Symphony No 21. He kicked off his shoes, checked the mail and decided on something to eat. For the first time in ages, he had a ferocious appetite.

He was suddenly agitated by a dull thumping on the ceiling from the flat above. It had happened before, as if a heavy object was being dragged across the floor. He vowed to leave a note on the door asking Ms Byrne to quiet things down a bit. His thoughts then returned to his meeting with Marcus which had gone well, against all expectations of obstinacy and ego causing friction between them. However, he couldn't decide who was obstinate and who had the bigger ego. Then he thought of the mysterious item wrapped in the blanket. What was Marcus hiding?

He extracted a ribeye steak from the fridge, prepared a mixed green salad and microwaved a jacket potato, settling into an evening of quiet reflection. Having Marcus on his team was a whole lot better than having him sniping from the sidelines. He fried the steak medium rare, refilled his glass, ate well, and caught the six o'clock news on the TV. All the talk was on sub-prime chaos over the pond. An economic advisor suggested that the tide of woes would wash up on the coast of Britain soon. He was loudly put in his place by an opposing politician, who refuted such panic-mongering. An argument ensued. Michael was convinced that there was a case for caution. After all, there was no smoke without a fire. He knew everything there was to know on that subject. Further news brought bad trading figures on the stock exchange and doubtful murmurings from the banking quarter.

This was getting serious, Michael concluded. He finished the wine, washed up and caught the end of *Have I Got News For You*. At last, he had something to amuse him: cheap laughs at the expense of the Government. Ian Hislop from *Private Eye* was in his element, as usual, satirising everyone in his beady sights. It made him smile. He then made coffee, dug out the telephone number he was looking for from a drawer in the hallway, grabbed his phone and dialled. There was an automated messaging service.

Michael spoke. 'Hi Martin, Michael Strange here. Remember me? I'd appreciate a call to discuss a job that you might be interested in. It's urgent.' He then left his phone number at home and work. He drank more coffee and scanned *The Times*. Later, he penned the outline for an article that he intended to publish for his art magazine *All The Rage*. It was a profile on the rise of Cuban painters, most notably from Havana. Michael could see the potential in investment opportunities, and hoped the market could be stimulated by his remarks. Toby and he had planned to travel over and discover new talent within the year. Provided the economy held.

The phone rang, and he answered quickly, turning the music down as he did so.

The metallic voice was north-east heavy, probably from Middlesbrough: 'Martin Penny, returning your call. Is that Michael?''

'It is, thanks for getting back so quickly. We've worked together before, many years ago. Do you recall?'

'I do, Michael. How can I help?'

'I'm looking for two things. Firstly, personal protection for a former colleague of mine, a woman and her new baby. Secondly, to investigate the whereabouts of a fugitive who I believe is stalking us.'

'I charge one hundred and fifty pounds per hour, plus

expenses.'

No small talk, Michael observed.

'Fine,' he gulped. He did the mental arithmetic. Not such a good idea perhaps.

'The fugitive: man or woman?'

'Woman.'

'Is she known to you?'

'Yes.'

'Do you have a name?'

'Yes.'

'Is the job home or overseas?'

'London.'

'Prepare a full dossier on her. I want everything you know written in a file. And I mean *everything*. A photograph of her would be helpful.'

'Done.'

'Shall we meet at your office or at your home? Maybe you prefer neutral ground.'

'Neutral ground it is.'

'When and where?'

'Tomorrow night, say eight, in the bar at the Tower Thistle Hotel. Does that suit you?'

'See you at eight.'

Then the line went dead.

Immediately after, Michael gathered a pile of loose leaf A4 writing paper from his desk, headlined the top copy MAGGIE CONLON and then started scribbling. It was going to be a long, arduous night. He reached for the whisky bottle.

His scrambled brain tried to recall an image of Mr Penny. Not exactly the most talkative person, thought Michael. But then again, he wanted action, not words from his new sidekick. Words never killed anyone. Maggie didn't understand words or reasoning. Martin Penny was just the kind to sort her out, once and for all. It was just going to cost a tidy packet.

CHAPTER SEVEN

Terry Miles had to do two things, both of which he hated. The first was to undertake a blood test at his local clinic and then, secondly, arrange an appointment with his consultant, who would give him an update on the condition of his cancer. The last MRI scan revealed a group of tumours central to the prostate gland, which indicated a T3 reading, meaning that the disease was non-evasive at present. It was a case of wait-and-see, according to Mr Callow, the urology specialist. According to Terry, it was a toss-up being caught between a short and long fuse. Both led to the same thing.

Michael had generously provided the funds to seek private alternative remedies, one being HIFU laser treatment, which was largely untested, but a viable cure for some. All in all, it was an unnerving experience going through this uncharted territory, trying desperately to understand the right course of action to take. It was that 'C' word. It terrified him. It terrified everyone. He suddenly felt lonely and vulnerable. The biopsy procedure was bad enough, intrusive and degrading. Then there was his morbid fear of needles. For the nurse at the clinic, it was routine stuff: A quick jab. For Terry, it represented his darkest irrational nightmare.

When it rained…

Something else jabbed at him too, this time at his subconscious. On his recent trip to the farm, he saw for the first time the momentous calamity that befell his friend, Michael Strange, and the home of the mysterious woman that he had loved and lost. What really happened to drag all these people to the barn on that fateful day? What secrets did each of them hold? How did the inferno start? Why did they need to fight each other with such venom? What became of Maggie, the sister to the dead woman? Much more damning: why did someone need to perish in such horrible circumstances…Was it simply a terrible accident? Terry began to see the bigger picture, murky as it was. This was a story of betrayal and greed and jealousy. At the heart of the conflict was Lauren O'Neill. Who was this alluring female? Why did she have such power over Michael and Kara? She too was like a cancer insidiously eating away at their flesh, all consuming...This suddenly made him feel squeamish, and utterly dispensable in the great scheme of things. Each of them was small beer, given that the world was fucked anyway. So was he.

Oddly, against this weird backcloth, he thought of Sheila Cox, the publican at The Royal Oak. It was after his impromptu visit to the pub that first set his mind wandering in her direction. She had gone missing, if you could seriously believe the teenage zombie called Lilly and her gossip. A far-fetched scenario: Someone so well-known to the community simply vanishing into thin air. Terry resolved to investigate this further. Something didn't add up. First things first, he vowed to take Michael back to the farm to confront his demons, which he knew his friend had locked away but couldn't quite discard the key. He was a haunted man. It was here that they could piece together the tragic events that unfolded that day. He knew Michael would be reluctant to do this, but Terry was determined that his friend would need to exorcise the loss of someone so close. After all, Michael and Lauren were intense lovers. He knew that Michael still carried her image like a beacon in his head. How did he know this? He knew Michael, knew how his mind worked. As an investigative journalist, it was his job to dig beneath the surface, and Michael, despite his serene manner, was a tortured human being: ready to explode. He kept his anger and frustration hidden, that was for sure. And here was the clue. Michael simply never spoke of her, to anyone, as far as he was aware. If the pain was locked away so deep, well, it was time to find the key to release it.

Terry underwent the jab the next day and arranged an appointment with the consultant in two weeks' time. Now he had to return to the job in hand. He had a deadline to meet. Normally, he would enlist the help of researchers for the story, but this was too risky if he wanted to protect his friend. He would do all the work himself, interview all those involved, aided by his internal source in the police department, happy that he could meet the deadline in six weeks' time. He opened a file on his laptop at home, rather than at work, and created a new password. He codenamed the article with the provisional working title:

The dealer and the devil:
The story of Michael Strange.

No one would see this file until it was absolutely finished and necessary for his editor to give it the green light for publication. Then the public would be hit with it, and the shit would hit the fan. He decided to write two versions, one for his editor which he would submit for her approval, and the alternative one which he would keep hidden from view. That is, until he learned the truth. The whole truth. Then he would decide on the course of action to take: publish and be damned? Yes, he had a loyalty to Michael, and yes, he had a professional duty to his newspaper readership but, more importantly, he had to look himself in the mirror each morning without hating the puppet that stared back.

Ultimately, he searched for the heart of the matter in a story and no one should be spared. Not even the author... Was he trying to protect Michael, or the integrity of the writer? Would their friendship be compromised, ruined beyond repair? Was he prepared to take that gamble? After all, he was an investigative journalist: he was in the business of uncovering the crap and nothing but the crap. He had done it all his life without suffering a bad conscience. Now it was personal, his friend about to be hung out to dry.

He silently groaned, and thought of cancer and his friend's unreserved offer of financial help. He was being compromised. *This fucking story.* He closed his eyes, and contemplated resigning from the commission. It was the easy option. But he knew that this would be like throwing Michael to the wolves. He had to write it. Where it led eventually was another matter entirely. Life was ugly, at the best of times.

***

The plush bar, a haven of slick black leather armchairs and

dark oak-panelled walls was largely empty, save for two late-night female shoppers, surrounded by expensive-looking shopping bags. As they sipped exotic cocktails, a man on his own, hugging a small lager, gazed forlornly out of the window, unaware of their high spirited giggling nearby. A tall, lean stranger entered, checked his surroundings carefully before approaching the seated man, and spoke above the din. 'I wasn't sure if I would recognise you.'

Michael was jolted from his malaise and lifted his head. He was cloaked under the menacing shadow cast from this large hulk of a man who suddenly loomed over him: the singular tough figure of Martin Penny. Slowly, he stood and shook hands firmly. They then sat opposite each other in the panoramic window bay, overlooking the churning black and silver waters of the Thames. The tide was high. The mighty towers of the bridge which spanned to the south bank at Butler's Wharf soared skyward, lit by powerful beams of light which added to their majesty. Michael diverted his attention back to his visitor. The light from the moon reflected on top of the private investigator's smooth-shaven skull. There was something odd about him: hard head, soft face, killer eyes. Michael was aware of his highly decorated army record. He was a baby- faced assassin. It was a little unnerving being in his company. Both the women at the nearby table threw sidelong admiring glances in the ex-soldier's direction, he noticed, aware suddenly of the intoxicating effect this man had over the opposite sex. He declined alcohol and settled on bottled water, which Michael ordered from the waiter.

Michael got down to business, mindful of Mr Penny's costs per hour, and passed over two sealed unmarked A4 brown envelopes. He cleared his throat.

'One file contains information on the woman I want protected, my former secretary, Kara. She has a live-in boyfriend, and they have a child, just weeks old. She's vulnerable, and I want to keep her and her baby safe. The other file contains as much as I know of a woman, Maggie Conlon, who I believe is a danger to Kara. In fact, she is a danger to me. We have history, and recently she has made her presence known to the both of us with implied threats of a sort…'

'What type of threats?'

'Principally, windows smashed at two galleries, which I and Marcus own independently of each other. He is Kara's boyfriend, by the way. We have each received numerous heavy breathing phone calls, which we believe come from Maggie. Kara is convinced she is being followed as well. Our movements are definitely being monitored. At the moment, our stalker is keeping her distance, but she is a force to be reckoned with. She blames me, in particular, for the death of her sister, Lauren.'

'Does she have a case?'

'She would argue an emphatic *yes*.'

'And what does she blame Kara for?'

'Nothing, but to harm her is to harm me. Maggie's sister wrongly thought that Kara and I had a thing going on. Not so. But Maggie would still hold this notion perhaps. She's a mad one, I should warn you'

Martin smiled coldly. 'Like an everyday plot from an episode of *EastEnders*.'

Michael nodded, and added: 'More deadly than that. This isn't fiction.'

'Have you informed the police that you feel threatened?'

'No.'

'Why not?'

'Although the case has been closed with regard to Lauren's untimely death, we are implicated, and remain under suspicion, if you get my meaning. I do not want to have the investigation reopened. It is finished, and Kara in particular needs closure. Besides, I know how you operate. Your skills at hunting prey and keeping a low profile will reassure me that Kara can bring up her baby without forever looking over her shoulder…I know you will be discreet, and professional. Also, a police presence will only alert this woman to the danger of capture, which in turn will make her operate from deeper underground. I want her to feel secure in her superiority.' He then raised his eyebrows, and added: 'For the time being.'

'Do you want Kara to know I am her bodyguard?'

'No. She will think I'm overreacting. Keep close but

invisible, if that is possible.'

'Everything is possible. And the boyfriend?'

'I have mentioned your name. Yes, keep him in the loop. He's a bit headstrong though. Watch him, he has a temperamental side.'

'Are you engaging me to solely protect Kara or find this woman?'

'Both. She will surface very soon. I just want you to be ready…'

'To do what precisely? I only operate to specific orders.'

Michael thought long and hard. The truth was that he didn't know what the order was. 'Do what is necessary. Serve and protect and…eliminate.' He couldn't quite believe his last word. Sweat seeped into his shirt. *Where did that come from?* Then he knew. It was fear.

Martin Penny didn't move a muscle. His steel blue eyes penetrated through Michael's rising panic, and calculated what had just been put on the table. It took a few seconds to digest. Then he leaned forward, and whispered, 'This isn't Belfast, Michael. Nor Baghdad. This is London, and this is where I work and the line between what I can do and cannot do is, how shall I say, a little more defined. In other words, I can't get away with murder.'

Michael shook when he heard this part. Their eyes never wavered in the intensity of the stare. They were locked together in complicity. The world stopped, as Martin emphasised his point still further.

'To protect is one thing, and I get paid accordingly. I report back to you. I monitor. To protect at all costs is another thing altogether. I do not monitor, I act. Point blank. No questions asked. The risk is to me. For that, I get paid a different rate.'

'And that rate is?' Michael surprised himself with his new-found confidence. Fear had no price.

'Fifty thousand pounds, in advance.'

'What do I get for that kind of money?'

Penny punched the words out, 'A soldier's promise: An allegiance that will never let you down. You have my word. This woman will not trouble you again.'

For some reason, Michael diverted his attention from the killer eyes and caught sight of a circular metal badge of a smiley face on Penny's jacket. It read:

Happy Birthday, Daddy.

He didn't know whether to laugh or cry, such was the paradox of this improbable situation he found himself in. A child only sees innocence in all things, especially in the unerring bond with their parents. Mummy and Daddy: The two greatest words in the world. At what point does life betray these children, and take away this purity? Mr Penny, the Daddy. Mr Penny the assassin.

Michael recovered his composure. Unnerved, he said, 'You'll have the money within the week.'

In turn, Martin stood, gathering the envelopes. 'I'll read these this evening, and get to work tomorrow. Do you have a decent photograph of this woman?

'Maggie?'

'Maggie.'

'No. But the police will. Besides, I believe she could have disguised her identity. She has money. In the envelope you will find the address where she last lived in Limerick. I believe her husband knows of her whereabouts, and is protecting her movements. They have children. It would be inconceivable for her to not want to see them. He and the kids have made two trips to the UK in the past three months. Draw your own conclusions, but I think she has been here all along. She did not attend her sister's funeral, or that of her dear mother in Ireland. She was never going to be caught, even though she would have been desperate to attend. She's too clever. Find her, Mr Penny, and quickly, but don't underestimate the woman. She is a murderer.'

'I never underestimate anyone, Mr Strange. That's why I'm still alive.'

Michael stared at him. 'You served in Bosnia, is that right?'

'That's right.'

'So you've seen and done everything, yes?'

'Enough for anyone to...' He picked the next word carefully: '...endure.'

'Why do this then?'

123

'It's all I know.'

Michael examined his ruddy cheeks, soft mouth, domed head and glacial eyes and tried to imagine the horrors of warfare contained within. He couldn't even put an age to him. He was a seemingly regular guy, with memories still buried deep, like his victims still hidden in the burnt soil of distant foreign lands. His child would never know of the haunting. The child just wanted that dependable person named Daddy. 'Watch out for this woman,' Michael said. 'If she had been in combat, she would be your worst enemy on the front line.'

'I'm used to working undercover behind the line, Mr Strange, but I take your words seriously.'

Michael watched as the man departed. He then knocked back his lager, buttoned his jacket and ambled down the arced staircase of the hotel and made his way into the clear night. If only his mind could be so clear. The moon glistened on the dark waters of the dock. All he saw was turbulent waters. Music blasted from a nearby bar. From afar, a police siren wailed. Michael felt good having Martin Penny on board, a way of doing his bit for Kara and Marcus. His stride lengthened as he moved speedily into the bowels of the NCP car park nearby. He withdrew his key fob and bleeped the door release of his BMW coupé as he approached.

His echoing footsteps suddenly stopped beneath him. His eyes widened, and his breath shortened. What the fuck was that?

Daubed across the bonnet, it what appeared to be whitewash paint was the stark message:

THE TIME HAS COME...
SAY GOODBYE TO KARA

Jesus. His first reaction was to turn abruptly and search for hidden eyes. Where was she, the bitch? She was following his every move. She had to be. Always so close but…Suddenly, bile reached into his mouth, and the petrol fumes in the confined space made him spin. His secondary reaction was to search the car park, but that was madness. She would be long gone. He managed to get inside the car and re-lock the doors, sweat pouring down his face. He checked the interior mirror and saw his grotesque features, ghostly pale and etched with dread. Igniting the engine, he drove from the car park recklessly fast, screeching the tyre tread as he went. Burnt rubber lingered in the air.

The invisible enemy was here, right now, directing from the front line.

***

Michael showered rigorously, as if attempting to scrub away this evil woman from his skin. He felt she was that close. He wanted rid of her. He wanted her dead. Now.

There. He said it. It didn't seem bad. *She was bad.*

Earlier, after getting back to his apartment, he took a photograph of the offending message before washing it clean from his bonnet. Then he cleaned himself. Now, slightly more relaxed, he took stock of the situation. Maybe he should call the police. Instead, he rang Martin, got a recorded voice and left a message relaying what had just happened. Then he ate. Rather, he finished off the leftover beef stew from the night before, washed down with copious amounts of red wine. He inspected his hands: they were still shaking. He moved to the window, his eyes narrowing as he surveyed the streets below. Where are you hiding, you bitch? Give me a sign and I'll bury you...

A pathetic response, he knew. She was far too smart to reveal herself so soon. She was playing a waiting game, based on her rules of engagement: Slow torture. He rechecked the front door again, making sure it was locked. He sneaked a glance through the peep hole: Nothing. Was this overreaction... paranoia...or drunkenness? He could live with the latter, and uncorked another fine Saint Emilion. His brain whizzed. How did she know of his meeting at the Tower Hotel? How did she know it was his vehicle in the car park unless...she was following him. In that case, was she aware of where he lived? It gave him the creeps. Was she that close, all of the time? From now on, he would need eyes in the back of his head. And a gun in his hand.

He moved to the bedroom, searched the bottom of the

wardrobe and extracted a box. Inside, he felt the heavy oily metal of a Walther CP 88 air pistol: lethal enough to put a pellet through a rabbit's head. The good news? You didn't need a licence for one of these things. He loaded the 8 piece chamber and inserted the gas cartridge which would propel the 4.5mm calibre pellets at awesome velocity. He was ready. Was she?

It was time for action. He rang Kara, nervously.

'How's my gorgeous god-child?' he asked.

'Funny time to call,' came the response. She seemed half-asleep.

'Just checking...'

'Harvey is wonderful. You should try having him, I'm dead on my feet.'

'Where is Marcus?'

'Playing squash at the gym.'

Michael was aware of the need to bring Marcus up to speed with Martin Penny's plans, and mention the evil message scrawled on his car. He'd have to ring him at the gallery tomorrow with the latest developments. He couldn't risk bringing Kara into the loop, so kept silent on the matter, fearful of her reaction.

'Everything fine with you two?'

'What is this: twenty questions?'

'I'm sorry...'

'You seem agitated, Michael.'

'Just concerned. Making sure you are OK.'

She yawned, which made him do the same.

'Harvey is to be baptised soon,' she said. 'When I get the date I'll let you know. Then you can truly call yourself a godfather.'

'I'll be there, although I'm fitting in the trip to Venice in the next two weeks. I'll be away two or three days. That shouldn't be a problem, I hope?'

'No, Michael. The service will be towards the end of next month. Is this trip necessary, or even wise?'

'Wise?'

'It's just that...well, isn't it a case of stirring up bitter memories?'

'It's a business trip.'

'So you said.'

Michael hesitated, catching the chill in her voice.

'Are you doubting me?' he asked.

'I think you are holding something back from me. After what's happened just recently, Venice seems a little too convenient, what with *them* living over there as well.'

Julius and Antonia. It seemed to him that it was impossible to escape the past.

He tried. 'It's a simple valuation job, but it pays well. If the painting in question goes to market, I also stand to make a decent commission.'

'I'm tired, Michael, and it's late. We'll talk again. Hold on.' There was a silence, and Michael heard a commotion in the background. Then she spoke again. 'It's Marcus, he's home.'

'Good night Kara. Say hi to everyone.'

'Will do. Michael?'

'Yes?'

'Be careful, please. I have a bad feeling about this trip.'

He put the phone down. He had a bad feeling as well, but there was the small matter of finding fifty thousand pounds fast, so the proposition from Theo intrigued him more than before…now it was a matter of extreme urgency. He could beg, steal or borrow the money to pay Martin, but any private income from the Venice connection was welcome and could provide the necessary means to redress his losses.

He checked the time: Nearly midnight. He phoned Terry, unconcerned by the fragility of his friend. If he was asleep, then he would wake him. He should have been more sympathetic with Kara, although he was wishing that Marcus had answered his call. He wouldn't make that mistake again. Kara was picking up on everything and nothing, forever paranoid, and it made sense therefore to always phone Marcus at work from now on. They had a pact.

'How you doin'?' Terry asked.

'Enjoying a fine bottle of wine. What's your poison?'

'Jack Daniels.'

'Are you alone?'

'Yep, the escort girl has just done a runner. What's up?'

'Developments.'

'Property?'

'Very funny.' Michael could tell Terry was worse for wear. 'I've had another calling card: A message on the bonnet of my car, from Maggie I reckon. I've also taken on the services of a private detective, just so you know. His name is Martin Penny. Ex-SAS.'

'Not his real name then.'

'No, I guess not.'

'Are you paying for protection, or eradication?'

He heard Terry slurp. He bit his lip.

'Both.'

'Expensive.'

'But necessary.'

There was a silence.

Eventually, Terry said, 'I'm dying, Michael.'

'That's the drink talking…'

'No, my friend, that's the cancer talking.'

'I have the money for the laser treatment, so use it. See the surgeon, Terry, now. How much have you had to drink?'

'Enough…to drop a horse.'

'Get to bed. We'll speak tomorrow.'

'What did you want…?'

'It can wait.'

'What did you want?' His tone was harsh and argumentative, as drunks usually tend to be, especially at this late hour.

'There is a man I need investigating.'

'Name?'

'Theo Britton. He has Russian connections.'

Terry laughed.

'What's so funny?' It was Michael's turn to be short-tempered.

He was left wide-eyed long into the night with Terry's last words reverberating around his frazzled brain:

'Not his real name then.'

CHAPTER EIGHT

The flight to Venice was booked for the Friday. Michael didn't want to hang around...He was now in the business of chasing any serious dosh on offer. Toby agreed to cover for his absence, which Michael explained away as a short break to recharge his batteries. At this stage, he elected to conceal the real motive for the trip from his son for fear of ridicule. After all, it could be a wasted journey of sorts. Equally, it could open up a whole new can of worms. Potentially, a substantial financial reward was on offer, one he couldn't turn down in the current economic climate. He'd bring Toby into the picture when needs must. Firstly, he'd survey the scene and give Theo the benefit of the doubt. In the meantime, Michael had three days to kill. It was game on.

After speaking to Terry again to catch up on things (more notably to find out what exactly his sidekick was digging up on him behind the scenes), Michael emailed Martin Penny and explained once more about the graffiti on his car bonnet, attaching a photo of the chilling message which he had taken on his mobile. He then arranged a temporary loan of thirty-five thousand pounds from his bank, and made up the difference from savings and shares, bringing the total to fifty thousand pounds: Martin Penny's fee. He transferred the funds into the account specified by Martin from an earlier email between the two of them. He then rang Marcus and filled him in with the relevant details of his meeting with Martin, and passed on a contact number to be used if necessary while he was away. Marcus was not impressed with his diversion abroad, particularly to La Serenissima, which conjured up negative vibes in his head, and he expressed these sentiments forcibly during their conversation. Michael listened, held counsel, and knew his defence was weak. He always found trouble, wherever he went or whoever he met. After Marcus's lengthy tirade, Michael shrewdly remained passive and then assured him that he and

Kara were safe from harm's way, but needed to be vigilant at the same time. Martin, he explained carefully, was an expert marksman and a former SAS member, and they should trust in his cold, hard professionalism. Marcus didn't buy into this. In retort he flippantly mentioned James Bond under his breath but Michael let it go this time. Anger boiling within him, he refrained from screaming obscenities down the phone in retort... with the added bonus that it was *he* and only *he* who was shelling out the extortionate fee for Martin's services...although sorely tempted. A little guilt on Marcus's pious conscience would be no bad thing.

Dear Marcus: Fucking amateur.

There was one final call to Venice. He spoke to Agnes, who was surprised and delighted to hear from him, and arranged to meet her for lunch on the Saturday, in the hope that she might help him with the valuation of the Italian paintings to be disposed of. He would visit the house on his own in the morning to see what all the fuss was about regarding the so called masterpiece. A great painting, Theo had stated. He was excited by the prospect. Agnes needn't know of this intriguing find, unless he required her considerable expertise. Then and only then would he involve her further: The masterpiece could turn out to be a dud.

There was another reason for his mounting excitement, and it was only now, after speaking to her, that he finally confronted his mixed emotions. He warmed to the thought of seeing her again. He hadn't thought of a woman in that sense since Lauren, his libido somewhat stunted. This then was a shock. Why did he suddenly think in these terms... with a married woman, to boot? He was merely meeting up with an old friend and colleague for a simple bite to eat, surely? Cut it out.

He banished such thoughts. While in the office, he dug up the new address for Julius and Antonio, who had moved to a different district in Venice to start life afresh. The past for them conjured up terrible images which they needed to vanquish from their heads. Michael knew he would be a stark reminder of those dark days, but it was they who had wanted to keep in touch. Only the distance between them prevented it, until now. The three of them had not met up since the inquest into Lauren's death. Was this then a good time to reacquaint old memories, as Kara had warned? Were the wounds still too raw? He pondered. The decision could come later, when he had a little more time on his hands.

In spite of the misgivings, he instinctively threw caution to the wind and rattled off an email to them with an invitation to the Venetian Ball as his guests. It was a long-shot. He pressed 'send' and then stuffed the handwritten paper containing their new address in his jacket pocket and returned to more mundane matters. The gallery still needed his attention. He worked on the brochure for the forthcoming exhibition by the Peruvian artist, Mora. This would be their big Christmas showstopper. Later, after coffee, he and Roland changed all the window displays with new stock, mainly expressive colourful floral work by a new artist from Budapest. These paintings, executed by the use of broad knife strokes, certainly caught the eye of the passers-by on the street.

Within an hour, they had sold a small delightful one of lavender in a terracotta pot for £1250. A promising start. In the meantime, Gemma concentrated on the VAT returns, a job Michael knew she hated but someone had to do it. Hours passed slowly. A large framing order arrived, which Roland took charge of. They were a good team, Michael acknowledged. Efficient, energetic, quiet. And there was the problem. Where was the spark? The old crack. Michael stopped what he was doing and looked around. Something was missing, something big in their lives. He wanted noise and colour and gaiety in the gallery, just like the flower paintings which they had just put on display. He wanted. He needed… No, he *yearned* for Kara to come back.

The day finished uneventfully. He had a quick Guinness with Ronald at the corner pub, grabbed a *Metro* freebie to read on the tube and was back at the apartment at seven. He ordered an Indian takeaway over the phone, a combination of four starters from the menu, to be delivered at eight. This allowed him time to settle into more comfortable clothes, jeans and T-shirt for the hours that remained before sleep. It didn't take long for the wine to be opened.

There were two messages on the answerphone and several

emails, most of them unwanted. Of special appeal was one from Agnes, expressing her excitement at meeting up again at the weekend. Inexplicably, his heart pounded. Another email brought him down to earth: a request from his accountant for overdue settlement of payment relating to his divorce from Adele. She was always there hovering in the background like a bat out of hell.

He turned his attention to the messaging machine. The first bleep was a reminder of his dry cleaning which the delivery man had twice tried to deliver without success. The suits now required collection. He swore. Then the following bleep caught his attention:

'Hi Michael, it's Martin Penny here. I've had a chance to do some digging around, and I've now put into place the surveillance team which we discussed earlier. Rest assured I have the operation under control, and have put protective security into place with regard to your apartment and that of Kara and Marcus. I need additional information in regard to Maggie Conlon's background, and any sightings from the CCTV cameras from outside or in the vicinity of the two galleries which were vandalised. I can liaise with the police on this and I'll report back with any information I receive. I got the email and photo attachment of your vehicle... interesting. Things are moving closer to home, eh? We all need to be extra vigilant from now on. I'll check CCTV at the NCP car park and speak to the staff. I'm compiling my own dossier and have employed a few chums to help track down our target, to make the job of apprehension a quicker one. The more I look though, the more I don't like this one. This woman is clever. However, I do not believe that she works entirely alone. I'm already thinking of an accomplice, or at the very least someone who is hiding her in the vicinity. She moves too quickly to be holed up outside a two or three mile gap. Who knows, she could be living right under your nose? I'm checking local hostels and bedsits to see if we can locate her lair. Oh, funds received. Many thanks.'

The connection went dead. *The more I look, the more I don't like this one.* The words were chilling. The doorbell rang, which startled him. He relaxed, knowing the delivery man with the Indian takeaway was imminent. Sure enough, the aroma reached his nostrils before he even opened the door. He didn't somehow enjoy the feast. His appetite was shot through. He thoughts returned to one of Martin's suggestions. *He had intimated an accomplice.* Things were looking bleak. First he had the bitter taste of Adele and her financial demands stuck in his throat, now the spectre of Maggie and her devoted army invading his space.

He ditched the leftover food, read a Harlan Coben paperback for an hour, finished the last dregs of wine and cleaned up. He retired and slept fitfully, dreaming of demons and sorcerer's magic and wished he too had the supernatural powers to defeat the fabled beast. In this case, one he had fought and duelled with before. No fable. He knew the enemy, or did he? Was she more capable than even he reluctantly gave her credit for? He had to admit it: she scared him. He awoke one time, listening intently, convinced there was someone sneaking around in the apartment. That was the affect she had on him. He checked each room.

Nothing. The front door was double-locked, just as he had left it. He peered through the peephole into the dimly lit communal corridor. It was empty, although he detected the distant hum of the lift moving between floors. Satisfied but not entirely settled, he padded back to bed, drank water and laid down once again. It was 3am on the bedside table clock. This time sleep came quickly, without dreams.

***

The next day, Michael penned a simple message on a notepad which read:

I would appreciate it if you could kindly keep the noise down in the evening. Many thanks, Michael from flat 26.

He took the stairs to the floor above and placed the note under the relevant door. He was tempted to knock but decided against it. Then he returned to the safety of his domain, forgetting the matter in hand. He had more pressing things to attend to. Two days to kill.

This day though was going to be a difficult one. He knew

what he had to do next, but he dreaded the prospect of what was required: His confession. More to the point: his admission of guilt to Terry. How long would it take to retell the whole sorry saga? A saga which in turn would form the basis for his own demise: In the shape of the very story that his pal was then going to write for all and sundry to read? The magazine exposé, in all its glory, would do just that. Destroy him, and destroy all those around him. He couldn't avoid it any longer. It was a uniquely long chronicle, but how much should he keep from his pal in order to protect those he so wished to protect? Terry had insisted from the very start that cooperation and honesty was essential if they were to be partners in this charade of sorts: Because in reality the bitter truth didn't shine a good light on any of them, particularly Michael himself.

He was acutely ashamed of his motives and past actions. He had ruthlessly pursued an avenue of such monumental greed with this woman called Lauren O'Neill. He had manipulated her and she had manipulated him, both of them showing a callous disregard for the safety and wellbeing of all others who were sucked into their world of betrayal and jealousy. These were the people he loved, who were themselves drawn inadvertently into his murky world of obsession and deceit. He behaved appallingly, putting all their lives at risk. And for what? A dubious profit and a quick shag. It was time to seek forgiveness, but from whom? Betrayal cut deep. It was time to face the music.

As previously arranged, he met with Terry at a secret location, a safe house in North London, and for the next 48 hours laid bare his soul, revealing everything – *everything* – until he had nothing else to say. He was spent of every last ounce of emotion. His story was the truth, the whole truth, and nothing but the truth. He was shocked that he revealed every detail, even aspects which he desperately wanted to keep hidden, in a declaration of brutal honesty and intensity. At the end of his rant, amid tears and physical shaking and cold sweats, he could barely look Terry squarely in the face, such was his shame.

It was all down on tape. There was nowhere to hide.

'In a nutshell,' Terry said finally, 'you sold your soul to the devil.'

'That about sums it up…'

'First you get involved with a temptress. She ensnares you and drags you into a plan to sell artwork under the counter.'

'I didn't need dragging…I wanted the money for my divorce.'

Terry shook his head. 'A desperate situation, no doubt. The deal was worth a million quid, give or take a bob or two. Her estranged husband, Julius, gets wind of this deal and tries to stop the sale, knowing that he too has entitlement to the proceeds. She, jealous of his unfaithfulness with Antonia, had decided to shaft him, hence the secrecy involved with bringing you on board. He can't confront his estranged wife because he and his girlfriend have run away to hide in Venice, for fear of retaliation from her insane jealousy and rage. He wanted a new life, a quiet life. After all, she had tried to kill him on numerous occasions. But enough was enough when he found out about her deception with the artwork. How am I doing so far?'

'You have the makings of a decent journalist.'

'Julius couldn't go to the police because he was complicit in the charade of who the infamous Patrick Porter was…which was Lauren herself. They were manipulating the art market and made a lot of money over the years until they separated acrimoniously after Julius cheated on her with Antonia. Lauren vowed to take revenge for his betrayal. Later, she decided to sell the remaining Porter paintings that she held at Laburnum Farm and pocket the money without sharing it with her husband. The farm would have been next to go, no doubt. Again, it was worth a million or more. Julius was broke and had a family to support. Okay with this…?'

'Pretty much.'

'It was at this point that Julius secretly approached you by means of cryptic messages, warning you of the danger you faced if you dealt with Lauren, the devil in his eyes. She had a destructive past, found guilty of battering her abusive father to death while a minor. Her trial caused an uproar back in the seventies, as the public were largely on her side at the time. He deserved his fate, after evidence at the trial revealed he had raped her. But the guilty verdict scarred her, the trauma of which bestowed upon her a split-personality. In later life, Julius found out the hard way just how vindictive this disorder could be. Eventually, he escaped from her clutches. By working undercover he was at first able to remain hidden from retaliation by his wife. The ruse worked, pulling you into his game plan. He used you, Michael. The hapless Marcus was his go-between who delivered the messages to you, an old friend of his from way back who had temporarily camped out at the farm in the wacko years of booze and drugs. Happy days.'

Michael cut in. 'It was only after I deciphered the messages that I finally understood the mental anguish that Lauren endured during her life, a life of family abuse and judicial injustice. Was it any wonder that she hid this trauma behind the illness that ultimately led to her downfall.'

'...And so nearly yours.'

'As you say, I was desperate and allowed the money to sway my judgment. Greed got the better of me. The funny thing: We so nearly got away with it.'

'Perversely, you did. You evaded prison. How much of the story have you revealed to the police?'

'All of it, except the secret sale of the paintings. I led them to believe that it was a gallery exhibition, all above board. That got us off the hook. They couldn't dispute this point.'

'Was Kara in on this?'

'Not at first.'

'Christ. Let me get this straight: You intended to sell the entire works by Patrick Porter for cash, thus avoiding tax and VAT?'

'Most of it, anyway. I have clients who deal in cash. I have the means and I wanted to keep the money from the clutches of Adele, who, as you know, was a partner in the gallery. I needed the cash to pay her off, settle debts and help save the business.'

'You have clients with *that* amount of cash?'

'In many cases, yes. They need to offload the readies. Buying art is a good way of doing this. I had already set up the private exhibition in the gallery basement, away from prying eyes, and tempted the selected punters! The date was set when the shit finally hit the fan...'

'What happened?'

'It's a long story. Wary of Maggie, who was becoming a troublemaker, I went to Ireland where the sisters were born, and investigated the family history, and especially the police prosecution and trial at the time when Lauren was convicted. I interviewed several people who were connected with the case during my trip over, all retired by now of course. I even spoke with their mother before she died. Incredibly, I discovered from psychiatric papers that it was Maggie who told a pack of lies in court and had in fact killed their abusive father, and it was she who duped the police, allowing Lauren to take the rap. She was called Laura Porter back then. Tragically, she served her sentence in a prison hospital while the real culprit, her sister, escaped punishment and led a normal family life. Eventually, after her release, Lauren, as she was now called, moved to England under this assumed name, within the protection of the Home Office. She met Julius and set up home at the farm, which in those days became a commune for artists and musicians. It was here that Lauren, with the help of Julius, a painter himself, first created Patrick Porter, her alter ego. This homage became an obsession, and the sublime work she produced became a symbol of recognition to her dead brother. Over the years, they made a huge amount of money selling these paintings.'

'What came between them then?'

'Antonia. She was a model for many of the paintings. Julius fell in love with her and Lauren resented it. The old story of plain jealousy, really. So they did a runner. It was only later that Julius felt cheated out of what was rightfully his…half the farm, entitlement to the valuable paintings left behind…but Lauren was not approachable to do a deal. She would have preferred to kill him.'

'So he took another approach, and tried to destroy her plan of selling the paintings behind his back.'

'Yes, by manipulating me. It worked.'

'How?'

'Because I discovered the truth…and much more into the bargain. The confrontation at the barn brought it all to the surface. For instance, on the day of the fire Lauren found out from me that it was her own flesh and blood who had betrayed her, namely Maggie. On top of that she also discovered that her cherished baby brother died at the hands of her father while a toddler, when she had always been led to believe that it was an accident. Another tragedy. The past marked her deeply and pushed her over the edge, culminating in the kidnapping of Kara. Her sweet personality in childhood had changed irrevocably to a flawed one in later life. Stupidly, I thought I could save her. But she mistrusted anyone who crossed her, including me.'

'Julius, in particular. Then you, then Kara.'

'She mistakenly believed we were having an affair...'

'Were you?'

'We were – *are* – very close, but our relationship is more like father and daughter. Lauren's twisted viewpoint refused to believe this...she felt threatened. That's why she kidnapped Kara and came so close to nearly killing her.'

'Is that the reason you were all at the farm?'

'Partly. It was my fault. I should never have allowed Kara to go there to do the inventory. But once there, it became a stand-off. The sisters trapped Marcus and Kara and used them as bait to lure me in as well...'

'I'm curious: What happened to the surviving paintings after the fire? How many were you trying to sell?'

'Twelve. From my understanding, they were put into storage by Julius until he could establish rightful ownership of them.'

'Are they still in storage?'

Michael shrugged. 'I believe so.'

'A fortune to contest, am I right?'

'A huge amount of money, even more so now because of the notoriety of Lauren and the publicity she received. A will is yet to be found, so Maggie could stake a claim.'

Terry changed tack. 'Who started the fire?'

Michael froze. He had to be careful. An image of Marcus recklessly throwing the ignited bottle of white spirits to threaten Lauren suddenly flashed into his head. It all happened so quickly, then chaos. Sweat poured down his neck. He hesitated, trying to banish such visions, before replying unconvincingly: 'I can't recall... someone probably knocked over the lamp. Tension was high. It could even have been the dog, Bruno. He went on the rampage and we all scattered…so who knows?'

Terry wasn't fooled, but concluded that the pact the three of them – Michael, Marcus and Kara – made was unbreakable. They each shared the guilt and the sorrow. Only they knew what really occurred that fateful day. They had to live with the dire consequences of their actions.

Michael stared into nothingness.

'Go home,' his friend advised.

'What do you make of it all?' Michael asked, his eyes reddened and swollen.

Terry gulped the remains of his whisky, switched off the Dictaphone, and stretched his aching limbs. He was fucked, too exhausted for deep analysis and the offering of absolution. He spoke candidly.

'Though he'd have struggled with the complexity of such a plot, Hemingway would have relished writing this epic,' Terry replied. 'But no one would have believed a single word of it. Even a master storyteller as he would hardly dared make fiction so sordid and get away with it even with his devoted readers.'

'I need you to believe every word of it.'

'No one could have that much vivid imagination, it's impossible. So, yes, I do believe every word of it.' He lied at this point, aware that the future of younger lives depended on his acceptance of the story he had been told. He wasn't about to destroy the dreams and aspirations of others. He had less sympathy with Michael. 'I thought I knew you. I really did, but even I'd have struggled to make such a venomous deal with the devil, however desperate I felt at the time.'

'I was out of my mind.'

Terry gathered up the mass of files spread across the table that he had meticulously written up and set them in a box together with the Dictaphone. He then discarded the empty whisky bottle and two glasses into the kitchen sink. He studied his friend with part-pity and part-loathing.

'You had to be,' he said finally, before turning off the light.

***

Kara was aware that she was being followed, but by whom she did not know. It was easy to speculate though. This shadowy figure seemed to slip in and out of spaces undetected whenever she felt vulnerable (which was every fucking second) and her mistrust extended to everyone in her vicinity, either on the street, in the library or in her local supermarket. Who was this person? What did they want? The mind played tricks. For example, just yesterday at the bookshop, she got nervous when a woman stood too closely behind her, which in turn made her assume guilt: Have I seen you before? Are you stalking me? Why are you crowding me?

Christ. This was getting scary. On top of that, Marcus was evasive and unsettled at home, forever peering out from the curtains. What was he looking for? Michael, too, had kept his distance. Had she offended him in any way? She knew of his trip to Venice…was he there already on his secretive mission? Was this the reason for his silence?

Paranoia seeped into her every thought. And then there was the man. She had spotted him twice now, and searching the dimly lit street from her bedroom window, peeping from behind the drawn curtains while Marcus sat glued to the TV, she saw him again standing in the darkened recess of an alleyway maybe fifty feet away to her right. Was this the same man she saw last night? He was as usual smoking a cigarette, the red needle point flaring every now and again in the night sky. He was bald-headed, shaven to be exact and possessed a muscular body. He was perhaps thirty-six, probably older, but the word soldier sprang into her mind when she tried to sum him up. Was Marcus aware of this stranger in their midst? Was that why he, too, habitually stared beyond the window, seemingly on edge, which was not his usual style. What on earth was going on?

***

He never made the flight. Too exhausted from the brutal interrogation by Terry, instead Michael slept and hid from the world he thought he knew. It took another 48 hours before he resurfaced, goaded mainly by repeated phone messages from Toby asking where he was (each call becoming more and more agitated), and concerned calls from the concierge checking his whereabouts as he had not detected his usual coming-and-goings over the past two days.

Unshaven, Michael sat around in his dressing gown, becoming more and more morose. The meeting in the safe house had knocked the stuffing right out of him. He was feeling sorry for himself and that sickened him still further. What was happening to him?

His troubled thoughts were interrupted by the phone ringing. He was slow to get to it and the voice message kicked in. He expected to hear the voice of Toby; instead, it was Martin Penny. Michael's ears pricked as he listened intently to the significance of the words:

'No sightings on CCTV, Michael. As you are aware, those positioned near the gallery are swivel cameras which rotate at regular intervals to monitor traffic at each end of the road. The culprit who smashed the window used this to their advantage, coming and going as the camera panned away from your shop-front. Easy to do. Looking at the plan of the street, he or she escaped down the alleyway between streets, the one just down from your location. This way, no one from the flats opposite would have seen the person responsible. It would have taken just seconds. In the case of Marcus's gallery, they don't have CCTV at that spot. They rely on security manning the dock, but this only occurs every hour or so. Again, we cannot pinpoint who the person was, or why this identical incident was seemingly reserved exclusively to the both of you. Of course, we do know the reason but the police have nothing to go on, simply because...'

Michael pressed the button and interrupted his flow. 'I know, I know, because a jackass idiot like me thinks he knows better! What the fuck do I really know? Perhaps the police should be brought in after all.'

'I'm making good progress, Michael. I've established that a thick-set woman was spotted moving between floors in the NCP underground car park, just twenty minutes before you discovered the graffiti on your bonnet. This woman was spotted by security and questioned. She departed soon after on foot. Interestingly, she was of Irish descent, carried a holdall and had scar tissue on her face. Ring any bells?'

'Maggie,' Michael announced. He then slumped into a chair, defeated.

'We are checking all the local hotels and bed and breakfast establishments to try to locate this woman. This is our first sighting, Michael, and a good one, I think. I'm dropping off the radar for a few days so you will not be able to contact me. I'm going to call up a few favours from my Irish friends, and pass the word around the bars in the area. Let her know that we are also in on the game plan...this might spook her into making a mistake. Then we'll be ready. OK with this?'

Michael was crestfallen, barely taking the words in. He was ready for a fight, but his iron will, which he thought was impregnable, was now shattered. Where had his strength evaporated to?

'OK with this?' Martin repeated; his voice stern.

'Yeah...'

'Good. I need you to hold firm.'

The conversation was terminated.

Michael managed to reach the bathroom, and then threw up in the toilet basin. He stared closely at his waxy features in the mirror. He didn't recognise the man who stared back. He chastised himself quietly: *God, get a grip and hold firm.* Martin was right. Slowly, he showered, shaved and cleaned his teeth, the first time in two days. It took three goes to get rid of the vile taste in his mouth and throat. He dressed without enthusiasm, putting on whatever came to hand: corduroy pants, plain white shirt and moss green v-neck sweater. He ran his fingers through his damp silver hair and suddenly thought of Agnes...

'Bollocks!' he barked, and grabbed for the phone, keying in her number in frantic prods. No answer. He left a muddled message, explaining lamely his reason for missing the flight to Venice, and more importantly, their dinner date. He concluded with a pathetic plea for forgiveness and over used the word 'Sorry' four times before ending the message. He hated letting her down and felt like shit.

Then he did something which he had fought against for ten years. The craving had never left him. He found what he was looking for in a top drawer in the kitchen. The unopened packet lay in idle temptation. At first, he closed the drawer slowly, then reopened it quickly. Fuck. The packet stared him in the face, compelling him to destroy in one split-second the very thing he had stayed defiant against for so long. The vow to give up smoking. The wickedness of desire tore at his weakening mind. Go on. *Just one...*

He removed a cigarette, felt its smoothness between his fingers and became intoxicated with the over-riding need to light it and inhale deeply...*Go on, Stop it idiot, Go on, Stop...*his brain then moved into automatic drive as he snatched the box of matches and eagerly slid back the patio doors to the balcony. Just then, in the exact same moment it seemed, he heard the same movement higher up, and was aware that the doors above had closed as his had opened. Odd. He moved to the handrail, turned, peered up and cast his gaze between the gaps in the hardwood floor to the balcony above his. Nothing, but someone had been there. Just coincidence? Or was he being watched...?

Crazy. He held the cigarette to his lips. The taste of tobacco was overwhelming. His hands trembled, fumbling with the matches. Lighting up, he leaned over the balcony and was suddenly distracted. He realised that he could peer into the apartment below, and a good deal into the next room along, which featured full length windows. Stretching a little further, he could make out a leather armchair, a stereo system, part of a rug and the beginnings...of a sofa? The point was, with a little imagination and maneuverability he could quite easily scan half of the damn room. He pulled back from the edge, thought long and hard, and imagined Marcus laughing at him with the words *James Bond* ringing around his insane head. This was getting ridiculous. This was getting beyond the realms of normality. What else was he going to start imagining next? He again looked at the apartment above his. Just suppose he was being snooped upon...he often moved around his home with the curtains drawn back. Why would he close them, being so high up? It was absurd, this paranoia. But he didn't laugh. Instead, he quietly extinguished the discarded cigarette, slid the balcony doors shut and drew the curtains in broad daylight. Madness.

***

At Churchill Fine Art, Gemma took a phone call at the same moment Michael refrained from reacquainting himself with an old sinful habit. While he was away, she had held the fort brilliantly, working front of house with assured confidence. She was beginning to win over Ronald (who generally kept his distance), and felt comfortable with customer enquiries. She logged everything in a notepad for Michael's return, including a potential fifteen thousand pound commission from a new client. That would impress her boss. He was a hard nut to crack, especially as she was aware of how brilliant miss goody two shoes had been as her predecessor. She could barely bring herself to say the name. So she didn't. Gemma was the new girl on the block. Fuck that what's-her-name…she was history.

'Churchill Fine Art, how may I help you?' Her voice radiated supreme confidence. Nothing could faze her.

A man's voice said: 'I need to speak to Michael Strange: Now.'

'Mr Strange is currently unavailable. May I take a message?'

'When will he be available?'

Gemma detected a shortening fuse from the caller.

'He is out of the office at present. May I take a phone number…'

'Get him to a phone within one hour. One hour, do you understand me?'

She tried to remain cool. 'Can I at least take your name and ph-'

'My name is Theo. He will know who I am. Tell that deceitful little piece of shit that he has betrayed me, that he has stolen money from me and that I expect a fucking explanation from him in exactly one hour from now, without fail. Tell him we had a deal and I don't take kindly to anyone who reneges on a contract of honour. He owes me, so make sure you give him the message, because I will make you equally accountable as that little shit if he doesn't answer my call in…58 minutes from now. Get it?'

Gemma froze.

'Do we have an understanding, cunt?'

She almost dropped the phone. *What did he just say?* Shocked to the core, she mumbled something about needing his surname but this man was on a roll.

'Fuckass, lady. Theo is all you need to know. Mess with me and I'll mess with you, and Theo is a name you are never likely to forget. You now have under 56 minutes sweetheart.'

He clicked off.

Gemma was speechless, left standing with the telephone hanging by her side, the dialling tone still audible above her shallow breathing. Her legs turned to jelly as she held onto the desk top for support.

Looking around, she was alone. Had this call really happened? Was this some kind of prank, a weird initiation test dreamt up by Ronald? Was he that sick? She imagined that his face would suddenly pop from around the door in uncontrollable fits of laughter...

But he didn't. This was no game. This was a sicko weirdo mental case psychopath on the loose...and what did he just call her? What disgusting word did he use? Was that even allowed?

Heart pounding, Gemma realised that she still had a lot to learn from this profession. That call certainly came from leftfield. Any imagined confidence was now shot to pieces. She checked the time and tried frantically to locate her errant boss, and fast. Boy, was he in trouble.

***

Michael got the message on his mobile, took the tube and arrived at the gallery with five minutes to spare. Gemma was on another planet, sitting in the staff room drinking copious cups of tea. She was ashen-faced and still shaking. Michael got her to relay the conversation – *every word* – and ordered a taxi to take her home. By way of compensation he offered her the day off tomorrow which she duly accepted. He was aware the abusive phone call was a hard lesson to endure but she had handled it pretty assuredly in the circumstances. Theo would have to deal with him now, and he was ready for a battle. He wasn't having any of his staff being intimidated and insulted. It was late, and Michael wanted to be alone to take the call so he sent Ronald home as well, who was equally upset at the abuse Gemma was subjected to. Michael decided he could then close the gallery a little early; after all, he would be in no frame of mind to talk to customers after his slanging match with Theo. And that's what it would be: Guaranteed. Who did this shitty little upstart think he was?

The time of the supposed phone call elapsed. Michael waited, sure that Theo had something up his sleeve. *Come on.* Half an hour passed. It was four-thirty. Michael lost patience, cleared his desk, closed the shutters and dimmed the lights. He moved downstairs to the kitchen and washed the dirty cups. He was suddenly aware of a noise upstairs. Fuck, he had forgotten to lock the main entrance door, his mind racing around: he wasn't thinking straight. He listened again and heard movement. Searching around, he picked up a kitchen knife and ascended the stairs.

He moved silently into the main showroom, which was still half-lit from the overhead spotlights. Nothing untoward. Then he spotted it. The front door was ajar. Christ. He saw a shadow move across the floor to the adjoining gallery. He held firm (recalling Martin's words) and shifted his emphasis by sneaking down the corridor at the rear of the building where he could then surprise the intruder, who would surely not expect a confrontation from this angle of attack. He suddenly had a terrifying vision invade his brain: *Please, please do not let this be Vlad the impaler.* His heart sank at the very notion. He needed a bigger knife. He reached the end of the corridor, hardly daring to breathe. Should he call out? Turn back and make for the exit door? Where was this foolhardy bravery coming from?

He edged behind a large podium which displayed an impressive bronze of a polo player on horseback. He crouched down and listened. *There it was again...* The shuffling sound seemed to come from the main showroom. Damn. Michael tiptoed across the floor, taking a stance behind a hanging partition. A fine nude painting by the Russian artist, Krutov, hung close to his face as he waited for either divine inspiration or a panic attack to hit him. He did a double-take. He couldn't help but notice that the figure of the female had her legs spread apart, his eyes level with her exposed vagina, just inches away. He felt like Inspector Clouseau. *Christ, I just don't need this...*

Then he felt the hairs on the back of his neck stand up. Someone was right behind him. He could sense it. Although he felt paralysed with fear he managed to clasp the knife tightly and steadied himself to strike. Quickly, he turned, and raising his hand, prepared to confront Vladimir, Theo's henchman. He could hardly draw breath. His life flashed before him as he faced his nemesis.

'For fuck's sake!' he screamed. He wasn't expecting this situation...

'Why am I not surprised to find you in a position of carnal absurdity, Michael,' the woman said, suppressing a giggle.

He lowered the knife in a hurry.

She in turn raised her eyebrows and stared beyond him to the lewd painting behind his head. 'Having a good look, I see. Sex and depravity is the story of your life, I hear on the grapevine.'

He didn't know whether to laugh or cry. 'Jesus...what are you doing here?'

'I was hoping for a slightly better welcome, to be honest with you.'

Michael reached out to hug her, his relief palpable.

The woman stood back. 'Is the knife really necessary?'

'You scared the shit out of me, creeping around,' he replied.

'Expecting trouble?'

He smiled for the first time, hugely relieved, aware though that a cold sweat varnished his body beneath his clothes. This was a happy turn-up for the books, it had to be said. It certainly was preferable to a fight with the mad Russian.

Although caught off-guard by her remark, he murmured: 'Certainly not expecting you, Agnes.'

CHAPTER NINE

'It's like this,' Michael explained, desperately hoping that Agnes would sympathise with his predicament. 'On the one hand I have a madman on the loose, chasing me for money which he thinks I owe him. Being of nervous disposition, I naturally thought it was him or his henchman sneaking around the gallery. It turned out to be you, thankfully.' He hesitated, hoping she was on his wavelength, before continuing, 'And on the other hand I have a mad bad woman on the prowl trying to cut my balls off...which I was half-expecting when I saw the door open. Now you can begin to appreciate why I was brandishing a knife.'

'I hope I am not the mad woman in question, and I certainly was not sneaking around the gallery. The door wasn't locked and I knew it was not normal closing time...so I entered, but quietly.'

'So you were sneaking around!'

Agnes smiled, beautifully. 'I was cautious, something didn't look right...the lights were dimmed so I came in to check if everything was OK...like a good citizen, no?'

'...And nearly got killed in the process.'

'Not the normal welcome one would expect when entering into a prestigious London gallery.'

Finally, after sparring for a few more minutes, they laughed and hugged warmly once more. He then made tea to calm their nerves. An hour passed in a flash, as he tried to make sense of things, with Agnes looking on incredulously as she listened to his preposterous story of skulduggery with much bafflement. After Michael finally switched off the lights to the gallery, set the alarm and locked the door behind them, he strolled arm in arm with Agnes to a Thai restaurant nearly. It was a chance to unwind and chill out in the company of a dear, dear friend. The feeling was mutual, he hoped. Theo, for the time being was forgotten. Why hadn't he phoned? What was he up to now?

'I'm so pleased you are here,' Michael said, taking her hand instinctively as they sat down at a table. 'What brings you to London?'

'To be honest with you, I was worried. Your message on the answerphone was garbled. First you were coming to Venice, and then you were not. What is a girl supposed to think?'

Michael was surprised. 'You came to London for me?'

Agnes lowered her eyes. 'Yes.'

He was momentarily taken aback and tried to explain. 'I panicked, I'm afraid. Everything is up in the air these days. I hated the thought of letting you down, but I allowed problems to pile up. For instance, I have the dubious pleasure of being the headline feature in a high profile magazine next month. This could kill me, Agnes. I'm collaborating with the journalist – an old friend – to assert damage limitation on the story and unfortunately everything got on top of me. I let you down.'

'I could hear the fear in your voice,' Agnes said, holding onto his hand without letting go. 'I'm here now.'

'You're here now...'

'I had to come...'

'I can't think of anyone better.'

He wanted desperately to kiss her on the mouth, but such an inappropriate desire had to be dismissed: she was a married woman. It was unthinkable to try it on with her. They drank chilled Pinot and ordered the food from the set menu. Michael sat back and marvelled at how young and vibrant she appeared, with new blond highlights in her hair and a navy blue velvet dress adorning her slim body. In truth, he was bowled over at how good she looked: Fabulous, actually.

During dinner, he was more shocked to discover, late into the dessert, that she and her husband, Adriano, were now separated. He didn't see that one coming. Agnes explained, awkwardly, that they had slowly drifted apart over the years. Their relationship was still strong, for the sake of their only child, but they were more like brother and sister these days. She still retained the gallery and workshop, and lived in the apartment above. He helped on a part-time basis. Life carried on, she insisted.

He detected an embarrassment in her demeanour, which was natural in the circumstances. He just wished he had shaved a little more carefully earlier and felt a little grubby with his choice of clothes, which he had largely just slung together. This was not normally his style. He never suspected that he had strong feelings for Agnes, but sitting here in the little restaurant and seeing the ambient lighting softly catch her face, he just knew that he had to be careful not to make a fool of himself. He was hopeless at reading the so-called signals between the sexes but... there was *something* there. He just had to play safe. He'd had enough passion and lust in his previous relationship to last a lifetime, and that nearly destroyed him. Agnes was sweet and endearing and he didn't want to hurt her or misread their close friendship. He could fantasise about his cravings for her but in reality he wasn't prepared to cross the boundaries and lose her friendship. It didn't help that she often stretched out her hand longingly to his.

Then she asked: 'How are you and Adele?'

'I think you already know the answer to that question...'

'I didn't want to be so forward...'

'We are divorced.'

'Do you still see her?'

'It's finished.'

He detected a hidden smile flicker across her face.

'Is she with anyone?'

'Johnny...I think you met him once.'

'Is it serious?'

'Who knows? Good riddance to the both of them.'

Agnes put her hand to her mouth, and muttered, 'I'm sorry I shouldn't – what do you say in England – pry?'

'Adele wanted to destroy me. She failed.'

He refilled their glasses. An awkwardness sat between them.

Then he said sharply, 'This is how it happened.'

They drunk more wine and over time he revealed painfully the terrible events that had shaped his life over the preceding months. He just had to tell her about his all-consuming battle with Adele and the intense relationship with Lauren. Both had damaged him to the core. His history of guilt carried a serious excess baggage allowance warning. He wanted to be honest with her. It didn't make for a romantic interlude.

Agnes was horrified by the catalogue of disasters, and this he noted was a genuine reaction to his deliberately diluted version of events, which touched him deeply. She wouldn't be able to take the full version. That would nullify any respect that she had for him. She wasn't as strong as Terry, he guessed, a man who could handle anything however depraved. He dealt with human failings every working day. It came with the territory.

Michael felt the need to change the subject. It was all getting too heavy. He idly mentioned the need to appraise the works of art in Theo's newly acquired house, omitting to tell her of the impending row that was about to erupt with his mysterious client. She was intrigued enough and agreed to meet up with him on his proposed journey to Venice to help form an inventory of sale, for a fee to be agreed, of course. At this stage, he also decided to conceal the so-called hidden masterpiece from her, which was always his intention. That transaction was between him and Theo. And in the meantime, he would have to speak with Theo to settle their differences. The deal could easily implode, as it probably had already. He was still hopping mad with the abuse thrown at Gemma. The guy was a rattlesnake.

He checked the time and was stunned to discover they had been in the restaurant for over four hours. Agnes excused herself and Michael noticed that she had applied fresh lipstick on her return from the powder room. They finished with a cognac for him and a Bailey's on ice for her. Agnes insisted on settling the bill. This was a woman he was seriously falling for.

He felt light-headed walking back in the direction of his apartment, arm in arm, and still chatting nonstop to her. It felt great, but surreal. He had no idea where they were heading. He looked for a bar. They passed close to a hotel near Jermyn Street. Then she stopped abruptly.

'This is me' she said, hovering outside the revolving doors.

'Oh,' he replied, halting in his tracks. He felt like a complete prat, his jaw aquiver.

'Can we get together tomorrow?' he asked.

'I'd like that, Michael.'

Signals. 'Right...right...tomorrow it will be.'

Neither of them moved.

Bashfully, she suggested: 'Would you care to come in?'

Oddly, she turned and pointed upwards rather than in, beyond the grand entrance. It took him a few seconds to twig.

He fumbled a response. 'Well, yes...'

'Then that's where we'll go,' she whispered, taking his hand.

And that's exactly where they went. Straight to her room: all night long.

***

Seeing Agnes asleep, lying naked beside him, he could scarcely believe it. He marvelled as the mellow dawn light slowly crept through the window slats and bathed her flawless skin in alternating parallel patterns, reminiscent of a glossy photoshoot in a fashion magazine. He kissed her shoulder, then her dry mouth and she murmured softly. This was all too soon but he wished for it to never end. He now had a better grasp on the signals, but was so grateful to be led like a child to his first day at school. He knew how it worked of course but still he was nervous of the expectation but delighted with the outcome. Agnes had brought him home. They showered together, and later had warm croissants and freshly squeezed orange juice in the Terrace Breakfast Bar on the first floor of the hotel. They sat in companionable silence, their eyes firmly fixed upon each other, as if devouring this precious moment...and the night they just had.

'Any regrets?' she asked, finally.

He smiled, and whispered: 'Absolutely none.'

***

It was her idea to take the train to Brighton for the day, just the two of them. It was a mad, impulsive gesture and she loved it that he responded so enthusiastically.

It was sunny and sharp as they ambled along the seafront

wrapped in each other's arms. Later, they took tea and scones in a café overlooking the seafront and then picked their way through the tiny antique and book shops which occupied The Lanes, a fashionable area for locals, tourists…and lovers.

It was a great day, with a great woman, Michael concluded. They still had several hours to enjoy together before her flight home. His mobile interrupted his thoughts, momentarily. He anticipated a call from Theo. Instead, it was Nick, the concierge at the apartments where he lived on Chelsea Harbour. A rare occurrence, he had to concede.

'What's the problem, Nick?' Michael asked cagily. He stood on the pebbled beach, gulls encircling his head, the busy promenade glistening in the sunlight. Agnes walked ahead, turning her head in his direction every now and again. He thought of her naked body and then came back to earth as the conversation kicked in.

'Sorry, Mr Strange, I wouldn't normally bother you.'

Michael knew the reference to his surname made this an official call. Normally they were on Christian name terms.

'What's the problem?' he insisted.

'I've had to gain access to your apartment. The washing machine from one of the flats above leaked water and flooded your kitchen.'

'Let me guess…Ms Byrne?'

'The very one. She informed me of the situation and luckily we rectified the problem and stopped more damage occurring. I've had the maintenance team over and they've cleaned up. It could have been a disaster but everything is back to normal, just a little damp patch on the ceiling.'

'Have the electrics been affected?'

'No.'

'Thanks Nick, for acting so promptly.'

'No probs. Didn't want you to come home and find mess and stuff, and thought that someone had snooped around your property.'

'Appreciate the call. Has the washing machine been replaced?'

'Yeah, they came down afterwards and inspected the damage and offered to pay for any repairs, but it's cosmetic as we acted so promptly. When are you back in London?'

'Tonight, if everything goes smoothly.'

'See you then, sorry to bring bad news.'

'Perhaps you could just keep an eye out in case of lightning striking twice…'

'Will do.'

Michael clicked off and slowly walked in the direction of the woman who waved back at him from further down the beach: The crazy Italian woman with the radiant smile.

Inexplicably, Nick's words re-entered his thoughts, and spoilt the moment. Something in their conversation nagged at him, but he couldn't think what.

***

Terry re-read his notes and listened to Michael's confession over and over, trying to form the basis of his magazine piece, which would run to six pages of text. This was a big story, the first to hit the headlines since the daily tabloids eased down on the initial explosion of interest at the time of the fire. The death of a mysterious and alluring woman in suspicious circumstances hogged the front pages for several weeks.

Michael weathered the first storm, Terry concluded, mainly because the police were complicit in protecting the real identity of Lauren O'Neill. She had a brutal past, one that the authorities wanted to keep hidden. The media soon uncovered the truth. Now the gloves were off again. How would his friend react to this latest and more intimate portrayal? After hearing every gruesome detail, he realised that he had a truly sensational story to rival any of the most notorious ones of the past fifty years. Christ, he could write a four hundred page book on all this debauchery. There were lies and then *these* lies. How could Michael sleep at night? How did he live with this shame?

Terry made a decision. Straight from the off, he elected to put the blame squarely at the feet of the sisters of doom. This way he could protect his friend but, more to the point, shield both Kara and Marcus, who now had a baby boy to look after. This was Michael's wish, but he had stressed that Terry could throw the book at him if this then had the desired effect in cushioning the lives of the two young parents. Pull every trick in the book, he asked. After all, Michael had explained, what was the worst that could happen to him? The worst had already happened. He could then simply retire from life and bury himself in solitude and drink. Not a bad compromise, he argued.

Terry saw it differently. The Press could and would crucify Michael if he, as a journalist, didn't do his job correctly. He needed to balance the story, but at the same time making his friend the real victim. If he left gaping holes in the testimonies of those involved then they would be buried up to their necks by those in the business who knew how to use spades. It took one to know one.

This intrepid journalist was ahead of the game, but only just. So far, the tabloids had tired of the story, after the initial impact, simply because the police had hastily closed the case. However, his editor-in-chief smelt a rat in the works, and was convinced there was a huge scandal to unearth. After hearing what Michael had to say, she was right. This story – a powder keg – would explode and circle the globe with its dynamic release.

Knowing this, Terry wanted to tread very carefully. Hence, his need for two versions: the truth and the near-truth. He had spoken to the main protagonist. He had visited Laburnum Farm. He had read all the news stories from the other national tabloids, watched the TV coverage at the time from the library archives and had gained access to some (but not all) of the police files from an unnamed source from within his trusted circle. Ideally, he wished to interview Kara and Marcus and Julius Gray and his girlfriend, Antonia. Would they all cooperate on his terms? Would Michael smooth the path clear for him to do his job properly? Or would they recoil from him...this persistent man with the awkward questions?

Michael had been adamant that Kara and her boyfriend should be protected...but they held the key, without a shadow of doubt. Marcus was a mystery to him: what did he have to hide? And what of Julius, the oddball artist, the boy wonder with the golden touch...a naïve boy who became a husband who then sought revenge against the woman he once

155

loved…the devil incarnate, Lauren O'Neill. This was the same man who also managed to manipulate all those around him, including Michael. He was a clever one, dictating events from the sidelines, keeping his hands clean while Michael and Kara were sucked into danger.

Terry tried to picture Lauren. What would he have made of her if she was still alive? She was indeed a master without equal when she was alive. A woman with a corrupt heart, a black heart. Only Maggie, her sister, could control her unrepentant rage and bring her back down to earth where she would simmer for a while, hiding behind one of her many crazy split-personalities. This calm before the storm lasted for only so long, though. Then the volcano would erupt again, her wrath cascading down like burning hot lava on the pathetic sinners who dared to cross her path. Against the odds, he calculated, his friend was one of the lucky few to survive this maelstrom of wickedness.

And finally there was Maggie. With her sister now dead, it was she who carried the threat of revenge upon all of their lives. Was this her only motive? Could Terry believe in this portrait of a killer, painted in graphic detail by Michael, a man who by his own admission was bordering on the insane at that time? Was Maggie real or a figment of Michael's imagination? Who could Terry trust in his quest for the truth? Could he track Maggie down, assuming Michael was correct in his assumption that she was stalking him in London and hell-bent on wanton destruction?

His head pounded. After examining all the information he had at his disposal, certain issues began to gnaw at him. For instance, how did the fire *really* start at the barn? Michael said (and the police corroborated on this in all their statements), that it was an accidental fire, started when an oil lamp toppled over as Bruno, the dog, went berserk. This seemed reasonable, but the fire department suggested that the seat of the fire ignited at the far end of the barn, where Marcus stood after he had gained entry from the secret tunnel which led from the main house. Surely the lamp would have been in the middle of the barn, where Lauren held Kara captive? And if the fire had originated at this point, then it would have stopped Marcus escaping by this route, especially as the fireball was sudden and fearsome. This led Terry to agree with the theory that the inferno started behind where Marcus stood. How could this be so? If this was the case, what really happened and what were they all hiding? Had Marcus started the fire deliberately…and if so, was he therefore responsible for the death of Lauren? Was this the real reason for Michael's insistence on protecting this young man?

The Coroner's verdict was 'death by misadventure'. The police file was unofficially closed. The only issue unresolved was which sister perished, as forensic evidence was inconclusive. Michael was convinced that Maggie had escaped. He swore by it, insisting that he saw Lauren succumb to the flames, hit by a blazing roof timber. This image still haunted him, he confided to Terry. But how could he be so positive as to which sister fell, with thick, toxic smoke hindering his view? Marcus, in the mayhem, told the inquest that could not recall this fateful moment with any real clarity, concentrating instead on saving Michael from inevitable death. It was only afterwards, dragging themselves to safety, that they all understood that the barn had become a tomb. All that mattered was that the three of them (Kara included) were alive and out of harm's way.

Terry tried to imagine the utter chaos and panic during these vital seconds. He had visited the farm and saw first-hand the devastation. Oddly, Marcus and Kara stuck to their stories, word for word, according to police files. Almost as if they had rehearsed their version of events, rather like the actors learning their lines from a script. It was too contrived. But did it really matter? Nothing would bring Lauren back from the dead.

But there was something that didn't quite add up, according to Terry, as he reworked the testimonies and tried to analyse the chain of events. If Maggie had escaped, where did she go? More importantly, how did she flee from the farm? If Michael was to be believed, there was a horde of cash and two passports in the bedroom in the main house, which disappeared after Maggie escaped. Had she the presence of mind, while badly wounded, to recover these items? And if so, why would she take both passports, if she was aware that her sister was dead? Also, Maggie had no means of transport, having been collected from Gatwick airport by her sister just days earlier. The vehicle in question was discovered by police still parked up at the house after they arrived on the scene. The police report confirmed this. It was inconceivable that Maggie, wounded and weak, could have picked up the money and somehow ran off across the fields...and to where? The farm was in the middle of nowhere. It was winter. She wouldn't have got far, unless she had an accomplice. Was this possible? What really happened in those mad and bad seconds which allowed a wounded fugitive to suddenly vanish into thin air?

Terry deduced that this was an impossibility...unless, unless. *Think.* There were five people at the barn that day. They were all implicated in the death of one of their number. They were all guilty. It was a miracle that any of them had survived, but four of them did. Now each of them had to face the consequences of their actions, however unpalatable this now seemed.

They were tortured souls, living with the lies they all told. Beyond that, they had to move on. The evil game they played meant that the final dice had not been thrown. It was payback time. A person or persons unknown had either been in on the plan and was part of the escape or had been innocently drawn in against their better judgment.

Which made Terry rethink his natural take on things and spin them around. Ever the cynic, his intuition and professional training smelt a rat. Sure, Michael had told his version of events...as he had seen them at the time. But the truth of the matter was that he couldn't be positive, especially as he was on the verge of dying. Yes, he saw Maggie escape. Or so he thought in the confusion. But the rest of the story was pure conjecture...

Suppose, suppose? Terry's brain was on overload. Maggie had no means of transport, or had she? Then he thought of something that happened to him just a few days ago, a conversation of sorts, that at first appeared unrelated to what happened at the barn. But this small thread began to connect with the main chain of events, and subsequently offer a different conclusion to Michael's testimony. Now it seemed pertinent to ask the right questions, talk to all those at the scene (and those on the fringe) and start to look at things slightly differently. *There were five people at the barn that day.*

Terry was now convinced there had been six.

CHAPTER TEN

On the return trip from Brighton, Michael dropped Agnes off at Gatwick Airport so she could make her early evening flight back home. It was an emotional farewell, but one filled with joy. He promised to clear his desk and get over to see her within a matter of days. He longed to see her again and of course he had the small matter of fulfilling his broken promise to Theo. Now he had a more valid reason to go to Venice. He was perplexed as to why he had not heard from Theo, considering the anger directed at his distressed assistant.

After taking the M25 back to London, he got onto the hands-free mobile in his car and conferred with Ronald to see if Theo had contacted them again via the gallery. He had not. The first priority was to check his apartment after the damage to his kitchen. He also wanted to shower and change. Before leaving for Brighton, all he had time to do was grab a pair of jeans, T-shirt, a fresh pack of briefs and a sweater which he purchased in haste from the hotel shop in London. He remained unshaven and shared Agnes's toothbrush before they departed for the south coast. This was love. Big time. Now it was back to reality. He parked up and took the lift to his apartment, relieved to find minimal damage, just an unsightly watermark on the ceiling in the kitchen. He checked each room, satisfied that everything appeared OK, including the balcony. He was becoming jittery. After checking his messages, he showered and then made tea and pondered his next move. Without thinking, he took the stairs and knocked on the door above his. He intended to introduce himself to the elusive occupant, which was the least he could do. No answer.

He took the lift to the ground floor and found Nick at his desk.

'Hi, Michael,' he said. 'Everything all right?'

Michael noted that normal service had resumed with first

name terms. 'Yeah, thanks for springing into action earlier. The ceiling just needs a spot of paint when it dries out.'

'Shall I get maintenance onto it?'

'Give it a few days...'

'Will do. Had a good couple of days?'

'Pretty good,' Michael replied. 'I've just tried knocking on Ms Byrne's door.'

Nick shook his head. 'Now there's a thing. Just after installing a new washing machine, as per the lease agreement, she suddenly departed the flat at lunch-time today.'

'Away for a few days...?'

'No. She's gone for good. Seemed in a fluster, settled matters, returned the keys and left in a taxi without explanation with just a suitcase...'

'Was she alone?'

'Yes.'

Michael shrugged. 'I was hoping to say hello.'

'Not going to happen, I'm afraid.'

'Have you a forwarding address?'

'No. She settled her rent in cash. I've notified the landlord, who is satisfied with the arrangement and will get the cleaners in over the weekend before any new tenants arrive.'

'Quick work.'

'Needs to be, she was paying £2000 per month in rent. The landlord can't afford to lose that kind of money with an empty flat on his hands.'

'Will the landlord have a forwarding address?'

'You would think so, or the management company. I assume a sizeable deposit was put down.'

'No doubt. Anyway, thanks, Nick. Let me know if she turns up again.'

'No probs.'

Michael turned toward the lift, then remembered the anxiety he felt from the earlier phone conversation with the Concierge when he was in Brighton.

He called back: 'Nick, you said Ms Byrne came down to inspect the damage to my kitchen...'

'Yes, she did.'

'How did she appear?'

'In what way?'

'I don't know. You tell me.'

'Well, she appeared upset…but thinking about it, she seemed agitated.'

'Agitated?'

'As if, well, she felt uncomfortable, nervous even.'

'On edge..?'

'I guess so. He was more calm and collected.'

Michael suddenly felt the unease shoot through his veins.

'That's the thing, Nick. When you phoned me you said that *they* had come down to my apartment. Is that not unusual? Why would two people come down? It's almost an invasion of my privacy. Can you remember who he was and what he wanted?'

It was Nick who looked agitated now, as if his judgment in the matter was being questioned.

'I didn't see a problem, Mr Strange.'

Mr Strange. He was now defensive in his manner. Michael remained silent, allowing his eyes to do the work.

Nick seemed uncomfortable with this. 'I don't actually know who he was…I assumed he was her boyfriend, although I hadn't met him before. The tenancy was in her sole name.'

'You assumed?'

'I should have checked.'

'Did you leave them alone?'

'No, not under any circumstances.'

'Where were you?'

'In the kitchen.'

'With the two of them.'

'Well, yes.'

'Are you sure?'

Nick squirmed in his chair.

'I'm sure…' Then he turned white.

'What is it Nick?'

'Well, he asked to use the bathroom.'

Michael moved closer, looming over the desk.

'So. The point is you weren't with them all of the time…that's right, isn't it, Nick?'

'I guess so.'

'In truth he could have been anyone…that's right, isn't it, Nick?

'I fucked up big time, Mr Strange.'

'You certainly did.'

'Is anything missing?'

'Not that I can tell, but I will look much closer now, especially as they have done an apparent runner…'

'Shit.'

'Could you recognise him again if I need you to?'

Nick blew out air and gestured with his hands in a manner of futility. 'I guess so, although I only saw him briefly, and that was for a matter of seconds. He left before she did. He was a regular guy, stocky, around fifty, I guess, well-dressed, very polite and concerned. I had nothing to be wary of, to be honest. But now you've got me thinking.'

'Think some more, Nick. I'm going back to my apartment. I'll let you know if anything is amiss.'

Michael retreated, leaving Nick embarrassed. It was probably nothing to worry about, just Michael being ultra-cautious. Then he remembered his concern when he thought he was being spied upon from the balcony above. Where was the evidence? He was tired. Give it a rest. *Chill.*

He pushed the button for the lift and waited for the door to open.

Nick suddenly came up behind him.

'A diamond,' he said.

'Pardon?' Michael replied, preoccupied with thoughts alternating between deeds of trickery in his apartment and the utter delights of Agnes's body. He couldn't help but concentrate on the latter.

'You asked if I would recognise him again…'

Michael turned to face him. 'I did.'

'Well, here's the thing.'

Michael waited. 'Spit it out, man.'

'He had a diamond in his teeth.'

Michael was taken aback, trying to grasp what Nick was saying. 'A single diamond? he asked, dreading the answer.

'A single diamond, right here.' Nick raised his lip and pointed to his upper row of teeth.

Theo. Fucking Theo. No wonder he hadn't phoned. What

the hell was his connection to the elusive Ms Byrne? Michael left Nick standing there, shaking somewhat as he closed the door to the lift and hurried to his apartment. He'd been shafted.

* * *

Terry returned home from International House, exhausted from a heavy workload. His day had largely been occupied by the breaking news from the USA: Sub-prime mortgage lending had crippled the economy over there, and sent the dollar crashing. The repercussions were heading across the Atlantic at breakneck speed. He'd had enough at work, grabbed a McDonald's takeaway and got in to be confronted by a ghastly sight. His flat was a pigsty, all of his own making, he had to admit. For the past two weeks he had neglected his cleaning duties, much to his disgust. Since the cancer scare, he didn't much care for anything. Normally house proud, he was still angered and punch drunk from the news of his illness. He had lost his wife to the same fucker. Looking around, he was ashamed at the state of his home, and knew that she too would have been appalled to see him living like this. He ate the quarter pounder and French fries and drank the tepid Coke with little enthusiasm. It was just fuel. Hell. He gathered the post from the mat, opened a black refuse bag and started the cleaning up operation. It took the whole evening to wash the pots and fill four black bags that he lugged to the communal bin area before he could relax, grab a beer and sit down on an uncluttered sofa at last.

That's better, he thought. A degree of pride returned. Whatever surprises the future had in store for him, he knew that his beloved wife would always insist on dealing with things with dignity and decency. All things considered, that's how she faced adversity and that's how he was going to remember her until his final days. Their home had always been kept immaculate. This was how he intended to keep it. In memory of her.

He opened the mail, one letter catching his eye. It was from the hospital, with an appointment to attend the MRI unit for a urinary scan on his tumour.

He sat for a moment, and downed his beer. Then another. He slept on the sofa, tears rolling down his cheeks. In his fitful dream, he saw an image of his wife, the same as the one in the photograph that sat atop the sideboard. She smiled reassuringly, offering hope and dignity and decency in what lay ahead. Dark days, he was sure. He hoped he had the same courage that she possessed, but he doubted it. He was exhausted, beaten and, if the truth was known, no longer able or willing to fight the ills of the world any longer.

He awoke in the early hours of the morning and suddenly thought of Michael, and the injustice that was about to befall him in the name of journalism. Terry was determined that this would not happen. This would be his last fight.

***

Michael had one singular thought. What was Theo up to? He spent the entire evening scrupulously going through drawers, jacket pockets, his briefcase, the mail, accounts and old files...convinced that his personal belongings had been tampered with. Everything, thankfully, seemed intact. Strangely, this made him even more uncomfortable. Theo had invaded his home. There had to be a reason for it: Had to be. The question had to be addressed: Was the leak from the washing machine simply a ruse to gain access to his apartment? If it was, then they also knew he was away.

How did they know this? And just who was Ms Byrne? Her name began to chill him to the bone. He phoned down to Nick. No answer. He'd get him in the morning and make a request: He had to get access to her apartment. Check her out. Find out if there were any clues to her identity...Nick described her as somewhat reclusive. Who was she? Was it Maggie?

He'd have to wait to find out. He opened a bottle of cheap Merlot, and raided the fridge for sustenance. All he mustered up was some French Brie, a slice of ham and a crusty loaf from the bread bin. It would do.

Then he turned his attention to Agnes. Wow, where did that sudden lust come from? He was absolutely stunned as to what happened with her...simply unbelievable. He was uplifted to have her in his life on an entirely different level to their past relationship. It was inspiring. The wine was pretty good too. Not everything had to come in expensive wrappings.

He switched on the TV to catch the late news. The usual crap appeared: the US dollar collapse, the Northern Rock fiasco, murmurings in the city that other banks were now under threat of monetary starvation...Michael ranted at the screen. Impossible, was his initial reaction to such hysteria. There was then a startling piece about the foreclosure of an Icelandic bank that was in trouble too. They were attempting to raise funds to stay afloat. Christ. Terry's dire warnings were rapidly coming home to roost.

Fiona Bruce, the newsreader, moved on to more mundane domestic matters. The price of petrol was set to increase, the Government was under pressure to stall on a VAT hike to ease the burden on the besieged motorist. Michael swore again. It was all doom and gloom. His eyes closed. He started to nod...

A story broke of an unidentified body recovered earlier in the evening from the Thames at Bermondsey. Michael stirred. The newscaster confirmed that the victim was a Caucasian male, aged in his mid-thirties and of muscular build. Michael opened his eyes and stared at the screen. What was she saying..? The police stated that the body had only been in the water for a short time, washed up on the tide. The male, shaven-headed, had been killed by a severe head wound, and DS Keene, in charge of investigations, appealed to local inhabitants to come forward if they had seen anything suspicious or were aware of a missing person fitting this description. Michael was now wide awake. He took in every word: The site of the discovery was now a crime scene. Police were appealing for witnesses to come forward if they were aware of an altercation in the area. What got Michael out of his chair was the announcement that this may have a military connection, as the body could have been that of a soldier or former soldier. The DS, on screen, added that he had evidence which he would not reveal to the public at this stage that confirmed this suspicion as to the profession of the deceased.

Michael's blood ran cold. Surely this was just a coincidence... but Martin had disappeared off the radar, currently working undercover and therefore operating incommunicado... now a dead body fitting his description was being highlighted on the national news. Fuck. He dialled Martin's office number and then his mobile. No response.

Calm down. He paced the room. This was difficult to comprehend...it couldn't be him surely? Martin had promised to contact him shortly. He had to hang on to that assurance. This guy was an experienced war veteran, ex-SAS, a man who had served in Bosnia and Afghanistan. A man like this doesn't suddenly turn up in the Thames mud with his skull smashed in, he reasoned. But still Michael felt nauseous. He rang Marcus and checked to see if Martin had been in touch with him. The answer was negative. Was there a problem? Marcus asked. Michael didn't want to raise any false alarm bells. No problem, he answered flatly.

He poured himself a brandy. There was nothing he could do at this late hour, except sleep and start again in the morning. Everything would be fine in the morning, wouldn't it? He continued this futile argument until his brain was numb, his confidence now washed down the drain.

***

He slept badly. At just after eight, he phoned Terry and informed him of the news item highlighting the suspected killing, and asked his friend to dig up what he could on the story. It was vital to eliminate the possibility that Martin was the victim. However, this was going to be hard to do. He knew the police would be tight-lipped at this stage of the investigation, and he also knew that if Martin was still undercover then nothing would make him jeopardise his precarious position. Certainly not to reassure his client that he was indeed alive.

He was stuffed, Terry concurred after listening to him, but he gave an assurance that he would do what he could in the circumstances. At this stage he suggested that Michael remained calm and focused until he had a chance to establish the facts.

Michael reluctantly agreed, although he was not convinced that he could achieve this. He was a bag of nerves. After all, he had Theo to deal with as well as finding Maggie, who had weirdly gone to ground as well. This really spooked him, he confided to Terry.

Then Terry dropped an extraordinary bombshell into the equation.

'Michael, cast your mind back to the day of the fire.'

'What do you need to know?' More fucking questions…

Terry pushed: 'There were five people at Laburnum Farm, I don't need to list them.'

'Yes, five of us plus the devil dog of course.'

'Bruno.'

'The family pet,' Michael said sarcastically.

'Think carefully. Did you see anyone else at the house that day?'

No. Who could you possibly be referring to..?'

'When you arrived on the scene, were you aware of a strange car parked up, or evidence that someone else was living at the house?'

Michael was stunned. 'No! Where is this leading, Terry?'

'A line of enquiry, that's all.'

'Jesus. Lauren is history…I bitterly regret ever meeting the woman.' He sighed, and whispered: 'What line of enquiry?'

'A hunch…'

'There was no one, I'm positive of that. What kind of fucking hunch is this?'

'Are you absolutely sure that there was no other person on or around the premises on that particular day…especially during the confrontation between Lauren and Maggie?'

Michael was incensed. 'I searched the house. There was no one else, absol…no, for Christ's sake!' He shook his head in bewilderment, his mind in a whirl. 'What are you implying?'

'Nothing that I can elaborate on at this moment: Just a wild stab in the dark…'

'Not the most appropriate comment.' Michael moaned, recoiling at the flashback of what happened at the barn and the raging vision of Maggie brandishing the scissors at him.

'Perhaps not,' Terry was contrite. 'Sorry.'

'I'm having difficulty with this conjecture, Terry. What

evidence is there to support this and what bearing does it have on Lauren's death?'

'No evidence. I just asked the question, that's all.'

Michael lost it.

'Well, I'll ask you to piss off then, that's all. I can't take much more of this shit.'

With that, he cut the connection dead.

***

Checking his watch, Michael turned his attention to Nick, who would be behind his desk by now. He met him at reception within ten minutes of shouting down Terry. A sixth person? Where was Terry going with this? It was insane.

'You want me to do what?' Nick asked.

'I want to gain access to the flat above mine.'

'I can't do that, Mr Strange.'

Here we go again. 'You can, and you will.'

Nick raised his eyebrows and shuffled his feet. 'On what pretext? We can't just enter into private property.'

'You took total strangers into my apartment...'

'There was a legitimate reason, as you know. I viewed it as an emergency.'

'This is an emergency. You have keys, I assume.'

'Well, yes. I have duplicate keys to all the apartments. What is the emergency?'

'Ordinarily, the water damage from upstairs wouldn't have caused me anxiety, Nick. These things happen. However, you let a man into my home and he was allowed to roam around freely...'

'Hell, Mr Strange, he just asked to use the bathroom. He wasn't allowed to just roam around at will.'

'Nick, he had his own bathroom. I know this man. His name is Theo Britton, and he isn't someone on my Christmas list. I can identify him from the diamond in his teeth. He's not someone who would be welcome into my home either.'

'I can only apologise once again,' Nick stressed.

Michael moved closer, their eyes locked. 'I need to find out what they were up to. I think the washing machine problem was an excuse to gain entry into my apartment.'

'Is anything missing?'

'Not that I can establish at the moment. But something isn't right. The keys, Nick?'

Nick retreated from the discussion and folded his arms. Michael sensed his loyalties being torn over this dilemma so he had to be firm.

'I need the keys,' Michael repeated.

The young man audibly blew out the wind from his chest. Sweat formed on his brow. He hesitated, and then said, 'I need my job, Mr Strange. Not a word to anyone.'

Michael nodded his agreement.

'I'll get the keys from the safe.' Then Nick disappeared quietly into another room.

Michael stood his ground. His bullying tactic had worked.

***

They stood outside the door like two bungling burglars, nervously scanning the corridor as Nick fumbled with the key. He was the first to enter. Michael checked the corridor once more (he was half-expecting to see Maggie charging toward him with a machete in her hand, such was his unease) and quietly followed in behind him.

The curtains in all the rooms were pulled tight, dulling natural daylight into the interior. Nick flicked the light switch. On first inspection, nothing seemed untoward. Just an abandoned nest.

'Five minutes,' Nick instructed.

The apartment was stylishly furnished: Marble floors, white leather sofas and silver framed decorative mirrors. A theme of black and white prevailed. The apartment consisted of an open plan lounge and kitchen, plus two bedrooms, one double with en-suite and one single. Michael was surprised to find the double untouched, the bed immaculately made.

The single bed was unkempt. The lady in question clearly lived alone. He checked under the bed, searched the bedside drawers. Nothing. Within the fitted wardrobe was a collection of empty hangers. He moved to the main bathroom. Beside the sink was a cheap hair clip and a discarded tube of toothpaste. In the kitchen, he opened each cupboard, looking…looking for what?

'Well?' Nick asked.

'Nothing,' he admitted with a shrug.

'Time to go...'

Michael gave a last glance and then followed Nick to the door. He felt rather foolish. Then he remembered the balcony. It was a long shot, his eagerness borne from desperation rather than any hopeful gain.

'What are you doing?' Nick asked with a twitch of his mouth.

Michael threw back the silk thread curtains, instantly blinded by the sunlight.

'Fuck,' he heard Nick shout.

Michael stood back, aghast. His eyes refocused.

They stared at each other and then reaffixed their eyes on the sliding doors.

'Fuck,' Michael repeated.

Scrawled across the glass, in what appeared to be white shaving foam, was the weirdest message imaginable:

Byrne in Hell

Nick regained his composure and spoke first.

'Not the normal parting gift that I've had to sort out,' he said. 'Usually I find a blocked loo or rotting food thrown in the sink...'

Michael barely registered his words. Maggie was living here. Right above him! Surely this message was a direct signal from this wicked bitch. His skin crawled with the vision of her stalking him, unseen, just feet away from where he lived. She was that close. She hadn't gone to ground...she had moved in right under his nose, as Martin had predicted. The fucking arrogance of the woman. What had she been planning?

He then thought of Theo. They were partners in crime. They had to be. The evil bastards...

Who was this Ms Byrne, if it wasn't Maggie? Who else would leave such a hideous message? They must have suspected that their lair of sorts had been uncovered, and escaped when they had a chance to do so...when he was in Brighton. How did they know all this information? How could they be aware of precisely what was going on? It was as if...

He opened the sliding door and stepped onto the balcony. Sure enough, if he leaned over, and at the right angle, he could peer down and see into his apartment below. Then he saw a tiny cable extending across the wooden floor slats. A portable camera lead...Oh, bollocks. A much worse proposition crossed his mind: Had Theo bugged his apartment?

Michael retraced his steps and closed the glass door, locking it. Something suddenly caught his eye. It was a small circular disc of some kind, sellotaped to the window.

He and Nick moved closer, examining it.

Michael then understood. His heart pounded. He could have died on the spot, the air punched from his lungs. He had been rumbled. Kara and Marcus had been rumbled. They were in grave danger, beyond what he could have imagined.

'What is that?' Nick said, unaware of how Michael was piecing all the facts together, and painting a picture in his head of what Hell surely looked like.

Michael then thought of Martin Penny, and the body in the Thames.

'It's a badge,' Michael said simply. He unpeeled it from the glass, the shiny surface sticky from the adhesive.

'How odd...' Nick said. He took it from Michael, and slowly read the inscription:

'HAPPY BIRTHDAY, DADDY.'

Michael stood frozen to the floor, a tear forming in his eye: This was Maggie's lair. No doubt about it. And this cheery badge was Martin's sad epitaph.

It was all the proof he needed as to the fate of a good man.

CHAPTER ELEVEN

It was Friday. Ronald manned the gallery on his own. This was usually a quiet day, as he knew the office workers in the locality just wanted to clear their desks and get away for the weekend. Hence, his day alone, and it suited him perfectly. Toby was somewhere, Michael was God knows where and Gemma, well, she was still spooked from the abusive client...and if the truth was known, he couldn't deal with her sob story anyway. He preferred it this way. Nice and peaceful. A gradual chance to unwind from the stress of the week he had just had.

He dusted down display shelves, printed off a couple of bio details to be posted on to clients on the coming Monday, and took two minor phone calls in the morning shift. For lunch he ate a sandwich that he had put together in the morning at home: bacon and chicken on rye bread with mayo. He also indulged in a packet of Kettle crisps and a chocolate éclair, bought from the bakery just round the corner. Normally he hid this indulgence from the others. Alone, with no one to judge him, it was his sin day.

Just after lunch, a woman entered the gallery, looked around, and engaged in convivial conversation. She was interested in a particular painting, and noted politely that he was very knowledgeable about the artist in question. He thanked her, and suggested that on another day he could deliver it to her house if she lived locally. He explained that today was not possible, as he was working on his own. The woman raised her delicate eyebrows, declined his offer and asked when the gallery closed.

At five, he replied. He walked her to the door and held it open for her. She smiled and indicated that she would mull things over and be back before closing time.

He smiled too, and suggested that he could reserve the painting for her. She declined and departed. He noticed her statuesque poise, the large sunglasses and silk headscarf which hid her hair and forehead. Her make-up though was rather... weird: Far too heavy for her pale skin.

Then he forgot about her.

***

Kara went for a stroll in the park, pushing her son in the pram. Harvey slept, blissfully unaware of his mother's misgivings about the world in which they lived. It was a fearful place as far as she was concerned. Michael had warned her to get away for a holiday because an exposé was about to impact on their lives. Marcus was adamant that they would not run from the flak. He had a business to operate. She was thankful that the persistent phantom phone calls had ceased. Things were too quiet, though. At least she was back on speaking terms with her mother, after the debacle with the inadvertently abusive phone call.

During her walk, she was forever conscious of prying eyes. She scanned the park, which contained the usual suspects: joggers, cyclists and other young mums out with their babies. In particular, she looked for the man she had spotted loitering outside her flat. It was odd. He was nowhere to be seen these past two nights. Who was he? What did he want? Was he friend or foe?

Exhausted from too little sleep, she slowly ambled across the common, perused the shops for an hour, bought a little blue dungaree outfit for her son, and decided on a spot of self-indulgence. She had earned the right: All this riveting conversation of gurgle-gurgle ("who's a pretty boy then!") was dispiriting to say the least. She needed stimulation. Her brain had diminished since the birth. This then would be a treat to savour. The shop beckoned. Fuck the world and its hang-ups, she had enough of her own. She crossed the street and entered her favourite French patisserie (a little bit of paradise) and stuffed her face with chocolate gateau and cream. That always worked.

***

Marcus was pissed off. First he had the broken window to contend with, then the crap from Michael about the need for protection. All this unnecessary SAS hokum! Then, out of the blue, Michael wanted to know if he had been approached by this mysterious Martin Penny (did he really exist?), who he himself couldn't get in touch with! He had tried but the line appeared to be disconnected. It was all very frustrating. Was everything and everyone going totally bonkers?

He and only he would look after his family. He was the only one of them with his feet firmly grounded in reality. Michael deluded himself, Kara was just plain scared. He could handle it, whatever it was that needed sorting. Here was the challenge: If Maggie was around, let her show her face. He was ready, armed and equally dangerous. He kept a claw hammer beside his desk and a baseball bat under the bed at home. Ready and waiting, bitch. It suddenly occurred to him...perhaps his feet weren't so grounded after all.

The point was this: He was also running scared, despite his outwardly hard-man image. He had to face facts. The net was closing in, and fast. He had done a bad thing. Not even Kara knew of his secret. But it was *bad*. If Maggie was snooping around, he figured that revenge for Lauren's death was not the only motive...she was after something else, a certain something that only he knew about. He thought he was being clever, now he was not so sure. How long could he keep this Mr Cool "I can handle anything" demeanour up before he finally panicked? He was getting closer to it.

Then he saw the news story about the unidentified body washed up in the river. It was suggested that the man had a military background, but as yet he had not been identified. A young and muscular man, found dead, bludgeoned to death. It was the emphasis on the word *bludgeoned* which had caught his attention. He had heard that story before... somewhere from the past...a violent father was bludgeoned to death by his abused daughter. A picture of the two deranged sisters came into his head. His throat cramped tight. It was Maggie's preferred choice of attack. He decided to get himself a bigger hammer.

***

Michael phoned Terry and arranged an urgent meeting. Over a pint at the Wig and Mitre, he told Terry everything he had discovered over the preceding twenty-four hours. It was the stuff of fiction straight from the pages of the latest Michael Connelly novel. Only this time it was so close to home that they could smell the hot breath of the dragon breathing down their necks.

Terry listened, downed another pint of Guinness and then gave his considered opinion.

'Call the cops.'

***

Ronald plodded through the afternoon, entertaining mostly dumb Americans who wanted mementos of London to take home. *No*, he had nothing for around 50 dollars, at the fifth time of asking, and directed them to the little gift shop on the corner of Piccadilly. He wearily suggested that they purchased a lovely 'bronze' model of Big Ben, which would undoubtedly become a fine collectible in the future. *Just the thing*. Jesus.

Later, he struck gold. A loyal client, absent for a year, wandered in and bought a small oil of a coastal scene, priced at £1000. He let it go for £900, as a gesture of goodwill, which clinched the sale.

'Haven't seen you for several months,' Ronald remarked. 'Where have you been?'

The client was a rough sort with an East End drawl. Expensive suit, mind. Ronald admired fine tailoring. He guessed Savile Row. He couldn't have guessed the reply even if he had tried:

'In the nick... out in nine months for good behaviour.'

He wished he hadn't asked.

The man – known locally as Mildred – then sidled up to him and whispered: 'What's a Patrick Porter original making these days?'

Ronald was taken aback. 'Are you buying or selling?'

'I've been offered one.'

'Really? Who's selling?'

Mildred tapped his nose.

Ronald persisted. 'What are they asking for it?'

'Forty K.'

'Hmm. Depends on the size and subject matter, and provenance of course but, in the wise old words of Mark Twain, they aren't making any more.'

'My thoughts entirely.'

'Is it a private sale?' Ronald was fishing. He knew that none had been offered around the London galleries. The work was like gold dust.

'Sort of, but I need to check it out to make sure it's genuine…'

'Tell you what, if you decline the offer let Michael know. He would be interested in buying. A commission, I'm sure, could come your way.'

'I know a bit about the artist. What's the big deal, anyway?'

Ronald smiled. 'The demand for such work is sky high. With what we now know, it's the notoriety of the artist and the tragic background of his demise that intrigues collectors…and the rarity value, of course. This ensures the price keeps rising…'

'I plead ignorance.'

Like hell you do, thought Ronald.

'Humour me.'

Ronald cleared his throat. 'Any painting by Patrick Porter was and is worth purchasing, particularly the nudes. They are sumptuous, grand and desirable. In the beginning a mystery surrounded the artist though. It was only later, quite recently actually, that his real identity became known to the outside world. His name was used as a pseudonym by his sister, Lauren O'Neill. She was an artist who painted secretly in homage to her dead brother. She suffered from a multiple split-personality disorder from shock she suffered in childhood and took on the persona of him… bringing him back to life, if you like. When she painted in his name, she seriously believed she was Patrick.'

'Fucking weird.'

'You could say that. She was deluded. Patrick died as a young child at the hands of his father, who was a thug and brutalised all the family, including Lauren. She was traumatised by the abuse and as a minor took her revenge by killing him. Even though it was in self-defence, she spent several years in a psychiatric ward before being released with a new identity. She moved to England eventually.'

'And this was the wacko who died in the fire, right?'

'Right.'

Mildred laughed. 'And she really believed she was Patrick Porter?'

'Only when she was painting, yes. It truly inspired her. It was her way of hiding from the harshness of the world, the pain she was subjected to as a child. A split-personality takes many guises. She could never truly trust anyone but over the years it got worse. Later, of course, she discovered that her sister had actually killed the father and never confessed, leaving her to take the punishment. An injustice if ever there was one. She felt very much alone in her mind. No wonder she was twisted.''

'A tortured soul, I guess.'

'That about sums it up. It was well documented...'

'And Michael was giving the bitch one, yeah?'

Ronald squirmed.

'Takes all sorts,' Mildred said, shaking his head. He then walked out as happy as Larry, his purchase in hand.

Ronald wondered at the inference to the Patrick Porter painting: Perhaps 40k wasn't so bad after all. This was indeed odd though: Was this the first to come to market since the death of Lauren O'Neill? Who could be trying to sell one? Usually, the galleries get first option...he concluded that this was being sold behind closed doors, and Mildred (just as suspicious as he would be in the same circumstances), was asking the right questions.

Ronald vowed to have a word with Michael sooner rather than later. He watched the client swagger across the road and thought: Great taste in art, great taste in suits. Shoes were pretty smart too. That got him thinking:

Crime does pay.

Takes all sorts, he mused.

***

Back at his apartment, Michael showered and changed, his shirt reeking of stale beer and exhaust fumes. He suddenly realised he was starving and decided to eat up the road at Carluccio's. Down at reception, he dropped Nick a £50 note for his troubles of late, an unexpected payment that he didn't refuse, Michael observed. It was the least he could do for the guy's assistance in their little snooping exercise.

Nick said, 'I had to clean up the offending mess on the window. However, you might be interested in this...' He leaned forward over his desk and handed Michael his mobile phone, with the screen in full view. 'Took a pic, just in case you ever needed the evidence.'

'Appreciated, Nick.'

'Everything OK, Mr Strange?'

'We'll soon find out. Not your problem though.' He mulled things over in his mind, and added: 'Keep all this to yourself, Nick. If either Theo or the woman resurface, contact me immediately. Can you do this for me?'

Nick folded the crisp note and placed it in his jacket pocket, and grinned broadly.

'You can count on it,' he said.

Out on the street, it was raining. Michael checked his watch: four-forty. The gallery would be closing soon, so he wasn't going to check in. Ronald could and would handle anything that came his way. It was a little early to eat, but what the hell. He walked briskly, his coat collar pulled up. On the way he saw a payphone, thought of Terry's last comment, and inserted the appropriate coins. He punched in the numbers and waited for a response.

'Chelsea police station.'

'Listen carefully,' Michael said, muffling his voice with a handkerchief, 'I'll only say this once –'

'Please can I have your name and contact number, sir.'

'Listen! I have information as to the identity of the man found dead in the Thames.' He felt the badge between his fingers. 'I believe his name is Martin Penny, ex-army.'

'Sir, please...'

Michael replaced the receiver, satisfied that he had done his civic duty.

Kara did the shopping at her local Tesco, and ambled back in the direction she came. The park was quiet, and bathed in the last remnants of light. She instantly regretted her decision, feeling vulnerable, but moved on regardless, quickening her step, relieved to suddenly spot a police car parked up close to her exit. Two officers were out on the street, talking to a gang of teenagers. She passed them by, knowing she was but moments from home.

Her heart missed a beat as a stranger, a man, stood by the communal entrance to her block of flats. He saw her coming and approached her.

'Kara Scott?'

He looked respectable enough, middle-aged and without menace. He had a card in his hand and offered it to her. She suspected he was a detective. Not what she wished for, preferring to get indoors, change Harvey's nappy, grab a glass of wine and prepare dinner. She craved just a simple life.

'Y-e-s,' she replied cagily.

'Sorry to startle you. My name is Terry; I'm a friend of Michael's.'

She examined the card. It read: Terence Miles, News International.

'I know of you,' she said cautiously.

He moved closer, the overhead security light bathing him in a yellow pallor.

'Kara, the point is, we need to talk…'

She knew this day would come. She'd warned Marcus that their little secret would one day be exposed. Michael had told her that a news story was about to break. And now here was this Terry, and his persuasive line of questioning. Why couldn't they just be left alone? No fucking chance.

This was just the start. This was the reckoning.

***

Kara cut the journalist short and sent him packing. Now was not the time. The baby was crying. Later, she prepared dinner as best she could, her thoughts interrupted by the sudden appearance of this fella called Terry, and decided on a whim to lay the table with candles as a surprise for when Marcus got in. Normally, they ate from trays, sitting in front of the TV, surrounded by toys. Not tonight.

This time she was organised. The floor was free of clutter and fresh flowers adorned the table, which was covered by a newly ironed white linen cloth. She was in the mood, feeling guilty for treating Marcus like shit recently. She'd checked with him earlier, and agreed that he would be home by seven. She insisted he call in on the way home and buy a bottle of vintage Burgundy, the one with the yellow label. That's all she could remember. He laughed. She laughed too: he was bound to get the wrong one.

She immersed herself in the kitchen, making stuffed mushrooms with stilton, an apricot and marsala based chicken dish with roasted vegetables, followed by jam roly-poly and custard. That would get him in a romantic mood, hopefully.

She made a decision to not mention the confrontation with the journalist. It would create a terrible tension between her and Marcus. Instead, she agreed to meet up with Terry, alone, to discuss the events at Laburnum Farm in a couple of days' time. Although a friend of Michael's he was still a stranger to her, and she felt uneasy inviting him into her home. Instead, he'd arranged to be in touch within the next twenty-four hours: Fine by her. Just time to get my head straight, Kara thought.

***

Terry moved on to a pub closer to home and settled in for a marathon drinking session, determined to forget his prostate bollocks thing and hopefully meet up with a few colleagues for a bit of banter. He needed to lighten up. All the talk of Martin Penny supposedly missing and this Theo and Maggie duo living above Michael was proof enough that things were really hotting up. It was evident that there were people out there serious in their intent to cause harm. He needed to up the game too. He spoke to Michael on the phone and hinted at his bizarre theory of what might have happened at the farm, but he needed proof to confirm this. Michael was perplexed, and dismissed what he had to say on the subject, describing it as "crackpot journalism". He was probably right. The tosser…

In the morning, he had a little more detective work to do. He was heading back down to the farm.

***

Ronald cashed up and checked the time: ten minutes to go. The street was empty. He momentarily stood outside and breathed in fresh air and decided to check with his boyfriend to suggest they splash out on dinner at the nearby Atlantic Bar. He phoned, made his proposition. More to the point: His treat. The answer was a resounding yes. He had a date.

Great.

***

Michael ate lightly, a salmon pasta dish with a glass of chilled Muscadet. The restaurant was busy, buzzing with hip young things. He felt old and a little sad. He wished Agnes was with him. There was something else too, but he couldn't put a finger on it, probably the stress of the phone call to the police. Somehow though, he felt that a terrible thing was about to happen. A black mood descended. Where did that come from?

He finished with coffee, paid with cash, and walked home, thinking of everyone and everything. His life was one colossal mess. Could Maggie, this monster incarnate, really have been camping out above him? Where was the evidence, apart from a deranged message of sorts? He could not establish categorically that it was her living there. There were plenty more crazy people about. He laughed, nervously: why did they *all* have to follow him about?

He crossed the road in front of a line of taxis and took the short cut through an alley. He regretted it instantly. He was grabbed from behind and pushed to his knees. At first he thought he was being mugged, and instinctively reached for his wallet. He didn't want a fight. He remembered that only three months ago a barrister was knifed just a quarter of a mile away in similar circumstances.

'Take it, take it!' he yelled, tossing the wallet in front of him. He knew it contained little in the way of cash. Luckily, he'd left his credit cards on the bed. Wise move, he knew.

He felt the grip on his throat tighten. This was no ordinary mugging. His head was suddenly yanked around, giving him a view of his attacker: Vladimir the impaler. Oh, Christ...

'Theo sends his regards. He rather thinks you owe him something.'

'Tell Theo I'll repay the cash. Our deal is off...' The pain intensified. His eyes turned bloodshot.

'He decides that, not you. He doesn't want the cash. He expects you to fulfill your side of the bargain.'

'Tell Theo to fuck off, shithead.' It was the wrong response.

The henchman picked him up and slammed him against the wall, then punched him hard in the gut.

The lights went out. Michael buckled over, bile flooding his mouth. The fucker could punch, that was for sure.

'What part don't you understand?' Vladimir asked through gritted teeth. 'He expects you in Venice within three days, without fail. He will be waiting.'

'Waiting? I thought I was to go alone...'

'Change of plan. He wants assurance that you will be there. So far you have not carried out your promise. My boss doesn't take kindly to that.'

Michael was aware of his attacker's clenched fist, ready to strike again in the event of any more wisecracks. He kept his response simple.

'And if I decline his generous offer?'

Vladimir smiled, released Michael, who crumpled to the floor, and slowly dusted down his long black leather overcoat. He looked the part and acted the part, Michael had to admit.

'You will not decline, Mr Strange. In fact, you will be in a decent hurry to comply with his request. It is in your express interest to do so.'

'Why would that be?' He got up, his trousers torn at the

knees.

'Mr Theo has taken a particular shine to a...friend...of yours?'

Michael's heart turned to stone. The air was sucked from his body.

Vlad grinned. 'Her name is Agnes, I believe.'

Michael watched as his attacker swiftly vanished from his view, his coat swishing. He grabbed his wallet from the cobbled floor and steadied himself, using the wall as a prop. There was blood on his knuckles.

Fuck. Fuck. Fuck. Then he threw up.

***

Ronald closed the entrance door, and washed his hands and face in the kitchen sink. He wasn't expecting anyone at this late hour. The street was still deserted.

He always kept a clean shirt in the staff room, which he now changed into. He dabbed Ted Baker aftershave on his ruddy cheeks. He combed his hair and checked himself in the mirror. Not bad for an old geezer. *The two Ronnies were about to hit the town.*

He heard the doorbell chime...a last customer perhaps?

Gathering his coat, he switched off the downstairs lights and climbed the short flight of steps. A woman stood in the gallery. He instantly recognised her.

'I came back, as promised,' she said keenly.

'Indeed you did...' he replied. He walked to the small painting that she had earlier admired, removed it from the wall mounting, and brought it for her to inspect once again.

'Delightful' she enthused.

She returned the painting to his safe pair of hands. He cradled it and waited for her instruction. It looked a done deal, but he was now anxious to lock-up and meet with his boyfriend. A double gin/tonic and lime beckoned.

He studied her face again: Too much make-up. He couldn't help but look closer. Her eyebrows were missing, drawn on with pencil. Again, weird.

He took a step back. *Was that a scar running down her cheek? Was that a burn mark on her neck?* Suddenly, he realised she was wearing a…a… partial face mask. It was a damn clever fit. He caught the steely look in her eyes and the toughened stance in her body. He tried to make small talk, waiting for the negotiation to start, but was aghast at her injuries. Frankly, it was off-putting to say the least. He wasn't going to play hardball with her…he was running late. Now something had changed in her demeanour. For the first time he felt…unsure of things. He tried small talk again.

'What part of Ireland are you from?' He had distant family connections himself, and recognised her accent. All he was trying to do was lighten the atmosphere which was now charged with electricity. His eyes affixed themselves to her neck for confirmation of the scar… It was a nasty one.

'Limerick,' she confided.

It was the last word he ever heard.

He felt the blow, but had no idea of what it was, or where it came from. It was an instant sharp pain, which ricocheted around his head, scrambling his brain. He rotated, fell like a stone, his head crashing against the wooden floor with a sickening thud. The painting clattered to the ground too, spinning away from him, wooden splinters breaking from the frame and scattering across the floor.

Everything happened in a split-second. He remained motionless, eyes alert but dead all the same. He stared into nothingness, baffled, his last breath cruelly exhaling into finality. *What the hell was happening to him?* As darkness enclosed all around, he could see the fading image of the woman standing over him, a mocking grin erupting across her lop-sided face.

For her part, she watched in silent fascination as a widening arc of crimson sticky blood slowly encircled his battered head. Then she left him to die alone.

CHAPTER TWELVE

'Dad, it's Toby.'

His tone was odd, almost urgent.

'I'm listening,' Michael said. He stood in the bathroom, naked save for a white towel around his waist. He was inspecting the giant bruise spreading across his stomach. He stopped inspecting...Toby sounded distraught.

'I have some awful news to tell you.'

'Give it to me.'

'It's Ronald.' A moment's hesitation: 'He's dead...'

Michael almost stopped breathing. *Christ.* The walls closed in, making him tumble with dizziness. 'How...How is that possible?'

'His boyfriend found him at the gallery after closing time.'

'Was it a heart attack?'

'No, Dad. It's as bad as it can get, I'm afraid. Ronald was murdered.'

'Jesus...what happened? Are you at the gallery now?'

'I am. Apparently Ronnie was due to meet up with him for dinner and he failed to show. He didn't answer his mobile, or the gallery number. He was worried, naturally, and came over and found the door ajar. Ronald was lying on the floor, his head bashed in. You can imagine how hysterical he is...'

'Have the police been notified?'

'They're here now, with forensics. I think you should come over immediately.'

'I'm on the way.'

'Be warned, Dad. The press have got wind.'

'Are they there now?'

'The place is swarming.'

Hell.

***

Michael parked up in the underground NCP and walked the last two hundred yards to the gallery. Cork Street was cordoned off. The press had gathered, and the photographers immediately started snapping when they recognised him. He explained his presence to a policeman on duty, who escorted him to the guarded entrance. Inside, it was chaos.

Toby came over and gripped his arm, pointing to Ronnie who sat slumped in the corner being interviewed by a detective. They exchanged glances. Several men in white overalls, slipovers on their feet, hovered over the stricken body in the middle of the gallery. Ronald. Dear Ronald.

Michael felt sick, unable to grasp the horrible sight that confronted him. It was all so senseless. Who could do such an appalling thing?

'The police want to interview us down at the local station,' Toby said, adding: 'As of now, the gallery is closed until further notice.'

'Of course,' Michael muttered, numb.

A tall balding man approached. Michael recognised him from a TV news bulletin a few nights ago.

'Detective Sergeant Keene,' the man announced. 'I understand you jointly own the gallery with your son?'

'Yes.'

'Until further notice, this gallery is not to be open to the public until we have concluded our forensic investigations.'

'I understand...'

'This is a crime scene. Your colleague was murdered. We suspect he was killed by a fatal wound to the head. A needless killing. So far, your son has found nothing missing so we can rule out robbery. The safe is intact. Just one damaged painting. However, from your recent history, which is well documented, it seems we already have a clue to the identity of the killer...do you agree with this assumption?'

Michael couldn't have agreed more. It was *her*.

'Could this be Maggie Conlon?' Keene said specifically.

Michael nodded weakly.

'I need to conduct an urgent interview with all those who knew the deceased. We also need to inform next-of-kin...perhaps you can help?'

Michael stared at Toby, and then answered: 'Ronald was

an only child. Both his parents died years ago. Only friends would need to be informed. His boyfriend would be able to do this, I'm sure.'

'Of course, and thank you for that information. It makes our job more tolerable...'

Michael excused himself and spoke with Ronnie in a quiet corner. They hugged. What could he say? It was a nightmare.

'Shall we go?' Keene said, approaching. 'I have a vehicle waiting.'

Michael and Toby were escorted to the police station. Keene interviewed Michael separately for over two hours, conducting the investigation into Lauren O'Neill's death which he had previously agreed to cooperate on. He felt pushed into a corner, victimised, as if forced to go over old ground. What more did they want from him? He was exhausted by the interrogation.

Eventually, Toby joined them. This second interview lasted for over an hour. It centred on Ronald's life and work. Michael revealed all he knew that was relevant to the crime, and after finding out how his colleague was murdered, readily agreed with the police suggestion that Maggie was the main suspect. The finger of blame for Ronald's death was pointed squarely in her direction. Who else could it be?

'A revenge killing? Keene suggested.

Michael looked at his son, and was thankful that he was unharmed...so far. They were all targets now.

'More like a sacrifice,' he replied quietly, his brain scrambled.

It seemed to him that his son aged ten years in that second.

***

Later, they returned to the gallery (camera lights flashing) under police supervision and locked up the premises, providing the police with duplicate keys. The forensic team had gone, leaving one man who diligently powdered down the door handles and work tops. By then, Ronald's body had been removed in a bag. All that remained was a white chalk outline at the spot where he had been slaughtered.

***

Michael started to drive home, then diverted to East London. He had to do this now, while he still had the courage.

Marcus sat, strangely impassive, as Kara cried her eyes out, comforted only by the mug of tea that her boyfriend provided. Michael didn't get one.

At this stage, there was nothing else to do except grieve. Everyone who knew Ronald, Michael felt, would be deeply affected by the tragic loss. Words of comfort didn't seem enough.

Time to go, he reasoned. Marcus accompanied him to the door and gave him a withering look of contempt as he departed. No words of comfort from him. He had his own demons to conquer.

***

At home, Michael drank a quarter bottle of whisky. Straight. It helped dull the pain. His ribs still hurt as well. The phone rang. It was gone midnight.

'I've just heard. You OK?'

'I'm fine, Terry.'

'We need to talk urgently. Was it Maggie?'

'It had to be…'

'This was vindictive and senseless, Michael. Why Ronald?'

'She's showing me who is in control, Terry.' He thought: First Martin, then Ronald. 'Who's next?'

'You all need police protection.'

'I'll sort it in the morning…'

'Do so. Get some rest, OK?'

'That's the idea.'

'And listen, lock the door and put a chair against the handle.'

Then he was gone.

Ha Fucking Ha. Then he did precisely that.

He was shattered. Then the phone rang again.

'I thought you told me everything was in the past?' Toby

189

snarled. 'That it was finished with these people…'

Michael could detect the hostility in his son's voice.

'I thought so too,' he replied wearily.

'This could close down the business.'

'I'm aware of that.'

'The publicity will hurt.'

'I'm aware of that as well.' His patience was wearing thin. He changed the subject. 'We need to inform Gemma of what's happened.'

'Already done.'

'How has she taken it?'

'She's shaken up, of course.'

'Not the best of starts for her in a new job…'

'You could say that,' Toby hissed, but he wouldn't be deflected. 'Is there anything else I should know, Dad?'

He could smell the fear down the phone line. Michael reflected on the police interview, which his son had attended jointly. The questions thrown at him from Keene would have shocked anyone within earshot, even hardened coppers. It had all the hallmarks of an Oliver Stone movie. Only this was for real.

'I reckon I covered everything, Toby.'

'Everything…?'

'Yes.' He didn't dare mention the news story that was about to explode across the globe, nor the attack by Vlad, nor…Oh, shit, the list went on and on.

'I'm pretty pissed, Dad. These things don't just happen for no fucking reason. We have a murder on our premises. Can you imagine the headlines tomorrow? This will ruin us…'

Michael thought of Theo and Maggie and their little twisted minds, then Agnes and the implied threat to her life. She too needed his protection. There was nothing he could do now for poor lifeless Ronald.

Peering through the curtains, he could see the gathering Press hovering like wolves at the security gates. This was never ever going to go away, unless he took the law into his own hands and personally brought Maggie to her knees. He just had to think of a way to bring her out into the open. A cog turned in his head…

'I'm scared too, son,' he said. 'But rest assured I will sort it once and for all.'

***

Next morning, the dawn broke with relentless rain, adding to the overwhelming gloom that filled Michael's head as his eyes gradually focused on the ceiling. Then it hit him: Ronald's killing. Difficult to believe it really happened.

The effects of the whisky raddled his brain. Sleep, and wayward dreams, did not solve any problems. If anything, the starkness of the day merely magnified the sheer horror of the equation. An equation that had two possible outcomes: kill or be killed.

He showered, dressed on automatic pilot and drank a carton of cold milk from the fridge. He was ready for action, although his aching bones told him otherwise. His ribs were still sore. *Fuck Maggie. Fuck Theo. Fuck Vladimir.* Which one of them had killed Ronald in cold blood?

He needed a bullet-proof strategy.

His first thought was to go the gallery, check everything out, search for clues, but that was out of bounds for the present. Toby could deal with the police instead. Besides, he wasn't in the right frame of mind to have to stare at the patch of crimson floor, which couldn't be avoided if he went back.

Next on the agenda was organising police protection for his son and Kara and her baby. He couldn't care less for himself and Marcus, the idiot. He phoned Toby, who agreed to try to arrange this, if Keene would cooperate.

Then he phoned Kara. Bad idea. Marcus had taken the day off to comfort her, and suggested politely for Michael to take a running jump. Par for the course.

Agnes! Oh, God... That bastard Theo was supposedly over there, which was an implied threat to her safety if he was to believe in what Vlad had said. And he believed him.

He had a plan, of sorts: Meet the fucker's fire with fire. The funeral would not be for several days. Just enough time. He went online and booked a flight to Venice for that afternoon. No time like the present.

Over the next thirty minutes, he packed a holdall and grabbed a fistful of euros from the wall safe, together with his passport and credit cards. He ordered a taxi for 11.30am, and warned the driver to park up at the back of the apartment block. Michael could take the lift to the garage and use the rear exit, thus avoiding the hungry mob at the front. He felt like a spy on the run. A spy? Fanciful, or fact? Then he turned his attention to what Theo had been up to...

He swiftly moved into the lounge and took hold of the wall-mounted telephone, his suspicions aroused by Theo's intrusion. He listened to the dialling tone. Then he made a call to the taxi firm again, on the pretext of bringing the time of his pick-up forward by fifteen minutes. He listened carefully. *There it was again.* A click of some kind. A faint electronic click. He retrieved a tiny screwdriver from the kitchen drawer and removed the cover mounting from the wall. What was he looking for? Then he saw it, a small disc adhered to the inner lining, with a wire attached to the main fuse board. He was being electronically bugged. That's what Theo's ruse was about. He ripped out the offending disc and stamped it underfoot.

So that's how they knew of his movements. That's how they planned ahead, with a listening device on his phone and an upstairs mini-camera which monitored his movements from the balcony above. Clever sods.

No longer. Now the lines of battle were drawn from a level playing field. A conquering grin formed on his lips. He was getting used to this desperate game of espionage. He was even beginning to enjoy it.

Then he noticed that the incoming messaging light on the answering machine was flashing. This had to be a call received in the early hours, as the light was dormant when he went to bed. He listened to the single message.

His grin was soon wiped from his face. It was Maggie's voice. Cold, vile, insidious. This is what he heard:

"Was that close enough for you, Michael?"

His head swam. He knew instinctively that something was missing when they found Ronald's stricken body: Her calling card of triumph.

Now he had it.

CHAPTER THIRTEEN

Impressive, thought Terry.

He stood in the car park of the Royal Oak at Old Hampton, and admired the slick revamp to the property. Outside, a new fascia board, highlighted by funky down lights and modern colour scheme, greeted the visitor. And by the number of cars parked up, there were a lot of patrons ready to sample the hospitality within the pub. He eagerly took refuge to enjoy the beer. He was more than impressed by the set-up. At least a quarter of a million had been lavished on the interior alone, he reckoned.

It was now cool and hip, with all the old fixtures and fittings ripped out, replaced by distressed panelling, modern abstract prints and French style upholstered chairs and scrubbed chic maple tables. Soft fusion music filtered down from hidden speakers in the ceiling. Too flash for me, Terry decided, after counting the number of Mercs and Beemers in the overflowing car park. The money spent was well invested though: the place was buzzing.

He was here now, so he had to make the best of it. He largely felt like a fossil found on the beach: A thing of curiosity. He sat at the bar, ordered a pint of Ruddles and checked the Daily Specials on the board propped against the wall. There was no scampi and chips.

A woman approached, a shiny thing who looked like she had polished herself in oil. She was trim, tall and elegantly dressed, with a hint of cleavage showing through the unbuttoned black silk blouse. Her hair too was black and fashionably cut into a slick bob. *Some girl.*

'Can I take your order, sir?' she asked, her teeth gleaming like pearls behind expertly applied red lipstick. He was almost lost for words.

'Soup,' he said. 'French onion.'

'With croutons?'

'With croutons.'

She flashed a smile.

'I'm afraid there will be a little delay. As you can see, we're a touch busy.'

'When did you reopen?'

'Yesterday.'

'An encouraging start...'

'Very.'

'Are you the owner?'

'The tenant.' She held out her hand. 'I'm Pippa.'

'Terry,' he said, returning her delicate caress.

'I'll place your order, Terry.'

The soup was delicious, although a little heavy for his taste. He amused himself with a newspaper crossword. It was forty minutes before he engaged her in conversation again. She looked a little flustered now, her workload unrelenting.

'I was here a few weeks back, before the renovation. There was a young girl behind the bar...'

'She was a stand-in, long gone now.'

'Before that I understand the tenants were Sheila Cox and her husband, Dougie.'

'I wouldn't have that information...'

'I'm trying to locate them. How do I go about that, Pippa?'

'I suppose through the brewery, they'd know.'

'Do you have a number?'

She flashed that smile again.

'I can do better than that. I can introduce you to one of the directors. He's overseeing things until I get my feet under the table.'

'Excellent,' he said.

Pippa hobbled off again on five inch heels. The girl had a lot to learn, Terry observed. She'll be in flats within a week. In the meantime, he was happy to admire her pins while it lasted. They went on forever.

A man in rolled-up shirt sleeves and sweaty brow approached. He looked distinctly frazzled, unlike the resplendent head girl.

'The kitchen needed extra hands,' he said, with a jovial smile. 'My name is Ian Banks. The new tenant said you wanted to see me.'

'Well, not you in particular, Mr Banks...'

'Ian.'

'Terry.' They shook hands.

'What can I do for you, Terry?'

Terry was always prepared. He extracted a bogus business card from his pocket, one of hundreds he kept at home. They always fooled the foolish.

Ian read: Terry Wilson/ Probate/ Wilson & Finch, London. The gold edging always added weight to the illusion. Who would go to that much trouble if they were a petty crook?

Terry smiled. 'I am required to contact the previous tenants, as a death in the family has resulted in a small legacy coming their way. Their last known address was this pub. Obviously, they have moved on. Could you provide the forwarding address to help locate them?'

'Dougie, yes. Sheila, sadly no.'

'Oh?'

'They split up, but Dougie still works with us. After his wife left he couldn't cope here alone and didn't want the responsibility of the new plans we had, plus the hike in rent. He took on a new tenancy nearer to his original home.'

'Which is where exactly?'

'He took over a smaller pub, The Cricketers at Wellington.'

'Wellington, Shropshire?' It was like trying to get blood from a stone.

'Yes.'

'Can I trouble you for the details so I can make contact?'

'I'll bring them up on the computer. Give me ten minutes, but first I just need to check on the kitchen. It's a bit of a panic back there.'

'Of course.' Terry held out his hand, indicating he wanted his card returned. He got it.

It was another half an hour before Ian came back. He slipped Terry a folded piece of paper.

'Telephone number, address and email. All that you need, but perhaps I can suggest you go a little easy as any mention of his wife will cause further distress. Dougie has been fantastically loyal over the years and has only recently got back on his feet. The split with his wife hit him hard.'

'Any chance of a reconciliation?'

Ian shook his head. 'Not likely, I feel. They had a history of marital difficulties. It's what often happens in the pub trade: long stressful hours and the pressure of combating falling profits from deserting punters which inevitably happens in a recession. Sheila moving out was not unexpected, as she had packed her bags on several occasions in the past.'

'But she had always returned?'

'Yes, but not this time. There was rumour that she had fallen in with a travelling salesman she had met at this very bar.'

'So you have no idea of her whereabouts?'

'None at all. The strange thing is we still have her P45.'

'I'll make enquiries, and see where it leads…'

'Dougie might know, but as I said…'

'Go easy.'

'It would make my job a lot easier. I don't want my tenants distracted, or complaining to me. The job's hard enough as it is.'

Terry had what he had come for and they shook hands again. He paid his bill, caught Pippa's eye and waved nonchalantly. She responded with a winning smile. The girl would go far. But not in those killer shoes.

Of a more pressing matter, how far would he go to find Sheila Cox?

***

Michael checked *Sky News* before departing for the airport.

It was the fifth item on the agenda:

'Police have received an anonymous tip-off as to the identity of the body found in the river Thames at Bermondsey. However, they are not releasing the dead man's name at this stage.. It is believed the victim was connected to the military, and his identity will remain a secret for now.' Then the announcer said, 'This story will grow and grow…now over to the sport.'

Michael switched off, concerned that he had done more damage than good by making his call to the police. Nick buzzed up. His taxi was in position at the rear of the building.

He grabbed his bag and made for the elevator. He was on his way.

He had no idea what was in store for him in Venice, he just knew he had to be with Agnes and deal with Theo once and for all. His ribs still hurt: Time to give a little pain back in sweet retaliation.

***

Laburnum Farm. It still gave Terry the spooks. It was a place of death, a macabre house that seemed to defy natural welcome and homeliness. Instead the very fabric of the imposing walls seemed to repel the intruder. The Devil once lived here, Michael had hinted on several occasions. Terry didn't doubt it.

On his previous visit he had concentrated on examining the barn. Now he turned his attention to the main house. Its low-slung roof hung heavy over the ochre timber-clad exterior. It sat hunched and brooding, silent and abandoned. Green damp seeped up the walls from the ancient foundations, like long, groping fingers. He shuddered. Although it was quiet, save for the circling crows, Terry thought he could hear the distant screams of the dead. But it was a trick of the mind, just the timbers slowly creaking under the weight of history. A wretched history.

He wandered at will, and realised for the first time of looking that the house was also damaged in the fire. The thatch roof had obviously ignited from the flames carrying on the wind. The west wing (nearest to the barn) was largely destroyed, the windows boarded up. The east side survived. He peeped through cobwebbed windows and strained his eyes to see into the murk...searching, for what he did not truly know. The house appeared empty of furniture. Moving to the rear, he noticed that the kitchen door had been broken into and subsequently repaired. Vandals perhaps? Recalling Michael's confession, he understood that the paintings by Patrick Porter (or should he say Lauren O'Neill?) were worth considerable money: More so now, given their notoriety as the truth of the provenance became known to the wider public. What happened to them? According to Michael, they were in storage. Beyond what Michael had told him, which was a confession of sorts while they holed up at the safe house, Terry felt that there was a missing element to the story, and to understand the monstrous events of that day, the day a woman was burnt to death, he strongly felt the desire to grasp the events from a different perspective. It was here that the truth would be found. It was here that the sixth person would be unveiled. He looked at it this way: Those that were so closely involved, Michael, Kara, Marcus and the two sisters, could not in any way be aware of what actually happened, to themselves or to each other amid such terror, being overwhelmed so completely by the inferno that engulfed them. No way. They only knew what they thought they knew.

And now, standing here amid the blackened debris, the remnants of the stricken barn, this house, he saw that different perspective. He played out the scene as best he could. He knew that it was Kara who alerted the police, and she at the time was in the house, away from the fire. Marcus had escaped, regained his senses and returned to help Michael, dragging him unconscious to safety. Maggie had managed to escape as well, before Marcus had reached Michael. This was all documented in the police files. Also, Michael was adamant that it was Lauren who perished in the fire, and the police had bought into this version of events, even though they could not identify the body through forensics.

Terry looked around, standing on the very spot that Maggie would have stood on, having made her getaway. For a few brief seconds she would have been alone. She could not have entered the house to retrieve the cash and passports as Kara would have seen her, or at the very least, heard her clattering around. Therefore, it was reasonable to assume that she had these items with her, retrieved earlier.

How then did she get away? It was a difficult terrain. She was injured. The cars belonging to Michael and Marcus were later recovered on the drive. Lauren's old truck, used to collect her sister from the airport, was still in the garage. Maggie then had no transport. So, how did she simply vanish into thin air?

The police had no knowledge of the missing cash and passports (which were originally seen by Michael in the bedroom) as they arrived on the scene after Maggie's escape. At the time, they were only concerned with saving lives. From the information they gathered from the witnesses, they were soon searching for one woman, on foot. How hard would that be? But they failed to apprehend her. What if…? Something else puzzled Terry. The fire brigade were alerted by an anonymous phone call. Who was the good Samaritan?

Retracing his footsteps, Terry quickly concluded that Maggie, hurt and bewildered, could not have escaped over the fields, through dense overgrown foliage, over slippery and steep fields. Could she have found refuge in one of the neighbouring properties? The police search found no evidence. She simply disappeared. Terry concluded that her only route to freedom was to drive away. And for that, she needed a car.

Whose car?

***

Kara had awoken late, after a fretful night of tears and sadness. The morning brought no respite. What had happened to Ronald was just unbelievable. She now genuinely feared for her life, and that of her family. It was time to bolt for cover. She discussed the possibility with Marcus, who felt it was better if she and Harvey went to stay with her mother. He would remain and run the gallery – after all, they had to make a living. He refused to retreat from the enemy forever. This bravado was bordering on the reckless, she reckoned. Why was he acting like this?

Michael had explained, in the meantime, that he was making the trip to Venice and would be away for just a couple of days. Another reckless act. Why the urgency to go there? She had forgotten, after all the horror of the previous night, to tell Michael that Terry had been in contact. He had always assured her that she could rely on his friend's help and loyalty. This she would do willingly when he made contact again.

She nibbled at the breakfast that Marcus had prepared, her

appetite dwindling. She could only think of Ronald, a man who wouldn't hurt a fly. Who could do such a vile act? She knew the answer and asked the question:

Why the fuck should this bitch control all their lives to the point of such hysteria?

She too vowed to stay put and fight fire with fire. From somewhere, a huge surge of strength enveloped her. She suddenly felt invincible. No one was going to mess with her. Marcus was right. They would refuse point-blank to be intimidated by this criminal. Now they needed a battle plan. But it would need to be a bloody good one.

***

The flight from Gatwick to Italy was smooth and uneventful, the journey on the water taxi to Venice choppy and cloaked in mist. This was how his mind felt as he approached his destination, a mystical place of crumbling façades, shrouded alleyways and echoing footsteps. As the horizon slowly loomed into view, the taxi engine throttled back and the peal of church bells lifted high into the leaden skies. He alighted from the dockside and as he made his way across St Mark's Square, suitcase in hand, a flock of gulls exploded into the air with their familiar screeching sound. Rain fell in cold, heavy droplets, forcing him to shelter under the wide arches that ran the length of the concourse. Finally, he quick-stepped over the Rialto Bridge and arrived at his hotel soaked through, a bedraggled figure on the brooding landscape.

Taking shelter in his room, he immediately discarded wet clothes. Never had a blistering hot shower felt so good to cold and aching limbs. On reflection, he knew that his marathon confession to Terry, the scary message on the balcony window, an unfortunate episode with Vlad in the alleyway and the murder of a dear work colleague had sucked out all the inner strength he possessed and left him feeling emotionally and physically drained. He was spent. Standing naked and feeling utterly exposed, he allowed the force of the water to cascade over him and drown his sorrows until the intense heat turned to a comfortable warmth and then to a temperature bordering on freezing. But still he stood there, unaware of how or why he began to shiver. It took him a while to discover that during this enforced respite he had been silently crying.

Later, he unpacked, took a light afternoon tea in his room and tried on his mobile to contact Agnes for an update. Silence. He left a message that he had arrived at his hotel, and suggested they meet up at seven. Damn, this silence made him nervous.

At reception he was handed an envelope which contained the directions to the house he was going to explore. This package wasn't a surprise, but how did Theo know he had arrived, and at this hotel? He was clearly being watched secretly. This proposed house search made him more than apprehensive, but he had a job to do. He couldn't do anything which threatened Agnes's life. She too, according to Vlad, was under observation, only she didn't necessarily know it. He had to warn her.

His immediate thoughts now turned to the Theo's house. What he was about to discover there just heightened the trepidation that crept into his bones. Was this a trap? He checked the time and decided to walk to his destination, which was in the locality, and get the damned search over and done with, giving him a little over two hours to uncover the masterpiece before meeting up with Agnes, assuming she got back to him.

Please phone, Agnes.

The weather was kinder now, with a diffused sunlight breaking cover through the thinning clouds. Folding a raincoat over his arm, he grabbed a notebook and small digital camera from his case and stepped out into the amber light that shrouded this wondrous city of interlocking canals.

He walked briskly, following the instructions that Theo had given him. In his pocket, the keys jangled. So did his heart.

The three-storey house stood at the centre of a terrace of fifteen, each a different shade of faded ochre and green. The avenue was tight, with a narrow waterway separating the terrace from the church opposite, which cast a giant shadow over their past grandeur. These were fine houses which had not succumbed to conversion into cramped apartments. Old money lived here, Michael was sure.

On entering through the handsome oak door, he was initially hit by the aroma of stale air and damp. The light switch failed and in the gloom of abandonment he could just make out a horde of exquisite, dusty objets d'art adorning the mahogany sideboards in the hallway, from bronze animals to Chinese ceramic figurines, he guessed. His eyes gradually adjusted. Each floor was overcrowded with individual antique chairs, sofas and a huge walnut dining table on the middle level. On the walls, an array of modern and old paintings stared back at him as he explored a labyrinth of corridors. To gain light, he cranked open the tall shutters as he went from room to room. Several times he caught his breath and coughed as the dust rose and clogged his dry throat. He vowed to bring bottled water on his next visit, if he dared to ever return.

He searched high and low, but the mysterious treasure eluded him, hidden among the many beautiful and desirable collectables contained within these walls. In the cellar he found the wine stock, perhaps four thousand bottles in total. On the top floor, a library of maybe ten thousand titles. Theo's father was obviously a man of refinement and intelligence. The contents of the house were worth over a million pounds on a conservative estimate. Strangely, on his search he found no family photos or personal knick-knacks, just an ebony cane and top hat. He refrained from poking his nose into drawers and wardrobes as a sign of respect to someone else's possessions. But the more he explored, the more he became wholly frustrated.

He retraced his steps to get a better perspective of the layout. Eventually he climbed the stairs again and came to an attic room. The door was locked. He scrambled around in a display of old bronze lidded pots on a hallway table.

Nothing. Then he rubbed his hand atop a cobwebbed Cabinet and found what he wanted: the key. Inserting it, the door opened reluctantly on its rusty hinges. A shaft of yellow light penetrated the darkness from a roof skylight. Michael adjusted his vision and wished he'd had the foresight to bring a torch with him. In the corner stood an ornate easel, displaying a heavy but empty gold leaf Dutch frame.

Where was the painting? He moved furniture, looked under

the floor rug, opened cupboards – but to no avail. There was nothing of any value in the room, nor a discarded canvas that would fit into the frame size required. He swore.

Where had Theo hidden the canvas? What game was he playing? Michael was irritated. And thirsty. He had but thirty minutes before he had arranged to meet with Agnes at her favourite trattoria. He moved swiftly from room to room, floor to floor, checking above and behind tall sideboards, under beds, behind sofas. Eventually, he re-entered the main hallway which led to the front door and stood silently, thinking that he had failed spectacularly.

His phone rang. He jumped.

'Well, what do you think?'

Michael cursed the name under his breath. *Theo.*

'Are you monitoring my every move?' Michael retorted.

'I know you are in the house…'

'Well, I can't find what you want me to fucking find.'

'You need to calm down, Mr Strange. Your health will suffer with all this stress…'

'My health is suffering from the attack by your henchman. I have the bruises to prove it.'

'A minor altercation…'

'And your health will suffer if you as much as lay a hand on Agnes, do you understand?'

'She's perfectly safe…for now. Just do your job, and we can all go home.'

'What am I searching for?'

'Look more closely.'

'Why are you playing a game with me?'

'Because I can, and the anticipation of your find is worth waiting for.'

Michael hesitated, and then said wearily: 'Help me out, Theo.'

Theo laughed. 'Why don't you enjoy a little hospitality on my behalf…may I suggest a fine bottle of vintage Champagne from my father's collection?'

Then he clicked off. Michael mouthed the word *bollocks* and then descended the narrow concrete stairs to the cellar. It was musty and dimly lit from a single air shaft which extended to the street above, covered by a metal grille. Huge drooping cobwebs spanned the vaulted ceiling like suspended shredded parachutes. His footsteps echoed across the tiled terracotta floor. He peered behind the rows of wine racks, struggling to see into the murky depths. He was seriously pissed off by now. There was no Champagne down here...then he remembered something.

He dashed upstairs and entered the kitchen. In the corner, beside the oven range, stood a pallet containing crates of the bubbly stuff. He peered behind. Again, nothing. He moved each heavy crate, until the wooden floor was exposed. There was a hidden latch. He pulled eagerly and lifted a trap-door, which in turn revealed a shallow recess. Inside, a flat rectangular object was tightly wrapped in sack-cloth. His heart pulsated.

With great care, he removed the object and settled by the open window, sitting down to calm his nerves. Unpicking the string, he peeled back the protective covering and at last examined the linen canvas, one which he knew instinctively would fit exactly the bulky frame in the attic.

For a second, he couldn't really make out what he was witnessing. He tilted the canvas toward the light and suddenly the image came into focus. At first he could hardly believe his eyes. What in Hell's name was this? He could hardly draw breath. He took a few moments to reflect on what he was looking at. It was a painting that he was familiar with. It depicted a naked young girl lying upon a silk bedspread. The model was unmistakably Antonia. He searched for the signature, one he already knew: Patrick Porter. Then it dawned on him. This was one of the paintings that hung on the wall in Laburnum Farm. It was one of the twelve that Lauren had so desperately implored him to sell when she was broke and needed the money. He tried to make sense of it. They were all supposed to be in storage. What had happened here?

His stomach churned, and his instinct told him he was indeed the victim of an elaborate ploy. Was he holding something so rare, so priceless that people would kill to possess it, cherish it...To own it? Was it was worth untold millions? Was it the treasure of a lifetime, as Theo had indicated?

Not a chance. It was another message from the joker in the pack. On the reverse was an enlarged black and white photograph of Michael and Kara hugging in the park in London: A snapshot taken by telescopic lens. There was a scrawled message in red lipstick written across the image.

He read the inscription again, this time aloud:

'Are we getting close enough, Michael?'

With trembling hands, he threw the offending canvas against the floor, creating an explosion of dust. He didn't care for its true value. He had to get out, and quickly. He reached the hallway and locked the door behind him, swiftly disappearing into the darkness of the alleyways, checking behind him as he went. Out onto the busy promenade, he found a bar and ordered a double brandy and Americano coffee. He was in Venice, Kara was in London. They had been separated. Why? Fear crept up on him. Everyone was in danger. He felt utterly helpless, like a puppet on a string. He needed to think things through. First things first: He checked his watch, downed both drinks and decided to go to the restaurant in the hope Agnes was waiting for him. She was, much to his relief. They kissed, and then kissed again.

'Why didn't you answer your mobile?' he asked.

'Why didn't you answer yours?'

He checked his pockets and realised, to his horror, that he had somehow dropped his phone in the house in a rush to get out.

Fuck, he said under his breath. 'I left it behind in the house. I'll need to go back and get it...'

He felt a shiver of absolute dread course through his veins.

Agnes smiled, kissed him longingly, and unaware of his fears, said: 'Not tonight, Michael. We have better things to do tonight.'

Then she grabbed his hand and led him away, breathless. Dinner and the missing phone could wait until later.

CHAPTER FOURTEEN

Terry decided to drive to Shropshire and talk directly to Dougie, rather than scare him off with a random phone call. He arrived in Wellington just after midday, and found The Cricketers pub on the fringe of the town, near the local landmark *The Wrekin*. The mountain stood bold and dark against the slate sky.

He made small talk with the barmaid, and was aware that the man who periodically came out from the kitchen with the food orders was probably Dougie, a slim man in his late fifties, with receding grey hair and a tattoo on his bare arm.

Later, Terry engaged him in conversation and took a different tack to the one he sold to Ian Banks.

'Basically,' he said, 'I'm selling life assurance, and wondered if you and your wife had adequate cover for loss of profits in the event of illness?' He handed Dougie a card, another with gold edging.

Dougie barely glanced at it.

'Talk to the brewery,' he snapped, 'they usually deal with that aspect of things.'

'I'm talking about joint personal cover, Mr Cox. How would you make the rent on this place if either of you were involved in, say, a car accident and weren't able to work? Suppose you were both unable to work?'

'There is no joint necessity, I live alone.'

'Oh, I understood that you were married...'

'I am, but we are separated.'

'Divorced?'

'I said separated...do you have a hearing problem?'

Terry sensed the hostility right from the start. He wasn't winning the man over. Ian had warned him to tread carefully. He opted for the sympathy card.

'Actually, I do. I was involved in an accident several years ago, lost my hearing temporarily and my job permanently and got into serious debt. I learnt my lesson the hard way.

Anyway, I'll be on my way…thanks for the time. Good food by the way.' He spotted the team photograph behind the bar. 'Hope the season goes well. We're in trouble, my bloody lot.'

He stood to go, and Dougie stopped him.

'Who do you support?'

'The Orient.'

'Thought from your accent you were from London. What brings you all the way up here?'

'Visiting my sister, but I always look for a business opportunity.'

'You need to…have you seen the news? The world's fucked.'

'Tell me about it: All the more reason to look after number one, Mr Cox.'

'It's Dougie. Can I take out a single insurance policy?'

'Sure can.'

'Can you leave me a pamphlet or something?'

'I'll arrange to have one sent in the post, Dougie.'

'It's just…well…being on my own, I can see where you are coming from.'

Terry had hooked him at last. He laid it on thick. 'I lost my wife.'

'She's dead?'

'In a manner of speaking.' He left the sentence to dangle in the air, and put on his best hound-dog expression. 'Left me for some slick smooth-talking bastard who promised her the earth.'

'Did she get it?'

Terry waited, and shook his head. 'Nah, she slums it up in a two million pound house in Hampstead and drives a SLK Mercedes convertible. So you see, these things always come home to roost.'

Dougie was slow on the uptake. Then he saw the ironic joke and burst out laughing. 'Fuck me,' he said, shaking his head in merriment, 'fuck me!'

Terry moved in with subtle grace. 'So what happened with you?'

Dougie narrowed his eyes, took the measure of the man and grabbed two glasses down from the shelf. 'It's a long story, do you want to hear it?'

'I've got the time if you have…'

'Pull up a stool, mister. What's your poison?'

***

'How long have you been awake?'

Michael turned from the window at his hotel, and smiled. Agnes was lying naked on the bed, staring at him.

'Since dawn, I guess,' he said.

'What's been troubling you?'

'I've been set up, and I feel a complete prick.'

She stood, gathered a sheet around her, and held him in a tight embrace as they looked out over the lagoon. A sudden shaft of light broke through the clouds and bathed them in lemon sunshine.

'Not by me, I hope,' she countered.

He kissed her lightly.

'Not by you, Agnes.'

'You need to tell me what's going on, Michael.'

He had thought long and hard, and knew the reason for the hoax painting. It was to get him to Venice, away from London. The photo on the reverse was a piss take, to demonstrate who had the upper hand. Maggie had played on his greed, knowing he would follow his instincts. He was a soldier of fortune. Actually, he was led like a lamb to the slaughter. And now he had implicated Agnes as well. But why was it so vital to draw him over here? He had to warn Kara…

'Agnes, do you know this man by the name of Theo Britton?'

'Should I?'

'I spoke with him yesterday. He suggested that you had met…'

She stroked his hair. 'Other than you telling me about him on the phone, and the deal with the proposed inventory at his deceased father's house, the answer is no.'

'He has a diamond in his teeth.'

She laughed, 'Now *that* I would remember.'

'I need to go back to the house to retrieve my phone.'

'Now?'

208

'Yes.'

'Well, not on your own. I'm coming too…'

That's what he was afraid of, but he knew he couldn't persuade her otherwise. They were now a team, and not to be messed with.

***

Marcus got to work late, making sure Kara was emotionally settled in her head. The immense shock of Ronald's death messed everyone up, but Kara took it very badly. It was as if she took the blame for what happened. He needed a little space and elected to go to the gallery for a couple of hours, as he had arranged to meet a client who wanted to purchase a painting for his private collection. And not just *any* painting. Hopefully, after several weeks of negotiation, he was about to close the deal at a considerable profit. His biggest sale to date. No mean feat. It would set him up, and his family. He wasn't going to blow this sale. Eat your heart out, Michael.

He opened the gallery, settled down and made coffee. He arranged the painting, a sizeable oil, on the main easel which took centre stage in the gallery, with good overhead lighting ensuring maximum effect to the appeal of the subject. It was a nude. He covered the front of the canvas with a white dust sheet which concealed it from prying eyes. Perfect. He checked the time and put a couple of red dots on other expensive paintings to add weight to the desirability of the work he carried and for the client to notice that he was a successful operator. A good trick to have up his sleeve.

He put Radio Five on to catch up on the news and sport and busied himself with bringing the weekly invoicing up to date. Nerves were getting the better of him, his concentration lapsing. Much depended on this deal. He thought of phoning Kara but decided against it. He knew what the topic of conversation would be. He grimaced. No matter. Tonight he would cook the meal in celebration of his success and make a fuss over Kara, as she had done previously for him with a dinner made in heaven. For the first time in ages, they had found the energy and desire to make love. Maybe, just maybe, he could get lucky tonight as well. A bottle of

Champagne would be the order of the day as well.

He was feeling smug, then disaster struck. His client phoned, cancelling his appointment due to unforeseen circumstances. Marcus was crushed, although the client did rearrange another appointment for the following week. He had to keep cool. These things happen. If the truth was known, Marcus needed to off-load the painting ASAP. It was too hot to handle.

At closing time, he balanced the credit card machine totals, switched off the lights and washed his coffee cup, which was unusual for him. Normally, he allowed them to gather in the sink, dirty, until he got sick of the sight of the clutter which built up over a period of time. In the background, a news item on the radio caught his attention.

He dashed over and increased the volume.

'...it has just been confirmed that police have released the name of the man recovered from the River Thames, after close relatives had been informed of his identity earlier in the day. His name is Mitch Hill, who was formerly a private in the army stationed at Aldershot. He was killed by a brutal assault to the head. The murder weapon has not been found. Police are now seeking help from the public in the hunt for the killer or killers...'

Marcus's heart jumped. Who was Mitch Hill? He continued to listen:

'...it was first thought that the unidentified body was that of a former SAS member, and a terrorist link was strongly suspected. This theory has now been eliminated from official enquiries and the anonymous call to this effect has now been discounted as a hoax. Police are appealing...'

Marcus switched off, stunned. *Mitch Hill?* What was all that about? He paced the floor and tried to make sense of what he had just heard...the body had been identified...and it wasn't that of Martin Penny, as Michael had indicated earlier. What the hell was going on?

***

'Is this the piazza?' Agnes asked.

Her eyes searched slowly over the grand façade of the

terraced house, admiring its mixture of fine balconies, green wooden shutters and decaying yellow paint wash. In the past, this would have been the home of a local merchant in the area, and was today worth a great deal of money.

She waited while Michael fumbled for the key.

He climbed the steps and entered, followed gingerly by Agnes, who checked the street before crossing the threshold. She shivered as the stale air invaded her nostrils.

Michael turned, and said quietly: 'Have a quick look around. We're not stopping. I'll get the phone and then we leave. There's nothing here for us, except a house of deception.'

Agnes took his arm. 'Michael...'

'Yes?'

'Why are we whispering?'

'I don't know,' he said guardedly.

It was that kind of place.

***

Terry had heard enough about the marital fall-out between Dougie and Sheila Cox. It was worse than a soap opera on TV. Now back in London, he sat rooted to his seat at work, trying to decipher the complex financial news that was erupting across his screen. This was a serious fall-out.

Alistair Darling had just announced the collapse of Northern Rock, after rejecting overtures from Richard Branson, who wanted to buy it at a discount. As a result of this collapse, the private shareholders had lost all the value of their shares. The taxpayer was now left carrying the can.

Terry was perplexed. This was all bollocks, in fact, financial suicide fuelled by global panic. He would lay a wager that one day in the future Branson would come back and claim his prize, and pay a much smaller premium for his troubles. *Watch this space*, Terry concluded with a wry smile.

Later, he pondered on what he had learned about Sheila Cox, the errant wife. It was the oldest story in the book. She had simply upped sticks and left for a better life...but where had she gone?

Her husband was hurt, but not baffled, by another walk out. They had been together, on and off, for over twenty-five years Terry learnt. She had several affairs ("a good looking woman," Dougie had said with pride) over the years, and had walked out on him on two previous occasions. In the past, she had gone to live with her sister in Sevenoaks when things had imploded.

An obvious choice, Terry thought. Sevenoaks was just down the road from Old Hampton. An easy refuge for a troubled mind. Is that where she had fled this time as well?

It was a resounding no, according to Dougie during their chat. He had spoken to the sister, Suzy, who confirmed that she had not heard from her on this occasion. They had argued previously, and hadn't spoken since: Sisters at war. Dougie looked for her elsewhere, but to no avail. Eventually, frustrated and desperate for a new start, he relocated to Wellington. Good riddance to her, was his final say on the matter.

Terry could see his point of view: Enough was enough. However, it was difficult to hide anywhere even in the best of circumstances...but to disappear entirely? Now that was a clever trick. Terry was far from convinced by this, unless...and the idea that swam around his head was beginning to gain momentum. *Six, not five.*

***

Michael discovered his phone on the windowsill. He checked for calls. There was one from Marcus. *Marcus?* That was unexpected. He logged it in his brain to return the call. More to the point: What was Theo playing at?

He found Agnes in the dining room, shaking dust from her shoulders.

'Well?' he said.

'Decent artwork, good bronze figurines, wonderful Asian ceramics,' she remarked, picking up a small Chinese cup of dull colour and then placing it down again. 'Whoever lived here had expensive tastes.'

'Oh...?'

'Look at this,' she continued, taking his hand and leading

him into the small library. The aroma of old leather and parchment clung in the gloomy air. On a small side table stood a small, pale green vessel, unremarkable to Michael's eye.

'Jade?' he asked, picking it up.

'Careful,' she said, 'It's from the Qianlong dynasty.'

It was barely six inches tall, plain, with loose ring handles.

'How do you know that?'

'By the curled dragon finial on the domed cover and taotie-style motifs, a really beautiful and rare piece.'

'Japanese?'

'Chinese.'

'Valuable?'

Agnes shrugged. 'To the right collector, yes. I'd say £40,000 at auction…'

'Wow.'

'Indeed. Put in down, Michael.'

Nervously, he did as instructed.

'I think we should go,' they both echoed in unison.

***

Kara answered the door, perplexed to see a young woman standing on the doorstep, a stranger to her. But she looked harmless enough, even a little pathetic.

'Yes?' Kara said, pulling a strand of hair from her face. Harvey was whimpering behind her in his cot.

'We haven't met, but I feel we should have done. My name is Gemma, your replacement…'

'Oh. This is somewhat of a surprise…'

'I wasn't sure…of what to do.'

'About the death of Ronald?'

'Just about *everything.*' She had a tear in her eye. 'May I come in, please?'

Kara settled Harvey and made a pot of tea, accompanied by a plate of biscuits.

'I'm sorry to burden you, Kara, but I feel I need to talk to someone. Michael is away…'

Kara had always imagined that she would hate Gemma, but she recognised the frailty in her and saw the bewilderment behind her eyes.

'It's been tough for everyone, Gemma,' she responded, 'but especially for you, having been thrown in the deep end. Why don't you tell me what the problem is, OK? I'm a good listener, but Harvey may not have the same patience...'

They laughed, and then Gemma talked non-stop.

At the end, Kara was sickened by what she had learned. Since resigning from the gallery she was definitely out of the loop. Who was this Theo Britton? Who was responsible for the killing of Ronald? Why was Michael so evasive, and at odds with Marcus? More importantly, was Maggie alive and seeking revenge, or was she a figment of their imagination? Who was pulling the strings that made them all dance the tune of the devil?

Then gentle Gemma dropped a bigger bombshell.

'I don't like being threatened...' she announced. 'We have a family tradition of fighting our own battles.'

Kara's ears pricked.

'I've been doing some research,' Gemma said, 'with a little help from my brothers...'

'Oh?'

'Theo Britton is in fact a petty crook. He masquerades behind a façade of being Mr Bigshot, which is a sham. His father, who is now dead, was the real brains. He ran a criminal fraternity for over thirty years which stretched from London to Glasgow. Theo inherited millions, stolen millions it has to be said. But he's spent most of it.'

'Christ,' said Kara, open-mouthed. 'How do you know this?'

'My family history,' Gemma said, biting her lip, 'my family has certain connections...'

'What kind of...connections?'

'My uncle worked with Reginald and Ronnie.'

Kara was aghast. *Not so gentle Gemma.* 'Fuck, you mean the Kray twins?'

'My Dad worked with them in the sixties too, and my brother has written a book on them. Bizarrely, he has gone on to become a criminal barrister-in-law in the city.'

'That *is* bizarre...I bet you never said any of that in your interview with Michael?'

'He never asked,' Gemma said, smiling cutely. 'Besides, it's not something you brag about, but it has its uses.'

'You need to tell Michael what you know. That little shit Theo has to be brought down a peg or two. Knowing Michael, he'll be relieved to know this information. It's a big breakthrough. You'll get a kiss from him, I bet.'

'Then he needs to be careful, I could take him to a tribunal if he tries that on.'

Kara suddenly liked this girl. She had balls.

***

Michael waited patiently, knowing he was under surveillance. He didn't like being watched from afar but he was determined to get the last laugh.

He sat in a coffee shop overlooking the Grand Canal. The call came within two hours of vacating the house. His mobile bleeped and he quickly answered.

'How did you like my little joke?' Theo asked.

'I'm ecstatic,' Michael replied. 'I thought you said the so-called hidden treasure was priceless.'

'It is, to those who treasure it, as you once did.'

'Are you and Maggie old acquaintances? Or do you do all the running around for her, like a good little boy?'

'All will be answered in the fullness of time, my friend.'

'I'm not your friend, Theo. Perhaps you can now explain what all this is about?' He kept his calm, knowing there was a further price to be paid somewhere down the line. He had also been remunerated considerably for little return so far. What was the trade-off?

'I would like you and Agnes to be my guest at a little dinner party I have especially organised in your honour. Would you humour me?'

'A dinner party…who are the other guests?'

'That will remain a surprise, Mr Strange.'

Michael looked to Agnes, who was sitting beside him and had been listening closely. She nodded.

'When and where?' he asked.

'Pier 14. Your girlfriend will be aware of its location. I have a motor launch, called *Zebra One*. Shall we say tomorrow night, around eight?'

'I'm leaving tomorrow, first thing.'

'Unwise.'

'Because..?'

'Because we have much to discuss. There is the small matter of what to do with young Marcus.'

'*Marcus*?'

'We believe he has been a very naughty boy…but we can discuss that over dinner, agreed?'

'Perfect,' Michael said, bewildered by this new development.

'Gracious of you to cooperate,' Theo said, 'or wise may be a better term.'

'Pier 14,' Michael confirmed. He nodded to Agnes, who began texting on her mobile. He added, 'Are we expected to bring anything?'

'Not a thing.'

'I didn't pack a formal dinner suit.'

'Not required. Come casual, the both of you.'

'The pleasure is all mine.'

Michael clicked off and took Agnes by the hand. *Marcus? What the fuck had he been up to? Was it just another of Theo's little games?*

'All done,' he said.

Then Agnes made a call to Adriano's brother.

Michael vaguely recalled him as the police officer who originally helped in tracking down Antonia Forlani on his last visit to Venice.

She spoke at length, and signed off: 'Ciao'.

'Theo might be equally surprised by the welcome party we have planned for him,' she said with a smirk.

CHAPTER FIFTEEN

Terry attended the MRI unit for the second time. He still hated it and was shitting himself, if the truth was known. He loathed the idea of being injected in the arm – he had a big phobia about this – then spending thirty minutes trapped in a narrow plastic tube with weird noises resounding around his head. The nurse reassured him that everything would be fine, then stuck a needle into him and strapped him to the bed, ready for the machine. This was going to be just great.

The scan lasted half an hour as promised, but felt like a lifetime. The magnitude of the whole damn cancer thing hit home, big time. He felt very much alone.

The next day he attended the hospital for an appointment with a consultant urologist, Fraser Smith, to find out the extent of the prostate problem.

'The good news,' Mr Smith said, removing his glasses after carefully reading through Terry's file, 'is that your PSA reading has increased only marginally, now up to 9.8. The scan reveals that the malignant tumour, a 3.3 carcinoma on the Gleason scale, is central to the gland, meaning, I am happy to say, that it is localised…and surgery at this stage is not required. We can therefore monitor the tumour by way of future MRI scans and regular PSA readings.'

Terry was struggling with this. He'd thought he was dying.

'Come again?' he said.

'I would recommend a watch-and-wait policy, as the cancer is not evasive to other vital organs or to your bones at this stage. This could take ten years perhaps…or even longer. Of course, you can elect to have surgery to remove the growth, or we can do a course of radiotherapy, which you can also consider, but there are side-effects with every treatment that you undertake.'

'Consider?'

'Mr Miles, if you have no other related problems, say, being unable to urinate for instance, then you actually need do nothing, except undergo regular check-ups. You'll probably live to be ninety.'

'What if the cancer suddenly grows and affects my bones?'

'Not likely for many years to come, as it is slow growing and we can watch it and measure it by means of the MRI scan. It is not aggressive...'

'Jesus...'

'He won't help you, I'm afraid. You're stuck with me, unless you wish for a second opinion, and Jesus can't help you there either. Be happy with the prognosis.'

Terry was dumbfounded, and vowed to get pissed at the nearest pub in celebration. Was this a celebration? He frowned.

'The good news, you said. What is the bad news?'

Fraser Smith gave a wry smile. 'I'm joining the club. I too have a malignant tumour. We are the same age, Mr Miles, and I thought I should practise what I preach, so I underwent tests as well. I had a biopsy.' Then he added, 'Mine is a worse prognosis, and I will be undergoing surgery within two weeks...'

Christ. This was like a sketch from a black comedy on TV, Terry thought. For the first time he was speechless.

'...So naturally I will refer you to a colleague of mine until I return to work, which hopefully will be in six to eight weeks' time.'

Terry too offered a wry smile. You couldn't make it up if you tried.

***

He had got a *Get Out of Jail* card free, and wasn't exactly complaining. He had a limited reprieve before a decision had to be made concerning the surgical removal of the prostate gland. The side-effects he didn't actually give a hoot about, because he wasn't in a relationship and wasn't likely to be either. He could live without an erection.

Back at the office, a vast open-plan modern complex displaying what looked like a thousand computer screens, numerous overhead TV monitors relaying world breaking news every second of the day and the incessant noisy gaggle of journalists interacting with each other, Terry reflected on the joy such atmosphere and intensity in this place brought to his life. He simply loved it. It was where his heart beat the fastest.

He needed to call in a favour, and spoke quietly to an informant at the local police headquarters, who had assisted him down the years with inside information whenever a news story was floundering. A wad of cash usually exchanged hands. *You scratch my back...*

Terry now considered Sheila Cox a missing person. She wasn't working, having not taken possession of her P45 from her previous employers. Her sister hadn't heard from her, and they had a close relationship, normally. Was Sheila living the life of luxury, fuelled by a rich sugar daddy somewhere in these shores? He doubted it, but it was an outside bet. According to the sister, the marriage between Dougie and Sheila was always going to be doomed: Her sister was simply bored and longed for adventure. She always talked of moving to Tenerife in the Canary Islands, having met a Spanish businessman at the Royal Oak one year, who tried to entice her away. Sheila had taken a holiday there on two occasions, without her husband.

That, thought Terry, sounded more likely...she had done a runner abroad in search of a romantic idyll. He could check that out as well, over time. But he didn't have time, as the news spread fast concerning the terrible killing of a member of staff at Churchill Fine Arts. The papers were having a field day. This put the spotlight firmly upon Michael Strange again and his deadline for the magazine piece was fast approaching. Hence, the required favour. Time was a luxury he didn't have.

He thought hard. If Sheila Cox was a peripheral figure to the main story: why this obsession in finding her? Terry now knew that, by an extraordinary coincidence, she had decided to walk out on her marriage, suitcase packed, a reserve of cash saved from money taken from the bar sales, passport in hand, on the very day the fire started at the farm. Where was she going, and with whom? Perhaps she was alone and meeting up with her lover at a secret destination. Very plausible, it happened every day in every corner of the land.

But something else happened on that fateful day, something which distracted her as she drove away for the last time...what was it? He now thought he knew.

Her car, a Vauxhall Astra, had never been found. Like her, it too had simply vanished. He needed a big favour from his contact. He therefore needed a big wad of cash.

And another thing: He could no longer pussyfoot around with other people's fragile egos. A chat with Marcus Heath was next on the agenda.

He was convinced this young man had something to hide.

***

Michael could hardly enjoy this enforced stay in Venice. The only good thing was Agnes. He felt imprisoned in a deadly game of sorts, with Theo pulling the strings. He didn't like losing control and felt vulnerable. But he had Agnes, and she was exhilaratingly wonderful, if not a little distant with him. Had she got cold feet in their new relationship? He too wondered if there was a future for them. Life was too damn complicated.

He decided to phone Marcus to get to the bottom of things, but was distracted by an incoming call. It was Nick.

'What is it, Nick?'

'Thought you should know, Michael: I was cleaning the CCTV tape, which operates on a rewind system, when it suddenly occurred to me that I have a reasonably decent image of Ms Byrne coming through reception. However, it's only a back view. Any use to you?'

'Definitely! Can you keep it for me...I'll be back within twenty-four hours.'

'Will do.'

'Thanks, Nick. Great work.'

Unexpected good news, and at last a potential sighting of Maggie. He was on to her. The net was slowly tightening. In his excitement, he forgot to ring Marcus.

***

Kara and Gemma decided to join forces, eager to find out everything they could about Theo Britton. They were a potent duo, and Kara was thrilled to be of some use in the real world again. They were, she decided with a giggle, the formidable Special Forces 'A' team: Although all this undercover skulduggery was hardly the real world, it was terrifying. Where was Mr T when you needed him?

But still, it made her feel valued, and needed. She liked Gemma, and hoped the feeling was mutual. While the gallery still remained closed to the public, pending police enquiries, Gemma called over again for a couple of hours and used Kara's apartment as a base for their secret operation, which they codenamed "The Crazy One" in reference to you know who...

Kara filled Gemma in with all the scandal from the past eighteen months. Well, nearly all the scandal. There were some things she simply couldn't reveal. But after filling her in with the exploits of Lauren O'Neill and her sister, Maggie, Gemma's face was a picture. Gape-mouthed, she couldn't think of anything to say. Her mouth just twitched stupidly.

'Still think this art lark is for you?' Kara asked.

'Any chance of a drink?' Gemma said eventually. 'Neat Bourbon would be good...'

Kara searched the drinks cabinet, found a bottle of Jack Daniels and happily obliged.

'You not joining me?'

Harvey started to cry. Great timing.

'Just water for me, I'm afraid,' Kara said sadly.

Later, she relented and had a small glass of red wine and noticed that her new best buddy was somewhat merry.

Kara laughed: They were useless detectives, it had to be said.

***

Marcus was seriously hacked off. Michael had ignored him, business on this day was non-existent and to top it all off, Kara had just informed him over the phone that her mum was on the way over to help for a few days. His silence spoke volumes. Kara picked up on his dread and reminded him that it was his idea originally to invite her over. Some ideas are just not thought through properly, he reflected quietly to himself. He was at odds with the world. Why was he the only sane voice on the planet?

And then he thought of Martin Penny, this elusive figure who for one minute was presumed dead, now assumed alive and kicking. If that was the case, and he was on their side, why had he not made contact with him or Michael, as he was expected to do? After all, wasn't he their saviour? Fuck that.

Something was wrong, very wrong.

***

It was getting dark, the light fading fast, day turning to night. Kara's mother arrived by taxi, flustered by the stop/start journey and was immediately put out by the fact her daughter had a friend over, a slightly tipsy friend at that. She didn't need the hassle.

Kara saw the disapproving frown and bundled Gemma out of the apartment, using the same taxi her mother arrived in. She made Earl Grey tea (nothing else would please her mum) and waited for the lecture on the chaotic state of her home. She tried to tidy up, but gave in without a fight, as her mother took over the task with a tut-tut here and a tut-tut there. Happy days.

The phone rang. She answered, expecting Marcus.

'It's Terry.'

'Oh.'

'I said I'd be in touch. Short notice, but can I come over? It's to do with Michael. He's in Venice and needs you to do something for him…'

'Not a good time…Why didn't Michael phone me?'

'I'll explain later.'

Kara checked the time, and rolled her eyes as she witnessed her mother attacking the almighty mess in the kitchen. She was ready to explode.

'OK, but you need to be quick.'

'I need ten minutes, that's all.'

'Ten minutes…?'

'See you shortly.'

She stood with the phone still stuck to her ear, the buzzing tone doing weird things to her brain. She seriously wanted to murder the woman at the sink.

***

Marcus made a late sale. It didn't change his general mood of foreboding. Minutes earlier, Kara phoned and asked when he would be expected home. Never, he joked, much to her annoyance. He had a legitimate reason for his remark: The fearsome dragon had taken up residence.

That wasn't all. Kara explained that Terry Miles, the journalist, had called and wanted her to help with the forthcoming story he was writing which concentrated on the fire at the farm. Michael had forewarned her of his approach. She held her breath and waited: Was he all right with this?

He was weary of such intrusions. What choice did he have? His opinion didn't seem to count these days. The story was going to be written come what may. At least Kara could put her perspective on it, but in his view all journalists were wankers anyway. He was fed up fighting the system. Kara should make her own decisions. She just had to be wary of his questions.

'Be careful,' he concluded, 'he'll be out to trick you. Think before you speak…'

He ended the call and vowed to phone Michael again and give him hell. Interfering bastard.

Then a stranger came in, a scruffy jerk in a duffle coat and corduroy slacks, carrying a holdall over his shoulder which looked like a computer bag. He instantly didn't like the look of him.

***

Michael took a call.

'Good evening, is all well with you?'

'Theo,' he hissed, 'what a pleasant surprise.'

'Indeed.'

'Is this a social call or another attempt at playing havoc at our expense with these idiotic mind games of yours?'

'Be more cordial, Michael. A speedboat will be landing at Pier 14 at seven-thirty, which according to my watch is half an hour from now. Will you be on time?'

'We will.'

'Vladimir will meet you and escort you to *Zebra One*. I can promise you a memorable evening.'

I can promise you a memorable evening as well, Michael said under his breath. Vladimir too.

'It will be good to reacquaint ourselves...' Michael remarked.

'Alas, that will not be possible on this occasion.'

'Oh?' Michael smelt a rat, but was reassured by Agnes's insistence that police surveillance was on red alert.

'I cannot join you, but my esteemed host will extend a warm welcome and provide lavish entertainment for you and your fine lady friend.'

'And who exactly is my esteemed host, Theo?'

'A mutual friend of ours and his exquisite girlfriend: Julius Gray and Antonia. They eagerly await this reunion, a chance for old friends to get together and talk over old times...'

Michael was shocked. He didn't see this one coming. Julius and Antonia? Surely not...

He then caught the fear rising in his chest.

'How are you acquainted with Julius and Antonia, Theo?'

'I'm not, but I know a person who is.'

This made the situation worse. His mouth was dry, his heart racing. 'Where are you, Theo?'

He knew the answer.

Theo laughed. 'Why, London of course.'

Another game, but the stakes were now far deadlier than he imagined.

He clicked off and immediately punched in familiar numbers with a London prefix.

***

Kara heard the doorbell and opened the door.

'Come in, Terry.'

'Can't do that, Kara.'

'I thought you wanted to talk.'

'I do, but I would prefer to discuss things in my car. It's a delicate matter. I don't want anyone overhearing our conversation and I can see you have company.'

Kara almost giggled. 'It's only my mother...' She could tell he wasn't buying into it.

He impatiently looked over his shoulder. 'My car is just parked at the front entrance...Can you spare a few seconds?'

Kara moved to the communal window and looked down.

'A red Corolla,' he said.

Sure enough, she noticed that he had parked at the head of a line of cars on the street. Three back was an unmarked police vehicle, thankfully manned by two officers on 24-hour patrol who she knew were there for her protection. Earlier in the day she had taken them coffee and cakes. She felt safe enough.

'Just a minute,' she said.

Terry smiled and shuffled his feet.

Kara looked in on her mother and Harvey, who were joyfully playing on the floor in the lounge. She grabbed a cardigan, pulled the door behind her and followed Terry to his car. She nodded to the police officers and waited while her companion politely opened her door. Ever the gentleman. She settled in and waited for a barrage of questions. Terry got in and set the heater on high, and started the engine.

'Are we going somewhere?' she asked, confused.

The beam of an oncoming car's headlamps suddenly lit up the interior where Kara sat beside the driver. Terry turned to her, engaged gear, and grinned. In the sudden flash of light, she saw an odd glint in his teeth.

'No need to panic,' the driver said calmly, and then sped away and quickly joined the flow of rush hour traffic. They were gone and out of sight in under ten seconds. Kara began to panic.

Unbeknown to her, in the kitchen of the apartment, her mobile phone bleeped, unanswered.

***

The veins on Marcus's neck bulged. His eyes widened.

'What did you just say?'

The stranger confronted him, equally transfixed by the widening eyes, aware that he had just somehow startled the young man. 'I said my name is Terry. Terry Miles. I'm a friend of Michael...'

'I know who you are...Michael has mentioned your name. Have you ID?'

The man passed him a business card and various credit cards.

Marcus looked baffled, and said: 'I can't get my head around how you can be with me when –'

His blood ran cold.

'Jesus fucking Christ!' he suddenly screamed.

The man took a step back in surprise.

Marcus fumbled in his pocket and tossed the shop keys over the counter towards the journalist, then grabbed his mobile phone and made for the door.

'My gut instinct tells me you are telling the truth...I'm out of here, lock up as you leave.'

With that, Marcus ran like the wind from his place of work. He ran blindly for all his life was worth without stopping to catch his breath.

He was on a mission.

Kara. Just what had they planned for Kara?

CHAPTER SIXTEEN

Michael and Agnes stood apprehensively on the pier. A small motor boat approached, the pilot hidden from view by the fixed canopy at the fore. Rather more unnerving, Vladimir steadied himself at the stern by way of a metal railing. The engine throttled back.

In the distance, the shimmering lights from a handsome one hundred and forty foot yacht reflected in the smooth lagoon. Vlad pointed with his finger. *Zebra One*, Michael surmised. Faint music could just be detected from the alluring vessel as it gently swayed on its anchor, its three tall masts striking majestically skyward.

Michael scanned the harbour. It was busy. Tourists ambled along, oblivious to the fact that the police were among them, lying in wait. Michael prayed that they were. He felt utterly sick in the stomach. The call from Theo disturbed him, and Kara wasn't answering her phone.

Agnes tried to calm him. Beyond the lagoon, magical under a full moon, he wondered what was in store once they reached the yacht. Would Julius really be on board? This didn't add up...

Vladimir stepped ashore and took Agnes's hand and supported her as she stepped down on the tiny deck. Michael followed, pushing the henchman's hand away forcibly. He didn't need assistance, and certainly not from a thug. Later, it would be payback time. He hadn't forgotten what happened in the alley.

The light wind caught in their hair as the small craft revved up and pulled away from Pier 14. Michael sat back and placed an arm around Agnes's shoulder as they huddled together. There was no going back on this one. Courage was the order of the day, but for Michael, a sense of terror began to strangle the very power surge he had felt earlier. He looked back toward the pier, hoping to spot another boat following at a distance. There was none. Had the police cocked up? For now, he was just one man against the odds. And he didn't like the odds one bit.

As they approached *Zebra One*, he could hear jovial voices and saw many people on the deck. It was a party of sorts. Couples were dancing.

He felt more at ease. Then his mobile bleeped.

Curiously, it was Marcus. His distant voice was straining, and difficult to grasp against the noise of the whining engine.

'Speak more slowly, Marcus...'

'I said why the fuck didn't you return my call?'

'What's the problem? You sound agitated.'

'The shit has hit the fan. Where are you?'

Michael tried to shield his phone. 'The shit...*what*? Oh, Christ, what has happened, Marcus?'

Agnes stared at him with a deep, quizzical frown. Just then the tiny boat swung to the stern of *Zebra One* and disappeared on the blind side. Michael could read the banner tied to the railings on the yacht, which announced gleefully:

"THE LOVE BOAT: HAPPY WEDDING DAY!"

Something definitely wasn't right. He could hear Marcus screaming in his ear, as he quickly realised that they were now out of sight of anyone on their tail...assuming the police boat that should be following at a safe distance was in fact there. Oh fuck.

He heard Marcus's abrupt words slam home: 'Martin Penny isn't dead...he's alive... and Kara has gone missing...I think she has been abducted. Where are you? Are you still listening to me?'

Suddenly, before he could answer Marcus, the speedboat increased power and veered away from *Zebra One*, its frothing wake cascading against the side of the steep black hull as it receded into the background. Those on board ignored the minor commotion, hell-bent on enjoying the party, blissfully dancing to the rhythmic blast from the disco music.

The line to Marcus suddenly disconnected. Michael now knew the brutal truth...*Zebra One* was a clever diversion. They were never going to step aboard... It was a decoy, intended to act as an elaborate cover to lure them into a false sense of security. *But for what dreadful purpose?*

Instinctively, Michael quickly removed the SIM card from his phone and stuck it in his jacket pocket just as Vladimir lunged menacingly forward, his immense bulk bearing down on them.

Vladimir grabbed Michael by the shoulder, yanked the now defunct phone from his grip and tossed it into the churning water. Agnes tried to intervene but was slapped down by the force of the henchman's trigger-happy backhand swipe across the face.

Michael was horrified. They were in dire trouble, trapped in a speeding boat at full throttle with a madman and heading into nothingness, the lights from the distant yacht diminishing by the second. It couldn't possibly get any worse.

Then, to his utter disbelief, a familiar hulking figure loomed into view from the cabin brandishing a shotgun. A satanic grin creased the wild-eyed face, her piercing laughter chilling the night air.

Agnes had never seen such a murderous expression. Michael had.

Maggie.

***

Marcus was in a sheer panic, unable to get his head straight. *Think, man!*

After phoning Michael, he searched the apartment for any clue which would help to find out what happened to Kara. There was nothing. She had been snatched in a second. All he knew was that she was missing, taken by a stranger. He frantically questioned Kara's mother but she was in no fit state to understand how serious this had become, attempting to calm a bawling baby at the same time as trying to make sense of why her daughter had been snatched. She kept repeating the name *Terry.*

Marcus cleared his head. Kara had been kidnapped, but by whom? It certainly wasn't Terry Miles.

Luckily, the police in the undercover vehicle saw what had

happened and recorded the registration number of the departing car. An APB had been put out over London, but Marcus knew it was a long-shot to be able to chase them down, or even find them in the rush hour. Kara had been taken and the police were powerless to act. She had simply vanished into thin air. Little Harvey cried hysterically. Kara's mum paced the floor, crying too, desperately comforting the baby in her soothing embrace and failing miserably. A woman police officer made tea as Marcus tried to fathom out what he could do next. It was mayhem.

Outside, the road was overflowing with police cars, their blue lights fracturing the blackness of the night. Uniformed officers crowded the room. Earlier, Marcus felt strong and in control…and thought he knew what he was doing. Now he was reduced to a quivering wreck. He took hold of his son and began to sob too. He felt worthless and foolish: Whatever made him believe he could somehow defeat this evil on his own?

***

Kara knelt on an oily concrete floor, frightened and cold. In the semi-darkness she could make out a single mattress next to her, covered by a thin blanket. Atop a tea chest, a mug of water was just within her reach. Her movement was restricted by her left wrist handcuffed to an old creaking radiator, which was barely lukewarm. She shivered and silently prayed for her life.

She heard footsteps and bit her lip. She was at the mercy of this madman. The door inched open. The man who called himself Terry entered the room, shining a torch in her face. Momentarily, she was blinded.

'Who are you?' Kara demanded.

'My name is Theo.'

'Well, fuck you, Theo!'

He smirked: '*That* I would enjoy…'

'I want to see my son.'

'You'll need divine intervention for that to happen.'

She wouldn't back down, defiant to the last.

'What do you want, wacko?'

'Patience, my dear. All will be revealed to you in good time…'

'I haven't done anything to you.'

'A fair point, but you need to meet with someone who does have a grievance.'

Maggie.

'Tell her to go fuck herself…'

'Oh, you can do that yourself, face to face tomorrow but unfortunately for you I won't be around to be the referee…you see, this room is soundproof and any screams will be lost to the outside world. And believe me, there will be screams, but I'll be away, attending to other business.'

'…And what business will that be?'

He laughed.

'I'll be digging a grave. You should get some sleep…it will be a long night for you.'

***

Marcus was aware of a sudden commotion at the front door. A girl burst in, shouting his name. A police woman stopped her in her tracks.

'Who the hell are you?' Marcus asked, catching sight of the intruder for the first time.

She was breathless. 'My name is Gemma. I saw Kara earlier this afternoon and we were working on something together…I have information which was important to her, so I was calling by. Then I saw the police cordon at the end of the road, and they told me what had happened. I blagged my way in…'

Marcus was bewildered. 'What information?'

'Has she been kidnapped?' the girl asked.

Marcus looked shell-shocked. 'What did you say your name was..?'

'Gemma, I work with Michael Strange.'

Not another one. 'And you've met Kara…?'

She was growing impatient: 'Yes! Has Kara been…'

He nodded in desperation. 'We believe so, by a man who called himself Terry Miles, but I know that was a lie.'

One of the policemen asked: 'What is this information you

have…?'

'This man is called Theo Britton.'

'How do you know that?' Marcus said, confused. He was joined by a detective in plain clothes.

'You need to trust me on this, Marcus,' the girl said. 'I've had a run-in with him and he's a very nasty character.'

'That doesn't make me feel better, Gemma.'

'I've been doing some research on the internet. You get nothing on Theo Britton or his associates. However, my family have ties with him. His real name is Theo Lakis, a Greek hoodlum who works mainly in the London and Birmingham areas. His father was at one time a big crime lord in the East End of the city.'

'Your family? How the hell…'

'It doesn't matter how I know…let's just say I have contacts.'

The detective smirked. 'Are you for real?'

She caught his eye. 'You'd better believe it.'

Marcus had nothing else to hold onto. He lowered his head, defeated.

Gemma pitched in, ignoring the withering looks that surrounded her.

'I've found out that Theo owns a disused lock-up warehouse at Shoreditch.'

The detective rolled his eyes. Marcus looked up and caught her gaze.

'It's called Britton House,' she said.

'That's it!' the detective shouted, grabbing for his phone and rushing for the door. Suddenly she was super-hero number one.

Marcus too rushed forward and kissed Gemma on the lips, leaving the poor girl staring into space. In a flash, he was gone too as he brushed past her and raced after the waiting police car.

He just had to believe…

***

The solitary landing light came into view, stuck on the end of an old, rickety, wooden jetty. Beyond, Michael could make out a small strip of land of some kind appearing slowly through the mist over the lagoon. A single fisherman's hut, built of stone and planks, stood as the only landmark on the island.

Vlad steered in. Maggie, shotgun in hand, yelled her orders to disembark as the tiny boat came alongside the jetty. As he did so, Michael glanced over his shoulder, searching for any activity on the water...any sign of help. There was none. They were prisoners of their own making.

Vladimir led the way over the shingle, dragging Agnes as he went. Maggie prodded Michael in the back with the barrel of the weapon, gleefully aware of her overpowering control of the situation. At the hut, Vladimir unlocked the huge padlock, flung open the rusty door and pushed his captive into the blackness. Michael followed reluctantly, after enduring a sharp crack to the spine from the gun butt. The door shut firmly behind them. In the gloom, he felt sure that they were not alone.

'Who's in here?' he asked warily, lifting Agnes to her feet.

He was met by a whimpering, frightened response.

'There are two of us – our names are Julius and Antonia. Who are you?'

'Christ,' Michael said in shock. 'Julius, it's Michael...Michael Strange!'

'My God...'

Michael suddenly felt a fumbled embrace in the black and damp air.

'How long have you been trapped here?' Michael asked.

'A few hours, hard to tell...who are you with?'

Ghostly human shapes began to materialise as their eyes adjusted in the darkness that surrounded them.

Michael spoke first. 'This is Agnes, a dear friend...she has a gallery just off St Mark's Square.'

'I know of it. Did Maggie drag you here, on the pretext of a party?' Julius asked.

'You guessed correctly, although we were duped by her accomplice, Theo, and his gorilla.'

'This is one clever trap...' Julius whispered.

'…And I don't think the planned outcome is a happy one,' Agnes said. She summed up their predicament, offering hope and despair in the same breath, adding: 'The police will be looking for us, and are probably searching *Zebra One* as we speak. However, they will be unaware at this stage that the yacht was simply a decoy.'

'They wouldn't have a clue where we have been taken,' Michael said, finishing her line of thought. Cold reality struck home. Then he thought of what Marcus had said: *Kara was missing...*

Somehow they had to find a way to escape, and fast.

'The police know of this?' Julius asked, his voice heightened in renewed optimism.

'Not exactly,' Agnes responded quickly. 'We gave them a tip-off that something was likely to happen, but…'

Her voice trailed off.

Silence prevailed, as the four of them realised the awful mess they were in. They were at the mercy of Maggie.

Antonia finally dared to speak: 'What's going to happen to us?'

No one wanted to answer her.

***

The police quietly closed in on the perimeter fence which surrounded the warehouse, one of a dozen run-down buildings on an industrial estate near Shoreditch. They manoeuvered stealthily and silently until the place was under total surveillance. Snipers hid on the flat roof opposite the main entrance to the building which, they believed, held captive the woman named Kara Scott. What was unknown, and caused the biggest concern, was just who else was in there with her and what firearms they possessed.

The police operation so far was quick, slick and deadly in its intent.

For the first time, Marcus felt a sense of hope.

***

At the perimeter fence, a tramp wrapped in a filthy blanket dozed, mumbling and cursing to himself in the cold. Without warning, he was kicked awake.

To his astonishment, he was confronted by a uniformed officer, covered head to foot in black camouflage with his face masked, brandishing a short muzzle machine-gun. The order was specific: scarper in double quick time.

He did, without protest. But his astonishment was merely a pretence.

If the officer had engaged in him in conversation, he would no doubt have been surprised by the expensive diamond lodged in the tramp's perfect set of white teeth. But no one cared about this seemingly bedraggled man…he was but a small distraction in the great scheme of things. They were after bigger fish. He was just one of life's losers.

***

Michael frantically searched for a weapon, but he was quickly disappointed.

'I have this,' Julius volunteered, holding up a rope in the gloom.

'That'll do, Michael said. 'We need to get them to open the door, and entice them in.'

'One of us can pretend to be ill,' Antonia suggested, raising all their spirits for a few fleeting moments.

'I'll do it,' Agnes said, 'I can scream with the best of them. I always fancied myself as an actress…'

'We'll take them by surprise, as it is very dark and our movements are not easy to detect,' Michael added.

'It's all we have,' Julius said weakly.

***

The signal came, deadly and silent. The storming of the warehouse by the police began as the armed teams moved in, smashing down the steel doors with force and speed, with the intent of bewildering Kara's abductors and causing chaos as smoke bombs filled the air.

The operation lasted less than sixty seconds. There was no

resistance. They soon discovered the captive alone and hysterical, chained like a dog to a radiator in a darkened locked room at the rear of the building. There was no guard, long gone no doubt. Had there been a tip-off?

Moments later, having been given the all clear, Marcus raced across the car park and into Kara's trembling embrace. Wrapped in a silver security blanket, she sobbed and held him tight. Both knew that she was lucky to escape with her life. The thought of what might have happened made them hold on to each other and shudder. Gemma had saved Kara's life, Marcus was sure of that.

'You're safe now,' he murmured.

'Take me home…please.'

A waiting police car whisked them away from the site.

Marcus thought of Theo, her captor. He was still free, and holed up with Maggie no doubt. They would not stop their vicious witch hunt…this was only the beginning unless he could halt this nightmare once and for all. They were relentless in this warfare they conducted against them. He would never beat them. Perhaps it was time to come clean. But how could he explain to Kara the lie he was living?

They weren't safe, as he had pretended moments earlier, but he had to make her believe the impossible.

Where was Martin Penny when he needed him?

***

Out of sight and long gone, Theo found his car, discarded the blanket, dirty overcoat and scarf on the back seat and took stock of the situation. He'd had a lucky getaway and he cursed how quickly the police armed unit had found Kara. How was that possible? Who could have known of the disused warehouse? He had been rumbled. Thankfully, he had the foresight to watch over the warehouse from afar and in disguise, knowing this was an easier escape route if everything went pear-shaped. Better that than be stuck in the building. He was proved right. Smart bugger, he thought smugly. He would find out later who snitched on him. The plan had misfired, and now he was standing alone taking stock. Vladimir was with Maggie in Venice. He was supposed to look after things here, holding Kara captive until their victorious return. Then Kara's fate would be decided. Now his fate was in the balance. Where was plan B?

Sweat poured down his face. He had to get away and regroup and await the wrath of Maggie later. She would be furious. And how would he deal with the *other*...?

He suddenly became aware of someone standing behind him. He turned slowly, pissed off that his henchman wasn't there to protect him. What else could go wrong?

Now he knew the answer.

The stranger stood so close that his breath cooled the sweat on his skin, and Theo instinctively knew he wasn't in a good place. This man stared with cold hard eyes: killer eyes. He was built like a soldier, his shaven head glistening under the moonlight.

Theo tried to speak but his futile utterings turned to a pitiful squeal. The final breath from his body was removed expertly as the unknown man quietly and methodically tightened a massive grip around his throat. His feet involuntarily began to kick. His brain was shutting down.

'This is for Mitch,' he heard the man say.

Theo's eyes began to bulge. A red mist descended as hundreds of blood vessels began to pop and cloud his vision. *Who the bollocks was..?* He was sinking fast, kicking wildly. Then his arms and legs lost their strength, his hands and feet twitching. He exhaled for the last time. His body went limp. Then pitch black overcame him.

***

The plan was simple...and all they had at their disposal. Fuck this up and they were all dead, Michael was convinced of it.

At the count of three, Agnes began to wail, her voice intensifying as the seconds ticked down. Antonia banged on the door, shouting for help. Either side of her, the two men crouched with the rope lying loosely across the threshold, but tucked back and hidden against the lowest of the three steps that led down into the hut. The trap was laid.

They waited for a response. Nothing. Michael left his position and banged frantically on the door as well.

'We need assistance!' he shouted.

Agnes screamed again. Even Michael was convinced by her performance.

'A woman is pregnant and needs medical help...can you hear me Maggie?'

Still nothing.

'Vladimir, are you there?'

They each held their breath.

'Have pity!' Michael implored. 'Agnes is not part of this, Maggie. You have no business to hurt her...you have me, surely that's enough!'

They waited and then Michael signalled to Agnes to intensify the drama.

This time her scream echoed around the hut, forcing Antonia to cover her ears. It was the last chance saloon.

It wasn't working.

'I'll offer them the paintings,' Julius said.

'What paintings?' Michael asked, but then he understood. It was the only currency they had to trade with.

Julius made his offer repeatedly and waited. He thought he detected a shuffling outside the door and grabbed Michael by the arm. He listened too and silently resumed his position holding tight the rope.

The door unbolted and creaked inward, a tiny shaft of light penetrating the gloom.

'Get back and shut that woman up,' Vladimir instructed, 'there is a fishing boat nearby. Keep her quiet, or I'll do it for you!'

Agnes cranked up the distress by whimpering and huddling in a corner but Vlad wasn't buying it.

'This woman needs help urgently,' Antonia pleaded, stooping beside her stricken body. The door widened.

'Where are the remaining paintings kept?' Vlad demanded.

'I can show you,' Julius said, gaining precious seconds.

Michael took a chance and left his position, knowing that if he spoke out his voice would betray his stance close to the door. A dead giveaway of a planned counter attack for sure, and then their game would be up if the Russian cottoned onto it. The fishing boat was their salvation. Nothing would happen while it sailed close by.

He could hear a muffled discussion from outside. Come on, come on...

Shit! The door started to close. The ploy had failed.

'Maggie!' Julius screamed. 'I can give you the paintings...''

The door held its position. Michael stared at Julius, who murmured:

'You win, Maggie...just let us go.'

Gradually, the door began to reopen.

It was Vlad who spoke: 'Come out, but just you. The rest stay put.'

Michael sensed a trick. He waved his finger at Julius. Sweat trickled down his neck.

'No deal,' Michael shouted. *This was the moment.*

He then slid across the stone floor, smoothly regaining the rope in his grip. It was up to Agnes to play her role again.

She groaned convincingly as the door opened further and Vladimir moved onto the first step.

'All of you, stand at the rear so the woman can come forward,' he barked. 'Julius can follow after...'

Michael knew the henchman's eyes would adjust to the darkness in a few seconds. His heart pounded. Hold steady, Julius. Just one more step...

'We need help to lift her,' Antonia pleaded. 'My boyfriend has hurt his arm and Agnes cannot stand...I'm afraid for her life and that of her baby if she doesn't get to a hospital soon.'

Michael assumed that Vlad didn't give a stuff for any of them but the fishing boat could potentially be alerted to the plight of the captives with another scream and somehow Julius's words had worked their trick on the kidnappers.

'I'm armed,' Vladimir said, his warning a veiled threat. 'Get her to the door and I'll lift her through...'

Christ, he stepped down! Michael could see the glint of his pistol and the profile of his ugly mug as he dropped down into the hut just inches away. Instinctively, he and Julius yanked violently on the rope so that it lifted behind Vladimir's knees. Before he could react, they both snapped the line forward, which brought his legs up from the floor. He tumbled backwards with a clipped curse – and then silence as his head crashed against the concrete step. He was out cold.

There was a delayed reaction from all of them, then a collective gasp, followed by utter mayhem.

Michael grabbed the gun, kicked out at the stricken figure to make sure he was unconscious and then braced himself against the wall for added protection for fear of Maggie being alerted. Julius in turn grabbed both women and brought them to his side out of harm's way. There was still the small matter of one fucked-up crazy mamma with a loaded shotgun waiting for them...

The noise was deafening as the gunshot exploded into the hut, followed by a blinding flash which lit up the entire universe, it seemed. Splinters of wood and chunks of stone flew out from the back wall as the missile made impact. Julius was caught on the arm and face as he shielded the women. He could feel blood slowly dripping from several shrapnel wounds to his body.

Clearly the fishing boat had disappeared from view, Michael deduced. He knew Maggie couldn't care who heard them now. She was beyond reason. She always had been. Crazy cow. It was the mad hatter's tea party.

'Everyone OK?' Michael asked, regaining his composure. His ears were ringing from the blast.

'OK,' Julius said unconvincingly.

Then it was Maggie's turn to join in.

'Be a good thing if you could step outside, Michael.'

Her voice sent a chill through his bones. He had been in a similar situation at the farm. He weighed up his options. He had a small handgun, she possessed a mighty shotgun. He had nowhere to run, she stood above him with a full view of his only escape route. Not good.

'Do you want me to come and get you?' she hollered. 'Or shall I simply burn you all to hell, which is my preferred choice?'

Through the crack in the door, Michael could detect the outline of bales of straw jammed up against the side of the hut. She wasn't kidding. They were in massive trouble, and alone and isolated. Hadn't the police heard the gunshot? Where the fuck were they?

Somehow he had to gain the upper hand, but how? It would be impossible to entice her in, as she was aware of Vlad's fate. If they stayed in the hut for much longer, they ran the risk of her setting fire to the straw. The police were hopefully coming...but when? Michael was sure that her beef was with him, and him alone. Why the need to kill all of them? Then he recalled Julius's odd reference to the paintings... what was that about? They must have had a deal, which he had reneged on. That's why they too were held captive. What was the motive? Why did Maggie have such a thirst for revenge? His mind buzzed. Then he had a masterstroke of a thought.

Had she reloaded? So far she had fired off one round. If he could get her to shoot again then her gun would be empty, giving him the opportunity to fight back on his terms. But had she reloaded? Not likely, he guessed. This was lunacy – but he had to find out the hard way...

He signalled silently for Julius to help lift Vladimir up so that he was in a sitting position propped up against the wall. He was still unconscious, perhaps dead, Michael didn't care. Between them, they lifted him just enough so that Michael could prop the body over his shoulder. It was an immense weight to support, and he could feel the sweat on his skin from the exertion. He was panting like an animal. This had better work...

He gave Julius the gun and whispered his instructions on the count of three. His life flashed before him, but the thought of Kara's fate gave him the strength of will to try anything.

One, two, three.

Julius fired two shots into the air as Michael shouted, 'I'm coming out, Maggie. See you in hell!'

Julius fired again and with one massive heave Michael lifted Vladimir upright and propelled him through the door. The sudden movement just after the shots from Julius had the desired effect. Maggie panicked.

A huge boom filled the night as a flash and then gunshot pellets peppered Vladimir's body, sending him spiralling to the earth. Michael grabbed the pistol from Julius and ran up the steps, hurtling over the lifeless bloody form of his captor and, in a swirl of choking smoke from the shotgun's blast, searched for the elusive Maggie. He heard retreating footsteps. Beyond, he could see her at the speedboat, untying the mooring rope. She looked back and grinned in his direction. Michael charged over the damp grass and onto the jetty as she jumped down and started the engine. Within a second, the motors roared into life and the boat lurched forward with a spray of foam flying into the air behind it. Michael leapt forward in the knowledge that it was now or never. This deranged monster was not getting away. It would be over his dead body.

He crashed down on the tiny deck and rolled over to protect his fall. He tried to stand but Maggie twisted the wheel and sent the boat into a series of turns. He fell and slammed his shoulder into the sidewall and dropped his gun. He watched in horror as it slid toward her.

She laughed hysterically and made a grab for it. The boat zigzagged crazily, its speed at full throttle as it skimmed the black waters. In the distance, Michael could see the lights from the shoreline. They were heading back to the mainland. And fast.

Maggie raised her arm and pointed the gun at his head.

'Time to meet your maker!' she shouted.

He spread his legs to gain balance. Anchored boats were coming into view at an alarming rate. They were out of control in the little boat and Maggie, he knew, was out of her mind. He was a dead man if she pulled the trigger – and she wasn't going to miss from that range.

What he wanted was precious seconds as he frantically mapped the path of the speeding boat and calculated his only possible escape route. He grabbed the handrail. *Think.* Then he prepared his risky exit. It was preferable to a hail of bullets and the watery grave that was about to come his way.

'Maggie! Maggie!' he screamed back, counting down the seconds in his head. *Think .Think.* 'You won't get away with this…the police are after you.'

'Die, you fucker…' she said coldly, and then her grin disappeared as her eyes turned to cold steel. She was about to pull the trigger in another second. The boat tilted.

'You can't kill us all. Too many people know your game.'

She laughed insanely. 'By morning you'll all be dead…including that bitch Kara. We have something special planned just for her… and that boyfriend thief, the self-righteous little prick. As for you, I should have finished you in the barn. You're a cat with nine lives. You won't get another chance.'

The boat veered the other way. He saw the massive steel hull of a dredger loom into view ahead of them. This was it. *Now.*

Michael turned and dived headlong into the churning sea as the gunshots flew past his head and into the black depths beyond. He hit the icy water and sank fast. His lungs fought desperately for air. He kicked and swam upwards toward the surface. Just as he raised his head above the waves, he watched as the boat slammed into the stern of the dredger and exploded into a fierce ball of orange and white light. The tiny speed boat fragmented into a million shards of burning splinters. Maggie disintegrated in that same moment. A black oily plume shot skyward, choking the night air. Flaming wreckage floated on the lagoon. Above, red-hot debris slowly cascaded down like red rain, leaving vapour trails in the sky. No one could survive that, Michael knew.

Exhausted and cold, he trod water and tried to stay afloat in the choppy waves, his brain a whirl of confusion. Did he hear her right? *A thief..?* What was that supposed to mean? In the distance, he could just make out the flashing blue lights of a patrol boat skimming into view. This hell – his hell – was finally over.

He closed his eyes and imagined how death must feel, and how calm it would be... and when he finally opened them he felt his aching body being lifted forcibly by willing hands into a waiting boat.

He'd thought he was a goner...but today was not his day to die.

CHAPTER SEVENTEEN

The debriefing at the police headquarters in Venice took four hours before Michael was finally released. He was utterly spent from the incessant questioning about how two people were found dead, in suspicious circumstances, without explanation. How could he get out of this one? He urgently needed to see Agnes, who had been rescued earlier with Julius and Antonia when he guided the police boat back to the island to pick them up. For the time being they were being interrogated separately, Antonia was in hospital suffering from shock. He knew the feeling. He was also frantic. He needed to get back to London and find out what had happened to Kara and Martin Penny. Marcus sounded hysterical. He hoped Agnes had smoothed things over with the authorities. If not, he was in deep shit.

Later, he found her in the corridor, sipping coffee. He froze. She was not alone. Next to her was her estranged husband. It was a difficult moment. What could he say? How could he explain himself? He was a foreigner in a strange land.

She did the talking. Slowly, she lifted herself from her chair and faced him. The saddened eyes betrayed her. He knew what was coming.

'Go home, Michael. We somehow escaped... Now we need to survive. I have a husband to look after...'

She slowly turned and smiled faintly at Adriano. He stared past her and caught Michael's awkward gaze, then ambled out into the street and lit a cigarette, looking lost and bewildered. Had Agnes told him of their affair?

Michael too felt bewildered, and ashamed of his conduct.

'I'm sorry,' was all he could muster.

Agnes stroked his battered face. 'It's over for us, can you understand that, Michael? If anything has come out of all this, it is that I have found my family again. Will you forgive me?'

He nodded. He knew she was right. Their worlds collided for a brief, beautiful moment, but this was her life, right here, and he had no desire to invade it still further and take what wasn't his. If only...

Michael took her hand and squeezed it. A tear crawled down her cheek. There were no further words to be said. He moved past her and walked into the sunlight and felt the warmth on his face. Adriano turned away from him, without acknowledgement. Across the promenade he saw Julius sitting in a café. He wanted to reach out to him, offer comfort, tell him what it all meant. He could not. They knew the truth, the lies, the betrayal and the greed... and the intolerable burden of guilt they all shared. Now it was over. Maggie was dead. They were free at last, and anything that he dared impart on these poor souls was another cross to bear. The ghosts were buried. It was over at long last for each of them. Once again, he walked away alone, as it had always been for him. He had no more argument in him. He was going home. Julius caught his eye. Momentarily they shared a fleeting recognition of what they had endured. But there was something else too...perhaps bafflement, or maybe a little gratitude? Contempt. That was probably it.

He was surprised to see Julius amble over, his right arm in a sling, a bandage on his forehead. They were lucky to be alive.

'How is Antonia?' Michael asked.

'They'll keep her in hospital overnight, but she'll be fine.'

He had to say it: 'Now that we know Lauren died in the fire, you can close the book at long last. Laburnum Farm is rightfully yours. Will you sell it?'

'I guess. We certainly don't intend to live in it.'

'That's understandable. It might be difficult to market, given the tragic circumstances of what happened there.'

'We'll sell at a massive discount. It's still a desirable area...'

Michael pondered. 'What will happen to the twelve paintings by Patrick Porter?'

'Thought you'd never ask,' Julius said sheepishly. He shoved his left hand into his jeans pocket. 'There aren't twelve paintings anymore.'

'I thought they were in storage?'

'I have a legal claim, I also have the key to gain access to them.' Julius shrugged. 'I needed to live...'

'So you sold them?'

'Not all. I managed to secretly off-load three cheaply which kept us afloat, bearing in mind that it could have taken up to seven years to lay claim to the estate. We were broke. I then disposed of another three when my girlfriend and our daughter were threatened if we didn't comply...'

'By Maggie? She wanted the paintings?'

'Yes. The threat came from our friend Theo. He was the go-between who bought the first paintings. It was only later that I made the connection with Maggie. She too needed money. She was on the run. That can be costly, so she came a' calling using Theo as her front man and I was happy to sell to him.'

'That's why you mentioned the paintings in the hut.'

'I had refused her the remainder of the paintings, and so she threatened to kidnap us. She was desperate for cash as she was about to have cosmetic surgery to alter her looks. We felt pressured and I knew what she was capable of . However, there was a problem...'

'Oh?'

'There were only eleven paintings in storage, and she accused me of holding back on her. That's when she came to England, in search of revenge for the missing picture. Somehow, she fathomed out that someone else had taken it...before they went into safe-keeping. I knew nothing of this. Maggie was greedy, as if there was another driving force behind this quest, but I never got to the bottom of it. Perhaps we never will now...'

Michael was startled by this story. *The thief.* His brain began to turn cogs, slowly. 'Perhaps we never will,' he repeated.

Then Julius looked away for the last time.

***

Michael packed his things at the hotel and headed for the airport, where he bought a new mobile from a kiosk and inserted his old SIM card. Thankfully, although the police investigation was ongoing, he was free to go home, courtesy of Agnes who had managed to smooth his departure by way of her brother's help in the force. Michael had to sign the necessary paperwork to agree to return to Venice if further testimony was required. At the debriefing he learnt that Maggie had lured them to the fishermen's hut with the intention of burning it down with all of them inside. She had constructed a bonfire of hay bales around the perimeter and as a diversion, she and Vladimir were going to send up a huge display of fireworks. No one would have been bothered about a simple bonfire on a faraway island. It would have been just entertainment for the passing boats.

He killed time and bought a paperback by John Grisham and some mints and headed for the coffee bar. Out of the blue, Agnes phoned him at the departure terminal just as his flight was called. She wept... wept for forgiveness, and for the second chance she had been given with her family. She wept too for the end of their affair. He knew she had made the right decision, and was grateful that it was she who had the final courage to finish things. He, on the other hand, would have let things linger on...and caused even more damage.

'Ciao,' she said quietly. Then he was left holding the phone, with dreams of what might have been. Everything was a fucking mess. A fucking car crash of sorts, largely of his making. He was instrumental in all manner of destruction and death. The only redeeming feature was that Kara was now safe. Earlier, after activating his phone, he had spoken to Marcus...rather, he listened silently as Marcus tore into him with a tirade of non-stop abuse, with a final warning to keep out of their lives, once and for all. How many times had he heard that? This time he took it to heart. He got the gist of the story which was blunt enough for him: Kara was in safe hands again. In other words, butt out.

He was shocked to then discover a text message from Martin Penny. It read:

I'm back from the dead. Good work on Maggie. Theo is now otherwise detained. Permanently. MP

Michael almost laughed: *Permanently?* He took this to read dead. Just like Maggie. It had a good ring to it. It was great having Martin alive and kicking once more.

He stood in the queue as the flight boarded and let his mind wander. Beyond the torment of losing Agnes, he was privately pleased for himself in a smug way.

He always had an angle to follow.

This was it. He had decided, in a moment of madness, to make it up to her in a manner that was both bizarre and daring, as only he would think appropriate. After he had checked out of the hotel early, he vowed to do one last thing before catching his flight to London. He had the time and inclination. It would take just a half an hour for what he wanted to do, then he was gone from this country once and for all, he hoped. He decided to take a walk . He had a job to do.

Sure enough, within the allotted time he completed his task and edged back alongside one of the narrow canals. He smiled, his overnight holdall heavier for the return journey than it was for the trip out. Usually this bag was just hand luggage for the flight (thus avoiding the queue at the check-out desk) but on this occasion it would go in the hold for added security. He didn't want to attract customs. He found a local shop and bought a padlock, secured the bag and carried on with his solitary walk just like any other tourist. Then he stopped, glanced first to his left then to his right as his free hand tossed a set of keys (belonging to a certain house) into the murky water. He smiled as they sank without trace.

He was quite positive that Theo Britton wouldn't be in need of them again. He had a strong feeling about that.

Then he took a taxi to the airport. Job done.

***

The funeral of Ronald Frederick Wilson took place the following day. He was buried at Chiswick cemetery on a beautiful sunny morning, surrounded by all the friends who loved and cherished him. The chief mourners comprised, unsurprisingly, a group of over forty male friends and colleagues who gathered to show their respects, with just

Kara, Gemma and Adele in attendance to break the gender ranks. His partner, Ronnie, led the service with great dignity. Michael read an effecting eulogy, reflecting on Ronald's unswerving loyalty and professionalism to the gallery. The manner of his death was not spoken of, pending the police investigation which was still ongoing into his mysterious murder. An elite group now suspected the identity of the killer but her name was not mentioned. It still remained a strained situation, given that everyone was sidestepping recent history to avoid confrontation and accusations. Marcus wasn't talking to Michael, he in turn was avoiding Marcus, with piggy in the middle Kara trying to keep the peace between them. Toby was angry with his father. Adele posed in delicate fashion, ignoring Michael and Kara, looking as usual the perfect victim for everyone to identify with. She wept, but they were cold, uncaring tears.

After the service, Toby took charge of events, ushering those present to a nearby hotel for the customary wake.

Beside the grave, Michael stood next to Kara as the mourners gradually dispersed, leaving them alone for a short respite. Marcus was fast approaching, looking for a fight.

'You OK?' Michael whispered to her.

She smiled and nodded. 'We'll talk privately…but another time, eh?' she managed to say before Marcus took her arm and marched her away to where her mother stood patiently cradling their baby.

Terry then sidled over.

'We need a stiff drink…and a serious chat,' he said.

Michael caught his eye and vowed to down a bottle or two, such was his sadness, pain and confusion as to why Ronald had to sacrifice his life for nothing. After all, what did Maggie have against him…this noble and innocent man? It made him question her intended motives, the sickness in her mind… Did she think he had the missing painting?

He suddenly looked beyond Terry and caught sight of a man standing beside the church steps, in the shadow of the Norman tower.

'We have a problem,' Terry said, but he knew his friend wasn't listening. He let it go for now. 'You look like shit,' Terry added, following Michael's gaze. He didn't recognise the stranger and had to ask: 'Do you know him?'

'Feel like shit too,' Michael replied. He patted his old friend on the shoulder. 'We'll talk soon enough.' Then he made for the church entrance and stopped to greet the man.

'So glad to see you in one piece,' Michael said.

'I could say the same thing,' Martin Penny remarked.

They shook hands and began a slow walk through the cemetery.

Michael spoke first.

'After you disappeared off the radar I thought it was your body pulled from the Thames.'

'He was a close colleague of mine, who was working undercover for me. I was on to Maggie and she knew I was on to her, but she hadn't seen me up close and personal. We were following her. Mitch had the idea to swap characters, including our clothes. We were the same build. That way I kept my identity secret, which allowed me to eventually latch on to Theo and track down Kara to the warehouse. I thought I had them exactly where I wanted...all under one roof. Then the police turned up in force and spoiled the party, much to my surprise. I had my day though.'

'I saw the headline about a man found strangled on wasteland, near the kidnapping site. Theo had it coming; he was a nasty piece of work.'

'I had proximity and chance...'

'Story of our lives.'

'Take the opportunity when it presents itself,' Martin stated with obvious relish.

'I was shocked when I found the Happy Birthday badge in her apartment...she left it as a trophy for me to find, as a warning of her power over me. If she could dispose of you, she could dispose of anyone. I naturally thought you were dead.'

'Mitch paid the price, but it gave me a chance to find out who she was colluding with...one Theo Britton, a two-bit hoodlum with delusions of grandeur. Maggie had recruited him and they concocted the story of his inherited wealth, which was partly true, knowing it would suck you in and get you out of London. In truth, the criminal activities of the family were diminishing. They no longer had control over rival gangs, and their wealth was evaporating as well. Theo saw a way of making up his losses by stealing the last of the paintings by Patrick Porter from Julius and then sharing the profits with Maggie.'

Michael cut in. 'And Julius wasn't playing hardball anymore?'

'They pushed him too far. Theo was the go-between and eventually threatened to kill Antonia and her daughter if Julius didn't comply with their demands. Julius had little choice but to do as he was instructed. The house in Venice did actually belong to Theo's aging father, who had died the previous year, but had massive structural problems and would need to be sold at a big discount, which meant he would still be in debt. He certainly couldn't afford the repairs. He owed a lot of money to a lot of people, and the paintings would have realised perhaps a million pounds or more...but then you knew that part already, I gather. He needed to settle debts fast and the house wasn't the answer to his prayers. The paintings were...and he and Maggie wouldn't take no for an answer.'

Michael knew that Martin was referring to his own spurious claim on the paintings when Lauren was alive, but he brushed it aside. Everyone knew about the business of others, it seemed. He deflected his guilt. 'Julius told me about the threats, but he's now free to claim his estate. There is no one to challenge him again...it's all over, thank God. I'm tired.' Michael shook his head. 'I was dumbfounded to discover that Maggie was living directly above me...'

Martin took up the story. 'At first Theo and Maggie operated from a dingy flat above an Irish pub in Bermondsey, but later, by chance, discovered the apartment above you was empty and available to lease on a short-term let. It was too good an opportunity to miss, and allowed them to spy on you. I believe he rented it, paid the deposit in cash and Maggie moved in under an assumed name: Ms Byrne seems appropriate in hindsight, don't you think? It was the perfect bolt-hole. That way they could monitor your every movement, first with a hidden camera and later by bugging your phone. They soon legged it when you got wind of what they were up to...'

'Theo got me to Venice on the pretext of a mysterious and valuable painting which I was asked to value and sell for a fat commission. I foolishly fell for the hoax.'

'And when you first failed to go over to Venice they had to change tack, and used Agnes as the bait.'

'I was blinded by greed at first and saw a way to make serious money, but changed my mind. Then I wanted to protect Agnes…they were clever and knew I would respond.'

'They had planned to separate you and Kara so that Maggie could deal with each of you in turn. Theo kidnapped Kara but he was unaware that I was still alive and on his trail. When you left for Italy I needed to keep under the radar so I elected to protect Kara and Marcus as a priority, as you had instructed at our first meeting. Good job I did.'

'I'm very grateful…But why did Maggie want to kidnap Kara?'

'One of the paintings from the collection at Laburnum Farm was missing. Maggie was convinced that Kara had it, and was going to sell privately to the highest bidder. She wanted it back.'

'I don't buy into that…'

'Someone has it. Could it have been Ronald?'

'No. If a painting by Patrick Porter had come onto the market I would have known about it. Besides, only three people had access to the…'

Then he stopped.

'Go on,' Martin said. He was on a short fuse.

'I need to think about this,' Michael replied clumsily. A warning light flashed in his head.

'Well, don't take too long about it. People have died, including a great pal of mine. Your gratitude has a hollow sound, Michael. You've been a complete arsehole in this whole business, a loose cannon, and I nearly paid with my life as well. You tried to take the law into your own hands. Not for the first time, I should emphasise. I left you alone and reasoned that you could sort your own bloody mess out. Remember, I had your money but loyalty to the cause only stretches so far….'

Michael glued on a wry smile. 'Don't hold back. And thanks…for nothing.'

'I helped save Kara's life. You owe Marcus too.'

'I made mistakes. You and Marcus saved Kara, I know. And I hear that gentle Gemma has a story to tell as well. I underestimated her. Now it's all over, thankfully.'

'Is it?'

'What do you mean by that?'

'Maggie didn't kill Ronald Wilson.'

'Then surely Theo or Vladimir...

'At the time of his death, Maggie was being trailed closely by me and Theo was in Venice. Only later did they swap places. I elected to remain here and tag Theo. I left you to deal with Maggie...wasn't I kind? I cannot be sure of his henchman's whereabouts at the time but I assumed he was with Maggie in Venice, which indeed proved the case. Besides, the style of murder was not from his hand.'

Michael's blood ran cold as he muttered the dreaded word: 'Meaning?'

'You tell me.'

'Ronald didn't have enemies...'

'No, he didn't.'

'But I do, is that what you are saying?'

'The killing of Ronald was a marker put down by someone with a grudge against you. I think someone is trying to destroy not only your life but your business as well. They want to bring you down, and all those associated with you. This is clearly someone with an obsession bordering on insanity.'

'Maggie is dead.'

'I'm not talking about her. Who else do you know who has the heart of the devil? Because that's who you are fighting against...'

'Maggie is dead,' Michael repeated. Then the image of Adele imprinted itself on his brain. *The heart of the devil*... But he refrained from mentioning her name out loud. She was a vengeful cow. He was suddenly angry and swore to take the law into his own hands...again. Would he ever learn? He faced Martin again. 'We can recover from this, starting from now.'

'My job is done, Michael. Be warned though. I wish you good luck for the future.'

Then Martin Penny turned and walked from his life.

***

The following days passed in a fog. Michael was perturbed to discover that Nick, the concierge at his block of flats, was off sick indefinitely. He had been replaced by an elderly man called Cyril, who didn't know when Nick would be back on duty.

Michael wanted to see the CCTV loop which Nick had told him about. It would have to wait. Dear old Cyril couldn't even work the telephone entry system. Happy days…

Toby took charge of the gallery and reopened to the public after the police agreed to his request. It was no longer a crime scene. Gemma reluctantly returned and gradually the routine of a working day resumed. An advert in the window for an experienced salesman was a poignant reminder of the sad loss of Ronald.

Michael took a few days off to recover from his ordeal at the hands of Maggie. On the third day he contacted Kara by phone and they agreed to meet secretly in the afternoon at Hyde Park, near the Serpentine. It was a breezy day, low cloud matching their mood. Michael saw Kara pushing her pram beside the lake, a proud woman stopping to feed the geese like a hundred other mothers do on the same mission with their excited children. He felt awkward approaching her but was happy to find her doing normal everyday things once again, without any fear hanging over her head.

She smiled broadly as he reached her, flinging her arms around his shoulders. He hugged her tightly, kissing her on the cheek. They didn't talk for a few moments, just prolonging the embrace. Then they walked on, Michael tossing bread to the gathering wildlife. There was a chill in the air, matched by their conversation.

'You all right?' Kara asked.

'Better for seeing you.'

'Who was that you were talking to at the funeral?'

'At the end of the service?'

'Yes. He looked intimidating.'

'He was your protector, actually. His name is Martin.'

'He looked familiar…thought I saw him outside the apartment at night. Is he still protecting me?'

'Not any longer. It isn't necessary.'

'Are you sure of that?'

'As sure as can be…'

'You know, I've always had trust in you but this stretches credibility to the limit, Michael. I want to believe but I'm frankly fearful…'

'Maggie is dead.'

'And this man named Theo?'

'Taken care of.'

'Michael, stop talking in riddles! He took me prisoner, I have a right to know if we are safe. I have my family to protect.'

'Martin is ex-SAS. We can rely on his judgment, Kara. Theo will not be troubling us again.'

'Then why am I still scared?'

Michael was taken aback by this. 'Because…because it is still all so raw and numbing. You went to hell and back.'

'So did you. Aren't you still scared?'

'Only from what the Press can do to us, Kara,' Michael said, a tone of defeat in his voice. 'Now that does terrify me.'

They ambled further toward Marble Arch. A string of thoroughbred horses cantered past, their straight-backed riders resplendent in military uniform. A gaggle of geese took flight across the grey, calm water, which rippled in their foaming wake.

'Marcus hates you.,' Kara announced.

Michael wasn't surprised by this. 'He'll get over it,' he said.

'He blames you for everything.'

'Great.'

'Give it time, I'm confident he'll come round…eventually.'

'Better make that sooner rather than later. The international art gala is on in three weeks' time. I've booked a table for ten and you are both invited. I want you to be there, Kara. It's our chance to unwind and celebrate a new beginning. I've had a surprise email from Julius. He and Antonia have decided to attend as my guests. It's a big gesture from them. I think they are coming over anyway to sort out the legalities with the farm. We can draw a line under all the shit that has happened.'

'Sounds OK to me…let me work on Marcus, but I doubt he'll come. I need to get organised. I feel a shopping spree coming on. What's the theme this year?'

He hardly dared mention it: 'A Venetian mystery night, masks and all.' He caught the expression on her face.

'Oh, boy, you certainly know how to pick them,' she remarked, shaking her head in bewilderment.

***

'Is that finally the end of it?' Toby demanded.

Michael faced his son across the desk in his office at the gallery. He was stone-faced and tired by this continued barrage of questioning. What could he offer in terms of further reassurance? More futile words?

'Don't bullshit me, Dad. The gallery can't survive on bad publicity, especially in the midst of a recession. I've put considerable money into the business and I cannot afford to lose my investment. If I had known the truth…'

'…You'd have stayed in New York. I get where you are coming from.'

'I'm not sure you understand the gravity of the situation.'

'Michael stood. 'Don't try to lecture me, son.'

'Well, don't try and patronise me. We were just beginning to turn the corner financially. I saved the gallery, remember? I paid off mum and settled the tax demand, remember? I carried the business while you recovered from your injuries in hospital, remember? So please give me a degree of credit, OK? The shit really hit the fan with the death of Ronald, a highly suspicious death at that and one that is not solved as yet. The publicity and untimely closure lost us massive turnover. Even old clients are avoiding us. We need to regroup, and fast. I'll ask again: Is that the end of the matter?'

Michael paced the floor. 'Yes, it appears so,' he said unconvincingly.

'Christ, Dad! I need a better answer than that…'

'There's naturally going to be an inquest into Ronald's murder. I may have to go back to Venice to give evidence into the death of Maggie and her henchman. Then...'

'Jesus.'

'...Then there is a news story that is coming out in a national magazine shortly.'

'What news story?'

'A six-page all singing, all dancing exposé into my torrid affair with Lauren O'Neill. And the small matter of the fire at Laburnum Farm, which took her life. But you know all this, it's public knowledge.'

'Why is it being dragged up again?'

'Because someone smells a rat, and recent events have put us back on the front page.'

'This will kill us, Dad.'

'I know. You mentioned it before.'

'Don't you care? We're fucking finished. The bank will call in the loan if we don't meet the covenants. I can't put any more cash in. The gallery is losing money since the murder of Ronald. The bad publicity is relentless.'

'There's always a way out...I need time to think.'

'That's a luxury we don't have. I have people willing to invest...'

'There's a *but* coming I feel.'

'There is, as always.'

Michael read the script, and lowered his eyes. 'Then there is a way out.'

'And that is?'

'I resign, and distance myself from the gallery. You can appoint a new board of directors with money to burn. Damage limitation, yes? Bring in someone squeaky clean to wow the punters back. The gallery can then survive. Is that your proposal?'

'Are you prepared to do that?'

'Yes,' he said with a brittle undertone.

'When?'

When?

Michael was stunned by the suddenness of Toby's question. His son was now steely-eyed and deadly serious in his request. He was cornered.

'As of this minute,' he volunteered solemnly.

'Accepted,' Toby said.

***

Later, he drowned his sorrows in the Duke of Wessex. How many times had Ronald sat here with him over the years? It was the end of a chapter. It had been agreed with his son that the forthcoming Gala would be his final hurrah, his crowning glory. Some glory. It was now after work hours, and his defences were down. He was glum and seriously pissed off with Toby, but he knew it was for the best. It was the only way for the business to survive and his son had too much to lose if it failed. There was no choice in the matter. He was the architect of his own downfall.

He sat glumly in the company of his drinking pal Terry, whom he had phoned earlier to help prop up his failing ego.

'What will you do?' Terry asked, sipping his Guinness with a distinct lack of enthusiasm. This was no party.

'Fuck knows,' Michael said. 'I'll probably sell the house in the country and remain in Chelsea, possibly downsize and set up an art consultancy in the city.'

'You could do journalistic work.'

'Funnily enough, I've been approached by two publishing companies with a view to writing my side of the story, but I'm not sure if it appeals at this stage.'

'Good money, I bet.'

'Not bad.'

'Do you want a ghost writer?'

Michael laughed for the first time. 'I'll know where to come, Terry.'

'Bad news...My story breaks in a week's time.'

'Ouch.'

'Put your tin hat on.'

'I'll find a hole to crawl into.'

'My piece centres mainly on the fire at the farm and your relationship with Lauren. I need to do a postscript. Can you bring me up to date so I can rebalance the story for the readers? This is more explosive than the fall of Lehman Brothers, to be honest. Even I can't keep up with it.'

Michael refreshed the drinks and ordered two of the day's Specials: Grimsby fish and chips with mushy peas. His treat. It was the least he could do. Slowly, he recounted the story from the moment of the first act of vandalism at his gallery to to seeing Maggie obliterated in a speeding boat as it careered headlong into a dredger. Theo was gone too, but he kept Martin's name out of this one. That was one saga that could be put to bed. The death of Ronald was unresolved. Adele was still on his mind. All that mattered was that Kara had been miraculously rescued and now each of them had to find a way to deal with the aftermath, the wreckage that remained in their heads. Could Terry somehow fathom that one out? He doubted it.

'That's my job, Michael. I'm an investigative journalist...I deal in facts and figures and human frailty. It's called an emotional rollercoaster. That just adds to the futility and complexity of human greed and the need for revenge, as in the case of Maggie Conlon. I'm not a psychiatrist, nor do I want to be. I have enough on my plate without analysing the reasons behind someone's extreme reactions which often manifests itself in their own self-destruction.'

'Are you pointing a finger?'

'To be blunt, yes.'

'Don't worry about kicking a man when he's down, will you?'

'Sorry, pal, but you brought the whole sorry house down on yourself. You used a sledgehammer to crack a walnut and that's exactly what happened. The walnut is now just dust in your hand.'

'Who needs enemies...'

'I'm just telling you how it is.'

'Christ, Terry, I'll just go home and take the overdose of tablets, shall I?'

'Many have done just that, but not you. Ronald should not die in vain, and think of Kara and her family. Not forgetting your son. They need you, even though it may not seem that way. Yes, go home but brush yourself down and come out fighting as you always do. Tomorrow is another day.'

'Tomorrow is another day. Got it.'

'Stop wallowing in self-pity. You are alive, Ronald isn't,

got it?'

Terry then handed over an envelope.

'What's this?' Michael asked quietly.

'A cheque for twelve thousand pounds, returned to sender.' Terry grinned and raised his glass. 'According to my consultant I do not require surgery at this stage, nor laser treatment.'

'What's happened?'

'I am under supervision as the cancer has remained localised to the prostate gland. While this stays constant I do not need to go under the knife, yet.'

'A kind of remission?'

'No, unfortunately. But drastic measures are unnecessary…a bit like your choices in life.'

Michael thought long and hard and realised just how lucky they had all been. He was too harsh on himself, even though he had been a complete prick. He waved the envelope away but Terry forced it into his top pocket in defiance. Michael wasn't going to argue. He needed the money. He was out of work.

He asked, 'How is the world of finance…are we fucked?'

'Absolutely. The Euro is screwed.'

'Will we survive the apocalypse?

'Probably. We always find a way, but it will take ten years to recover.'

Michael raised his glass.

'I'll drink to that,' he said.

***

Outside the pub, they parted company with a prolonged drunken hug. Terry stood on the pavement as his friend clambered into a taxi and headed for home, and a new beginning. He still cradled a half-filled glass of the black stuff. It tasted good. He downed it with gusto and slowly made his way to the tube station. It was close to midnight, the sky sprinkled with a million jewels of light. The city throbbed with the intensity of a healthy beating heart, in spite of the catastrophic downturn in the economy. Somehow, there was always a way through a crisis, as Michael was now learning to his cost. There was always a price to pay. His mobile bleeped.

He listened intently, thanked the caller and felt a deep frown crease his forehead. His optimism for the survival of humanity began to falter. The heat was back on. Sheila Cox's car had been found. Somehow, he didn't think this would bring good news to anyone.

CHAPTER EIGHTEEN

The thing that bothered Terry most was the odd location of the abandoned Astra. It was discovered in a lock-up garage in Liverpool, the last place he would have expected, especially as Sheila was supposedly driving south at the time of her disappearance...wasn't that the original plan? Or was it so strange to find the car here? A complex picture was beginning to emerge. He knew this discovery meant trouble, but in what context? He just needed to fit in the last pieces of the jigsaw. This much he did know: During his earlier investigation into her disappearance, after talking to various kitchen staff at the pub, then village friends and finally her sister, he found out that Sheila had left home on the day of the fire for a new life in Jersey, in the Channel Isles. Her husband had been callously dumped for the promise of a better life. It turns out that she had met a businessman in The Royal Oak, struck up an immediate friendship with him and conducted their affair over many secretive months. They had planned their escape on this very day, the tragic consequences of which no one could possibly have foretold. Certainly not by her. Sheila packed, left home without fanfare and planned to head for Poole harbour to catch the ferry.

Why then had her car ended up in Liverpool? Had she driven there...or had the car been stolen? He had to examine the evidence.

Terry took the train out of London to the north west, met his police contact, handed over a wad of cash and was given brief unauthorised access to the vehicle. At this point, it was just a parked-up, dusty, nondescript car, with no one coming forward to claim it. It could have stayed hidden for years. Just so happened that a bunch of kids had broken into the garage, found the car, ransacked the CDs and then left the up-and-over door open for anyone to look inside and take pot luck. The tyres were taken next. Then the police got a tip-off.

Terry was the next to get the nod. That's how it worked.

Sniffing around, he noted the road tax had elapsed. The owner of the lock-up was unknown at this stage, which was unhelpful, but the police were on to it. But the registration number of the car showed that it belonged to one Sheila Sarah Cox, licensee of The Royal Oak, Old Hampton, Surrey.

The driver's door had been opened by force, the side window smashed, the keys missing. Inside, there was dried blood on the steering wheel and door handles and strange black smears across the front seats. This baffled Terry at first. Then the smell of the interior hit his nostrils: Soot. The evidence of a fire...This car had been at Laburnum Farm on the day the barn burnt to the ground. There was no other explanation. The fire coincided with the exact time she left her husband. He tried to imagine the scenario. She would have been in a hurry to leave the area, quickly and without fuss. Why would she go to the farm?

Terry tried to figure out what could have happened that fateful day. Then his inquisitive mind kicked in. He knew the answer instinctively. This changed everything...He needed to get back to London – and fast.

***

In spite of his professional embarrassment – he knew people would snigger behind his back – Michael decided to throw caution to the wind and attend the Gala dance on board the *Star Cruiser* moored at Excel. It would have been too easy to crawl under a table and hide, as many colleagues in his industry might expect him to do. News of his resignation had soon got around and he had heard the disapproving murmurings out on the street.

Well, he argued: Fuck them! Besides, he wanted to celebrate the important things in his life and show solidarity with his son and work employees. He wasn't out to pasture yet. The invitations had gone out for his selected table guests with only one refusal: Marcus. What a surprise. He was still playing hardball. The table comprised himself, Toby and his latest squeeze, Gemma and her boyfriend (whom he looked forward to meeting), Kara, two from the framing workshop

263

and, as always, an invited client (plus one) who had loyally supported the gallery down the years. They extended the guest list by two: Julius and Antonia. The Gala was an annual ritual, a chance to unwind and get drunk, and a way to say thank you to those who best deserved it. More importantly, this year the Chairman would make a special citation to celebrate the life of Ronald Wilson, who would have sat at Michael's table and been the life and soul of the party. He would be sadly missed, and was the main reason Michael had decided to attend. He wouldn't, couldn't, let dear Ronald down again; and it was vitally important that he got some kind of recognition from an industry he served so well. Michael feared he had unwittingly failed his colleague already. His death would haunt him to his own grave.

The dinner and dance event was in the grand theme of a Venetian Ball, and fancy dress was compulsory. As was usual, Champagne and nibbles would be served on arrival, to the accompaniment of a string quartet playing Puccini, followed by a feast of five extravagant Italian courses. Later, the dance music would be more up-tempo, performed by a ten-piece jazz band. Each year the gala surpassed itself in refinement and splendour, and the evening was topped off with an award ceremony to give recognition to those in the Fine Art Society across the capital. Photographers from *Tatler* would also be in attendance. The patron this year was Princess Anne. It was that kind of a glittering occasion.

Was Michael ready for this ridiculous exposure? The days had quickly passed. Tomorrow night would tell. He was in the spotlight once again.

***

Kara had argued with Marcus to the point of disgust. She was determined to go to the Gala and support Michael. Marcus, on the other hand, was as stubborn as a mule. He nobly elected to babysit instead, making her feel even worse about her emphatic decision to attend. She wanted him there, beside her at the table. What was the problem? It wasn't a big ask, in her view. To make matters worse, she ordered a beautiful sequined dress and short cape with a diamond encrusted emerald green mask from the designated fancy dress shop in Knightsbridge which every self-respecting person used for these special occasions. The upshot to all this? The outfit was costly to hire. Marcus was by now even more peeved. Well, sod him, she argued.

***

Gemma felt awkward returning to work, and kept herself apart from both Michael and Toby. She was unsure of her future.

Tomorrow night at the Gala was going to be a great occasion, a first for her, but in her pocket was a resignation letter. She couldn't hack it any longer, working in the gallery and constantly stepping over the exact spot where Ronald was killed. Although now removed from sight, the white outline of his stricken body was imprinted forever on her brain. Frankly, it spooked her to the point of keeping her awake at night. The simple answer was to leave. Things could never be the same again. The job was difficult enough, but having to deal with murder and kidnapping was beyond the job description. She wanted to laugh, she wanted to cry. Instead, she felt numb from head to toe. At closing time, she quietly placed her letter on Michael's desk and left for home. Tomorrow would be her last official day. The Gala would be a fitting conclusion, and she hoped Michael and Toby would understand her reasons for jumping ship so early in her career. A job at Tesco's was suddenly appealing.

***

Martin Penny was not a man to dwell on past cases, but this one had got to him. Michael Strange had paid him a lot of money to ensure the safety of Kara and Marcus, and he accomplished this goal. But something nagged at his subconscious. In the beginning, his task was also to find Maggie. She and her sidekick Theo had been eliminated messily, but the operation was finally closed. Now he should move on. But he couldn't. It was the unexpected killing of Ronald Wilson that bothered him, as he had tried to explain at the funeral when he discussed matters with Michael. But he also picked up that Michael wanted to draw a neat line over everything. So he did. Until now…

He couldn't let it go, baffled as to why Michael was lured to Venice when it was easier to kill him in London, baffled by his kidnapping alongside Julius and Antonia when Maggie didn't have an obvious gripe with them, especially as she had obtained most of the paintings and sold them for a profit. Was she that desperate? He could understand her thirst for exacting revenge on Michael for the death of her sister, but why complicate matters by including the young lovers? This was like a ritual killing, a mass murder.

Then it dawned on him. As Michael and he had discussed earlier, Michael was drawn to Venice to be separated from Kara. She was kidnapped at the same time and held prisoner, but for whom? Maggie was in Venice. It was almost as if she was one part of an equation. Certainly Theo was not the other part. He was just the go-between. The shapeshifter. Perhaps Maggie intended to massacre those held in Venice and then return to finish Kara. Highly unlikely and far too risky. Martin knew from army experience that an intended target should be removed quickly and efficiently for fear of being detected before the operation could be carried out. Which was exactly what happened: Kara was lucky to be alive.

He was convinced that Maggie had an accomplice other than Theo and whoever it was, he or she had murdered Roland. He was an innocent victim, chosen randomly at the gallery to send a signal to Michael that his predator was close and capable of inflicting damage. It could just as easily have been Michael's son or the new girl at the gallery, whose name he couldn't recall. Lucky girl though. It could have been her who died that fateful day.

Who then was the killer? Lauren was dead. He had tabs on Maggie and Theo, and his henchman was in Venice. Police had checked the CCTV cameras outside the gallery but they were not operational. Did Ronald know the identity of the killer, a killer who went about their business in brazen fashion in a public place on a busy street? This callous act was from the hands of someone either supremely confident or plain mad. What statement was the killer making? He pondered this point: To prove they could do anything, of course. To show they had the upper hand and to put the fear of God into Michael and Kara. The murder of Ronald would certainly bring home the message.

He returned to the pub in Bermondsey. The landlord allowed him access to the bedsit, as it was still paid up to the end of the month. It cost him a twenty. The room was a shambles, now vacant. However, in a black bin bag he found hundreds of discarded photos of Michael and a young woman, who he recognised as Kara Scott. Who had really lived here until recently? Certainly not Maggie. She was gone. The landlord mentioned another woman, but he was vague and unhelpful. In Martin's opinion it had to be someone off their rocker...a maniac. Someone with vengeance in their heart. And he was equally convinced that Mitch, like Ronald, had crossed their path too. And suffered the consequences.

He was back on the case.

***

Terry returned from Liverpool and went back to work, perplexed and overworked. His brain was ready to explode, such was the overload. As soon as time permitted he headed straight to Old Hampton, to The Royal Oak. From the car park he could just detect the chimneys of Laburnum Farm poking above the trees in the distance. He reasoned, therefore, that any smoke from the burning barn would have been easily spotted from here, especially an inferno of dense smoke blackening the sky. And if Sheila Cox was indeed in the car park at that precise moment, then she would have been aware of trouble on the horizon. Just supposing...

He continued his car journey to the farm. It took four minutes to arrive at the gates. The fire would have been raging by now. Did Sheila try to help, knowing that her friend Lauren was living there and possibly trapped and in need of help? That seemed logical.

It was inconceivable to imagine that she simply drove on. Terry tried to re-enact Sheila's response. He drove down the gravel drive and pulled up at the side of the house. No, the intensity of the flames meant she would have either turned round or parked behind the main house, perhaps even in the open fronted garaging space where Lauren kept her 4 x 4. It was likely that at this point Sheila called the fire brigade. Confused, and wanting to help, it is possible she investigated the house and then entered the barn. Was it possible to do this with the intensity of flames leaping all around? The jury was out.

What Terry did know from Michael's account was that Maggie somehow escaped, and there was no mention in the police files of another car parked up at the house. Was this Maggie's escape route? It began to appear so. This gave her mobility and anonymity. Proximity and chance. If this proved to be the case: Then what happened to Sheila Cox?

Terry's blood ran cold.

***

When he first undertook the task of helping Michael uncover the whereabouts of Maggie, Martin employed a team to work undercover to flush her out into the open. They concentrated on a 'golden square', which they had mapped out as an area she probably worked within. Then they slowly narrowed that area, squeezing her ability to move effectively without being detected. Working beneath the radar, Martin concentrated on how quickly she operated, on the assumption that she mainly walked between destinations, rather than being picked up on CCTV at train stations in particular. Although probably in disguise, she would also avoid taxis for fear of being remembered. Walking gave her the freedom to move largely unrecognised, surrounded by millions of people. Therefore, she had to be close to Michael's gallery and the one Marcus ran on the Docks. This was how she was able to break the windows and quickly vanish. Was she in disguise...or had she surgically changed her appearance? Doubtful. She had two children back in Ireland and the last thing she would want to do is freak them out. Besides, she was arrogant enough to make her presence known to Michael. She wanted to confront him, show him who was the Boss. So she strutted her stuff – brazen enough to even move in above him – and began planning his demise on her terms.

Before this discovery, Martin was convinced she was living locally and put word out in his search for a single Irish woman in the area of the golden square. It was like finding a needle in a haystack, but people in general follow natural habits, even killers. She would find cover in her own comfort zone, where she could mingle easily. Through his network of contacts, he found eleven women of her apparent description, eight of them employed full-time in the city. They were eliminated. Another was partially blind and relied on a walking stick. Another was in a wheelchair. One, without a P45, fitted the bill perfectly and lived in a bedsit above an Irish pub in Bermondsey. Her name was Annie Byrne and investigations showed she had been staying in London for just five weeks. According to staff, she had a regular visitor, a man with a diamond in his teeth.

His team was triumphant at first: They had got the bitch! But Martin and his team got too close. They made their first error. Another member of his gang, affectionately known as Havoc, introduced himself and befriended her as he had distant Irish connections. Initially, it seemed to work. He, in turn, introduced Martin as his brother. Martin should have known better: Never get too close to the enemy. She sussed them out, the clever cow. His cover was blown, without him knowing it. She arranged a meeting with Martin and enticed him to the spot beside the Thames, a little private jetty, and he agreed, to find out what she was capable of. It was midnight. He was nervous.

Just before the meeting, and even more disturbing, Maggie was then spotted elsewhere, and was clearly setting a trap for him. Was Theo lying in wait for him, with a bunch of psychotic hooligans? He couldn't back out of the meeting.

A new plan was devised. As they were of similar build, Mitch and he swapped clothing and assumed each other's identity (they could have been brothers, they were so alike), with Martin undertaking the task of tracking Maggie and finding out what she was up to. It was vital that she was kept under surveillance and he felt this was his direct responsibility. Mitch could look after himself if cornered. Sadly, he apparently couldn't. His body was later found bludgeoned to death, floating in the Thames.

Clearly, someone wanted Martin Penny dead but luckily the killer was duped convincingly by the late identity swap. Perhaps it was the darkness of the night ...

Like Ronald, Mitch's death wasn't at the hands of Maggie because on both occasions she was under tight surveillance. So who killed his colleague? Theo, as he first guessed? He was doubtful. It was someone who was either easily fooled or an assassin just doing their job cold-heartedly, without emotion. They killed whoever stood in front of them. It was someone that neither Mitch, Havoc or Martin had ever met: A rogue element of the worst kind.

The battle perameters had just been shifted.

He turned his thoughts to the Birthday badge displayed on the window, which Michael discovered. It was a trophy for sure. Why would Maggie dare to do such a thing? It wasn't her style. She had no emotional attachment to Michael. Who did? Was it someone else sending a message, someone with a clear need for personal vengeance? Who was this rogue element? Who was the real Ms Byrne?

***

Before leaving the death site, Terry tried to gain access to the house. The doors were locked, the windows boarded up. It was a sorrowful reminder of better days: now all that remained was grimy paintwork and cobwebs hanging under the dark eaves, whispers on the wind. He snapped the door handle at the rear and shoulder-charged it open. Inside, it was dark and dank. The remains of the furniture was covered in white sheets. No one appeared to live here...

He was perturbed to find smouldering embers in a fireplace. He wasn't expecting this...it was probably a tramp finding shelter, he figured. He was more perturbed when he found a woman's silver bracelet seemingly discarded on the mantel. It looked expensive. Odd. Who had been visiting here temporarily? It was now abandoned for sure, just like the spirit of Lauren. Even her estranged husband, Julius, hadn't the heart to return and claim what was rightfully his, which was, in truth, an impressive estate standing on prime land. Worth a packet. He guessed that the property would have been part of an ongoing legal battle between Maggie and Julius to gain eventual ownership. Although rightfully his, Terry was sure that over time she would have tried to get her claws into it. Now there was no dispute. Maggie was dead. She could no longer claim anything. Julius was the rightful legal claimant to the estate. No will could contest this. With Maggie exposed and later identified, Lauren's death was at last conclusive. Julius no longer needed to wait the seven years' time lapse to formally declare his wife dead. It would have been a long wait.

In the meantime, the house stood empty. Terry turned his attention to the question of what happened to the paintings by Patrick Porter, which were the subject of a tug of war between the warring couple. These paintings were worth nearly a million pounds. The walls were empty. Someone had removed the paintings. Michael had indicated that they were in storage, pending any legal claim. Terry wanted to verify this.

He had seen enough. He headed straight for Michael's home, anxious to discuss his findings. He had serious questions to ask. Just then, his mobile bleeped. He listened intently. The caller informed him that the lock-up in Liverpool belonged to a man of Greek origin called Theo Lakis.

***

Michael collected his hired costume for the Gala and dumped the items in the gallery. There was a letter waiting for him but he set it to one side. He arranged for a private limousine to arrive at the gallery at closing time tomorrow to pick him up, then pick up all the guests up en route. He wanted to do it in style.

He decided to stay in the West End and have some fun and let his hair down. He ended up at Annabel's for cocktails, followed by a feast at Momo's, the Moroccan restaurant just off Regent Street. He didn't want to be alone in the apartment, morose and jobless. Toby was right of course, the business would only survive if new blood was introduced, and quickly. His continued presence was rather like Terry's cancer...a black spot that wouldn't go away without it being removed. He was being removed.

There was only one thing to do. He picked up one of the waitresses and moved on to a nightclub. The rest of the night was a blur, but he remembered spending a lot of money and he got to keep the girl. He didn't go home. He went to her place.

***

Terry arrived at around seven in the evening to Michael's block of flats, just as the concierge was going home. They exchanged pleasantries as Terry headed for the lift.

'Could you give this to Mr Strange?' the elderly man asked.

Terry turned and was handed a slim package. It meant nothing to him, he'd just do the errand. Moments later he alighted from the lift and rang the doorbell. No answer. He waited, then phoned Michael's mobile. It was switched off. Damn. A wasted journey. Where the hell was he? He'd try again in the morning. He left the building in search of a burger bar, the package temporarily forgotten and shoved in his coat pocket. His mind was a whirl. He couldn't switch off. Where was Michael?

He got home, had a beer and watched TV. It took him three hours to finally get to sleep.

***

The next morning Michael awoke in a stranger's bed, a king-sized four poster covered by crumpled black satin sheets and pink cushions. A pair of French silk knickers and stockings were entwined around his arm. *Christ, now he remembered...*

The smell of cigarettes lingered in the air. His head felt like a crushed melon. An empty bottle of Champagne and two glass flutes stood on the carpeted floor beside him. He heard the shower from an adjoining room and guessed he wasn't alone...if only he could remember her name. What was he thinking of?

He climbed from the bed and steadied himself.

'Coffee?'

He turned and caught sight of a young woman standing by the bathroom door, her lissom naked body dripping wet. Slowly and unabashed, she towelled herself down in front of him as she repeated the question.

'That would be good...'

'Double espresso?'

He nodded as he watched her glide into the next room. He recovered his trousers, slipped them on and followed. He felt like shit, too old for this game. Under the harshness of the kitchen down-lights, he ruffled his hair, drank water and tried to avoid eye contact as best he could. She was perhaps twenty odd, for heaven's sake. He was old enough to be her father.

This auburn-haired beauty turned and laughed, handing him a small coffee cup.

'You don't even recall my name, do you?'

'I'm struggling,' he said.

'Snap.'

They both grinned and downed their coffee.

'What do we do now?' he asked.

She dropped the towel.

'Do it all again,' she said, 'only this time we should perhaps formally introduce ourselves first.' Her smile was infectious. 'Leah,' she volunteered.

'James.' He kissed her lightly and studied her deep set amber eyes, catching the devilment within them.

'Liar!' they both exclaimed simultaneously, wild laughter filling the room. This relationship wasn't going anywhere, and neither of them cared one jot.

She kissed his mouth, deeper this time and grabbed a bottle of Jack Daniels from the kitchen and then led him to the bedroom, slowly closing the door behind them.

***

Terry downed a chilled orange juice from the fridge, ate a packet of crisps and slumped on the sofa. He had slept right through, which was unusual for him. It was now midmorning. He flicked through the TV channels and decided to take a soak in the bath. He removed his coat and tossed it across the back rest. The package fell from the pocket. He'd forgotten about it. On inspection, it was a CCTV disc. Idly, he read the scrawled writing on one side: *For the attention of Michael Strange.* It didn't mean anything to him. He grabbed a lager this time, discarded the disc and went upstairs to run the water. An hour later he came down in his dressing gown, made tea and sandwiches and studied the package again. It was not sealed so he removed the disc. His investigative urge took over and he inserted the disc in his laptop and sat back on the sofa to watch. He immediately recognised the entrance door and communal area where Michael lived.

He waited and watched. The concierge, a young man, took the mail from the postman, and could be seen making a phone call. A couple ambled through, followed a minute later by a businessman taking the lift, carrying a briefcase. Two minutes later a van pulled up and a uniformed maintenance man came to the desk. There was a brief exchange of silent words, a form passed between them and then the man disappeared into the lift. Nothing unusual. Then the disc finished. Terry was perplexed. Why did Michael need to see this?

He checked again and concentrated on the couple: A man and a woman with their backs to him. They moved fast, with no acknowledgment toward the concierge. The man's arm was around the woman's waist but not lovingly, more in a manner of protection, as if he was guiding her...Was this Maggie and Theo?

He tried Michael again on his mobile. Silence. Then he thought of a someone who could give him an answer to this question. The rumours had been flying about, now he wanted to face this man...*The thief.*

***

Michael got back to his apartment at noon. He stripped off in the bathroom and inspected the scratch marks on his back and shoulders. Leah, or whatever her name was, was red-hot and a serious risk to his pulsating heart. She was too much to handle, and he vowed to avoid Momo's for the foreseeable future. He couldn't keep up with the pace.

He showered and dressed and made a cup of tea. That was more like it. Now he was on safer ground. All he needed was the slippers to complete the picture of middle-aged contentment. Still, it was reassuring to his fragile ego that he had what it takes…he just needed longer to recover from the exertions. Months, in fact.

He checked the time, had a word with Toby at the gallery and arranged the pick-up times to make the evening gala in the limo. Toby informed him of Gemma's resignation letter: *Just brilliant.* He made another brew.

His mobile rang. It was Terry.

'Michael, what happened to the paintings?'

'Paintings?'

'The Patrick Porters, the ones at the farm.'

'They were put into storage.' He remained defensive.

'By whom?'

'I can't answer that exactly. I suppose Julius or his solicitor arranged it. The house was smoke damaged and some of the paintings were badly affected.'

'How many were displayed there?'

'Twelve. What's this about, Terry?'

'Do you have an inventory of the titles and sizes…'

'The police will. Kara compiled a list at the time, so I presume they kept it for their records. The paintings were worth a huge sum of money.'

'Who else helped with this list?'

'Just Kara…oh, Marcus was there at the time of course.'

'Anyone else?'

'Yours truly…Do you want to tell me what's going on?'

'I've been to the farm. There are signs of a break-in.'

'Vandals, I reckon. It's a remote spot.'

Terry didn't buy this argument. 'Apart from you, Kara and Marcus, who else knew the total?'

'Lauren, of course. That's how many she asked me to sell when she first made contact.'

'Was Julius aware of this number?'

'Possibly, but he hadn't lived at the house for several years. Is there a problem?'

'I'm not convinced by many aspects of this case, Michael. Things don't add up.'

'Try me.'

'I'll check it out further and get back to you later tonight.'

'We're all at the gala from about eight.'

'We'll speak in the morning then. Is Marcus going?'

Michael laughed. 'No,' he said. 'We're not on speaking terms.'

'By the way, I have a CCTV disc for you to view…I called last night to your flat but you were out. The concierge asked me to pass it on.'

'I'm shattered. Shall we look at it tomorrow?'

'Yeah.'

'Come by the gallery, I'll be in around lunchtime…provided I don't have a hangover.'

'OK, see you then. Have a great night.'

Michael clicked off, baffled by Terry's odd line of enquiry. What trouble was he trying to rake up?

***

Terry immediately contacted the police. A word here and there, a favour promised, a favour forfeited and he had the information he required. His name still carried weight. He had a copy of the painting inventory emailed to his office within minutes. He checked the titles from this list which was originally compiled by Kara, all twelve of them. Spot on.

The police source also confirmed the name and address of the storage facility in Midhurst which held the household contents from the fire, including the paintings. Because of the complexity of the case (which was ongoing due to the suspicious death of an unidentified body), the dispute of ownership of assets was also unresolved between Lauren's sister and her estranged husband. Terry knew all this by now, of course, but still needed to clear his head and get a better take on things. Maggie at the time was on the run. Hence, the necessity to keep the contents secure until the identity of the victim (supposedly Lauren) could be officially named. Seemed reasonable: only then could the rightful heir take possession of the contested goods. This was now finally established with both sisters dead and at long last certified as such. The case should now be officially closed, but nothing was ever that easy.

There was another complication on the horizon, according to his informant. Ordinarily, Terry understood that Julius could now take possession of the remaining paintings finally. Except...and here was the rub...this was still proving impossible as the police lab could not match the DNA samples from Maggie's remains to the dead women in the barn because there wasn't any remains. Maggie had been blown to bits. There was nothing left of her. The body in the barn therefore remained defiantly unidentified. This latest development had only just come to light. Even Terry had a headache just trying to get his head around it. A seven year legal precedent to prove such matters was a long period to remain both patient and cool for those awaiting a definitive outcome. ...

Terry couldn't wait that long. He didn't have the patience either. But he did have the expertise to hack into the storage computer system of a certain company in Surrey. Which he did. Within the hour, he knew precisely the list of contents belonging to Laburnum Farm. Among the items were twenty six assorted paintings and prints. Of particular interest was the eleven Patrick Porters. Michael had said there was twelve. He scanned the titles. Bingo.

The one missing was called *Venetian interlude by moonlight:* The very same painting that he had seen in a certain gallery just a few weeks ago when he was left alone to lock up when the owner did a runner. The connection made sense now. Marcus had in his possession an original Patrick Porter kept under wraps, gained by illegal means.

Terry made a phone call to DS Keene, and told him his wacky theory surrounding the death of Lauren O'Neill and urged him to carry out an immediate sample test to help verify his beliefs. Keene protested at first, then agreed to comply and checked the DNA database. Minutes later he confirmed he already had the sample in question and would see if there was a match. Terry then closed down his computer, buttoned up his jacket and walked briskly in the direction of the docks. It was late afternoon, the sky threatening rain. The impending darkness matched his sombre mood.

His next step wasn't going to be easy. A confession was always difficult to extract, especially if the thief had already sold the painting, thus hiding the evidence.

***

It was six o'clock. Michael finished dressing, shrugged on his black cape, adjusted his sequinned mask and cradled his ebony walking stick in his right hand and then strode purposefully from the gallery in all his splendid finery.

The stretched limousine purred as it glided out into the traffic and headed east. Michael relaxed. He felt good. The Champagne on ice certainly helped. Soft music nullified the slight ache rumbling behind his temples. As the limo eased along, a thousand flickering images tormented his frazzled brain. Tonight, he would banish such demons and cast them aside. He was upset with Gemma though. He would try to get her to stay. Still, tonight was a night for fun and celebration. The past was consigned to damnation.

Nothing was going to spoil his party.

***

The Marcus Heath Gallery was closed, the lights out. A handwritten sign on the door signified that the doors had been shut early at four-thirty. It concluded 'Sorry for any inconvenience.'

Terry Miles swore. He checked his watch, and then marched across the dock toward Tower Hamlets. He wasn't going to be deterred.

***

The party was in full swing before the limo had even arrived at its destination at Excel. Michael sat hunched beside Kara as they toasted the evening's forthcoming frivolities. She looked stunning in a white full- length ball gown, split from the thigh, revealing a glimpse of her long legs. She wore a peacock feather hat atop her pinned-up hair and an emerald green diamond encrusted mask which contrasted with her red glossy lipstick and pale foundation. Her eyes shone brightly, a sense of wickedness prevailing over the other guests. Toby grinned, as if in another world, sharing a joke with his latest girlfriend... Michael could never keep up with the names. He was sure it was... Veronica? Or was it Veronique? He shrugged. He didn't care. Kara raised her glass.

She shouted, 'To Marcus...and his stupid stubborn streak!'

'I'll drink to that!' Michael echoed. At the back of his mind though, he knew that Marcus had every right to be pissed off with him. He was thankful therefore that the babysitter (baby was just about right!) had declined his invitation...the atmosphere would have been dulled. Let him stew in his anger. The rumbling in his head intensified.

The *Star Cruiser* loomed into view as they parked up on the dock, a sleek monster of a ship that sparkled from the onboard lights and twinkling decorative illuminations along the multi-decks. Clusters of giant red balloons swayed in the night breeze as the string quartet greeted their arrival. A long line of distinguished guests, resplendent in outrageous costumes, slowly climbed the gangway to the top deck, their idle chatter and laughter punctuating the sound of the music.

Michael alighted from the limo, the fabulous Kara on his arm. It didn't get any better than this.

***

'What do you want?'

Terry stood on the doorstep, eyeing up the young man who peered back at him suspiciously from behind a half-closed door. Terry said nothing until the request was repeated, this time in a much harsher tone.

'We need to talk,' Terry replied.

'What about?'

'Can I come in, Marcus?'

'No. You can talk from there. My son is sleeping...'

'Is Kara with you?'

'I'm alone, she's gone out for the evening.'

Terry edged forward. 'You need to listen to what I have to

say,' he whispered.

'Why is that? I'm sick of the sight of all of you…'

'We can do this the easy way or the hard way, Marcus.'

'Is that a threat?'

Terry was losing patience with the young man's brattish remarks. He put his foot into the gap and grabbed Marcus's hand and twisted, happy to hear the squeal from behind the door. Then he pushed his way in.

'Where is the painting you stole?' he asked. They stood face to face in the hallway. 'I saw it at the gallery that day when you charged off and asked me to lock up, remember?'

'You're off your rocker, granddad…'

'It was hidden under a dust sheet, on an easel. Were you attempting to sell it? How much did you expect to get for it…a painting by Patrick Porter, nicked from Laburnum Farm, eh? A tidy sum, I bet. Cash, no doubt. But it was proving tricky to sell, wasn't it? The truth of the matter was that you're just an amateur in a professional's game, and Maggie was on to you. She knew you, Kara or Michael had the painting…that's why she was after you all. You all believed that she was after revenge for Lauren's murder…but you would be wrong, Marcus. She wanted what she thought was rightfully hers…she couldn't easily get her hands on those held in storage, but she could claim back the one you had…and she was prepared to kill for it. What was it worth, fifty grand on a good day?'

Marcus recoiled, his defiance crumbling.

'You were hoping to make a killing yourself, correct? Do you want me to call the police and have you arrested?'

Marcus sneered: 'Where's your proof?'

Terry took out his mobile and scrolled down his camera shots. He pointed to an image. He didn't have to say anything else.

'Fuck!' Marcus turned white.

'Where is the painting?'

'In the gallery, locked in the loo.'

'Wow…slick. Does Kara know you have it?'

'No, I was trying to make some serious money… impress her…show her how good I was…I thought I knew what I was doing.'

'How did you acquire it?'

Marcus led Terry into the living room and removed a pile of toys from an armchair, inviting Terry to sit down. He did so and listened to the boy's confession.

'I took the opportunity to steal the picture on the day of the fire,' Marcus said, shaking his head. 'After dragging Michael clear, the ambulance and police arrived just after the fire brigade. It was chaotic and we initially took refuge to the side of the house, where the heat was less intense. Michael was the first to leave the scene. The police took Kara and me later.' Marcus hesitated and put the kettle on. 'I recovered my camera and Kara's phone from the house …I had time to lock them in the boot of my jeep. I was told to move my car to help gain access to the site because it was blocking the drive. I did this and then, while alone, wandered through the house again in a daze, shocked by what had happened…'

'Go on.'

Marcus filled the teapot with hot water and grabbed two cups from the cupboard. 'I saw the mess and the paintings lying scattered on the floor. I knew they were valuable. I knew that they would be in demand…who would miss one in the confusion? The flames had finally spread to the main house, where I was and I figured that everything was in danger of burning to the ground…so it was an easy decision to remove one.'

He filled the cups, brought one to Terry and sat opposite, his eyes affixed to the floor. 'I shoved the smallest one under my arm and put it in the rear of the jeep. No one noticed, no one cared. All around it was just madness…the smoke was intense, choking. We were lucky to get out alive. No one would miss a stupid picture, I figured.'

'Someone did,' Terry commented, 'you figured wrong.'

'Christ, what a fuck-up. Did Maggie really come back for that?'

'Not entirely…but had Maggie lived you would have paid with your life eventually. Whatever her true motives, she was a relentless machine and I believe that she was hell-bent on destroying everyone and everything that represented a threat to her and how she perceived the wrong-doing of others. Along with her sister, she was psychotic and vengeful. You picked the wrong artist to steal …Both Lauren and Maggie were possessive to the point of madness in regard to the work in the name of their dead brother. The reasoning behind their actions was impossible to fathom to us. Not surprising to them, mind you, when you consider the past horrors they had to endure.'

Marcus looked up: 'The beatings at the hands of their drunken father?'

Terry slowly breathed in. 'Worse than that: He was a rapist, and both daughters became his victims…'

Marcus buried his head in his hands. 'I was aware of the story…but not all of the details.'

'You need to return the painting to Julius, he will understand.'

'He's an old friend, so I doubt he will appreciate my treachery.'

'He'll see your point of view. The matter needs to go no further as far as I'm concerned. Get on with your life and look after those dearest to you…namely, your family.'

Terry finished the tea and rose from his chair, weary but gladdened that a serious wrong could be put right in this whole sorry saga.

'Oh, one last thing,' he said. 'You knew the sisters. Take a look at this and make of it what you will…it beats me.' He handed over the disc and watched as Marcus inserted it in his desktop Apple and examined the images.

'Stop just there,' Terry instructed. 'That couple…is that Maggie on the arm of that guy?'

Marcus leaned closer. 'No,' he muttered.

'No?' he asked, bewildered.

Marcus stood back and raised a hand to his mouth.

'Fuck,' he said. 'Fuck, fuck, fuck…'

'What is it, Marcus?' He just knew the fucking answer.

Suddenly his mobile bleeped and he took a text message from Keene as Marcus examined the image once again. Preoccupied with the message, he barely noticed Marcus, ashen-faced, retreat from the room to look in on his crying son in another room.

Terry stood transfixed, his eyes alternating between the screen on the Apple and the text on his phone. He had to read the message again and again:

**SON OF A BITCH...THE DNA SAMPLE
MATCHED...JUST AS YOU SUGGESTED.**

Terry was perplexed. Then it hit home. He had his answer.
He had the truth.

When Marcus returned to the hallway, he found it empty, the
door ajar. From somewhere, he could hear the clatter of fast
running steps descending the communal stairs. He shook his
head. This guy Terry was weird. One minute here, the
next...gone! What could be so urgent?

Then his eyes returned to the screen, with the image of a
woman held on pause: Where did this picture come from?
When was it taken? He tried to make sense of it, but the more
he tried the more his stomach churned with terror: He was
staring wide-eyed at a ghost from the past...

CHAPTER NINETEEN

The evening was going better than Michael had dared to hope. Surprisingly, Julius entered into the spirit of things and took it in turns to dance with all the ladies who sat at their table. Toby was merry, his girlfriend merrier...and Michael got to have a waltz with Gemma, who was dressed beautifully in a sequinned purple dress and silver feather boa.

'Resignation not accepted,' he shouted above the din, whirling her around in his arms.

'We'll talk in the morning,' she said, eyebrows raised.

'Speak to Toby, he's adamant.'

'Hm.'

'Things can only get better...'

'You think so?'

Michael was in mischievous mood. 'Well, ditch the boyfriend to start with.'

'Hey, what's wrong with Tarquin?'

'My case is closed.'

Gemma pushed him playfully and laughed.

Later, he danced with Antonia, who looked stunning in a strapless, scarlet satin dress slashed down the back, revealing her slender spine. As she danced, her black mane of hair swirled around her shoulders. The music was great, the Champagne flowed. Everyone laughed. The ballroom on the lower deck heaved with the gaiety of over four hundred people.

Eventually, Michael invited Kara onto the overcrowded dance floor, where they jostled with the other revellers. The atmosphere was hot and sticky. They hugged and mischievously caught the other's knowing eye...the past, and all the horrors that came with it, was finally put to rest.

'You're a mother!' he shouted above the music. 'Who would have believed it?'

She threw back her head in delight, purring: 'And a damn fine mother too!'

He swirled her around, not caring that their drunken antics caused those nearest to them to leap aside. But everyone laughed. A fellow gallery owner shook Michael's hand and wished him good luck in retirement.

'Bloody cheek,' he murmured to his companion.

'Well, you are getting on a bit,' Kara yelled.

Another female dancer reached over and patted him affectionately on the shoulder. Word had got around, he guessed.

He was suddenly ushered closer together with Kara from someone behind him. Turning, they were met by a blinding flash as a photographer snapped away merrily, dressed in white tuxedo, bow tie and fully-fitted mask. The man, tall and slim, swung elegantly away and engaged another couple, then another as the flash gun popped and illuminated those in the vicinity.

Michael led Kara from the dance floor, exhausted. As he reached their table, he suddenly felt uneasy...there was something about the photographer: His walk, his demeanour maybe..? He searched the sea of faces but to no avail...the man was gone. He shrugged, assuming it was the booze making his head spin.

A waitress appeared, holding a large plate containing a giant strawberry Pavlova, which she placed in the centre of their table.

'Bravo!' Toby exclaimed, knocking over a glass of Champagne in the process.

Michael grinned. Nothing was going to spoil this night. He sat down heavily and tucked into the dessert with gusto. Kara and the other girls followed with equal enthusiasm. The Pavlova disappeared as if by magic.

***

Terry reached the dockside in minutes as he raced along Wapping Highway to the Excel Exhibition Centre with scant regard to any vehicle blocking his path. It took longer to convince the bouncers to let him speak to someone in authority, after they barred him from entering onto the *Star Cruiser* without the necessary invitation pass. His agitation was not helping the cause, nor the general swearing as his increasingly desperate demands were met by stony resistance.

Eventually, a uniformed man approached down the gangway, arms folded, eyes set narrow.

'Problems?' He asked one of the men on sentry duty. He listened to the whisper in his ear. Then he looked at Terry, and demanded, 'Let me see your identification.'

For once, Terry had forgotten his press pass, such was his panic. He nearly kicked himself for being unprepared for such a moment. He tried to settle his head and remain cool. *Breathe in, breathe out. Be calm...*

Then he went on the attack. 'These two fucking gorillas are getting in my way. I have to get on board. People are in danger. I need to warn them...' He pushed forward, his arms restrained forcibly by the henchmen. 'Are you listening to a single thing I'm saying, shithead? You have a killer on your guest list...'

That wasn't quite what he had in mind when he first opened his mouth to speak. Something was lost in translation. He had seriously jerked them off. After more expletives, he was marched off the quayside. Inside his car, he tried to phone Michael on his mobile. No response. His phone was obviously switched off. He then scrolled his contacts page, dialled Marcus and got him to text Kara's number to him. Marcus attempted to argue but he cut him off. He tried to reach her, but she too wasn't answering either. He assumed her phone was in her handbag and probably on the floor and out of earshot. As a last resort, he'd call the police. He wasn't entirely convinced of his theory...and didn't want hundreds of irate party people heading his way if he set in motion an invasion of coppers to evacuate everyone and spoil things if he was wrong.

Whatever.

He just had to get on board the ship.

***

'Where's Kara?' Michael asked. He had returned to the table after a light-hearted chat with another gallery owner at the bar.

'Gone to the loo with Antonia,' Toby's girlfriend said, slurring her words.

He looked around and saw Gemma dancing with Tarquin. She hadn't taken his advice. He decided he needed fresh air. It was too damn hot in the ballroom. He moved to the upper deck, loosened his bow tie and breathed in the night air. His legs felt wobbly. He moved to the portside and peered down. A line of taxis waited on the quay, the drivers in a huddle of gossip and cigarette smoke. A few guests began to slowly depart. No stamina. He looked beyond them and spotted a familiar car. He tried to clear his head. Was that…was that Terry beside the vehicle? His friend appeared agitated, pacing up and down, a mobile stuck to his ear. Michael steadied himself. He searched his pockets and found his phone. He had switched it off during the awards ceremony. He clicked on. He had a 121 call.

He moved down a deck, then another until he reached the gangway which led to the dockside. He shouted Terry's name but the music drowned out his voice. Terry was still fiddling with his phone, so he descended the ramp and pushed past security and approached his friend nervously, enquiring as to why he was here in the first place.

The journalist looked up, startled.

'Michael, thank Christ for that…I've been trying to contact you.' He pointed at the bouncers. 'The buggers wouldn't let me on the ship.'

'What's so urgent that it couldn't wait till the morning?'

Terry's bullet-like stare pierced his skull.

'Maggie wasn't on her own, Michael…'

Michael shook his head in mock bewilderment. 'I know, I know. Theo won't be troubling us again. Come on board and have a drink, don't worry about the gorillas…'

'The police compared the DNA from the remains in the barn with Suzy Fowler, and they matched. This proves conclusively…'

'Who the hell is Suzy Fowler?'

Terry stepped forward. 'The sister of Sheila Cox.'

Michael was stunned, he could hardly comprehend what his friend had just announced. His words were a little slurred: 'Sheila, the bar lady from the Royal Oak…that's impossible!'

'You'd better believe it, pal.'

'That means…'

'It means Lauren O'Neill is alive. She survived the fire. It was Sheila who fell, it was Sheila who died trying to help you. In the confusion, you thought it was Lauren who collapsed under the falling timber. Do you remember me asking how many of you were at the farm that day? Well, there was an additional guest, and she ended up the victim, but it was impossible to identify the body until now.'

'How did you find this out?'

'No time for analysis, Michael. Let's just say I discovered Sheila's car in Liverpool. The sisters of doom stole it to escape and dumped it there. It was an obvious place to go. It gave them access to Ireland. Theo later got them false passports so they could travel freely. It cost them big, so the money they had, the money you saw that day at the house, soon ran out. When they needed more they chased down Julius…'

'Why didn't he go to the police?'

'Because the dumb fucker was already selling the Porter paintings to raise some cash for himself…they then threatened to kill Antonia and his daughter if he didn't cooperate with the remainder of the works.'

Michael shook his head, and moaned, 'No, no, no…'

Terry nodded to the *Star Cruiser*. 'You have a killer on board that ship, and she needs to be found quickly.'

Michael looked over his shoulder, the blood in his veins turning ice cold as he studied the glittering vessel. How the hell was he going to find Lauren among so many party-goers decked out in fancy dress? The masks made it almost impossible to identify anyone. He reasoned that Kara and Antonia were definitely a target, and they had suddenly disappeared. His pulse quickened. The girls had gone to the loo… Had they been taken already? Then something nagged at him from earlier in the evening, while on the dance floor. It suddenly hit him…it was the fragrance. His mind back-tracked: The scent, the familiar curl of the lip, the feline walk…the photographer!

'Fuck,' he shouted. The sudden image of the clever disguise hit him like a sledgehammer: The full face mask and hair tucked beneath the decorative hat had hidden her identity so cunningly. She had been there, right there, mocking them all. *Lauren.*

'What is it?' Terry asked.

Michael started to run frantically in the direction of the ship.

Terry followed, his pace slower and his throat gasping for air as he tried to keep up.

***

Julius was the first to react as Michael rejoined the party, accompanied by a sweaty stranger who was out of breath and seriously out of touch with the required attire.

'What's the matter?' Julius asked, eyeing the two of them suspiciously.

Michael searched around the sea of faces on the dance floor. His own expression, contorted by panic, telegraphed his fears to those in earshot.

'Where are the girls?' he demanded nervously.

Julius swigged a beer. 'They went to the loo. I presumed they were getting some fresh air…is there a problem, Michael?'

'They should be back by now. We need to find them…'

'I'm sure they are fine.'

'No, Julius.'

'They're probably at the bar,' Toby interrupted.

'They've been abducted.'

'What…at the bar?' Toby said, giggling. No one else caught the joke.

Then a nervous chorus resonated around the table:

'*Abducted?*'

Toby began to sober up, suddenly aware of the odd conversation. 'What the hell are you talking about…?'

'Exactly that.'

'Then we should call the police,' Toby said, raising himself unsteadily from the table.

'No time for that,' Terry said.

'Who are *you*?' Toby asked.

'We met at Ronald's funeral.'

'Ah, the journalist if I recall correctly...What are you doing here?'

Terry stared at Toby, then Julius, back to Toby. 'I have evidence to suggest that a woman on board this ship is fully intending to do harm to your father...by means of hurting Kara. She's possibly held captive already.'

'What woman?' Toby then looked at Michael, bewildered.

'Lauren O'Neill,' Michael announced.

'I thought you said she'd died in the fire?'

'She's alive, and she's here.'

'Fuck,' Julius shouted. 'That means ...'

Toby jumped in: 'Can someone explain what is going on?'

Julius caught his breath. 'Are you serious, Michael, or is this just drunken bullshit?'

'Deadly serious,' Terry cut in.

Julius was aghast: 'Then Lauren has Antonia as well.'

'Exactly, Julius.' Michael said. 'So we have to find them, and fast.'

'They could be anywhere. They could have been taken ashore...'

Terry interjected: 'No, they are here, on board.'

'Is that a guess?' Julius asked.

'He's right,' Michael said. 'This is her opportunity to make a statement of intent against me.'

'And that would be...? Toby replied.

'To punish me and Julius. As Terry mentioned, she will harm the girls to harm us, because of her irrational obsession with rejection. She can't handle it. The voices in her head control her. Lauren feels I betrayed her in the same manner as she feels Julius betrayed her...right now, this woman intends to hold captive the two people we hold most dear.'

'What do you suggest we do?' Julius said, shaking.

'Spread out, search the ship,' Michael said. 'Stay in pairs. I'll go with Terry. We start with the ladies' loo on this deck.'

'Keep in touch by mobile,' Terry announced, 'And don't panic the other guests...we could be wrong in our assumptions.'

'I sincerely hope you are,' Toby countered.

'We'll take this deck, you take the lower one,' Michael said. 'Gemma, you search the upper deck, but take Tarquin. Nobody should be alone, work in pairs. Lauren is extremely dangerous. Let's move it.'

'What can I do?' Toby's girlfriend suddenly perked up.

Michael had forgotten about her. 'Stay here in case the girls return. Ring the police if none of us gets back to you within thirty minutes, got it?'

She nodded. Then they were gone.

***

Kara strained to listen in the darkness. A bead of sweat ran down the hollow between her shoulder blades. Her mouth was taped. Her eyes covered. She could hear her own breathing. That was all.

She wanted to scream. She wanted to vomit, such was the fear rising in her throat which forced her to swallow hard. Where was she? Where was Antonia?

Slowly, her brain began to untangle the mess. She remembered going to the loo with her new-found best friend and finding it locked. An 'Out of Order' sign hung from the handle. They went in search of another, desperate for a pee. Suddenly, a photographer – the one she recalled from the dance floor – appeared and kindly led them to an operational one further up on the top deck. She remembered giggling as they encountered the maze of narrow corridors. They were grateful for the photographer's assistance, especially as Antonia was struggling to keep her balance as the alcohol had gone to her head. Once inside the loo, all hell broke loose as their knight in shining armour locked the door behind them and suddenly turned nasty and confrontational.

Tears welled up in her eyes at the memory. Her heart pounded as she recalled what happened next. Everything happened in seconds. Antonia was pushed to the ground. Shocked, Kara had thought at first that she had slipped on the wet tiles. Then the photographer turned on her and slapped her face. She fell. Bizarrely, she tried to retrieve her handbag which had fallen under a sink, the contents scattered in all directions. The slap hadn't initially registered. She was in denial. She felt foolish and cried out to Antonia, who was temporarily stunned and unaware of what was taking place. Kara tried to get to her knees but her assailant was too quick, first grapping her arms and taping them together and then applying the same technique to silence her scream.

They were helpless and trapped…and this apparent madman had the strength of a lion. Antonia was lifted to her feet and hand-cuffed to a down pipe, blood dripping from a wound on her head from where she fell.

The madman gave a shrieking laugh, a laugh of unbridled evil… and only then did Kara recognise that triumphant sound, one which pierced any resistance she had left. Her legs had buckled. Her heart momentarily stopped.

She saw the terror in Antonia's eyes as she too was haunted by that shrill: A noise to awaken the dead, or that was how it seemed. They were locked in a room, powerless to defend themselves against…against… *someone* with the devil in their soul. Kara could barely bring herself to conjure up the name, such was her mounting fear.

***

With the help of a steward, Michael soon located the ladies' toilet and, on entering, discovered that it was vacant. He cursed and searched the cubicles. Nothing. Terry pointed to a white placard discarded in the corridor. It simply read: Out of Order.

'Not so,' said the steward, shaking his head suspiciously.

'Where's the next one?' Michael asked.

They were led further down the maze of corridors before ascending a flight of steps. They came to a door. The steward knocked lightly and entered. Michael followed and instantly recoiled: There was blood on the floor. He peered around and picked up a lipstick which had rolled under the row of sinks. He looked closer, finding a nail file.

'There,' Terry said. He retrieved a handbag from the waste paper bin. 'Is it Kara's?'

Michael wished his powers of observation were better attuned to women's fashion. He gulped, closed his eyes and whispered: 'I'm pretty sure it is…'

'I'm calling the cops,' the steward announced, and reached for his two-way radio.

Michael looked at Terry. For once, he couldn't find the strength to disagree with the man.

***

A thin shaft of light allowed her a split-second to judge the situation, and make something of this hell on earth. They had been moved to another room. A door had been opened, just enough. She blinked, the tape over her eyes now thankfully removed. A split-second was all she had; then the darkness returned to smother all hope.

She now knew that Antonia was seated beside her, her head down, possibly from exhaustion or the bash to the head. Her breathing was shallow, so shallow that she had thought she was alone in the room. Not so. Somebody else was with them. Kara listened. Silence. Her hands were still bound but it dawned on her that she was sitting freely on her seat, not tied to it. This gave her hope. Had her attacker made an error? Was this the chance to fight back? Did she have the strength of will to do so?

The tiny hairs on the nape of her neck stood on end as panic engulfed her. She felt warm breath on her face. Fuck! Was that the eyes of Satan starring at her in the blackness of hell?

Then a rasping voice split the air: 'You cunt!'

Kara jerked.

'I have you now…' Then the light from a torch shone in her face, dazzling her. Beyond, she could just make out the outline of a blood-stained mask staring at her: a shiny white mask with ruby encrusted decorations. *The dream.* Slowly, the mask was removed. Oh God! No! Surely not… then Lauren's face came into view! She wanted to throw up.

'Look at me, cunt!'

On the left side of Lauren's ruined face Kara saw the hideous scar that reached from her eye line to her chin. Her eyebrows were missing. The skin below was taut and sickly yellow, pulled together in tight knots from the burn marks.

Her teeth and gums were exposed on this side too as her lips curled up into a grimace. Strangely, the right side of her face was untouched and retained its former exquisite beauty.

Kara shivered as their faces almost caressed.

'I wanted him,' Lauren hissed. 'He was mine, all mine, until you had to interfere, didn't you bitch?'

Lauren ripped the tape from Kara's mouth.

Kara almost spat the words out: 'I worked for him, for Christ's sake, that was all! He and I were never lovers...'

'Shut the fuck up!' Lauren snapped. 'I've been watching you, following you, seeing you with him...you disgust me! Why did you have to take him from me, you selfish little cunt?'

'I didn't, you crazy fucked-up freak.'

That did it. Kara recoiled as the clenched fist tore into her cheek and a hand grabbed her by the throat. Her tirade was not the best move of the night so far.

Lauren almost spat the words. 'Michael loved me, cherished me. Look at me! I've lost my lover, I've lost my looks! He said I was history. Well, now he will lose everything that is precious to him. We were meant to be together. I could have won him back, I just needed time to heal myself...but you interfered with my plan, alongside that greedy shitty little boyfriend of yours...'

'Marcus?'

The hand on her throat tightened. There was no reasoning with this mad woman. She had to do something...

She kicked out. Then again, harder this time. She put her full weight behind the second kick. Her heels tore into something...was it flesh? The roar of pain reached her ears and lay testament to this hopeful claim. She kicked again and sensed Lauren fall at her feet. Kara stood and brushed past the stricken figure and reached the door, which was still ajar. The small light led her way. The metal door was heavy and she struggled with the handle, her back turned, until her groping fingers swung it open. She stumbled into the corridor. Momentarily, she was free and felt utter elation...then gasped as a hand grabbed her ankle, sending her plummeting to the ground. This time the blood on her hands was her own.

***

Michael raced down the labyrinth of corridors, his shirt soaking wet from perspiration. He kicked open doors on the right side as he went, calling out Kara's name. Terry followed, mimicking his friend's actions on the doors to the left, this time shouting the name of Antonia. It was stiflingly hot. They were searching blindly, aware of just what mayhem Lauren was capable of creating.

They reached another deck level.

We need to split,' Terry said.

Michael didn't answer. He just took off in the direction in front of him, unaware of what his companion had elected to do. When he finally turned and looked back, he was alone. In front, he saw an object on the carpet. A woman's shoe. And droplets of blood leading further ahead.

***

Kara regained consciousness and felt the surge of power to fight back. A rage boiled up inside her. Twisting, and using her shoulder to climb to her feet she once again lunged with her foot. Her heel dug into skin and bone. As she pulled away, she recoiled in horror as her shoe dislodged from her foot and remained as a dagger sticking out of her attacker's neck. Blood pumped from the wound. But still the beast staggered, yelped and reached out in defiance. Kara kicked off her other shoe and ran as fast as she could. She didn't dare look back for fear of what the walking dead actually looked like. All she knew was that this thing was following hard in her footsteps, and her stride was getting slower.

***

Gently he opened the door. In the gloom he detected a figure slumped on a chair propped against a far wall. It was some kind of storage room. Michael lifted Antonia's head and checked her pulse. It was weak but she was alive, blood congealing down her face from a head wound. She needed

295

urgent medical help. He untied her arms and cradled her body as he gently lowered her to the floor. He called her name but she just murmured. He removed his cloak and draped it over her body. A noise reached him and he froze.

'It's OK,' Terry said.

Michael was utterly relieved to hear his friend's voice.

'I'll take over here, you find Kara.'

He didn't need further persuasion. He fumbled through the cupboards and found a wooden mallet, a weapon nonetheless. He then moved into the corridor, looked both ways and weighed up his options. Lowering his gaze to the floor, he picked up the blood trail and followed, quickening his pace to the frantic beat of his heart.

***

It was like the dream. The god-damn fucking dream, only this time she was stuck on a ship and not down the mystic alleyways of Venice. But the feeling was the same. Utter terror.

In the darkened corridor, she could smell the acrid breath of the demon, it was that close. She shuddered. Behind her, a shadow followed. Ahead, a wide staircase beckoned. Her hands were still tied, but the tape had loosened. She twisted her wrists and gained leverage. At last she was free of the restraint as she yanked her hands apart. She was no longer defenceless. Beyond the staircase was a set of glass double-doors…and beyond that the night sky! Her heart thumped. It was her only chance of escape. She hesitated, then listened to a distant roar

It was the scream that did it; a scream not of this earth…a deep guttural sound that first reached into and then echoed around her brain with an intensity that ensured madness to anyone who witnessed or heard such a notion of evil. The sound abated. And then from somewhere very close, it started again, reaching an even higher crescendo.

Kara ran. She ran for her life. And in her panic, she could see visions from her past…vivid scenes from her dream which intermingled with the reality of what was happening right now.

Gripping the iron railings, her clenched fists turned knuckle white with fear. She peered tentatively into the black water...

She reached the upper deck and momentarily stood over the unlit swimming pool, holding onto the handrail. Her ghostly face was reflected back in the mirror-like water. She could hear the distant throb of music. She turned and searched the shadows, desperate for someone *–Michael –* to appear and miraculously rescue her.

She hesitated on the precipice of the subconscious world and thought of...well, murder, and the consequences of her own demise. It scared her witless...

Then an unimaginable horror: Her attacker staggered from the top of the staircase, bloodied and howling from the wound in her neck. Rage engulfed her as their eyes locked.

For Kara, the bloody violence of the history between them was a burden too great to carry. Was she capable of a cold-blooded killing, when it really came down to it? Her own life was on the line. She had to be prepared to forsake it. A tooth for a tooth...

The attacker approached in a stagger and slowly removed the velvet hat from her head. Red hair tumbled down onto her shoulders. Kara gasped, reeling again from the sight of the hideous scars that disfigured the woman's face and neck. And in that instant, she knew too that the living curse that Lauren endured during every waking hour was focused upon avenging those who inflicted such terrible damage.

The stain from her past almost touched her now, so much so, she could even detect the stench from the breath of the beast who was now upon her ...

Suddenly, the strength of her resolve evaporated. Sheer terror crept up and began to render her defenceless against the impending onslaught.

This was it. In a moment of lingering defiance, Kara met Lauren's flaming eyes with the same intensity, just to finally demonstrate her contempt for such brutality. It wouldn't save her, this she knew.

The glinting blade came down upon her throat with lightning speed. This vision was death itself...

Kara wobbled, and felt her legs buckle beneath her.

***

Michael had just one chance to react. He charged across the deck and flung himself at Lauren as she held the knife aloft. Grabbing her around the waist, the momentum of his thrust pushed all three of them headlong over the handrail into the murky depths below. The impact of the icy water filled his lungs as he gasped for air. He surfaced, gulped, and felt his legs being pulled down by unseen hands. He lashed out to free himself as the clawing fingers pulled him deeper. In the swirling tumult, Michael tried to make sense of who he was fighting against…it was impossible to judge. What he did know was that Kara couldn't swim. Was it her desperate grip which pulled him down? He had to somehow get to the surface and regain his strength. He kicked out as his body somersaulted from the weight of another pulling on him, sending him spiralling downward again. His head cracked against the bottom. He spread his arms to gain leverage and touched an object. He grabbed it. The mallet. He pushed against the tiled floor and soared upward, breaking the surface in a rush. He looked around as the waves settled. *Christ, where was Kara?*

He dived and swivelled, searching frantically the bottom of the swimming pool for signs of her stricken body. Then he saw her dangling legs at the edge, next to the metal steps. He swam and caught her as she began to sink from exhaustion. He pushed her from below as she regained consciousness. Holding her tight, he helped as she instinctively climbed the steps to safety. He regained his strength and slowly followed her until they slumped beside each other, completely spent. *Where was Lauren…?*

He lifted his head and turned to peer down into the red water. He put his hand to his head and felt blood oozing down his neck. He still held the mallet tightly with the other hand, just in case…

But it was quiet. The water slowly flattened. It was over…

As he turned toward Kara, he was suddenly aware of a movement out of the corner of his eye, a rush, a flash of steel. His eyes suddenly widened involuntarily, horror contained within.

They affixed upon the impossible and breathtaking speed with which Lauren resurfaced and propelled herself from the water as she ascended the steps beside them. He had neither the strength nor the opportunity to react as she hovered above him, brandishing a knife above her head. In the gloom, he saw the angry scars which had ravaged her once stunning good looks. For a fleeting moment, he sensed a kind of pity behind her manic stare. All he could do in his panic was to scream her name and lift the mallet to protect himself and Kara, offering a feeble last line of defence.

'Lauren! Lauren!'

Startled, she hesitated and then uttered a howling scream that seemed to reach beyond sadness or rage. It was the final calling of a woman who only knew torment and torture; and a sound that signified the closure of her anguished past...and the prospect of a pitiful future. Alone.

Michael saw this futile moment and acknowledged the deep sorrow in her eyes as she looked down at him... for the last time.

The bullet ripped through the air and slammed into her head, sending her body in a backward arc as it first smashed into the water, sunk momentarily and then settled on the surface once more, a crimson stain widening around her as she gradually turned full circle in the centre of the pool. Then there was silence as the echo from the gunshot vanished into thin air. Michael and Kara turned and stared disbelievingly behind them.

The man with the gun stepped out from behind a gantry.

Michael dragged himself to his feet. Terry suddenly emerged behind the unexpected but welcome saviour, a soldier of fortune if ever there was one.

'What the fuck?' Terry yelled, approaching them, the moonlight illuminating his craggy face. Gemma too arrived on the scene and, in shock, held a hand over her mouth.

Michael raised his arm. 'It's fine, Terry, everything is just fine...'

Martin Penny helped Michael lift Kara to her feet and between them they shuffled her away, away from this forsaken place...a place for the dead. A final resting place that not even Lauren was ever going to return from. There was no coming back this time.

As they gradually descended the gangway, each wrapped in a blanket and accompanied by the ship's staff, the police sirens wailed from afar as the dockside became a scene of bedlam. Kara crouched down, exhausted, as the first ambulance arrived. Toby comforted her, unaware that Julius had arrived behind him and was watching anxiously as Antonia was laid on a stretcher, an oxygen mask attached over her mouth and nose.

'Is she going to be OK?' Julius asked, bewildered.

An ambulance man nodded reassuringly. Together, they supported her as she was lifted into the rear of the vehicle. Then they were gone.

Michael stood on wobbly bare feet, his head now bandaged, the blood flow stemmed.

'How did you know?' he asked, as Martin lit a cigarette and watched the smoke unfurl into the night sky. He passed it to Michael, who inhaled deeply. *He was allowed this one moment.*

'It was Marcus who alerted me, so thank him for saving your life. He saw an image of Lauren leaving your apartment block, from CCTV footage that Terry had provided. I always believed that Maggie had an accomplice other than Theo. It was Lauren who killed Ronald. It was Lauren who lived above you, not Maggie as we first suspected. Her motive was not to hurt you...but to be close to you. She was misguided, truly believing that you could be together again.'

'I can hardly grasp what you are saying. She lived above me..?'

'After Marcus warned me, I searched the underground car park where you live, hoping to find something in the refuse block...' He stopped and drew on the cigarette.

'*And?*' Michael asked.

'I found an easel, and a discarded canvas...It was a painting of you, with her by your side. She hadn't finished it, but I've kept it to show you.'

'Why a painting..?' he said, as he recalled the scraping noise above him as he tried to sleep one night. It was the easel being dragged across the floor, it had to be.

'Because that's how best she expressed herself, where her real talent lay and...she loved you, and even though she knew she couldn't have you, because of her disfigurement, it was her way to make the union permanent. She wanted to be close...to be able to share something of her life with someone who ultimately wanted to help her when she really needed it. It was she who tried to save you in the barn, if you recall. While all else failed in her life, she ultimately believed in you. After she left the flat she holed up for a few days in a bedsit, which she originally shared with Maggie. I found hundreds of photos of you and Kara there. This was her lair.'

'One thing that puzzles me,' Michael said. 'When you first took on the job, I understood that you put surveillance on my block of flats. Why didn't you pick up on Lauren?'

'We didn't know who we were looking for. People came and went...you gave me a description of Maggie, not Lauren. As far as everyone was concerned, she was dead and posed no threat. Why would anyone be alarmed by a woman coming and going from the building? After Marcus spoke to me, I checked the cameras and found her...but it was too late. She had vanished. That is why I searched the refuse, to see if I could find anything to link her with you. And of course, I did.'

'She was a fugitive, on the run...'

'Exactly. Her world was tortured, and she had visions of recapturing her time with you...but that all altered when she overheard you on the phone to Terry. You said she was history, and that you bitterly regretted ever meeting her.

Remember, she had your phone bugged. Kara was still around and then Agnes came back on the scene. That's when she changed. She flipped. That's when she sought revenge, and Ronald was the first to suffer her rage, because he was an easy target. Mitch too. It would have been Toby if he'd been working that day. It was her way of getting at you, to make you feel her pain. Kara was her next target, but Theo made a cock-up and she escaped with her life. But she would not be denied. If she couldn't have you, no one would have you. Everyone was in danger.'

Michael gathered the blanket tightly around him. He shivered from his wet clothes.

Martin continued. 'No one was safe. Julius and Antonia could go to hell as far as she was concerned. Agnes too. You had to understand her mindset. She was deluding herself, in self-denial, wrapped up in her traumatic past. She didn't care much for Maggie in the end. After you escaped from the hut and her sister perished she had only one thing on her mind...she planned to exploit this moment as her final solution, if I can use the term.'

Michael shook his head. 'And she so nearly succeeded,' he concluded.

Terry approached, having overheard the conversation. He put his hand on Michael's shoulder. 'Lauren also returned to the farm. I found this.' He handed over the bracelet. 'Is it hers'?'

Michael frowned. It looked familiar.

'You, of all people, understood the deep-seated problems that invaded her head,' Terry said. 'The abuse she suffered as a child from her father's hands. Her time in prison for his murder. The death of her baby brother. All this changed her for the worse. That's what trauma does. It was this split-personality disorder which ruled her life, and betrayal was something she could not forgive...and that extended to all those who crossed her path. No one was ever excluded from her radar of hate, and time was not a healer for her. In fact, it just festered within her head, building the intensity of misguided notions of what love was about for her... something she was denied in her childhood.'

'She put me on a pedestal,' Michael said, 'and I couldn't live up to her expectations. It was infatuation, nothing more. But ultimately I failed her.'

Terry added, 'No one could live up to her expectations, but is that so surprising if you consider her history? A history of mental anguish, and, to top it all...a wrongful conviction for a crime that she didn't commit. She was even shafted by her own flesh and blood, Maggie. Lauren was a victim of circumstance but in her troubled mind it was those she loved who ultimately let her down. Think about it, it started with her father, then her husband, then Maggie and the biggest sinner of all...you. But she didn't want to sacrifice you. She wanted to recapture you. Possess you. Nobody else was

302

going to have you.'

Michael thought about it, and cursed under his breath. 'The biggest sinner of all,' he repeated, his heart full of remorse. What had he done to all those he had loved? He closed his eyes, thought of the demons that had driven him to the point of insanity. He had quarrelled endlessly with his own conscience in regard to the ethical issues that had taken him down this path to near oblivion. He had hurt many people in the process, and sacrificed his right to judge others when his own moral compass was damaged and unreliable. This weakness carried him forward, on a daily basis, but ultimately it was a damning verdict on the way he conducted his life: A life imperfect, an existence without a clear conscience between what was good and what was evil. He was driven by hunger, putting the needs of himself above all others. He undermined those he cherished and put their lives at risk by his basic disregard for their safety. He let greed drive his desires in both love and financial matters. He felt morally bankrupt. Without honour.

Kara had survived her ordeal, again. She too stood wrapped in a blanket, held in a tight embrace with Gemma.

She caught Michael's eye, hobbled over and embraced him, tears flowing. It was all over at last.

He hugged her in return, fearful of letting her go, fearful of making empty promises once again. But this time his faith was restored, knowing that Lauren and Maggie were no longer able to assert their wicked dominance over all of their lives. Theo too. They had each paid the ultimate price. Theo was a thug. He lived and died by the sword. Maggie sinned by corrupting her own flesh and blood, going to her watery grave with a pious notion of believing she was above those who foolishly stood in her path. Including her sister. She never saw her own faults, only in those who she considered to be the enemy. And she had only one way of dealing with them. Her heart was black. Her mind callous and mean-spirited.

Only Lauren could truly seek forgiveness for crimes she did not commit, those she was not aware of, such was her gigantic struggle with the demons that infiltrated her mind. They controlled her, baited her and led her on a wayward path between beauty and destruction…the utter beauty of her inspired painting under the guise of her brother, Patrick, and the intended destruction of all those she loved and treasured, as if by killing them off somehow preserved the sanctuary – the wall of defence that she hid behind – that was so vital between the balance of reason and insanity in her twisted existence. It was this perpetual fight against the wrongdoing of a society that she couldn't fit into which ultimately conspired toward her downfall.

Lauren was dead: At peace with the world. Her fitting legacy was the great and majestic paintings of Patrick Porter. They would live on forever, perfect and grand – a kind of poetry in paint – from the hand of an artist untouched by any other notion than the innocence she found in her lost brother. This body of work would remain untarnished, unlike her brutal upbringing. Michael decided he would always honour her memory, if not her misguided and evil actions.

Lauren O'Neill, RIP.

Maggie Conlon could rot in hell. Revenge wasn't her motivation, as they first thought. Her needs were spitefulness and a murderous spirit. She wanted Michael silenced because of what he knew of her past…and she wanted the stolen painting back. One of them had it, she knew. Which one, she didn't care: They were all going to die, in her book. She was pure evil.

She had gradually plundered the paintings, and wanted every one of them back. Her sister could pursue her pathetic misguided notion of love. Julius could have the farm, she bargained. But how long would it have been before she wanted the proceeds from that too? She was relentless. She considered everyone else weak and expendable.

Michael knew something was amiss when he discovered the Patrick Porter in the Venetian house. It was one of the original twelve, held supposedly under lock and key for safekeeping. How could it suddenly reappear? He knew that someone was playing a game…of blackmail. And then it all fell into place when Julius confessed his complicity in raiding the collection. They were all desperate people, including himself.

Even the hapless Sheila Cox became a victim, trying to help other people in their hour of need.

Michael took a deep breath.

He felt renewed optimism, a heightening of his senses, a faith restored but where that inner strength came from he did not know. Beyond his gaze, a young man came into view and briskly walked towards them, a bundle in his arms and two police officers by his side.

Michael gradually pulled away from Kara, kissed her brow and silently turned her towards her future. She caught sight of Marcus and little Harvey Heath and bit down on her lip, her eyes moistening.

'Go,' Michael said, edging her forward with the palm of his hand. And in that moment, he imagined a little bird taking flight for the first time as its fragile wings spread and fluttered, and he smiled triumphantly as Kara took her first hesitant steps toward the rebirth of her trust in human kind and the search for new beginnings.

For Michael, in the company of Terry and his own precious son, it was a call to witness, a poignant moment to cherish. And in his mind he thought he saw Kara, like the little bird he imagined, soar into the sky and rejoice at the privilege of life and the family embrace which awaited her, such was her exhilaration at reuniting with those that she loved so dearly and so nearly lost.

It began to rain heavily, but Kara Scott didn't care. She was going to get married! Damn sure of it. Her pace quickened. Then she ran across the cobbles, hands outstretched, as Marcus eagerly walked into her arms.

EPILOGUE

THREE MONTHS LATER

'How much do you want for it?'

Michael remained calm and considered his options. His client was old school, old money. He knew the worth of things, especially art, and Asian art in particular. He stood beside the elderly client in a darkened room at the rear of the gallery and remained impassive, as they quietly examined the tiny ornament which sat modestly upon the illuminated blue velvet-lined table top.

'Sixty thousand, cash,' Michael ventured. He had done his research and felt confident in his valuation.

The man lifted the tiny jade vessel carefully to the light and turned it with his fingers. A thin smile crossed his lips as he marvelled at the exquisite craftsmanship.

Michael had known the collector for many years, first introduced by his father when he was wet behind the ears, but they had a fondness for each other... borne from the many successful dealings they shared over the course of the intervening years. They always conducted business in this manner: In secrecy and with hard cash. The man had impeccable taste, an eye for treasure and a lust for the seemingly unobtainable. It centred on *ownership.* Michael knew the feeling well.

'Fifty thousand, not a penny more, Michael.' He replaced the vessel on the ebony stand and pushed a leather briefcase with his foot across the floor to where Michael stood. Michael bent down and opened the case and leafed through the cash pile.

'You don't need to count it.'

Michael closed the lid and locked down the hinges. He deliberately pondered his reply for affect, but they both knew the game. He then extended his hand.

'Deal.'

They shook hands warmly. Michael placed the vessel gently in a cushioned wooden box, closed the lid and handed it over, escorting the man to the front door. A chauffeur driven Rolls-Royce waited outside on the street, engine purring. They bade farewell.

'To the next time,' the man said fondly. Then he was gone.

After his departure, Michael locked the door and poured himself a 12 year-old single malt whisky, savouring the rich smooth taste as it ignited joyfully in his mouth. He then switched on his laptop, hesitated, and emailed Agnes (careful to use her work address) and asked for her bank details, adding that he had a little reward for her. It was the first time that he had communicated with her since the end of the affair. So much had happened since then. Terry's lurid story had broken across the nation, bringing widespread notoriety to his life. He was now a newsworthy superstar as word spread to all corners of the planet. He was the hottest celebrity in town. He had a stark choice: Hide and be picked off by the ensuing media or relish the global attention and go with the flow.

He chose the latter route. His star was once again in the ascendancy, and on balance he rather enjoyed the attention. And rather enjoyed the painting that Lauren had done, which he now displayed on his wall at home. It was reminder of the sacrifices they had all made. As agreed with his son, he had resigned from Churchill Fine Art and set up his own art consultancy, advising on rare acquisitions, insurance valuations and building up corporate collections and private purchases for wealthy clients from around the world. Although he worked from home, he also acted as a consultant to the gallery on one day a week…thus enabling him the use of the premises whenever it suited him. His new business flourished. This was one such case, with a slight difference. The object of desire had personal history.

The response from Agnes came back quickly:

Why?
He was amused by her terse response and replied:
Because you earned it, big time.
She sent:

How?

He sent:

Because I screwed up. You don't need to ask how. Take it and enjoy.

She replied with the bank details.

No further encouragement was needed, he noted. He then added :

Thanks for everything. M.

He transferred online a twenty-five thousand pound deposit into her private account. It was the least he owed her. Then he refilled his glass, with a generous measure this time, and toasted his good fortune. He missed her, but she remained in Venice with her family and that was how it was going to be, he guessed with a heavy heart. Who knew what tomorrow would bring though? The thought struck him: Perhaps he would look up an old friend at Momo's. He lifted the case and placed it in his safe, then pondered his next move, a little richer and a little wiser. This is what he did know for sure: Theo would not be chasing him for the Chinese vessel, nor for the cash.

Not now, not ever.

An email came in which simply said:

Wow!!

He smiled, switched off the computer and lights, locked the gallery door and walked out into the cold air, unaccompanied once again. He sighed, looked up at the *Tobias Strange Fine Art* sign and smiled again. He then ambled into the night, aware that it was his own footsteps he could hear as he strode down the deserted street in the city he loved above all others.

Greed was a lonely warrior, he now knew.